Frankie

ANNIE JONES

Printed by CreateSpace

www.createspace.com

Copyright © 2018 by Annie Jones

ISBN-13:9781717455215
ISBN-10:1717455212

Photography and cover design courtesy of Mark Woolcott

For mum x

LOVE WAS...
the torn-up pieces inside of me,
all the scars, the burns, the wreckage.
Love is everything I wanted us to be.

    a.m. watson

EMBRACE THE PAIN, IN FACT, BUY IT A DRINK
And you, you're something else entirely.
You can't embrace the pain that comes with love.
You tremble in fear and throw away anything good.

    a.m. watson

CHAPTER ONE

I unlocked my front door, my possessions slowly sliding out of my arms, losing the battle to keep my mobile phone under my chin as I listened to my ex-husband's tirade to the counterpoint of my daughter Gracie's incessant chatter. Finally through the door, I unceremoniously dropped everything on the hall floor while ushering Gracie along in front of me.

'Please, sweetie,' I whispered to her as she tugged on my arm.

'I want to speak to Daddy,' she continued her tugging, starting to pout.

'Put Gracie on,' my ex-husband commanded in his "do as you're told" voice.

'Look,' I broke away from Gracie and quickly walked away from her, keeping my voice low, 'it's late, I've just got in. Ring her tomorrow, OK?'

I ended the call before he could begin to argue.

'Sorry sweetie,' I switched on the kitchen light and turned back to Gracie, 'Daddy had to go, he will speak to you tomorrow.'

'But I wanted to tell him about today,' she frowned up at me as she sat down at the kitchen table and started to take off her shoes, her reddish gold curls drooping over her face.

'Sorry sweetie,' I repeated. 'You can tell him all about it tomorrow.'

'Can I wear my dress to bed?' she asked brightly, recovering somewhat.

'No.'

'Can I wear it tomorrow then?'

'We'll see.'

'Can I go straight to bed without a bath?'

'Hmm, well you need to wash your face and brush your teeth.'

She slid off her chair and scampered upstairs. I filled the kettle, and kicking off my shoes, sat down wearily.

It had been a strange and never-ending day - a day I had been dreading despite it being a day of celebration: my stepson's wedding. I couldn't *not* have gone, even if Gracie hadn't had been a bridesmaid. Will would have been heartbroken, and in normal circumstances I would have loved to have seen him getting married. And it *had* been a beautiful day, despite feeling like the elephant in the room; the martyr.

Robert had persistently and emphatically forbidden us to attend. There had been countless, boring and circular arguments - I had been slightly ashamed to realise that I had revelled in my defiance.

I had spent too much time during our marriage backing down, not wanting to make waves… in fact doing everything I had always despised, that I had considered weak. *Does love do those things to you?* I think so. And I had loved him deeply. I *still* loved him.

Anyone who has suffered the cruel, crippling and demeaning experience of infidelity knows there is a lot of denial. Denial, self-loathing and detective work. And even when the evidence is too much to deny there is still more denial. And excuses. And questioning your sanity. But eventually, everybody has their limits.

My limit had been discovering that Robert had an affair with Will's girlfriend, now his wife - Lennie. I should add: *before* she had got together with Will. I didn't blame her, not really. I had been married to him long enough to know he could charm any woman, young or old. But the discovery had been devastating, sickening and probably the worst thing that had ever happened to me. The weird thing was that I didn't feel any jealousy or resentment towards her. In fact, I genuinely liked her. It was just a terrible, weary acceptance that I had to walk away. And soon.

In retrospect, it's possible that I might have confused my own grief with anger for Will. I met Will just before his twentieth birthday. I reckon a lot of people assume our closeness stems from me 'bringing him up' but I'm not even old enough to be his mother - we just hit it off from the start. He had a rather strange and distant relationship with Robert that I couldn't quite get my head around, but it didn't extend towards me.

I remember so clearly when Will first brought up Lennie with me. He had been out of our lives for a while - something that Robert was extremely closed about - but after moving away for nearly three years he returned and, at a time when my marriage was beginning to deteriorate, became my once again friend and confidante. That may sound strange, but we kind of had this unspoken agreement that Robert was actually a bit of a shit.

He had met Lennie through his friend, Daniel, with whom he had gone into business with - Lennie being Daniel's sister.
I think "smitten" is the correct word, and he suffered the pangs of disappointment that she was apparently involved with someone.

The awful irony was that that someone, as time told, was my very own husband and his father. I met her months later after they had got together and was amused to find that the "most beautiful girl in the world" was, OK, pretty enough, if slightly quirky and awkward but not the drop-dead-gorgeous girl I had been imagining. But then, love is blind and all that. Deaf, dumb, blind and bloody stupid.

I made myself a mug of tea, and leaving it on the table, I went upstairs to check on Gracie. She was changed into her 'Minions' pyjamas and laying across her bed, engrossed on her tablet.

'Hey you,' I crossed the room to her bed, pausing to pick up her discarded dress and underwear. 'No tablet after seven o'clock.'

'But Mummy, today doesn't count,' she said without looking up.

'Does it not?' I smiled despite myself.

There was no denying it, Gracie was spoiled, and my weak spot. Of course, I had a mother's bias, but she was a beautiful little girl - a precocious seven-year-old with her father's confidence and dark blue eyes, and my red hair, darker than mine with golden streaks. It didn't matter how much she played up and pushed all of my buttons, because when I looked at her at night, curled up in bed fast asleep, looking peaceful and innocent like an angel, I forgave her for everything. Of course, my guilt at disrupting her home-life played a part in that, but she really was adorable.

'Come on sweetie,' I sat on the edge of her bed, 'tablet off and into bed please.'

'OK Mummy,' she sighed, handing it to me and pulling back her duvet to crawl in.

'Did you have a lovely time today?' I asked, tucking her in.

'Yeah,' she snuggled down, 'I wish I could get married... if Will and Lennie have a baby, will I be its big sister?'

'No, you'll be an auntie,' I smoothed back her hair.

'Oh,' she blinked up at me, 'when I'm grown up, Mummy, can I have a tattoo like Lennie?'

'Mm,' I smiled, 'probably not.'

'Lennie was sick twice this morning,' she said, 'and the second time, she said 'fuck it'.'

'Gracie!' I gasped, shocked. 'That's a naughty word!'

'I heard you say a naughty word once to Daddy on the phone,' she looked totally unabashed.

'Oh,' I tried not to smile, feeling slightly ashamed but wanting to giggle all the same. 'Well, that was very naughty of Mummy, wasn't it?'

'Yes Mummy, it was,' she yawned.

'I think it's time to turn the light out and go to sleepy land,' I kissed her forehead and reached over to turn off her lamp.

'Goodnight Mummy,' she murmured, turning on her side.

'Goodnight sweetie.'

I went back downstairs, still feeling tickled, and picked up our bags and jackets from the hall and took them into the kitchen. I checked my phone and saw that there were three texts from Robert, probably very pissed-off texts I decided, and deleted them without reading them, with slight satisfaction. *Screw him*, I thought.

My tea was luke-warm and I poured it down the sink, deciding to pour a glass of wine to drink in the bath.

A hot bath and a glass of Shiraz later, I lay in bed mulling over the day and wishing I felt sleepier. I probably would have felt more relaxed and enjoyed the day if I hadn't felt so paranoid, wondering who knew my whole sorry situation… not that *I* felt sorry for myself -well, not anymore - but I hated the thought of people talking about me or pitying me. But everyone had been lovely to me.

I had previously met Lennie's parents, brother and wife, and her friend Adam - who had spent the evening pulling me up to dance and playing with Gracie who absolutely adored him. The other bridesmaids had been Will's half-sister from his mum's side and Lennie's friend, Rosie. They had been angelic, looking after Gracie and calming her down. There had been a little awkwardness with Will's mother and stepfather, I found them slightly *too* polite towards me. And I noticed that nobody asked where Robert was.

There's nothing like a wedding to make you feel lonely, especially when the happy couple are so obviously in love.

Will had looked so handsome and proud, he couldn't take his eyes off of Lennie, and she had looked radiant, although pale and fragile -

like a fairy in her floaty white and rose-gold dress and dark curls. For a brief moment, despite that I didn't feel the hatred that I maybe should have towards her, I couldn't help thinking: *there's the girl that slept with my husband. My Robert.* And my heart felt tight with misery.

Thankfully that moment passed. The ice was broken by soft laughter of those closest, as Adam promptly burst into tears, and his boyfriend awkwardly started shushing him.

I had then focused my attention onto Gracie. She had looked, at first excited and pleased with herself as she had trotted up the aisle holding Rosie's little boy's hand, then as the ceremony was underway, rather unimpressed and bored, swinging the skirt of her pale green dress around and fiddling with her posy - dropping it twice - the second time not even bothering to pick it up.

Another moment I found uncomfortable was during the photographs. I had discreetly sidled away, but had been pulled into a couple by Will, who had looked at me almost pleadingly. There was a slight sticky patch when Gracie requested loudly if she could "give Daddy a photo" so he could see her in her dress - because he had been "too busy" to come today.

As I smiled grimly at that memory, I wondered for the first time that day what Robert had actually done with himself all day and if he'd felt any regrets or sadness at being excluded from his own son's wedding. I automatically looked at my bare ring finger and sighed. He had probably felt angry and hard done by - that none of this was his fault. Because things were almost never Robert's fault.

I had been engaged to another man when Robert first burst into my life. Incredibly attractive and charming, I think he - as the expression goes - had me at 'hello'. I'm not proud of how I behaved.

I had met David, my fiancé, in my twenties whilst studying accountancy at college. It turned out we had a couple of mutual friends and we started hanging out together. He was kind of cute, not really my type, rather serious and had a vague ex-public-school boy air about him. We lost contact - easy back then in the days before Facebook.

Fast forward to my thirtieth birthday. I was out celebrating with some friends when I felt a hesitant tap on my arm at some bar in Cambridge, and there stood David. I won't bore you with the details:

we hit it off, started dating, moved in together after two years and got engaged.

Exactly a month before our wedding, I met Robert. I had been sitting alone in a wine bar, waiting for my best friend, Maggie, to meet me to discuss last minute wedding details. She had just rung to tell me she was running late - as usual - and I'd settled myself in a quiet corner with my notebook and a gin and tonic. I had glanced up as the door opened, and in strode Robert, sun-tanned, dark-haired, chatting on his mobile phone, tugging his tie off one-handed - exuding confidence. To my acute embarrassment, he caught me staring and grinned wickedly. I had quickly looked down and took a slug of my drink. When I dared to look up again, he was unashamedly studying me from the bar, now off his phone with a bottle of beer in his hand.

And not knowing what else to do, I made the mistake of smiling at him. Within twenty minutes, when Maggie finally turned up, we were chatting and laughing together... and I was probably half-way in love with the man. He had excused himself and left, but not before handing me his business card.

I vaguely remember Maggie saying - in true Maggie style - something like, *'fucking hell, that is one splendid piece of man meat,'* then telling me to *'keep my knickers on'* and I had laughed and casually dropped his card on the seat next to me. For the next hour I slowly slid my handbag over to cover it and hastily shoved it in as we left the bar.

I spent the next few days thinking about him; it was crazy. I can't even explain what was going through my head. The wedding plans were driving me mad. David, a constant worrier, was getting on my nerves fussing and going through things. One evening, I found myself getting increasingly irritated with him, and making some excuse about popping over to see Maggie - who I knew was working that evening - I drove into town, parked up and rang Robert. Thirty minutes later we were in a country pub, and an hour after that we knew how the evening was going to end. I could of, *should have*, stopped myself... the terrible part is that I didn't feel half as guilty as I should have.

Sex with Robert was incredible. David had never been the most adventurous lover: in bed, lights out, usually missionary position. Robert and I hardly made it through his front door. I remember returning home much later, already feeling like I wanted more. I had hurriedly showered, David was already asleep in bed, and I lay for a long time staring at him, suddenly feeling an odd, distant numbness towards him.

The upshot of it all is that two weeks before the big day, I left him. I took a day off work, packed my things and left a letter on the kitchen table along with my ring. Of course I felt awful, and for a long time after that I kept a low profile. My parents were furious, even Maggie who was always in my corner, gave me a dressing-down. And David? He accepted it with shocking docility. I think I would have felt better if he had shouted at me. I met up with him a few days after we should have been wed to sort out our flat. That's when it hit me - the enormity of my crime. Pale, unshaven and red-eyed, he quietly said what he had to say, and unable to look me in the eyes, handed me the keys to our flat, informing me in a hollow voice he was moving away and I could keep the deposit.

I wanted to comfort him. I wanted to know he didn't hate me. And when we parted, I told him again that I was sorry. He simply stared at me with wounded eyes and walked away.

As I lay awake, going over and over in my head just *some* of the horrors in my past, I reluctantly got up at around one o'clock in the morning and took one of my sleeping tablets that had been prescribed to me the year before - when I had left Robert.

My last thought was that I was going to have one hell of a headache in the morning, taking that on top of copious amounts of champagne and wine.

CHAPTER TWO

I woke up early the following morning, feeling groggy, with a face full of Gracie's hair - she must have snuck into bed with me at some point. I'd forgotten to draw the curtains the night before, and bright sunlight filled the room. Stretching and deciding my head wasn't in too much pain, I climbed out of bed and went over to the window. It looked like it was going to be another glorious summer day. My small back garden - a far cry from Robert's spacious lawn and immaculate flowerbeds - was nothing short of a playground. Leaving Robert had been hard - taking Gracie away from his sprawling house with her playroom, filled with every toy that a little girl could wish for and her two-storey wooden play-house in the garden, had nearly killed me. In my terrible guilt, I had spent a small fortune on a swing-set, a slide and a six- foot trampoline. Before we moved in, during the mission named "operation leaving Robert", Will and Daniel had built a huge wooden raised flowerbed for Gracie to plant her own flowers, which was currently filled with her pansies and plastic windmills.

'Morning Mummy.'

I turned around, Gracie was struggling out from under my duvet, looking wide-awake and clear-eyed in the way only children managed to look in the morning. I crossed the room and lay back down for a cuddle.

'Did you sleep OK?' I rested my chin on her head as she nodded. 'Mummy's going to run you a bath to have after breakfast.'

'Can we go and see Will and Lennie today?' she asked.

'Sweetie, they've gone on their honeymoon today,' I said, resisting a sigh.

'What's a honeymoon?'

'Well, it's like a holiday for when you've just got married,' I said.

'Did you and Daddy go and have a honeymoon?' she pulled back her head and looked up at me with her dark blue eyes - so much like her fathers.

'Yes,' I said cagily. I knew it was impossible not to talk about him, but often her behaviour became erratic when she did. 'Come on,' I climbed back out of bed, 'let's go and have breakfast. Maggie's coming over today.'

I had promised Maggie some lunch and wedding gossip. Normally she would have demanded a late-night phone call, but she had been working until midnight - she was a nurse on the children's ward at the local hospital. We had been friends since junior's school. Another girl had been bullying me since the year before, and one day Maggie decided to go and push her over and kick her on the bum. I can't really remember how much trouble she got into - I think her parents had to take her home - but after that we became best friends.

Now, both divorced, she had proclaimed that we were going to conquer the world, and the men of Fernberry "better watch out" … my part in that was failing miserably. Maggie, on the other hand, was having a whale of a time. Single life was easier for her; she had two teenage sons - Tyler, eighteen and Nathan, coming up to sixteen - no hassle of finding babysitters for her, and she had the slight advantage of not giving a rat's arse about her ex-husband. I wouldn't say she exactly *hated* him, but she certainly wasn't still in love with him. He was usually referred to as things like "pencil dick" and "that weasely bald fuck-face".

I envied her. I felt emotionally drained and sexually stunted. She constantly insisted that there was no way I could possibly still love Robert, not after all he had done. She also insisted a "good seeing to" would cure me "just like that". She had an enormous amount of confidence - incredibly pretty with thick, glossy blonde hair and wicked, knowing, dark eyes, and the fact she was barely over five-foot-tall and over-weight didn't dent her pursuit of men one bit, nor did it put men off her.

On time for once, she arrived just after twelve, laden down with cakes and a tub of Ben and Jerry's.

'Maggie!' Gracie yelled as soon as she walked in and threw herself at her.

'Hello princess,' Maggie ruffled her hair and pulled some chocolate buttons out of her bag, she held them out of reach and bent down for a kiss before handing them to her. Gracie skipped off towards the kitchen and out the back door.

'I really wish you'd stop giving my daughter sweets,' I shook my head, laughing, as Maggie hugged me.

'You alright then?' she studied me, frowning.

'Fine, I'm fine,' I assured her. 'Really, I am,' I added when she gave me a look.

We went into the kitchen and I continued cutting up some chicken that I'd been halfway through when she'd knocked at the door.

'What we having then?' she put the ice-cream in the freezer and then settled herself at the table.

'Pasta and chicken of some sort,' I said over my shoulder, 'it's too hot to go to a lot of faff.'

'Sounds good to me,' she paused, then said, 'so... how was it?'

'Not as bad as I thought it was going to be,' I could almost feel her eyes on my back. 'Gracie behaved, the ceremony was lovely, people were nice,' I shrugged. 'That's it really.'

'Hmm, well,' she said, 'you're a better person than me, that's all I can say.'

'Well it's over, it's history,' I shrugged again. 'What's the point in holding grudges and causing upset?'

'I suppose,' she agreed, although I could tell she didn't really agree. Maggie could probably hold a grudge forever.

'Robert rang me just as we were getting out of the taxi,' I told her. 'God, he pisses me off, he was going on that he couldn't believe that I had... what was it now?... "exposed our daughter to the very people that had *wrecked* our marriage."'

'Dick-head,' Maggie said venomously. 'I think it was his penis that wrecked your marriage.'

I laughed, Maggie always had a way of making things seem less awful.

'Yeah, well, try telling *him* that,' I put my knife in the sink and started to wash my hands. 'I couldn't even be bothered to argue. I know what's *really* bugging him,' I smiled grimly, 'it's the shame of not being invited, if any of his business buddies got wind of it... it's all appearances with him.'

I looked out of the window, Gracie was happily playing on her swing with Yellow Bunny. I took a bottle of Chardonnay out of the fridge and plonked it on the table and went to fetch two glasses. As I sat down, my eyes suddenly filled with tears.

'Come on,' Maggie said gently. 'I hate it when you get like this.'

'Sorry,' I muttered, trying to smile. 'Do you know what he said the other day?' Maggie shook her head. 'He said I'm spoiling her too much and not giving her proper attention - can you believe that?'

'And you know that's a complete and utter load of crap,' Maggie said, impatience in her voice.

'Is it?' I took a shuddering breath. 'In the week her childminder sees her more than I do.'

'Oh, for crying out loud,' Maggie sounded angry now. 'You've got to work, haven't you? You're supporting yourself *and* your child - and doing a bloody better job than some single parents. Robert's just a bully. Why do you let him get to you?'

'I don't know,' I shook my head slowly. 'It was all over that kitten she keeps asking for. I've told her a million times that I'm allergic to cats. Robert told her if I don't get one, he will, to keep at his house… he doesn't even like cats. I told him he shouldn't have promised her that.'

'He's just point scoring,' Maggie opened the wine and poured us a glass each, then tore me off some kitchen roll.

'Yeah, I know,' I blew my nose and took a sip of my wine. 'I just hate it when he turns on me like that… it's like we were never married.'

'Oh, for fuck sake Frankie,' Maggie chuckled. 'That's what happens when you split up. Don't take it so much to heart. You're still letting him hurt you.'

'But… I didn't do anything wrong,' I said. 'It was *him* that cheated - more than once - I don't get why he wants to punish me. It's been a whole year now.'

'Ah, but you *did* do something wrong,' Maggie said wisely. 'You showed him up by leaving him.'

Later that evening, after I'd put Gracie to bed, I went and sat outside on my tiny patio, as I liked to do when the weather was warm, before I got ready for bed myself. I felt depressed and slightly ashamed for breaking down like that - not ashamed that I'd done it in front of Maggie, she was used to it, but ashamed of myself. It had jolted me earlier when I had said it had been a whole year since I had left Robert. I should be over it, I thought sadly, I need to move on.

Leaving Robert had taken careful planning, to the point of it almost becoming farcical. I knew with a heavy certainty that I couldn't just sit him down, tell him it was "over" and that I was leaving him.

Firstly, there was no way, in any stretch of the imagination, that he would have allowed me to walk out with Gracie. And walking away without her was out of the question. Secondly, I knew that the moment I gave him my reasons, he would do some fast talking and I hadn't felt strong enough to argue my case. Any accusations thrown at him would have been denied, then he would have turned it around on me - it would have been my paranoia and insecurities. Then he would have turned on the charm and sweet-talked me. I simply couldn't face it.

I had suspected affairs before, with no real evidence, but you know... you just *know*. It seemed to me that our relationship had come in two parts: before Gracie and after Gracie. Don't get me wrong, he loved her, the only time I had seen him cry was after I had given birth, but things change when you have a child. Sadly, some men just can't handle it.

I wouldn't be the first woman to talk herself out of her worst fears. I didn't want to believe it, so I convinced myself it was all in my head - not my Robert. Not my handsome, funny, adoring husband.

His behaviour towards me slowly began to change - more impatience, a palpable irritation with me, a vague *withdrawal*. It was slow, and it was painful. I was constantly confused and hurting. His working hours became longer and his business trips more frequent. And somewhere in the midst of all this, he became more possessive of me. And I was foolish, telling myself that it must have meant he loved me.

When Gracie was approaching her third birthday, in defiance to his protests, I decided to go back to work part-time. I was nowhere near any kind of a decision about leaving him, I just wanted to claw back some of my independence. I went back to my old job, working for a property management company as Purchase and Sales Ledger, and at least felt that I had something else in my life, even though I missed Gracie terribly. As some sort of punishment, or so it seemed, Robert withdrew even more - added to the mix was increasingly frequent passive-aggressive hints that I wasn't cleaning the house as often and Gracie was suffering now I wasn't a full-time mother.

When Will returned from his three-year absence that summer, I was absolutely delighted. I had no idea what had happened between him and Robert. In fact, I'd given up trying to get to the bottom of it.

Will had cut all contact, he didn't even know that we had got married in that time. I'd felt too awkward approaching Will's mother to try and get a number or address... plus I knew that would have angered Robert.

One moment everything was fine… well, maybe not *exactly* fine between the pair of them, Will had dropped out of university and got engaged to his girlfriend Daisy, and Robert had predictably hit the roof, but Will seemed happy enough… then he just left.

Anyway, he returned home and contacted me, and we began meeting up when we could, Will implored me not to tell Robert, and I didn't. Also, I didn't question Will about what had made him leave. All I could gather was that him and Robert had had an almighty argument, and I didn't like the look of fury and hurt in Will's eyes when his father was mentioned.

In the New Year after Will had come home, Robert's behaviour changed again. I vaguely wondered at first if he'd gone to some sort of counselling. Starved of affection, I embraced his sudden improvement of mood and it took me a while to notice that longer absences from him coincided with this happier and more loving Robert. And finally, I realised I couldn't just close my eyes to it anymore.

Although, *what* I needed to do, I had no idea.

Maggie talked endlessly about private detectives and the such, but truth be told, I was petrified. Will suggested leaving him and going to live at his, but that terrified me too. Full of turmoil and a new anger that was foreign to me, I began to withdraw myself as Robert had before, and although I was in a miserable hell all of my own, I felt less like a victim.

I became fixated on his mobile phone. He had always been slightly secretive with it, but before, when things were good, it never entered my head that he was deliberately never leaving it unattended. I knew he wasn't stupid and the likelihood of him actually leaving any evidence on there was next to nothing - but I wanted that phone.

The last straw was on Valentine's night, not that we had anything planned, but when he announced the evening before that he had to be away overnight, I can't even remember where, I felt like my body had been filled with ice. It still over-whelmed me with bleakness - the memory of laying in our king-sized bed alone that night, sobbing like my heart was breaking, fighting out the awful images in my head of Robert making love to another woman.

It wasn't long after that awful night that I managed to get my hands on his phone. Rare for him, he had fallen asleep on the sofa whilst watching whatever film we had on, and his phone was poking slightly out of his trouser pocket. My heart hammering wildly, I had made myself wait for ten minutes before I went over and knelt down beside him, I watched him for another few minutes, then I eased his phone out slowly, looking at his face the whole time. When I finally had it, I ran upstairs and shut myself in the bathroom. With shaking hands, I began to go through his text messages. Nothing suspicious caught my eye. No surprise there. I scrolled through his contacts feeling a strange disappointment, and swearing quietly to myself, started towards the door, when on impulse I looked at his calls. Straight away I could see something wrong - very, very wrong. "K.D. Suppliers" had called him at 11.22 the evening before and again at 12.15 in the afternoon on the same day. I started to scroll back, some days he had called the same number three or four times - some of them late in the evening. And that number had called him, one of them, dated six weeks previous at 6.30 in the morning and just before midnight. I sat down numbly on the edge of the bath feeling a sob hitching in my chest. I kept scrolling, a buzzing was filling my ears - this wasn't right... I couldn't even begin to formulate an excuse.

I went into our bedroom and scribbled down the number clumsily, took his phone back downstairs, and not trusting myself to put it back in his pocket with my hands trembling so much, perched it on the side of the sofa next to him, then belted back upstairs and threw up again and again, feeling like I was going to pass out.

A few days later, feeling like a coward and chickening out of calling the number, I had texted it, simply asking who it was. No reply. I didn't even tell Maggie of my discovery. And with self-loathing and a hollow heart, I went back to ignoring the situation.

It wasn't until nine months later I made the gut-wrenching discovery about Lennie. Robert and I had become something like polite strangers. I'm ashamed to admit we still made love once or twice a month - a far cry from our early days, and to the outside world we probably seemed like a normal married couple. Him and Will had, not exactly made up, but were at least on speaking terms.

Will and Daniel had opened a restaurant together - I was so proud - and on opening night I finally got to meet Lennie. It was a strange evening. The atmosphere was tense. I had put it down to the awkwardness between father and son, but in retrospect I could see, *feel* that there was something else. Of course, I found out later that Lennie had absolutely no idea that Robert was Will's father, and Robert had been clueless that the love of Will's life was the girl he had slept with, and despite how terrible it was, I later was slightly impressed that they both held it together for the evening.

Two months later, still convinced that Robert's affair had been going on all year, I found a bank statement, and what a read that was. Expensive jewellery, hotels and meals all around the country, flowers, and even a spending spree of nearly three hundred pounds in Ann Summers. And pitifully, my first thought was: *that's it. It's serious. He's going to leave me.*

In desperation I had rung Will, calmly asking him to come over - Robert had been away - and when he turned up, I had hysterically broken down, showing him the statement that I had hidden away in my handbag, along with the phone number I had found all those months ago. And as I had tearfully showed him the number, telling him about all the calls, the penny started to drop. Because, straight away I could see something was very wrong with him. He'd looked at the number, then looked at me with the strangest expression, then stared at that scrap of paper again, his face visibly paling. Then without explanation he had left.

I can't explain how I knew, but it happened so fast… almost like I had read the script. My first thought was, *he knows that number…* followed by, *it's her. It's Lennie.* Then as my mind ran through Robert's behaviour all year, my next thought, with complete clarity was, *but now it's someone else…* I had no reason to defend her, but I knew she hadn't cheated on Will.

Will was beyond devastation and disappeared again. I went to see Lennie, and in all honesty, I felt pity for her. I could see she was sorry, and scared, and numb with misery. I had wanted to hate her, make her feel worse than she already did, but when I looked at her pale young face, her dark eyes shadowed and full of agony, I couldn't. She was as much as a victim as I was.

To cut a long story short… Will returned and eventually forgave her. They got their happily ever after. And I? Not so much. It took six months of plotting and planning and lying. I went full-time at work as company accountant and slowly saved my money and went hunting for somewhere for Gracie and me to live. I had help from my parents, they were over the moon that I was leaving Robert and helped me furnish my small two-bedroom house. Will and Daniel decorated it and tidied the gardens. I had to wait for Robert to go away on "business". Thankfully it was for two days, so I packed what I could and shipped Gracie off to my parents' as she had no idea of what was going on, and Will, Daniel, Adam and Maggie helped me with the frantic process of moving out. And I won't lie, it was horrible.

I had to cheerfully explain to a bewildered Gracie that we were going to live in a lovely new house, just me and her, and Daddy was going to stay at his house, so she would have *two* houses to play at… how lucky was she? And then, with a fear inside me that was huge and over-whelming, I turned off my phone and waited.

It was such a lovely early summer evening. I thought how nice it would be to be in love and share it with someone - walks in the countryside and cosy drinks in a pub garden. Or making dinner together like Robert and I had in the early days, sharing a bottle of wine, laughing… just being together.

I stood up abruptly. I had to stop these stupid thoughts, I was torturing myself. Feeling irritated with myself, I went back indoors to wearily iron school and work clothes, pushing away the solid weight of loneliness that was never far away.

CHAPTER THREE

I loved my weekends with Gracie, but sometimes it was a relief on a Monday morning to be able to switch off at work from my less-than-satisfactory personal life. That may sound like I was an incredibly selfish person. I knew that I was very lucky to have a daughter, and my own home, and friends... but I think most single parents, without even an at least casual love interest, will know precisely what I mean.

I loved my job. My boss, Scott Windsor, was, as far as bosses go, OK. He unnervingly reminded me of an older Robert. He had a big grin that he seemed to be able to flash on and off, without it ever reaching his eyes. He also had an eye for the younger girls in the office, something that didn't go unnoticed, and they nicknamed him "letch". However, that didn't extend to me - I wasn't the slightest bit insulted - he was an old pal of my father, and I had known him since I was a little girl... something we didn't advertise. And it made juggling work and motherhood a lot easier - if I was running a little late in the mornings after school drop-off or if, on the rare occasion, I had to pick Gracie up because she was poorly, he didn't mind.

I would have found him a little intimidating if I hadn't have known him from old. In fact, there was only one other person in the office that wasn't slightly wary of him, and that was Bea. She was another reason I enjoyed work. She'd been at the company forever as the bookkeeper and was practically part of the building. No-nonsense, kind and motherly, she never forgot a birthday and was relied on for organising card signings, gift collections, office parties and any out-of-work events. Her desk was like a home from home, with her biscuit tin and her framed photographs of her daughters, grandchildren and her Norwich Terrier, Prudence. A picture of her late husband, Alfie, was kept in her drawer. She once told me it was upsetting to have him looking at her all day but liked him to be at work with her. She was also Godmother to Gracie. I had worked there for a few years before I fell pregnant with her, and she had almost been like a proud grandma-to-be.

When I arrived at work she had already made me a mug of coffee and left a homemade flapjack on a napkin next to it.

'Thank you, Bea,' I said gratefully, putting my glasses on and settling myself in my chair. 'Did you have a nice weekend?'

'Yes, I did, thank you my dear,' she replied through a mouthful of flapjack. 'How was your Will's wedding? Did Gracie look beautiful?'

'It was lovely,' I replied, trying to sound happier than I felt about it. 'Gracie looked gorgeous, of course.'

'Naturally,' she chuckled. 'I love weddings, I always cry. I bet Will looked as handsome as a prince, you must bring in a photo.'

She had met Will on a couple of occasions and he had been my plus-one at our Christmas meal - she had been rather taken with him.

'Yeah, he did,' I assured her.

'Oh look, here comes your admirer,' she said in a low voice.

I glanced up and sighed, Jamie, my thorn in my side, was indeed strolling over in our direction. I stared intently at my monitor.

'Good morning ladies,' he said cheerfully, pausing at our desk.

He had started work just before Easter and was constantly chatting me up - not in any sort of worrying way, I had a slight suspicion he was sending me up half the time. In his early thirties, he was sweet looking - Maggie would have eaten him for breakfast - dark boyish hair with a trendy beard, innocent blue eyes and very white teeth - he reminded me of a slightly manlier and better-looking Jack Whitehall. He was a client property administrator, which meant he had the gift of the gab, and I found him slightly irritating. The two admin girls, Louise and Sophie, who happened to be friends with Mr Windsor's spoilt daughter, both shallow, but very pretty, were *big* fans of his. He'd nicknamed them Sharon and Tracy, which they found hysterical. I'm not sure why, I would have been rather affronted.

'Good morning, dear,' Bea beamed at him. I murmured a vague greeting and tried to look busy.

'You're looking nice this morning, Bea,' he said, 'and you look ravishing as usual, Frank. New dress?'

'No,' I looked at him over my glasses, 'and don't call me Frank.'

'I love it when you look at me like that, very school teacher-ish,' he winked, and went on his way out of the office.

'For God's sake,' I grumbled.

'Oh, bless him. He's got a little crush on you, that's all,' Bea looked warmly after him.

'Hmm,' I pushed my glasses up and got on with my work.

After work, I went to pick Gracie up from her childminder, Rachel. I liked Rachel. It took me a while to find someone suitable and it had been a dreadful wrench for me, entrusting someone to look after Gracie. One of the best things about her, apart from the fact that she was an excellent childminder and came highly recommended, was that she seemed immune to Robert's charms. We'd become good friends over the years and gradually, in bits and pieces, she knew most of our history.

'Hi, how's she been?' I asked when she opened the door. She stood back and let me in. She was in her thirties but looked a lot younger, with long fair hair permanently up in some sort of ponytail or bun, and usually with either food, paint or some child-related stain on her clothes - and yet she had a serene calmness about her. I suppose that was a requirement if you're going to look after other people's children all day. I certainly couldn't do it.

'Mm,' she smiled a small smile, and lowered her voice, 'tricky today, sorry hun.'

'Christ, what now?' I inwardly sighed.

'She hit Jake. She wouldn't tell me why, so she had time out for a bit,' she rubbed the top of my arm, looking apologetic. 'She refused to say sorry and at snack-time she threw her toast on the floor. But,' she added kindly, 'she's been OK for the last hour.'

'I'm so sorry,' I followed her through to the playroom off of her kitchen. Gracie was sitting cross-legged in front of a wooden doll's house, chatting merrily to herself.

'Gracie, Mummy's here,' Rachel called from the doorway.

'Mummy!' she scrambled up, dropping the doll that was in her hand and belted over, her arms out-stretched.

'Hello baby,' I knelt down and hugged her. It was hard to believe that my angelic-looking little girl could turn into the devil at will.

'I missed you Mummy,' she always said that when I picked her up. 'I had cottage pie at school for dinner and it was yukky,' she informed me. 'And Chantelle got told off by Miss Sutton for calling Harley a bum-face.'

'Oh dear,' I said, standing up, 'not the best day then,' I glanced at Rachel, who still looked apologetic. 'Go and get your things.'

'You OK?' she asked.

'Yeah,' I shrugged, 'she's been worse.'

At home, after we had read her school book, eaten our dinner together and she'd had her bath, I sat down with her in the living room, bracing myself.

'Gracie,' I began firmly, 'can you tell me why you hit Jake today?'

She blinked a few times, 'I'm sorry,' she said eventually.

'No, Gracie,' I said, 'you can't just say sorry. Rachel said you wouldn't say sorry to Jake... you can't just say sorry to me and think it's OK. It is not OK. What have I told you? Hitting is wrong.'

'Well, Jake's an idiot,' her eyes started to fill with tears and she set her jaw in very much the same way Robert did when he was angry.

'Gracie... that's not a very nice thing to say, and that's no excuse to hit anyone, ever.'

'Well,' she said loudly, 'he *is* an idiot and I don't like him,' she sprung up and ran from the room, thundering up the stairs.

'For fuck's sake,' I rubbed my temples. I went and took a painkiller and counted to a hundred before going upstairs.

I found her in her room, sitting cross-legged on her bed, her arms folded, bottom lip protruding.

'Gracie,' I said as evenly as I could and crossed the room to sit on the edge of her bed, 'you know you've been naughty. Tomorrow you *are* going to say sorry to Jake or I will take your tablet away for a whole week, OK?'

'Mummy,' she looked at me solemnly, 'why don't we live with Daddy anymore? Jake said *his* daddy lives with *him*. He said my daddy can't love me very much.'

'Oh, sweetie,' I sighed, 'we've been through this a million times. Jake shouldn't have said that, but you know it's not true. Daddy loves you very much.'

'But you and Daddy don't love each other anymore,' she said dully.

'No,' I murmured, feeling lost.

'Can I get into bed now?' she said quietly.

I had a bath and pottered about upstairs tidying until I was confident she was asleep, then went downstairs thinking I might ring Maggie, then decided I didn't feel like talking to anyone.

Gracie was breaking my heart. The guilt was eating me up and making me question my decisions. I knew *exactly* what Maggie would say... I shouldn't feel guilty, what I did was for self-preservation. If anyone should feel guilty, it should be Robert. His daughter was the last person he was thinking of when he was screwing around. I knew that was true, but I was the one that took her away from her home and her daddy and that's all she knew in her moments of despair.

One of the hardest things when I left Robert, was keeping him away from Gracie for a little while. Not out of spite - I wouldn't do any of the dreadful things that mothers can do to hurt the father of their child - simply because seeing Gracie would mean seeing me, and I won't lie, I was terrified. Terrified of his reaction, his fury and also that he would try and take her from me. So, I stayed in the house, my phone switched off, and waited for the dust to settle. Another fear was that he would go straight to my parents, assuming I would be there, a fear I voiced to them. My father was not daunted, said he'd like an excuse to tell Robert precisely what he thought of him.

I left on a Friday, and felt relatively safe all weekend, but was petrified he would turn up at Gracie's school. I had the intensely awkward task of talking to her head teacher and the family support worker about the situation. They were very sympathetic and assured me that she would be safe, and for a week or so she could be picked up twenty minutes earlier to avoid any confrontation. So then, unable to ask Rachel to do that, I had to explain to Scott too and leave work early for the next week.

I switched my phone back on late that first Sunday evening and there were countless missed calls and, surprisingly, only one text. That text made my blood run cold. It simply stated that he would make me sorry. If I was more melodramatic I would have been scared it was a violent threat - but I understood what he meant. I would be punished.

I left it for a whole week, constantly fearful he would come bursting into my office, or that he would, more his style, watch me and follow me home. However, he done none of those things. After slight relief that I was being left alone, I then became wary and suspicious as to why he was keeping quiet. Our first conversation was not a pleasant one. Will came to play with Gracie and kept her out of the way, while I shut myself in my bedroom with a large drink.

'You fucking bitch,' was the first thing he had said, followed by threats that he would do everything in his power to get custody of Gracie, and berating me for chucking away our marriage because of my paranoia and instability. I had been expecting all of that and let him rage on while I remained silent.

When he eventually had shouted himself hoarse, I calmly told him that I wasn't coming back, I didn't love him anymore, that if he hassled me in any way, shape or form, I would contact the police and that he could see Gracie the following weekend and then we could come to a suitable arrangement in regard to his contact with her.

'Contact?' he had snarled. 'Contact? She's my fucking daughter.'

'I will ring you in the week when you have calmed down,' I had replied and ended the call. Then, shaking from head to toe, I had broken down and sobbed.

Thank God for Will - he had, upon seeing my face when I had come back downstairs, promptly whisked Gracie off out for a Burger King, bathed her and read her a story, then spent the evening holding my hand while I cried some more and poured my heart out.

Of course, things eventually calmed down. I suspected that Robert had spoken to someone about fighting for custody of Gracie, and was told it wouldn't happen, as he never mentioned it again. We agreed that he could pick her up from Rachel's every Friday and have her until evening, and on alternate weekends he would have her for the whole weekend through until Sunday night. School holidays would be negotiable, as would Christmas.

I had filed for divorce straight away, on the grounds of unreasonable behaviour - expecting a fight, I was stunned that Robert agreed without a quibble. Despite my solicitor's exasperation, I wanted nothing from him - just a fair maintenance for Gracie. I received my decree absolute at the end of the following April and thinking it would devastate me, I felt a strange relief that it was over... only it wasn't over. He still had a hold over me, he was still in my thoughts and I knew until Gracie was *a lot* older, he would still act as though he still had possession of me. I hated him, and I loved him, and was always walking on that fine line between the two. And my poor, beloved Gracie was the victim of a marriage that should never have happened. That was the worst hurt of it all.

CHAPTER FOUR

The following weekend - Robert's weekend to have Gracie, was my birthday weekend. My birthday wasn't until the Monday, but Maggie insisted we were going to have a night out with the girls on Saturday, and Bea had arranged after-work drinks on Friday at the pub around the corner from our building, then onto an Italian restaurant in town. I didn't feel that turning forty-four was a reason to celebrate, but as my Gracie-free weekends usually involved housework, going to the gym and television binging with wine, I felt it would make a nice change.

Fridays at work were always busy, and as five o'clock approached I wasn't feeling much enthusiasm about the upcoming evening. As I was doing a quick make-up repair job in the ladies', Bea came bustling in.

'I've rounded up designated drivers tonight,' she joined me at the mirror and started applying pale pink lipstick, 'so you can have a little drink tonight.'

'Lovely... thank you Bea,' I murmured. I had been planning on one glass of wine at the pub and maybe one with my meal and making an early escape.

'Jamie isn't drinking, he said you can go with him,' she continued, fluffing up her hair.

'Did he now?' I looked at her in the mirror.

'He's a sweetheart, isn't he?'

Fifteen minutes later, I was reluctantly following Jamie to his silver BMW with Louise and Sophie in tow, the pair of them tittering.

'The birthday girl can sit in the front,' Jamie opened the passenger door and stood back grinning.

'Thanks,' I slid in.

'Ooo, I didn't know you had a kid,' Sophie exclaimed from behind, I twisted round and spotted a child's car-seat in the back.

'I have a little sister,' Jamie explained, taking off his tie and chucking it in the car-seat.

Louise whispered something to Sophie and she giggled.

I stifled a sigh and decided to sit very far away from the three of them at the restaurant.

'So how old are you going to be, Frankie?' Louise asked from behind me.

'Forty-four,' I told her shortly.

'You don't look that old,' she commented.

'Well... thank you,' I glanced at Jamie, he was smiling and shaking his head.

When we reached the pub, I shot out of the car, and mumbling my thanks. I spotted Bea getting out of her car with Joe - a young guy from the office who was painfully shy but lovely, Sarah, who he had a not-so-secret crush on, and Paul, who was a little younger than me with a beautiful wife and four sons - and looked permanently knackered.

'Come on you,' Paul threw an arm around my shoulders, 'let's get you good and drunk.'

'Yes, let's,' Jamie said from behind us, 'she might eventually agree to letting me take her out,' he had been asking me out at least once a week since he had started working with us.

As the evening was so beautiful and balmy, we decided to sit in the pub garden. Louise and Sophie trotted off after Jamie to the bar, along with Paul. Joe sat awkwardly opposite Sarah, who was looking ravishing in a short yellow sundress, her huge sunglasses on top of her head, pushing back her black glossy hair. Nearby, a group of five or six young guys were eyeing her up.

'So, what's the birthday girl got planned this weekend?' Bea asked.

'Not much,' I turned my attention away from Joe who was looking at Sarah with puppy-dog eyes. 'Going out tomorrow with Maggie, probably will need all of Sunday to recover from two nights out.'

'No Gracie this weekend?' Sarah asked, and I shook my head. 'What are you doing, Joe?' she asked.

'Paintballing,' he said blushing.

'No way!' she said grinning. 'I've always wanted to do that, it looks well fun.'

'Yeah, it is,' he looked delighted, and they started chatting.

'Gosh, I wish he would just ask her out,' Bea whispered, smiling at them.

'Yeah,' I agreed watching them. Joe wasn't bad looking - he was a bit on the chunky side, but he had a sweet face.

'Young Jamie could give him lessons,' Bea smirked as he appeared in the doorway, clutching three glasses and nearly getting knocked out by the ginormous hanging basket spilling over with crimson and yellow flowers next to the door.

I pulled a face as I watched him lope over with his fan club and Paul behind him. I supposed he *was* handsome in a cheeky chappie sort of way. A shame he was so young and annoying.

'Quadruple gin for you, lovely Frankie,' he placed my glass in front of me and sat down with his orange juice on the other side of Bea. He looked at Joe and Sarah, still in deep conversation, and grinned.

'Thank you, Jamie,' I said.

'Urghh, my mum drinks gin,' Louise said as she sat down with Sophie. The blokes that had been eyeing Sarah, turned their attention to the pair of them. Sophie wriggled her off-the-shoulder top down a little further and Louise crossed her very suntanned legs, showing off a lot of thigh. One of the men caught me looking over and he winked at me. I smiled blandly and turned away again.

'- and I only was meant to be popping out to fetch the coffees,' Jamie was in the middle of regaling an apparently funny story to the table at large, Paul was chuckling, and Louise and Sophie were giggling again, 'and the stupid arsehole said he'd have sacked me if three of his staff hadn't walked out the week before. I handed in my notice a week later.'

The girls both screamed with laughter. I drained half of my drink, deciding maybe I should get "good and drunk" to survive the evening.

We got to the restaurant an hour and a half later, I was well on the way to becoming tremendously drunk. Jamie promptly ordered four bottles of wine as we were seated, and a jug of fruit punch for himself and Bea. I was rather irritated that I found myself sitting between him and Paul, but maybe less so with alcohol inside me.

'Here's to the birthday girl,' Bea said raising a glass.

'Happy birthday,' everyone chorused, I half-heartedly raised my wine glass and knocked some back.

'We doing starters?' Paul asked, examining the menu.

'Yep, I'm starving,' I said at the same time as Sophie said, 'No, I'm dieting, I'm so fat.' Everyone ignored her and started deciding what to have.

'I don't want anything with garlic,' Jamie nudged my leg with his, 'just in case I get a kiss later.'

I shifted an inch away in my chair and turned to talk to Paul, asking him after his boys. When the waiter came and hovered by our table, I ordered the garlic bread and salad.

'I'll have the same,' Jamie said. 'It's OK if you both have it,' he grinned sideways at me.

'So how come Mr Windsor didn't come?' Louise called down the table.

'It's his wedding anniversary,' I said without thinking.

'Oh right,' she smirked and said something quietly to Sophie.

'Oh, shut up,' I muttered to myself, Jamie looked at me for a moment and then burst out laughing.

'What's funny?' Louise asked.

'Frankie is,' Jamie said, 'she's got me in stitches over here.'

I sighed and topped up my drink.

After the starters were cleared away, Paul, Joe and Sarah went outside for a cigarette.

'Joe and Sarah are getting on well,' Bea looked fondly after them.

'Ew, he's punching well above his weight,' Louise said, and Sophie laughed.

'Why's that?' Jamie said mildly. I glanced at him and was surprised to see him frowning.

'Oh,' Louise looked startled. 'Well... he's OK, well he would be if he lost a bit a weight and got a decent haircut.'

'Right,' Jamie said.

An awkward silence followed. I excused myself and went to the toilet, when I returned, the others were back and everyone was chatting noisily.

'Alright?' Jamie asked as I sat down.

'Yep,' I replied as he refilled my glass.

The main courses arrived, and I tucked into my pasta, finding that I was ravenous after   drinking on an empty stomach.

'So,' Jamie turned towards me, after a couple of bites of his pizza, 'when are you going to let me take you out?'

'I'm not,' I shook my head.

'You know how to hurt a man,' he said, not looking the slightest bit deterred. 'I tell you what, you give me three *really* good reasons why not, and I will give you three reasons why you should.'

I thought about it for a moment, 'Well, firstly, you're too young -'

'Over the age of consent,' he interrupted.

'Hush up,' I smiled a little, 'secondly, you're a player - I don't do players... and thirdly, I don't fancy you.'

'Ouch,' he grinned.

'Sorry,' I shrugged.

'Hmm well, as far as being a player, you know the last time I had a date?' he raised his eyebrows and I shook my head. 'Over a year ago.'

I laughed derisively.

'I'm serious!'

'Whatever,' I carried on eating, then said, 'OK, I will humour you, give me your three good reasons then.'

'Mmm, well...' he put his slice of pizza down. 'Firstly, I'm good-looking and I'm hilarious -'

'That's two things,' I interrupted.

'Nope,' he grinned, 'it's a package deal.'

'OK,' I rolled my eyes.

'Secondly, I know how to treat a lady,' he lowered his voice, 'and thirdly... I'm amazing in bed.'

I looked into his eyes for a moment, then burst out laughing.

'See?' he sat back in his seat. 'Hilarious all the way.'

'Still nope,' I turned back to my food, trying to hide a smile.

After our meal, Joe, Sarah, Louise and Sophie wanted to go on to somewhere else.

'Let's go to Coco's,' Sarah suggested. Coco's Bar was a music bar in town.

'Nope, I'm done,' Paul said, 'I've got to take Max to football practice early in the morning.'

Jamie, who was busy sorting out the bill looked up at me, 'Frankie?'

I shook my head. I'd only been in Coco's a couple of times and had felt like a pensioner.

'I'd better not,' I said, 'I'm out again tomorrow.'

'I'll decline,' he directed at the others. 'I've got to be up early too, got an early morning hot date.'

I watched him looking back down at the bill with a small smile on his lips and decided he was winding me up with one of his stupid jokes.

We went outside after the bill was settled, Paul kissed me goodnight and Bea hugged me before they got into Bea's car - Paul lived up the road from Bea. The others had drifted off after saying their goodbyes towards the town centre.

'Alone at last,' Jamie nudged me.

'I can get a taxi home if it's out your way,' I offered.

'It's not.'

'But you don't know where I live.'

He laughed and strode off towards his BMW - I reluctantly followed him.

As I did up my seatbelt, I gave him my street name and he pulled off, driving in silence for a little while.

'Enjoy yourself tonight?' he inquired politely.

'It was OK,' I said, then feeling I sounded ungrateful, 'nice of everyone to come out.'

'Yeah,' he swore quietly as another car pulled out on him. 'I prefer the Italian on the High Street though, the food's better.'

Glad that he wasn't flirting, and we were having a normal conversation, I agreed with him.

'Have you eaten at The Lounge Lizard?' he asked.

'Yeah… actually, my stepson owns it,' I said, trying not to sound boastful.

'For real?' he glanced over. 'That's cool… he a chef?'

'No, he just runs it with his friend.'

'Cool,' he repeated. 'Nice little goldmine he's got there. The food's fantastic.'

'Yeah, he's done good,' I said fondly, 'he's only twenty-nine.'

'Not much younger than me then,' he murmured.

I fell silent again and he started singing along to the radio, not particularly tunefully.

'I'm here, just in front of that Audi,' I said as he turned into my road.

'There we go, you gorgeous creature,' he said as he pulled over, 'delivered safely to your door, and I kept my hands to myself.'

'Enjoy your hot date tomorrow,' I said mockingly. *Not a player, my arse,* I thought.

'Jealous?' he winked, then laughed. 'My date is my six-year-old sister, we're going to the zoo.'

'Oh,' I opened the door and climbed out, then reached down to pick up my bag. 'Well, thanks for the lift.'

'Hey Frankie,' he said as I went to close the door, I bent back down. 'Guess what I was looking at when you got out?'

'Oh, for heaven's sake,' I shut the door firmly and walked towards my front door, without turning around, I put a hand up as I let myself in. He beeped his horn twice and pulled away - I could hear him singing through his open window.

The following evening, I decided to go and get ready at Maggie's house. I'd planned to crash there the night too, as she lived nearer to town. Just as I was leaving, Will rang me. He'd returned from his honeymoon late the night before.

'Hello,' I sat on the stairs, 'how are you? Did you have a lovely time?'

'Great,' he said, sounding cheerful, 'swam in the sea, ate like pigs and spent a fortune.'

I laughed, 'Back to the grindstone... you in the Lizard tonight? I might put my head in.'

'I might put in an appearance, although -' he lowered his voice, 'Lennie isn't very well, she was sick a couple of times, wondering if she ate something dodgy.'

'Oh really?' I glanced at my watch and stood up, 'Gracie said she was sick before the wedding... hope she's OK,' I added.

'Yeah, she looks like crap to be honest... might drag her to the doctors on Monday.'

'Yeah, I would - listen, I need to go, I'm on my way out,' I said apologetically.

'OK, maybe see you later,' he said. 'If not, I will come and see you Monday, you doing anything for your birthday?'

'I said I'd take Gracie to Pizza Hut, join us?'

'Yeah, great... OK. See you later Frankie.'

'See you,' I ended the call smiling. He was such a lovely lad... well, man... I often wondered how on earth he was Robert's son.

I loved Maggie's house. Despite her lack of a husband now, it felt like such a cosy, albeit slightly chaotic, family environment. A far cry from my organised and sometimes lonely little home. I sat in her large, untidy kitchen, doing my make-up at the table, while her eldest son, Tyler, a good-looking young lad with Maggie's blonde hair and, thankfully, his father's height, made a stack of sandwiches for him and his two friends who were playing the PlayStation in the living room. Maggie was arguing good-naturedly with him about him apparently teasing his brother Nathan earlier - he had a new girlfriend who had been over earlier in the day, and he was now upstairs sulking. Maggie had grounded him for telling Tyler to fuck off.

'Christ, be thankful you have a daughter,' she said, handing me a glass of wine as Tyler disappeared back into the living room, sniggering.

'They're lovely though,' I said examining my face in my mirror. 'Can I borrow your hair-straighteners?'

'They're in my room,' Maggie started wiping up crumbs. 'Lovely… sometimes,' she conceded, 'but, fuck me, I feel like a referee half the time.'

I finished getting ready in her bedroom - probably the tidiest room in the house - and we got a cab into town.

We were meeting up with our friend, Sally. I use the term friend loosely - she could be a bit of a nightmare. We had also invited our old school friend Debs, but she couldn't get a babysitter, and we both knew that if Sally had got wind of us going out and not being included, she would have sulked. The younger Sally had been a good laugh, but divorced Sally was a moaner and was constantly having a pity party all of her own. She had an annoying habit of comparing her problems to everyone else's, no matter how bad they were, and hers were always the most tragic. Also, if you had something good going on, she would make you feel guilty. I hid my exasperation better than what Maggie did, she was constantly rolling her eyes and loudly and indiscreetly changing the subject.

We went to our favourite wine bar - the wine bar that I had first met Robert in, and ordered large gin and tonics and waited for Sally to turn up. She wandered in, promptly at eight o'clock, and after morosely saying hello, and not asking how we were, started complaining about her ex-husband. After gathering that their daughter's maintenance had been late, *again,* and that she had spotted his new wife in Sainsbury's earlier, and "that fat bimbo" had definitely had a boob job, I began to switch off.

'Oh, my fucking God,' Maggie said when Sally had gone to the ladies', 'can't we ditch her? I'm seriously considering Harikari,'- I giggled, 'why are we friends with her again?'

'Shh,' I said. 'I feel sorry for her.'

Sally returned from the ladies' and sat down sighing, 'What have I missed?'

'We were just talking about Japanese rituals,' Maggie said seriously.

I turned my laugh into a cough and excused myself. In the ladies', I tidied my face and checked the time. Surprisingly it was only half past nine. I walked out, squeezing myself past a noisy group of people, when a hand shot out and caught the top of my arm.

'Frankie?'

I swung round, looking for the owner of the hand.

'David,' I gasped in surprise and shock.

'It *is* you,' he started to smile, his familiar dark eyes raking my face. 'God, it's good to see you.'

CHAPTER FIVE

I stared at him, temporarily lost for words, my first emotion was pleasure at seeing him, then a nudge of shame at what I had done to him.

'You look fantastic,' he said, 'really well. How long has it been?'

'Oh,' I regained my composure with effort, 'ten, eleven years? Wow...' I smiled, 'a long time. You're looking well too.'

And he did. He looked older - naturally, but it suited him. His face was thinner, his dark hair greying a little at the temples, but he looked more self-assured, and his eyes less innocent.

'What are you doing here?' I asked. 'I mean, in Fernberry?'

'I moved back last year,' he was still studying my face, then he grinned. 'God... sorry, I can't believe it's really you - although I'm surprised we haven't bumped into each other before now... sorry, how rude of me, how are you?'

'Yeah,' I nodded, 'I'm good, and you?'

'Good, really good,' he glanced over my shoulder. 'Is that... is that Maggie?'

I turned my head to look over at our table. Maggie had stood up and was squinting over at us, short-sighted and too vain to wear her glasses out.

'Yes... actually, I better get back to her,' I gestured awkwardly.

'Yes, of course,' he paused for a moment, then kissed me on the cheek. 'Well, nice to see you. Enjoy your evening, Frankie.'

'You too,' I murmured. He nodded and then turned back to the group of people he was with.

I went and sat back down.

'Who was that?' Maggie asked, now sitting down but craning her neck in David's direction.

'David.'

'David?' she frowned, then comprehension dawned on her face. 'David? *Your* David?'

'Yes,' I looked over at him, he had his back to us and was talking to a pretty Mediterranean-looking woman in a navy- blue dress.

Even Sally looked semi-interested.

'Is that his wife?' Maggie asked avidly.

The woman glanced over at us.

'Stop staring,' I turned slightly in my chair. 'I don't know, we spoke for like two minutes.'

'She's pretty,' Sally looked away. 'The one that got away, eh? I always liked David.'

'Well, we split up for a reason,' I shrugged. 'Obviously it wasn't meant to be - even if Robert hadn't have come along.'

David and his friends went over to a table at the other side of the bar and Maggie gave up trying to get a good look.

Just after half past ten, Sally decided to get a taxi home, claiming her sciatica was playing up. We waved her off and wandered up the road to The Lounge Lizard - Will's restaurant. Typically for a Saturday night, it was heaving.

'Hey, Frankie,' Adam appeared behind the bar as we squeezed our way in.

'What are you doing on that side of the bar?' I asked loudly.

'Doing a shift here and there,' he leant over, grabbed my hand and kissed it, then did the same to Maggie. 'Will said as I'm here most the time, I might as well.'

You couldn't help but love Adam. Ridiculously pretty, with his blonde hair, long-lashed bluey-green eyes, a body to die for and his charming, slightly outrageous personality. He always seemed to say the things that nobody else dared to, but in such a way you couldn't possibly be offended - he was simply hilarious and lovable. He was Lennie's best friend, and a perfect match for her slight socially awkward shyness - or so I had decided - he seemed to drag her out of herself. And he was fiercely loyal too - you upset Lennie, and you upset him.

'If you want a table, you're out of luck,' he continued. 'We are chocka.'

'No, just a drink,' I said.

'Cocktails? Sex on the Beach? A Porn Star Martini? Me, slathered in chocolate sauce?' he winked at Maggie. 'I know you're gagging, Maggie... Magging,' he laughed. 'Oh bloody hell, I'm funny... I'll get you a couple of G and T's on the house.'

'Stop giving drinks away to everyone you know,' Dom, Will's head barman and Adam's boyfriend grumbled as he squeezed past him to serve some girls on the other side of us.

'OK,' Adam said cheerfully. 'Don't tell on me,' he mouthed.

I shook my head, giggling.

'Oh, he's edible,' Maggie watched him waiting to use the optics.

'He's a pain in the arse,' Dom said, a slight smile behind his beard.

'Is Will about?' I asked him.

'No, sorry my lovely,' he finished serving and leant over the bar. 'He put his head in earlier but went home about an hour ago.'

Will had made a good decision employing Dom - I hadn't realised until the wedding that they knew each other from old - nobody, and I mean *nobody* was going to start any trouble in the bar when he was about. Tall, muscular and bearded, he reminded me of a big bear with his rumbling deep voice. However, I discovered at the wedding, he was actually a big softy. Still... I wouldn't have liked to get on the wrong side of him.

Maggie and I spent the rest of the evening sat at the bar, chatting to Adam in-between him serving, before we reluctantly went to find a taxi back to hers.

'So, weird bumping into David, eh?' she said as we both climbed into her bed.

'Yeah, a little,' I pondered on it for a moment. 'I'm glad he doesn't hate me.'

'He's an OK bloke,' Maggie mumbled, turning on her side.

'I suppose,' I pulled the duvet over and stared up at the darkened ceiling. 'You move on though, don't you?'

'Yeah,' she said sleepily.

A minute later she began to snore softly, and I turned over too.

I wondered if David and I would have still been together if Robert hadn't come between us and I hadn't lost my head. *Probably not*, I decided. Like I had voiced earlier, we split up for a reason, and that reason wasn't entirely Robert.

David had been picky, fussy, too sensible and if I were truthful, boring. I remembered thinking, when Robert and I were in the throes of love and passion, had David ever made me breathless with laughter, or made my heart race with just the thought of having sex with him? He hadn't. But, I loved him in my own way - well, enough to agree to marry him. But I knew now, being older and wiser, the flipside was this: *David would never have cheated on me.* And how did I know that? I just did. I wondered if such a thing was possible - someone who could excite the hell out of you *and* be faithful and loyal. Be dependable without being boring. Any woman that had found such a man, I thought wistfully, was lucky.

My thoughts drifted towards Will and Lennie. I hoped that she knew how very lucky she was... *I want what they have...* It had been like a classic love story - Will's unrequited love, then finally winning his fair lady's hand... overcoming the obstacle that had been Robert, then their happy ending.

As I drifted towards sleep, I thought to myself that if it went wrong between them, I would be very disappointed. Their love, somehow, gave me hope.

I woke up early on Sunday morning to the smell of bacon drifting through the house and loud voices from downstairs. I went to the toilet and brushed my teeth, wincing at my bloodshot eyes and pale face in the mirror, then wandered downstairs.

Maggie was stood at the cooker in an over-sized t-shirt and bare legs, frying bacon and chatting to her boys, both sat at the table.

'Good morning,' she said brightly, and handed me a mug of tea.

'Thanks,' I said gratefully, pulling up a chair.

'Bacon butty?' she asked.

'Oh God no,' I shuddered. 'I'll be sick.'

'Pisshead,' Tyler said, then catching a look from Maggie, said, 'sorry.'

In the end, she forced some toast on me, which I ate, then decided I felt better. She had work at midday, so I drove home after I had helped her wash up the breakfast things. Feeling slightly guilty, I had a lazy afternoon sunbathing and reading until Gracie was due home. Just before six o'clock, I threw on an old sundress over my bikini and mentally prepared myself for whatever mood Robert was going to be in.

He was, however, in one of his more "sunnier" moods.

'Mummy!' Gracie yelled as soon as I opened the door. 'I missed you... I had steak for dinner and chocolate ice-cream and Daddy has brought me a new paddling pool and it has a dolphin in it that squirts water. And guess what? I have another wiggly tooth and Daddy told me to eat apples to make it come out quicker.'

'Lovely, sweetie,' I hugged her as Robert stepped in uninvited and watched Gracie fondly.

'Did she read her school book?' I asked over her head.

'Yes, three times,' Robert said. 'And done all of her maths, and I bathed her and washed her hair after we got out of the pool, so she doesn't need one before bed.'

'Thanks.'

'And this is for you,' he pulled a small wrapped box out of his pocket. 'There's a card we made together in her school bag for tomorrow,' he smiled down at me.

'Thank you.'

'You're welcome,' he put a warm hand on my shoulder briefly, then bent down to scoop up Gracie. 'You be a good girl for Mummy, darling. Daddy will see you next week,' he kissed her forehead and squeezed her until she squealed.

'Bye Daddy,' she wrapped her arms around his neck.

'I love you,' he kissed her again and put her down.

'I love you too,' she said.

'OK, I'm off to tidy what is left of the house,' he grinned, 'have a nice birthday tomorrow.'

'Oh,' I said, 'yes, thank you.'

Gracie belted off to the living room to watch Robert drive off, he gave me a swift smile and left - I physically felt the tension leave my body.

'Goodbye Daddy,' Gracie yelled, even though he couldn't hear her. She pressed her face against the window until his car was out of sight.

'Come on you,' I said, 'shall we find a movie to watch until bedtime?'

'OK Mummy,' Gracie reluctantly turned away, looking a little sad as she always did after Robert had left.

I got to work the following morning to find a silver balloon tied to my desk and a pile of cards next to a boxed birthday cake.

'Happy birthday,' everyone chorused as I walked over.

'Thanks guys,' I smiled, feeling slightly embarrassed.

Jamie sauntered over, pulling a bunch of yellow roses out from behind his back.

'You shouldn't have,' I shook my head and took them off him. He grinned and leant forward, turning his head and prodding his cheek. I hesitated, then kissed him quickly.

'I got my birthday kiss,' he crowed. 'You owe me a tenner, Paul.'

I tutted and sat down, watching him walk back across the office.

'Did you have a lovely time with Maggie?' Bea asked.

'Yes, I did, thanks,' I lowered my voice and leant over. 'You'll never guess who I bumped into though,' I proceeded to tell her about David.

'Well, isn't that lovely though,' she whispered. 'That might have been awkward.'

'It was... a little bit,' I admitted, then spotting Scott on his way over, I sat up.

'Many happy returns Francine,' he plonked a bottle of champagne on my desk and patted my back.

'Thank you, Mr Windsor,' I smiled up at him.

He bent down a little and said quietly, 'I'm having lunch at your parents this Sunday, I will have a catch up with you then, sweetheart.'

I nodded, and he straightened up and went over to talk to Paul.

The morning went slowly - I didn't feel very focused after two nights out on the lash.

At lunchtime, I decided I needed some carbs, and nipped out to Greggs. On my return, Sarah, Louise, Sophie and Jamie were gathered around my desk.

'Here she is,' I heard one of the girls say. Puzzled, I walked over clutching my Greggs bag. As they parted, my mouth probably fell open. There, covering my desk, was the biggest bouquet of flowers I had ever seen. It was almost laughably so.

'What on earth...' I looked at Bea.

'They arrived ten minutes ago,' she chuckled. 'Subtle, aren't they?'

I searched for a card; there was none.

'Somebody has an admirer,' Sophie smirked.

Without thinking, I glanced at Jamie.

'Whoa,' he put his hands up. 'Don't look at me, they put my feeble little posy into the shade.'

'It puts the whole office in the shade,' I said appalled, and he laughed.

'David?' Bea whispered, after everyone had wandered back to their side of the office.

'No,' I picked it up, and not sure what else to do with it, I sat it my wastepaper bin. 'He doesn't know where I work.'

'Robert?'

'As if,' I said scornfully.

I ate my roll whilst Bea tried to guess who had sent my flowers. Paul returned from his lunchbreak and stopped in his tracks when he spotted them.

'Did you save someone's drowning child or something?' he chortled.

That evening, Gracie and I drove to Pizza Hut to meet Will, Gracie clutching my boxed gift that Robert had handed me the day before and had refused to let me open in the morning. Just as I was unclipping Gracie from her seat, Will pulled up in his dusty Range Rover.

'Will!' Gracie cried. 'Mummy, look, its Will,' as if she hadn't of known we were meeting him.

'Hello trouble,' he picked her up and leant over to kiss my cheek, then handed me a card. 'Happy birthday.'

'Thank you,' I smiled at him.

We went inside and waited to be seated, as Gracie talked non-stop. As we sat down, after a brief wait, I looked at Will properly and decided he looked pale beneath his honeymoon tan and a little tense.

'You OK?' I asked lightly, he glanced at Gracie and nodded, smiling his crooked smile.

'Mummy,' Gracie tugged my hand, 'open your present now,' she thrust the box at me.

'Thank you, sweetie.' I unwrapped it and opened the box. 'Oh, thank you,' I gasped. Inside was a beautiful gold bangle with tiny diamonds set in it.

'Daddy helped me choose it,' Gracie confided. 'Put it on.'

Will and I met eyes over the table and probably had the same expression on our faces. It was clearly expensive. Will helped me fastened the catch.

'I love it, thank you Gracie,' I kissed her forehead.

Will was looking at me with an odd light in his eyes, and I frowned.

Thankfully, he looked nothing like his father, although sometimes I could see Robert in certain facial expressions. I never shared that observation with Will. Nearly as tall as Robert, with dark blonde hair that never looked neat and tidy, and strange dark grey eyes, he wasn't classically handsome, but he had something about him.

'How's Len?' I asked.

'Yeah, she's good -' he trailed off and looked at Gracie again.

'Gracie,' I said, 'can you be a big girl and go and wash your hands all on your own before we eat, please?'

'Will?' I leant closer as Gracie slid off her seat and marched towards the toilets.

'She's pregnant,' he said, looking almost surprised as he said it.

'What?' I said loudly, then not sure whether he was happy or not, 'is that good... or -'

'Yeah,' he started to grin. 'Bloody brilliant - just, you know a bit of a shock. We weren't planning on starting a family for a while.'

'Well, you'll be OK, won't you?'

'Yeah, we will,' he nodded, 'that's not all though... she's eight weeks pregnant.'

'How did she not know?' I lowered my voice as I spotted Gracie approaching.

'She's never been regular. I guess that explains the throwing up before the wedding - she's panicking because she's drank alcohol - rather a lot of it.'

'It'll be fine,' I reassured him, then without thinking, 'I was two weeks pregnant with Gracie when I got married.'

Will's face tightened for a moment.

'Mummy, can we get our food now?' Gracie rubbed her tummy. 'I'm hungry.'

The rest of the evening was enjoyable. I could tell Will wanted to talk some more, but it wasn't possible with Gracie in tow. After we had eaten though, I told Gracie she could have ten minutes at the play area behind the restaurant. We sat together on a bench and watched Gracie for a moment in companionable silence. It was a glorious evening, the warmth of the day still lingering in the air, the sun low in the sky, casting a hazy glow.

'So,' I nudged his arm. 'How did Lennie take the news?'

'I think her words were something like, 'you've got to be shitting me,'' he chuckled.

'She'll be fine. It's always a shock when it's unplanned.'

'Yes, I expect it is,' he agreed. 'Listen, Frankie, keep it to yourself for a bit.'

'Of course,' I looked at his side profile and decided he still looked edgy.

'I'm telling Mum and Harry, and Len's telling her dad. Definitely not her mum yet,' he smiled grimly, 'and nobody else. Not even Adam, because... well, you know Adam.'

I laughed, 'Yes,' I watched Gracie laying belly down on the tire swing, her golden curls swaying with the motion. 'How come she's not telling her mum?'

'Her mum is a bit tricky,' he confided. 'They don't get on, and she will have an opinion on it that will turn into an argument. We're waiting until the twenty-week scan, unless she's showing by then.'

'Sounds like Robert,' I exhaled, wondering what he would say about it.

'Yeah. Talking of him, we don't want him to know at all,' Will said shortly.

'Never?' I asked incredulously.

'Never. Or as long as possible,' he began to fiddle with his watch strap and I could feel definite tension in his body now. I sighed sadly.

'Will, sweetie,' I said gently, 'Fernberry is a very small town. I'm not sure that's realistic. And then there's Gracie, you can't seriously expect her to not say anything... especially when the baby is born.'

'I know,' he said, that angry and hurt tone in his voice that I hated so much. 'But if he thinks that he is coming anywhere near Lennie or my child, he can think again. I mean that, Frankie.'

Tears filled my eyes, and I took his hand and squeezed it. I didn't believe for a second that Robert wouldn't make any attempt to be a part of his grandchild's life, but I didn't voice it. I probably didn't have to - Will knew Robert. For a moment, I felt such fury towards Robert that he still affected Will like this, usually so easy-going and happy, shrugging off life's small hassles with a positive attitude - then one mention of his father's name and it was like a bomb waiting to go off. His hatred was deep, and it was complicated, and I didn't fully understand it and honestly... I'm not sure that I wanted to. All I knew was, that his love for Lennie must have been immense to shake off their past.

Will looked at me, then gave a small smile when he saw my distress.

'Sorry Frankie,' he squeezed my hand back. 'Don't get upset over it, please. And hey... you're going to be a grandma.'

And he laughed as I lightly punched his arm.

CHAPTER SIX

For the rest of the week, I had to endure a fair amount of ribbing about my flowers from my work colleagues, and speculation as to whom had sent them. Everyone seemed to find the subject a lot more interesting than what I did. In the end, I hadn't wanted to throw them away - I had taken them home and divided them into four vases.

'I've got competition,' Jamie had commented. 'I must do better next time.'

I met up with Maggie for dinner after work on Friday, as Robert didn't bring Gracie back home until around nine o'clock. I'd invited Paul along, as his wife was away with the kids over-night, but he had declined, saying he was meeting up with a friend for a quick pint, then going home to 'enjoy the silence.'

We went to a quiet little Chinese restaurant in town, up the street from the Lizard. I was dying to tell her about Will's news, but I didn't. Instead I made the grand mistake of telling her about my flowers.

'Robert,' she said straight away as she tucked into her duck, 'always with the grand gestures... the dickhead,' she added.

'He would have put a card in there,' I argued. 'To make sure he got the credit for said grand gesture.'

'You sure you didn't tell David where you work?' she asked, pinching a forkful of my rice.

'Yes, I'm sure,' I gazed into space for a second, 'I definitely didn't, we didn't even have a proper conversation. Just hello and how are you and good to see you, kind of thing.'

'So that leaves Jamie, or unknown admirer,' she said happily, 'ooo I love a bit of mystery.'

'Mmm, well,' I started on my food before she helped herself to more, 'they need to take it down a notch, whoever it is. They were ridiculous.'

I changed the subject after that, and Maggie told me all about her date she had lined up the following evening, some guy she had met in Sainsbury's, of all places.

'Good place to meet a man,' she said, 'you can tell a lot by someone by what's in their basket. He had expensive wine and no supermarket branded items, which means either he's got money, or high standards.'

'Well, high standards are out the window,' I blew her a kiss, 'he asked you out, didn't he?'

'Fuck you,' she laughed her raucous laugh. 'I'm class with a capital 'C' and you know it.'

'You're certainly something,' I said affectionately.

She studied me for a moment, 'Isn't it about time you jumped back on the dating train Frankie?'

'Mmm, no,' I shook my head. 'I don't need a man.'

'Liar,' she smirked. 'Why don't you let that dishy little Jamie take you out? Seriously, you're too gorgeous to go un-ravished.'

'I think I can aim higher than him,' I frowned at her. 'Anyway, I'm fine as I am. I've got Gracie, I've got work, I've got *you*.'

'Yeah,' she agreed lightly, 'but -'

'But nothing,' I interrupted. 'I'll be ready when I'm ready. Don't nag.'

'God, you annoy me,' Maggie grumbled.

'*You* annoy me,' I said laughingly.

'I'm not talking about getting involved,' she tucked her hair behind her ears. 'Just get your knickers wet, woman.'

'Maggie!' I giggled. 'No… my days of casual sex are well and truly over.'

'Prude,' she sighed, and carried on eating, looking thoroughly exasperated.

We left the restaurant just before eight. I declined a quick drink elsewhere, wanting a shower before Gracie was dropped off home. The bars were starting to fill up, music drifted from the Lizard's open doors and there was a pleasant summer night's atmosphere, with the sounds of talking and laughter and people making their way to wherever they were heading. We crossed the road, passing a group of rowdy young guys, laughing and joking.

'Hey, Frankie,' a male voice called from outside a bar opposite, with a tiny cordoned off area with metal tables and chairs.

'It's David,' I whispered sideways to Maggie. Feeling it would be rude not to go over, I grabbed Maggie's arm.

'Hello again,' I stood awkwardly on the other side of the cordon.

'Well, hello,' he beamed. 'And hello Maggie, you're looking lovely.'

I studied David as he leant over to kiss Maggie - I couldn't decide if I still found him attractive or not. He had obviously come out straight from work, his striped shirt looked rumpled and I spotted a suit jacket behind him draped on a chair. Two men, slightly younger than him, were smoking and looking over inquisitively.

'Do you want a drink, ladies?' he asked. Maggie nudged me.

'Sorry, I need to get home for my daughter,' I explained.

'You have a daughter?' he smiled, 'that's nice... I've got a son now.'

'Oh, nice,' I said lamely and glanced at Maggie. 'Well, nice to see you again, I really must get home.'

'Sure,' he nodded. 'Bye Frankie, great to see you Maggie.'

'You too,' she called over her shoulder as I steered her away. 'Well, that wasn't awkward at all, eh?'

'Christ,' I muttered.

'He *is* looking good, I must say,' she mused, then giggled. 'There was a worrying over-use of the word 'nice' back there.'

'Don't,' I cringed. 'I feel so *weird* seeing him.'

'Doesn't seem to bother him,' she said.

'Well, it bothers me,' I said miserably. 'I was a bitch to him. It's embarrassing.'

'He's probably happily married and I'm sure he has recovered by now,' she said mockingly.

'More than me then,' I sighed. 'Got my comeuppance, didn't I?'

By the time Robert arrived with Gracie, I was showered, in my pyjamas and half-way down a glass of wine.

'Tough day?' he asked pleasantly as he walked in and followed me into the living room.

'So so,' I shrugged, taking Gracie's school things from him.

'You look tired,' he said lightly.

'I'm fine,' I frowned. 'Have you been a good girl today, Gracie?' I gathered her up and kissed her.

'Yes, Mummy,' she snuggled up to me. 'I got a sticker today for my maths and Daddy said I'm clever like you, Mummy.'

'Well, I won't argue with that,' I ruffled her hair. 'Give Daddy a kiss then, it's bath time
soon.'

I walked Robert to the door.

'She said you saw Will on your birthday,' he said in a low voice as she belted off to the window, ready to watch him drive off.

'Yes,' I looked at him evenly.

'How is he?'

'Very well,' I replied, almost defiantly.

'Good,' he rubbed his chin, looking at me up and down. 'OK, well, have a nice weekend then.'

I closed the door behind him, thinking how much I hated how he could make me feel like I was walking on uneven ground. What I hated even more was that I couldn't help wondering what he was thinking when he looked at me like that, almost with lazy lust. Then other times with cold indifference. Did he know deep down that I still loved him? I hoped not; that would give him power. I had told him a year ago that I didn't love him after I walked out - I sincerely hoped that he thought that was true.

As I ran Gracie's bath, I mulled over Maggie's words about dating again, wishing I could be more like her. I thought about that first date feeling - getting to know someone, the butterflies and the excitement, being intimate with them. Closing my eyes briefly, I thought about how Robert had made me feel and his rapturous love-making. Feeling like I was pushing a boulder off a cliff, I pushed those thoughts away. *No,* I told myself, *you keep those walls up, Frankie.*

On Saturday, I took Gracie to the outdoor pool for the afternoon and then we took a picnic to the boating lake which was situated more or less bang in the middle of Fernberry. Will lived literally across from the lake, the rest of the park stretched uphill towards the town end of Fernberry.

It was a hot and sultry day. Picnic blankets were dotted everywhere, occupied with families with children or couples sunbathing. I loved mine and Gracie's weekend activities but often felt lonely and like I had single parent stamped on my head. I watched a family nearby wistfully: the woman was sitting cross-legged breast feeding her baby, giving her husband instructions to put more sunblock on their two daughters. He playfully grabbed the smallest girl by the ankle as she tried to make a get-away and wrestled her to the ground, the girl squealing and giggling.

I spread out our blanket, telling Gracie to keep in the shade, and handed her some orange juice in a carton and her favourite cheese and cucumber sandwiches, and then helping myself to some crisps, I laid on my front and gazed out over the lake. Some children were having some kayaking lessons on the other side near the boathouses, a small dog was gambolling up and down yapping it's head off at them. I could of easily have dozed off after a while, so I sat up and watched Gracie happily munching away.

'Do you want to go and play on the swings?' I asked her.

'No,' she wiped her hands on her shorts. 'I'm too hot.'

'OK sweetie.'

'Why can't Daddy come out with us?' she suddenly asked.

'Oh,' I looked at her, taken by surprise. 'Well... Mummy and Daddy aren't together anymore, so that means you get to do things with Daddy and things with Mummy. That's OK isn't it?'

'Yeah,' she looked pensive for a moment. 'Will you marry somebody else? Because Julia told me her mummy is marrying her boyfriend, and he's not her real daddy, but she calls him daddy.'

'I can't really answer that right now,' I felt wary. 'I haven't got a boyfriend, so I won't be marrying anyone anytime soon.'

'Oh,' she squashed her empty juice carton up and handed it to me. 'I think Daddy has a girlfriend. I don't think I want *him* to get married.'

'Why do you think that?' I asked cautiously, feeling a little sick.

'Because I saw girls stuff in his bathroom,' she said, her eyes narrowing a little. 'I saw some girls shower gel and a pink razor, like what you have.'

'I see,' I tried to smile. 'Well, it's OK for him to have a girlfriend, isn't it?'

She shrugged and started pulling up blades of grass.

Gracie was exhausted from our busy day out and wanted to go to bed at seven - unheard of at the weekend. I bathed her and read her a story and left her snuggled up with Yellow Bunny, knowing she would be asleep soon. Not feeling much like watching a film, I went and sat outside to ponder on what she had said about Robert.

The truth was, it had wound me up and I felt upset and niggly; I had no idea why. I did not think for one moment that Robert had spent the last year celibate, if he had slept around when he had been married to me, I was damn sure that he was at it like a rabbit now he was single and free. And jealousy wasn't really an emotion I was feeling... just... something...

I couldn't even say that it was because he had moved on and I hadn't. Moved on from what? He couldn't have *really* loved me -

not like I had loved him… no, I hadn't broken his heart, not like I had broken David's. I had dented his pride, that was all. And I was still stuck, feeling hurt and under his spell - my life hadn't changed that much. I still had the same job, still looked after Gracie, still felt lonely as I had when I was married to him. The only difference was that I had my own house and wasn't rattling around in his big house.

I stood up abruptly and went back indoors, suddenly feeling an unplanned purpose. Things had to change. I went upstairs and after checking on Gracie, who was out for the count, I ran a bath and then stripped off and stood in front of my mirror. I had put on just over a stone since I had left Robert, but I wasn't complaining. I had always been the skinny kid at school and tall for my age. As an adult, I'd hated being tall, five-foot-eight, and felt self-conscious. It had only been in the last few months that I had felt comfortable showing my legs. I knew I wasn't in bad shape for my age and looked younger than what I was, but Robert had dented my confidence. Not that he had ever put me down - just his obvious preference for younger women.

I opened my wardrobe and let my gaze wander along the rail. Most of the clothes I had brought after I had moved in with Robert were designer - one thing about him was that he always had wanted me to look my best. More than half of them he had brought, and I wished I could have afforded to have left them behind. I rifled through my work clothes - sensible knee-length skirts and plain blouses. I swiped them to one side and randomly started yanking clothes off from their hangers and chucking them on my bed. I came across a pale blue maternity top and stopped for a moment and held it against me, looking in the mirror. Lost in wistful memories, I suddenly realised I was close to the onset of tears. Wondering briefly if I should keep it for Lennie, I decided it wasn't really her style and threw it behind me.

Next, I emptied my underwear drawer onto the bed, next to my pile of discarded clothes. I had a strange obsession with underwear… well, maybe not an obsession, but I loved buying it. Robert liked, what I considered, "tarty" underwear. I didn't, but had worn it anyway to please him. I picked out maybe a dozen black or red thongs, and four or five push-up bras and stuffed them in my wicker bin. I then opened my pyjama drawer and pulled out a scarlet Basque and two see-through short nighties and added them to my pile too.

I stood, hands on hips, surveying the mess I had made, feeling somehow like I accomplished something. I checked my watch, it was nearly nine o'clock and my bath water was probably freezing. I turned on my lamp, and realising my curtains were wide open, I crossed the room to close them and then froze as I heard a noise outside. It sounded like one of my garden chairs scraping on the patio. I quickly closed my curtains and threw on my dressing gown, feeling uneasy. I wasn't particularly wary living on my own - I had spent enough time alone in Robert's house with Gracie, but for some reason I felt the hairs on my arms standing up. I went downstairs and into the kitchen, by now it was growing dim and I couldn't see outside properly through my big kitchen window. I stood for a minute, then pulled down the blind and bolted the back door and checked that the side door in my minuscule utility room was locked. I left the light on in there as I went back into the kitchen, still feeling a little frightened. After another couple of minutes of listening for any noises outside, I decided I was being daft and headed back upstairs, after grabbing some black sacks to bag up my clothes.

I shoved them in unceremoniously and tied the tops up, I managed to fill up three of them. My bath water was indeed cold, so I emptied it out and had a hurried shower, still a little unsettled. After checking on Gracie, I collapsed into bed feeling exhausted but unable to get to sleep for ages, having childhood thoughts of a big bad monster creeping around outside.

CHAPTER SEVEN

The next morning, I was distressed to discover that one of my patio chairs was on its side and there were footprints on my flowerbed that ran along one side of the patio, with some of my red geraniums squashed flat. I checked my side gate and it was unbolted. I never left it unbolted.

Not knowing what else to do, I rang Will.

'Do you think you should call the police?' he asked, sounding concerned.

'No,' I said, although it had briefly crossed my mind. 'I'm being over-dramatic, there's not much they can do… it's hardly the crime of the century.'

'I suppose,' he paused for a moment. 'Are you home this afternoon?'

'No, I'm going over to my parents' for lunch.'

'Tell you what,' he said, 'I've got your spare key, I'll pop over later and fit a bolt on the bottom of your gate and later in the week I'm going to get you a security light, OK?'

'Thanks, Will,' I said gratefully.

He went on to say that him and Lennie were both working the lunchtime shift, but he would swing by around three o'clock after the rush. Feeling slightly better, I got Gracie and I ready and left for my parents'.

I had an enjoyable enough afternoon - Scott and his wife Brenda came for lunch and we chatted about work. On the pretence of helping my mum in the kitchen, I had a whispered conversation with her about David.

'I always liked David,' she stirred a large pan of gravy, bubbling away on the range.

'*Everyone* liked David,' I countered. 'But he wasn't for me in the end, was he?'

'Mmm,' I could tell she was biting back a retort about Robert.

I loved my parents dearly, but it rattled me a little that they both blamed Robert entirely for my actions. It didn't bother me that they were anti-Robert - it bothered me that they seemed to think I didn't act with a will of my own.

I sat at the breakfast bar watching her for a while, in her beige summer trousers and a vest top that she only wore at home and her greying faded-red hair tied in a bun. I got my height from my dad, he was way over six-foot, although I noticed as he approached his seventy-fifth birthday he seemed to have shrunk a little - my mum was tiny, just over five-foot.

'Frankie lovie,' she said over her shoulder, 'go and see what wine people want with their dinner.'

My dad and Scott were sat outside on the patio drinking whisky and smoking. My dad wasn't supposed to be doing either of those things, but I turned a blind eye.

Brenda was walking around the garden with Gracie trying to find some butterflies.

'So, what's this I'm hearing, then?' My dad patted a chair next to him. 'A young man having a little thing for you at work, eh?'

'Thanks for that, Scott,' I rolled my eyes and they both chuckled. 'Well, I'm guessing you mean Jamie. He's a pain in the arse.'

'He's a bright young lad,' Scott winked at me.

'Young being the operative word,' I said dismissively.

'Always gazing at her across the office, he is,' Scott directed at my dad.

'My Francine's always been a heart-breaker, prettiest girl in her class,' my dad nodded at me. 'About time you found yourself a man - now you're shot of that bastard.'

'Dad!' I looked meaningfully over at Gracie who was trotting back over, hanging onto Brenda's hand.

'Come and see your gramps,' my dad called to her. 'Did you find any butterflies?'

I sighed and went back indoors. He was as bad as Maggie, thinking that me being single was like some sort of disadvantage.

I returned home late in the afternoon, full to the brim, and hot and bothered. My mum's roast beef was probably my favourite dinner, ever - but not in the middle of a mini-heatwave. Gracie was tired and whiny; I was hopeful that she might want another early night. I thought grumpily about my pile of ironing I needed to do when all I felt like doing was having a cool shower and crashing out.

To my surprise, as I pulled up, Will's car was parked on my driveway. The side gate was ajar, so I wandered round the back, to find him and Daniel, Lennie's brother, both topless and drinking beer on the patio.

'Will!' Gracie ran to him and jumped on his lap.

'What are you doing here still?' I took in a toolbox open under my kitchen window and an extension lead trailing out of the door.

'We've been your knights in shining armour,' Will said grinning, shooing Gracie away. 'Sorry, trouble, I'm hot and sweaty.'

'Hi Frankie,' Daniel smiled at me from under his baseball cap.

You couldn't help fancying Daniel. Him and Lennie were nothing alike. Whereas she was rather short and very dark, Daniel was - I hate to use the expression - like a blonde Adonis, tall and muscular with bright blue eyes. And he was always smiling and chatting to everyone, roaring with laughter at his own jokes; he was very likeable.

I suddenly noticed a security light next to the backdoor.

'Oh my goodness,' I said, feeling rather touched. 'You didn't have to go to all this trouble.'

'Yes, we did,' Will stood up. 'You were worried this morning. That's a sensor light, so any movement, it will light up,' he pointed to the light. 'We've fitted another one by the gate, next to the utility room door. I've also fitted a bolt at the bottom of the gate, it looks like someone stood on your bin to open the top bolt, there's a dent on the lid.'

'Really?' I felt uneasy again.

'Yeah,' Will frowned. 'It was probably kids - but even so.'

I took a few paces back and looked up at my bedroom window, feeling slightly nauseous.

'Don't worry,' Daniel was watching me. 'Any bugger that comes near here will be lit up like Blackpool illuminations.'

'Well, thank you guys,' I looked at them both. 'What do I owe you for the lights and bolt?'

'Nothing,' Will glanced over at Gracie, who was now on her swing. 'Long as you two are safe.'

I started to argue but he put his hands over his ears.

'Fine,' I laughed.

'I just need to vacuum up some brick dust in the utility room and we'll get out of your way,' he picked up his t-shirt from the table and wiped his face.

He ignored my protests that I could do it, so I gave up and went inside to sort out Gracie's school clothes. As I watched Daniel through the window starting to pack up the tools with Gracie following him around, and listened to Will singing as he vacuumed, I thought that if nothing good had come out of my marriage - with the exception of Gracie, of course - how wonderful it was that I had somebody like Will in my life. Even if he was married to the biggest reminder of all of Robert's total lack of fidelity.

I definitely slept a lot easier that night and woke up Monday morning feeling refreshed and positive. I was finishing work early that afternoon, which lifted my mood even more - I had an optician's appointment and had snuck in a hairdresser's appointment, without mentioning it to Scott.

As I got dressed for work, I glanced at my sacks of discarded clothes, and decided that while I was on a bit of a roll, maybe I would have something more drastic than my usual trim done to my hair.

I arrived at work to find Jamie sitting at my desk chatting to Bea and Paul perched on the edge of Bea's desk.

'Hem hem,' I fake coughed.

Jamie jumped up and grinned at me, 'Sorry, gorgeous.'

'That's quite alright,' I sat down. 'Nice weekend, everyone?'

'Paul was just telling us he lost his mobile,' said Bea.

'Oh no,' I looked up at him.

'Got it back now,' he said. 'But it was really bloody weird.'

'Oh?' I raised my eyebrows.

'Yeah,' he scratched his neck frowning, 'I had a quick pint in town with a mate and realised when I got home that I didn't have my phone,' he patted his pockets, 'so I rang him on my house phone to see if I had left it behind, he said no… so I got him to see if anyone had handed it in at the bar, he said nobody had, so I thought, bloody hell, that's that gone then - '

'Didn't you try and ring it?' I interrupted.

'Yeah - it just rang and rang, so I thought, you stupid bugger, bet you've dropped it getting in the car or something,' he continued. 'So, I drove back to have a look and not a sausage. Then Chelsea came back Saturday with the boys and got all uppity, thinking I'd been somewhere I shouldn't,' he rolled his eyes. 'Then, bugger me, I got up Sunday morning, and someone had posted it through the door. How flipping weird is that?'

'Yeah,' I agreed. 'It is a bit… maybe they found your address somewhere on your phone?'

'That's what Bea said,' he shrugged. 'Weird though.'

'As long as you didn't have any incriminating photos on there,' Jamie sniggered.

'No such luck,' Paul grumbled.

I left work at two o'clock and drove into town. I had an hour to kill after my optician's appointment, and feeling slightly guilty, I had a little spending spree buying some new clothes. Loaded up with bags, I got to the hairdressers five minutes late and Bonnie, my hairdresser who had been cutting my hair since my early thirties, was sitting on the reception desk.

'The usual?' she took me through to the salon.

'No,' I settled myself in the chair and looked at her in the mirror. 'Cut it all off.'

Feeling nervous, I drove to Rachel's to pick Gracie up, constantly looking in my rear-view mirror.

When I had met Robert, my hair was shoulder length, and as I had naturally wavy hair, it was a lot curlier at that length. I remembered him saying once that he liked long hair and so I grew it out, and as it got longer, my curls had dropped into waves.

When I entered the hairdressers, my hair was half-way down my back. When I left, the back of my neck was bare, and my curls were back.

Bonnie, sensing a challenge, had promptly fetched some style books... and whilst she was gleefully rubbing her hands together, I had boldly decided to have my hair layered into my neck, leaving the sides longer in a sophisticated bob. Half-way through the cut I panicked that I would hate it - when she was done, I loved it. However, as not the most confident soul in the world, I was scared of people's reactions.

I knocked on Rachel's door, feeling horribly self-conscious.

'Hiya,' she greeted me, then - 'Oh my God... Frankie, you look stunning!'

'Not too short?' I smiled, despite myself.

'No,' she walked around me, looking gobsmacked. 'You're braver than me... but no, I love it.'

'Thank you,' I rubbed the back of neck, 'I hope I don't regret this in the morning.'

'Mummy,' Gracie appeared in the doorway. 'Where's your hair

gone?' She promptly burst into tears.

'Oh, sweetie,' I knelt down and looked up at Rachel, she smiled and shrugged. 'I've had a haircut, that's all… no need to cry.'

'But I liked your hair,' she really looked distraught.

'It will grow back,' I reassured her.

She glared at me, looking half cross, half devastated.

Later that evening, I asked Maggie to come over - I was slightly regretting such a drastic change already and if anyone would be brutally honest, it would be her.

'Fucking hell,' was her first response. 'What have you done?'

'Oh God,' my heart sank – then I saw that she was grinning.

'Very French chic,' she said, walking around me like Rachel had. 'I love it, very sexy.'

'Thanks,' I took her through to the kitchen. 'Wine?'

'Why are you asking?' she tutted. 'You been shopping?' she started rummaging through my bags that were still on the table.

'Yeah, fancied a few new things,' I poured two glasses and sat down.

'Hold on a minute,' she looked at me, smirking. 'New haircut… new clothes… you're taking my advice, aren't you? About bloody time.'

'Eh?'

'You're going on a man hunt,' she said, looking smug.

'No!' I laughed.

'Yeah, yeah,' she waved off my protests.

'I just fancied a change,' I shrugged. 'I had a monster clear-out, this isn't for any man, totally for me.'

She looked unconvinced, so I changed the subject and told her about my little scare on Saturday evening.

'Will's a babe, isn't he?' she said, then frowned. 'Worrying though. Perhaps Robert's fucking with you.'

'Nah, not really his style, probably just kids,' it hadn't entered my head that it might have actually been someone I knew.

'Ooo, perhaps David followed you home,' she looked intrigued. 'Poor David, been harbouring a grudge, yet still insanely in love with you.'

'Maggie,' I laughed. 'I think not - you're such a drama queen.'

'Not impossible though, is it?' she sipped her wine, looking thoughtful.

It worried me more, thinking it could have been somebody familiar to me, more than just somebody random prowling around.

'Like I said, probably kids, there's some right little shits on the estate behind the secondary school,' I said lightly, then distracted her by asking about her Saturday night date.

Just before ten, she decided to go home, as we were both yawning and she had an early shift the next day.

I chuckled to myself as I double-checked I was all locked up properly. I was, in truth, still a little nervous, but Maggie did make me laugh with her overactive imagination.

I parked up at work the following morning, feeling apprehensive again. As I locked my car, I heard a wolf-whistle - expecting to see Jamie's grinning face, I was surprised to see it was Paul. He was sat on the low wall to the side of the entrance smoking a cigarette.

'Good morning,' I walked over to him, I noticed he looked tired as normal, but his light blue eyes were rather more shadowed than usual.

'Looking good,' he nodded in approval. 'I like it… I could do with a make-over too,' he said wryly.

'Or sleep,' I smiled. 'Rough night with your little one?' I could never remember which kid had what name.

'No,' he flicked his cigarette into a bush and followed me into the building. 'Chel's still being funny about my phone,' he grumbled. 'Ended up having a row.'

'Really?' I rubbed his back. 'Sorry to hear that.'

'Ah well,' he looked morose. 'She'll get over it.'

'Of course she will,' I said. 'She knows you wouldn't mess her about,' I tugged my curls down nervously. 'Is Jamie in the office?'

'Yes,' we paused at the door and he smiled at me. 'Worried he'll take the piss?'

'A bit,' I shrugged. 'He usually does, at every opportunity.'

'Nah,' Paul chuckled. 'He really likes you, that's all. It's just his way - you know, you should give him a chance. He's actually a very decent chap once you get past all the banter, honestly.'

'Mmm,' I pushed open the door.

'Morning,' Bea looked up, then started. 'You look lovely, Frankie,' she beamed. 'Was that your optician's appointment, eh?'

'No,' I giggled. 'I actually had that first.'

'Love your hair, Frankie,' Sophie called over loudly - I smiled and then sighed as Jamie looked up from whatever he was engrossed in and predictably wandered over.

'I hope that's not for another man's benefit?' he put his head on one side. I suppressed a grin, thinking of Maggie's smug little face.

'Nope,' I rummaged in my bag for my glasses. 'All for me.'

'A little bit for me too?' he grinned his wide grin. 'Come on, you've got to let me take you out now, you're breaking my heart a little bit.'

'Jamie?' I looked up at him, he looked at me expectantly. 'Bugger off.' I shooed him away.

'Think about it?' he called over his shoulder as he made his way over to Scott's office. 'You can take your time, it's fine.'

Bea giggled.

'Honestly,' I grumbled, then noticed Bea looking at me with a peculiar expression on her face.

'You OK there, Bea?' I asked.

'You know what?' she started to smile slowly. 'I reckon you like him.'

'Who?' I said incredulously. 'Jamie?'

'Yeah,' she looked thoughtful. 'You are perfectly lovely to everyone - you are a very lovely girl - but you are a little less lovely to him… hmm, now that's interesting.'

'Bea,' I burst out laughing. 'No, you are very, very wrong, I'm afraid.'

Shaking my head, I started to get on with some work, ignoring her little sighs.

At lunchtime, not feeling that hungry, I decided to drive into town to pick up something for dinner that evening, and regretted it immediately after getting stuck in a queue at the supermarket. I drove back to work, absolutely dying for a pee and went straight into the ladies'. I sat checking my face in my compact mirror, when I heard Louise and Sophie come in, noisily chattering - then continued their conversation in their respective cubicles.

'So, do you reckon she's screwing him, or not?' Louise called, her voice full of laughter.

Intrigued, I stayed put.

'Oh, for sure.'

'One minute you're saying she's frigid, the next she's a slapper.'

'Or desperate,' a small noise of disgust. 'Can you imagine? He's so old and gross.'

'But rich -'

'So was her husband, but she got shot of him... and he's *gorgeous*.'

I suddenly went cold.

'Perhaps *he* kicked *her* out -you don't know what happened.'

'Perhaps she was screwing Mr Windsor then, and he got wind of it.'

I heard a flush, then a second one and they both came out and started washing their hands.

'She's so stuck up, don't know why Jamie's always sniffing around her.'

'He fancies a bit of posh - can I borrow your lip-gloss... ta - God it would be like going to bed with one of his mum's mates.'

As sick as I felt, I imagined the look on their faces if I chose that moment to open the door.

'Ew.'

They both left, giggling. Shakily, I put my hands to my face, my cheeks felt boiling hot. I felt horribly on the verge of tears. *Bloody nasty bitches*, I thought. I wished I was like Maggie - *she* would have strolled out and taken great relish in it. I walked to the sinks and looked in the mirror. I looked oddly flushed. Washing my hands, I willed my heart to stop racing. As I calmed down, I began to feel angry rather than upset. They were just stupid, shallow, little girls.

I went back into the office, blood ringing in my ears, and before I had time to think about it, I walked over to Jamie's desk.

'Can I have a word?' I asked, aware of Louise and Sophie watching me.

'Sure,' Jamie looked surprised, I beckoned him and walked away a little.

'You alright, Frankie?' he frowned at me as we stopped in the middle of the office.

'Yes,' I said quietly. 'I'm fine... and actually, I've changed my mind. Let's go out for a drink, Saturday night.'

'Really?' he started to smile, but then frowned again, seemingly confused.

'Yes, really,' I assured him, and smiled - probably a little stiffly, but he seemed delighted.

'Great,' he grinned broadly. 'Wow, OK - well, we'll sort that out later in the week.'

'Absolutely,' I touched his arm and turned back to my desk, aware of several pairs of eyes on me.

'What the fuck did I just do?' I whispered to myself from behind my monitor.

CHAPTER EIGHT

As the weekend approached, I felt more and more regretful of my impulsive decision. Maggie thought it was - after raging about Louise and Sophie, and telling me exactly what she would have said to them - deeply hilarious.

On Thursday morning, Jamie told me he had booked a table at the Italian restaurant that I had said I liked after my birthday meal, and he would pick me up at seven-thirty. Strangely, he had taken his flirting down a notch, and I wondered if he had after all, not been that serious about taking me out, and maybe was regretting it too.

However, Paul and I had a murmured conversation at lunchtime, and he had said that Jamie was thrilled. It made me feel guilty; my actions were not out of actually wanting to go out with him - I had simply been angry with Louise and Sophie.

Rescue came, or so I thought, in the unlikely shape of Robert. On Thursday evening, he rang me.

'Frankie,' he sounded harassed. 'I'm afraid I can't have Gracie this weekend, I've got to drive up to Birmingham first thing.'

'Business or pleasure?' I asked before I could stop myself.

'Business,' he sounded angry. 'As if I would blow off my own daughter... there's not much I can do about it.'

'She's not going to be happy,' I said shortly, 'but if it can't be helped... ring her though, please.'

He ended the call saying he would ring her Saturday morning and again on Sunday. I was already dreading telling her - last time he let her down at the last minute, she cried until she made herself sick. Then, very selfishly, my heart lifted as I realised I would have to cancel my date with Jamie. I decided, as I didn't want her to have a bad day at school, that I would tell her when I picked her up from Rachel's. I warned Rachel that, as Gracie would be expecting her father, there would be an epic tantrum. Rachel took it in her usual good-natured stride.

I sought Jamie first thing on Friday and told him that I was sorry, and explained that Robert had to go away. Despite not being the least bit disappointed that we wouldn't be going out, it suddenly occurred to me that I didn't want him to think I was lying.

'Oh,' he did look really crestfallen, 'that's crap, isn't it? OK, we can rearrange.'

'Yes,' I hadn't expected that. 'Of course, another time.'

Just as I was getting ready to leave work that afternoon, Jamie bounded up to me, looking slightly happier. I eyed him, feeling on guard.

'So,' he perched on my desk. 'You're at a loose end tomorrow then?'

'Oh, well,' I zipped up my bag, 'not ever so, I'll just have to change my plans, as I have Gracie.'

'How about we do something in the day?' he asked brightly.

'I have Gracie,' I repeated patiently.

'I know,' he rolled his eyes. 'But I have Jessie, my little sister… so I was wondering if you'd like to do something together. Maybe.'

'Well,' I cast around for a valid excuse - I was never very good when I was put on the spot. 'I suppose that would be OK. How old is she?'

'She's six,' he suddenly looked unsure, 'but there's… well not exactly a problem, but there *is* something -'

I looked pointedly at my watch.

'Oh, sorry,' he slid off my desk. 'I'll walk with you.'

'What was you thinking of doing?' I asked as I hurried out of the door.

'Picnic at the lake, maybe,' he followed me. 'But, it's not a biggie - Jess is autistic, so she might seem a little, um, shy at first.'

'Oh,' I stopped and looked at him, not sure how to respond. 'I see, I'm sorry to hear that.'

'Don't be,' he laughed. 'Sorry, we get that a lot.'

'Oh Christ,' I felt mortified, realising what I had said. 'Will she be OK with Gracie? Gracie is kind of… strident,' I felt myself blush. 'I'm sorry, I don't really know much about it - well I've kind of read articles, but I don't know anyone with it… I mean who has it -'

'She's just a normal kid,' he was still looking amused. 'I just thought I should tell you. Look, Frankie, if you're uncomfortable, we can wait until you're free for an evening, it's fine.'

'No,' I now felt embarrassed and awkward. 'It's a great idea,' I lied.

'OK,' he looked at me for a moment. 'It's nice to see you not so sure of yourself. You are human after all, eh?'

Lost for words, I folded my arms and frowned at him. Unabashed, he grinned at me.

'Meet us at the park,' he opened the door for me and we walked out into the carpark. 'I will bring food, Jessie is kind of picky... what does Gracie eat?'

'Everything,' I shrugged. 'But she likes cheese and cucumber... look, I can bring something -'

'Nope,' he stopped at my car. 'Leave it to me, meet me at eleven?'

'OK,' I relented.

As I watched him amble over to his car, I supposed I should have been thankful that it wasn't the kind of date he wanted - but I didn't much like the feeling I had just made myself look like an idiot.

Gracie looked surprised to see me instead of Robert, but she took the news that she wasn't seeing him all weekend better than I thought. She initially burst into tears but as she calmed down, and I explained we were going to play with another little girl and mummy's friend from work, she cheered up slightly.

'How old is she?' she asked on the drive home.

'She's six,' I replied.

'Can I be in charge because I'm nearly eight?'

'No, Gracie,' I sighed. 'Nobody's in charge. I want you to play nicely, OK?'

'What's her mummy called?'

'Oh... I don't know,' then I realised she thought my friend was Jessie's mum. 'My friend is her brother, he's grown up - so it's like you and Will,' I explained.

'What's his name? Do they have different mummies like me and Will?'

'I don't think so,' I said. 'His name's Jamie.'

'OK,' she said, and fell silent. I glanced in the mirror and she was staring out of the window. I often wished that I knew what she was thinking.

Just before eleven, I parked up on Will's driveway, as it was easier, and walked across the road to the park entrance, which was situated on the left-hand side of the lake. The day was a little cooler than it had been of late, but I wasn't complaining. We followed the tree-lined pathway to the play area - I noticed that Gracie seemed rather subdued and prayed that she would be on her best behaviour.

I spotted Jamie straight away. He was sitting cross-legged on the grass near one of the climbing frames, there were two or three little girls on there and a couple of boys. I hadn't expected him to be in a shirt and tie, of course, but he somehow looked younger in shorts and a T-shirt. As I drew closer, he suddenly turned his head and jumped up, brushing grass off his behind and grinned at us. I glanced at Gracie and she was looking at him from under her lashes, her face very solemn.

'Hello ladies,' he looked at Gracie. 'You must be Gracie, how are you sweetheart?'

'Fine,' she muttered, I squeezed her hand. 'Thank you,'

'Hello,' I said. 'She'll thaw out,' I added in a whisper.

'Sure,' he didn't seem fazed. 'Plonk yourself down, I'll go and get Jessie.'

He jogged over to the climbing frame and a dark-haired little girl approached him. He crouched down and spoke to her, pointing over to us. He stood back up, and taking her hand, led her over to us. I had to smile - she was a miniature version of her brother, with dark glossy hair in two plaits, and bright blue eyes.

'This little monster is Jessie,' he sat down and she knelt in front of him, not taking her eyes off of his face. 'Jess, this is my friend Frankie, and this is Gracie… say hello.'

'Hello,' she whispered, then leant forward, putting her arms around Jamie's neck.

'Hello, Jessie,' I looked at Jamie and he just smiled and winked.

'What do you girls want to do first?' he asked cheerfully. 'Shall we go and feed the ducks?'

Gracie shrugged and Jessie didn't respond. I decided it was going to be the longest afternoon ever and felt vaguely depressed.

'OK, we'll do that first,' he gently disengaged himself from Jessie and reached for his rucksack behind him. 'Come on then.'

Much to my surprise, he had Gracie eating out of the palm of his hand within ten minutes, and I'll give him his due - he knew how to make things fun. Jessie started to come out of her shell and was soon following Gracie around, and giggling at Jamie's antics. I reluctantly had to admit, I was enjoying myself. He produced some bird seed out of his rucksack and kept pretending to be scared of the ducks and geese, grabbing the girls and hiding behind them, making high-pitched shrieking noises. Then, to my horror, he suddenly ran up behind me and picked me up around my waist, threatening to throw me in the water - much to Gracie's amusement, who started yelling at him to do it. I wriggled and kicked, half laughing, half terrified he would actually do it, until he put me down.

'You idiot,' I giggled breathlessly, rubbing my ribs.

'Sorry,' he brushed a curl away from my forehead, and smiled lazily. Surprised by the over-familiar gesture I stopped laughing, then dropped my gaze quickly.

'Are you hungry, girls?' he called as I walked over to a nearby tree and flopped down in the shade.

They both came running over and sat very closely either side of Jamie.

'Back it up a bit, girls,' he wiggled until they moved over an inch. 'Blimey... right then, I've made seventeen different sorts of sandwiches -'

'No you haven't!' Gracie interrupted.

'Who says?' Jamie looked at her. 'Now, also I'm a little bit magic. Let me look into your eyes,' he gazed at her, getting closer and closer until they were touching foreheads, Gracie trying to hold in her giggles. 'Mm... I think that you like... hold on... cheese and cucumber?'

'How do you know?' she gasped, and I laughed at her expression.

'Because I'm magic,' Jamie said very seriously. 'And you,' he turned to Jessie, who was holding her small fists under her chin. 'Mm... tricky... I think... peanut butter?'

Jessie nodded rapidly, beaming at him in adoration.

'It's the only sandwich filling she's eaten in three years,' he said in an undertone to me as he pulled out the food.

I wasn't expecting much, but it seemed he had packed a feast - chicken and ham rolls for us with olives and feta cheese, two big bags of crisps, chocolate cupcakes and some fruit. I wasn't very hungry, but I nibbled on this and that as he messed around with the girls, pretending to steal their food.

I had, for months, labelled Jamie so wrongly, I decided. I'd just dismissed him as a flirt and a player, but seeing him with the children, I felt a small flicker of affection. Of course, that didn't mean he *wasn't* a flirt or a player, but I liked him. He caught me studying him and he gave me a swift smile. I looked down, feeling confused and wrong-footed.

After the girls had finished eating, Jamie pulled a Frisbee out from his rucksack and they ran off a short distance away and were soon joined by two little boys and a teenage girl. I helped him clear away the mess and then we sat in silence for a minute, watching the children play.

'She's like you,' he stretched his legs out in front of him, indicating towards Gracie. 'Very pretty.'

'Thanks,' I took a swig of water and turned towards him. 'You're very close, you and Jessie, aren't you?'

'Yeah,' he agreed.

'How come you look after her so much? I asked curiously.

'Because she won't stay with anyone else,' he said. 'She has a childminder in the week when my mum's working, but she does shifts, so weekends and evenings when she has to go in, I have her.'

'That must be hard work for you,' I said.

'Nah,' he shrugged. 'My mum has had it rough, and Jessie can be hard work. I don't mind though.'

'Are your parents divorced?'

'My dad died when Jess was a year old,' he said in a deliberately light tone.

'Oh God, I'm sorry,' I gasped. 'How sad.'

'Car accident,' he looked back at the girls. 'Jess doesn't remember him of course, but when she showed signs of autism, my mum thought it was some sort of trauma,' he smiled sadly. 'I moved back home, and now this is kind of it, for the time being anyway.'

'Wow,' I briefly touched his arm. 'I had no idea.'

'Why would you?' he smiled at me. 'It is what it is, I don't advertise it. Remember I told you that I hadn't dated for over a year?' I nodded. 'Well, that's why. The women I've met before get pissed off with it, that I'm not always free at the weekends when she's not even my kid.'

'It doesn't seem fair on you,' I said hesitantly.

'But I don't mind,' he shrugged. 'It's like being a dad, but not… and she's great, Jessie is.'

I stared at him, feeling even more guilty for being so dismissive of him. He looked like he was about to say something when my mobile started to ring. I rummaged in my bag and pulled it out, then tutted.

'What's up?' Jamie asked.

'Nothing,' I shoved my phone back in my bag. 'Withheld number. I had three calls this morning, I don't answer unknown numbers.'

'Probably someone trying to sell you insurance or make a PPI claim,' he said. 'So… what's the deal with Gracie's dad?'

'Oh,' I hesitated, feeling guarded. 'I left him last year.'

'Why?'

'Hmm, well mainly because he was having an affair,' I said hesitantly.

'That was silly of him,' Jamie grinned.

'Yeah,' I chuckled. 'It was very *silly* of him. Probably wasn't the first... actually, I *know* it wasn't the first. It just took me a while to leave him. He can be... difficult.'

'He must have been crazy,' Jamie's eyes moved over my face, and for once he wasn't smiling. 'What could any woman have that you don't?'

'Youth?' I tried not to sound bitter, but I probably did.

'Oh, come off it,' he shook his head. 'What are you? Twenty-one?'

'I wish,' I laughed. 'Actually, that's the bit that stung. He's ten years older than me.'

'And I'm ten years younger than you,' Jamie nudged me.

'Don't spoil it,' I tried not to smile. 'We've had a perfectly nice, flirt-free afternoon.'

'I've been good, haven't I?' he drew out a fake sigh. 'I do like you, Frankie. And I *really* fancy you, I can't help it. And I'm sorry if I've annoyed you at work - it's just how I am. I know you're not interested in me like that, but we can be friends, can't we?'

'Of course we can,' I nodded slowly, 'I would like to be. And I'm sorry that I've been -'

'Cold, dismissive, snobby,' he interrupted.

'Yes,' I admitted. 'All of them. Sorry.'

'Hug it out?' he spread his arms.

'Why not?' I laughed and leant towards him and hugged him briefly.

'I'll still fancy you, OK?' he said. 'But I will try and behave.'

'OK,' I giggled.

Suddenly a yell and then a scream rent the air, and we both instinctively looked at the girls, Jamie standing up.

'What the hell -' he started to jog over, me close behind him.

A boy, roughly Gracie's age was laying on the ground in front of her; she stood over him, hands on hips, looking furious. Jessie was kneeling on the ground some distance behind Gracie, her hands over her face, making quiet whimpering noises.

'Gracie?' I strode up to her, the boy got to his feet, glaring at her.

Out of the corner of my eye I could see a man running over.

Jamie went and crouched down beside Jessie and she started screaming incoherently.

'She pushed me over!' the boy yelled.

'He ripped my top,' Gracie snarled. I noticed the bow on the front of her top was hanging off.

'She kicked me,' the boy looked warily behind him as the man running over got nearer.

'He called Jessie stupid,' Gracie looked at me, her cheeks bright pink. 'And she's my best friend.'

'OK, OK, stop yelling,' I looked from one to the other.

'Frankie?'

I looked up and was shocked to see David standing there, breathing hard after his run.

'David?' I glanced behind me at Jamie; he was talking in a low voice to Jessie.

'Frankie, what the… Harry,' he strode over to the boy. 'What did I tell you?'

Utterly confused, I just stared at him.

'Daddy, she kicked me and pushed me over,' Harry went and stood next to David, glaring malevolently at Gracie.

'He was being horrible to Jessie,' Gracie followed suit and stood closer to me, her little face a picture of outrage.

'Only because she wouldn't answer me,' Harry looked up at David, 'she's dumb.'

Suddenly I felt terribly protective and felt anger filling my head, 'She's autistic,' I snapped.

'Right,' David looked at me and then to Harry, 'right… Harry go and sit over there,' he pointed towards a bench, looking stern.

Harry stormed away, muttering under his breath.

David and I looked at each other.

'Sorry,' we both said at the same time.

'Gracie, please go and sit near Jamie,' I ordered. She stomped off. 'I'm so sorry, I don't know what gets into her.'

'No, I'm sorry,' David walked over to me, his dark eyes kept darting over to Jamie. I looked around - he was still talking quietly to Jessie, she was stroking his beard and seemed to have calmed down, Gracie sat on the other side of him, glaring in the direction of Harry.

'Kids eh?' David said dryly. 'Please let me pay for a new top, I can't believe he did that,' he raked a hand through his hair. 'I only went to use the gents - I shouldn't have left him.'

'Really, it's fine, it's only a cheap T-shirt,' I said. 'I still can't believe she kicked him.'

'No, I insist,' he looked behind me again. 'Is that your husband?'

'Oh, no,' I shook my head. 'Just a friend from work and his little sister.'

'I'll go and apologise,' he started to walk over but I put a hand on his arm.

'I'll pass it on,' I looked up at him. 'Just let him sort her out.'

'Oh, OK,' he suddenly broke into a smile. 'We must stop meeting like this, eh?'

'Yes,' I laughed - we both looked at each other for a moment.

'Look, give me your address,' he said. 'I'll pay for the top, I've got no cash on me. Knowing you, it isn't a cheap top at all.'

'It really is,' I lied - it was actually brand new from Next and I wasn't happy about it in the slightest.

In the end, I reluctantly gave him my address, then we both called our respective children over, telling them to apologise to each other. They muttered 'sorry' to each other and walked off in opposite directions. We looked at each other and burst out laughing.

Gracie had wanted Jessie and Jamie to come back to ours, but Jamie gently declined, saying it would probably be better to take her home.

'Absolutely,' I agreed, ignoring Gracie's pout. I wondered if he was angry, but he didn't seem to be.

We walked out of the park together, Jamie was parked up the top of Will's road.

'I'm parked over there at my stepson's,' I pointed. 'Well, thanks for a lovely day, I hope she's OK.'

'She'll be fine,' Jamie stroked her head, then smiled at me. 'Thank you, Frankie, it was fun ... until world war three broke out.'

Suddenly, Jessie pulled away from Jamie and hugged me around the middle, then hugged Gracie.

'Aw, thank you Jess,' I said in surprise. 'We will see you again soon.'

'Yeah?' Jamie raised his eyebrows at me.

'Sure,' I took Gracie's hand. 'They seem to like each other, eh?'

'And we do too,' Jamie grinned.

'Yes, Jamie.'

CHAPTER NINE

David turned up at my house on Tuesday evening. Feeling awkward, I invited him in - it seemed rude not to.

'Is your husband about?' he asked. 'I want to apologise to him for Harry's behaviour.'

'No,' I took a deep breath. 'We're divorced actually.'

'Oh, I see,' he followed me through to the living room. 'Sorry to hear that.'

'Would you like a drink?' I asked, hoping he would decline.

'No thanks,' he glanced around the room. 'I won't keep you,' he fumbled in his back pocket and pulled out his wallet. 'Will a tenner cover it?'

'Really, you don't have to,' I said. 'It really doesn't matter.'

'Well... it does,' he insisted, frowning. 'I'm so embarrassed, he's having a few problems right now, but there's no excuse for what he did.'

'I understand,' I assured him. 'Gracie's not exactly being an angel right now. I reckon it was six of one and half a dozen of the other, please don't worry.'

'Thank you,' he smiled. 'You have every right to be angry. Look, at least let me buy you a drink one evening or something.'

'You don't have to,' I realised I might have sounded dismissive. 'But... OK, yes, I'd like that.'

'Great,' he replaced his wallet and pulled out his mobile phone. 'Give me your number, I'll call you sometime. Is your daughter OK?'

'Yeah, she's fine,' I smiled. 'And your son?'

'Yes,' he chuckled. 'On his best behaviour, he knows he's in the doghouse.'

I gave him my number and he left, saying he would ring me sometime soon, and apologising yet again for Harry's actions.

I went back into the living room after I had seen him out, feeling strange. It had all been very surreal, David standing in my living room, and I was very uneasy about us going out for a drink together. I wasn't sure how I felt towards him other than his presence made me feel guilty and ashamed.

I was shaken out of my reverie by my mobile phone ringing - it was Robert.

'Hello,' he sounded cheery.

'Gracie's in bed,' I said straight away.

'I was just ringing to see if I could pick her up tomorrow,' his tone wasn't really asking, it was telling.

'Yeah, sure,' I saw no point in arguing for the sake of it. 'As long as you don't bring her home too late.'

'Of course not,' he said mildly. 'Tell her minder I will pick her up after five.'

'Yep.'

'See you tomorrow then,' he said briskly.

I decided to head upstairs and have a soak and an early night - halfway up, my phone rang again, making me jump.

'Hello?' I answered without looking who it was, assuming Robert had forgotten something. Nobody answered and after a second, they ended the call. I looked at my screen and it was a withheld number again - I had had four or five more calls since Saturday.

A sense of unease washed over me, and I turned and went back downstairs, checking all my doors were locked. Feeling daft, I pulled the living room curtains open an inch, and peered outside. It was nearly dark, and the streetlights had come on, the one directly across the road from me flickering slightly. I jumped violently as a cat shot out from under my car and ran into next-doors garden.

For God's sake, woman I thought, yanking the curtains closed. Giving myself a mental shake, I ran a bath and tried to relax a little.

I started thinking about Jamie. His flirting at work had been minimal, but I was rather paranoid that people would notice the change. On Monday morning, I had inquired after Jessie and he had reassured me that she was absolutely fine and had not mentioned the incident on Saturday. We had spoken very little in the past two days, and I had wondered if he wasn't too keen after all on getting the girls together, or maybe his mum had said something - I wouldn't have blamed her, Gracie's behaviour hadn't done her any favours.

Paul and I had a chat over a coffee that morning - he told me that Jamie had said he had a good time with us, and was in high spirits.

'See?' he said, smirking a little. 'I told you he wasn't so bad.'

'No,' I agreed, slightly irritably. 'He's OK.'

He went on to tell me that Jamie had gone over to his house Sunday afternoon and was talking non-stop about me to Chelsea, who thought the whole thing was terribly sweet.

'You should be flattered,' Paul said. 'Chel thinks he's "fit" …
more than I get told,' he grumbled.

I wondered why I *didn't* feel more flattered. I sighed, turning the
hot tap on with my foot. Perhaps Robert had simply taken away my
capabilities to feel anything towards any man. And that, was a very
depressing thought.

The school holidays were approaching, and Robert and I had our
usual disagreement about who was having Gracie when. He brought
Gracie home after his weekend with her and as usual strode in, then
visibly got his back up when he spotted Maggie sat with her little
legs tucked under her on the sofa.

'Maggie,' he nodded coldly.

'Robert,' she gazed steadily at him.

'Gracie,' I said. 'Go and play in the garden for ten minutes, I just
need to sort something out with Daddy,' I subtly indicated with my
head for Maggie to follow her.

'How are you keeping then, Maggie?' Robert asked, injecting as
much indifference into his voice as possible, or so I thought.

'Very well,' she rose and looked at him for a moment. 'I trust
you're keeping well also? Dick not dropped off yet?'

I made the mistake of giggling, and Robert gave me a thunderous
look, then glared at Maggie's retreating back.

'Ridiculous woman,' he said contemptuously. 'So… when can I
have Gracie?'

'I've already told you,' I said evenly. 'I have the first and fourth
week booked off work, so any of the other weeks are fine, but I need
to know soon so I can let Rachel know.'

'Well, I was planning on taking her away the first week,' he said -
I knew he was just being awkward because he had the hump.

'You can take her away any of the other weeks, surely,' I folded
my arms and refused to drop my eyes.

'I am a very busy man, Frankie,' he said patronisingly. 'I can't
just rearrange myself around your plans.'

'Whatever Robert,' I suppressed a sigh. 'But if you take her away
the first week, I will miss out on spending time with her, and she will
lose out too. I think she would rather have two weeks with me than
one. And before you argue, no - I can't swap them.'

'Fine,' he looked at me like I was being the most unreasonable person on the planet. 'I will have to get back to you.'

'I'm not messing Rachel about,' I was having a hard time keeping my voice level. I could feel my temper rising. 'If you don't let me know soon, I will have to book her for all the weeks I'm working.'

'Don't be immature,' he snapped. 'You pay the woman, she should have Gracie when you want her to.'

And that just about summed up the whole of Robert's attitude to anyone he considered to be below him. Which was most people.

'Daddy,' Gracie came clattering through the kitchen from the garden, her cheeks rosy. Maggie followed her and leant against the archway between the living room and kitchen.

'Daddy is going now,' I told her brightly. 'Give him a kiss.'

Robert swept her up, narrowing his eyes at me at the same time.

'I love you,' Gracie wrapped herself around him, burying her face in his neck.

'And I love you, darling,' he squeezed her, then set her down. 'See you soon.'

As usual, Gracie positioned herself at the window to watch him.

'Wanker,' Maggie muttered under her breath.

I rubbed my eyes and flopped down onto the nearest chair, feeling like I had just done battle.

'Come on, trouble,' Maggie directed at Gracie. 'Let's run you a bath and let mummy have a rest.'

I smiled at her gratefully.

'Pour wine,' she mouthed as she headed toward the hall with Gracie in tow.

I decided to book a holiday for me and Gracie on the Norfolk coast on my first week off - I really felt the need to get away from it all.

I saw Will on the Monday of my last week of work: Lennie had just had her first scan and the baby's due date had been confirmed as the fourth of January. He proudly showed me the scan picture - an almost perfect image of the baby with the head in side profile and the curve of its back with indistinguishable shadows that I took for its legs tucked up. He informed me the baby was the size of a lime, according to the book he had been reading.

On the Wednesday, David rang me, asking if I was free on Friday for a bite to eat. With slight relief, I told him that as I was driving to Norfolk the following morning, so it wasn't really practical. He then suggested doing it on the Thursday night - realising that I would have to accept sooner or later, and feeling that I wanted to get it over and done with - I accepted and rang Maggie, asking her to watch Gracie for a couple of hours. I was half hoping she couldn't, but she was more than happy to.

As it happens, the evening wasn't as bad as I thought it was going to be. I met him at a restaurant in the neighbouring town, Chembury. Out of habit, I had spent ages getting ready, dressing in a tight black dress - one of my new purchases - then thinking it looked too seductive, changed into black jeans and a silk blouse, wanting to look like I hadn't particularly gone to any effort. I arrived ten minutes late, as Gracie had decided to play up and get clingy.

He was sitting at the bar when I arrived, drinking a coke and looking fidgety.

'Hi,' he stood up as I approached. 'Thought you were going to stand me up.'

'Sorry,' I smiled, 'Gracie was being a pain.'

'Our tables ready,' he looked me up and down. 'You look lovely by the way… shall we go through?'

The waitress took our drink orders and left us with the menus. I studied it intently, putting off small talk, feeling uncomfortable. When I set the menu down, he was smiling across the table at me.

'You always took forever to decide what to have,' he looked at me affectionately.

'Sorry,' I looked down, shaking my head. 'This is rather weird,' I looked back up. 'Can we just clear the air?'

'Clear the air?' he raised an eyebrow.

'Yes,' I looked at him steadily. 'We parted on bad terms - kind of - and I'll be honest,' I took a deep breath, 'I feel bloody awful every time I see you. And I'm sorry.'

'Frankie,' he chuckled, 'it was a long time ago. It doesn't matter… really.'

'It's weird though,' I studied his familiar face, different but oh so familiar. 'We were together a long time, yes it *was* a long time ago, but… oh, I don't know!'

'OK,' he leant back in his chair a little and considered me for a moment. 'It is a little strange. But I'm so glad we bumped into each other, I've thought about you on and off over the years… wondered how you are, what you're doing. But if I was holding on to some sort of resentment… well that would be ridiculous. It happened, and life went on.'

'Yeah,' I relaxed slightly. 'But I *am* sorry, David. What I did was horrible. Horrible and cruel.'

'Please,' he unexpectedly reached over and stroked the back of my hand. 'It doesn't matter anymore and look at it this way, you wouldn't have Gracie, and I wouldn't have Harry… although it's debatable whether that's a good thing or not at the moment.'

I giggled, 'You don't mean that.'

'No,' he looked up as the waitress approached with our drinks. 'But, my goodness, he's hard work.'

We ordered our meals and he raised his glass to me.

'Here's to shitty kids.'

I laughed and we clinked glasses.

'So,' I took a sip and set my glass down. 'Are you still married?'

'Separated,' he pulled a face. 'A weekend dad and forever in the doghouse.'

'Oh?' I felt curious despite myself. 'You don't have to discuss it.'

'No, it's fine,' he said. 'Nothing dramatic. I met her six months after we, um, parted… she was, I'm ashamed to say, a rebound. But, I did have feelings for her, genuine feelings, just way too soon and it kind of snowballed and like the fool I am, I asked her to marry me. Then Harry came along, and after a while it was obvious we were both really bloody unhappy. We kind of just drifted along until I decided one of us had to address it,' he shrugged. 'And that ended up being yours truly… so I'm the bad guy. We split up last year - Harry took it badly, so she hates me even more.'

'I'm sure she doesn't,' I frowned. 'It's just tricky when it's still raw.'

'Yeah,' he agreed. 'Maybe. So, how about you?'

'I left him last year,' I fiddled with the stem of my glass. 'We had drifted apart, and he wasn't faithful. That's all there is to it really. My divorce came through three months ago.'

'Sorry to hear that,' he said sincerely.

Our food arrived, and we started to chat about our jobs and things in general. I was glad, I didn't feel it was appropriate to discuss Robert with him, despite him saying it was all in the past. I realised, as the evening went on, that I had forgotten what good company David was. He didn't have me in fits of giggles, like Robert had, but he had a dry sense of humour and was intelligent and could start a conversation out of thin air. I suppressed a smile when he kept clearing his throat - an old habit of his that used to irritate me - a big throat clear, two small ones and then another big one.

'What?' he smiled bemusedly at me.

'Nothing,' I looked down.

'Another drink?' he asked as the plates were taken away.

'No, thank you,' I looked at my watch. 'I must get home, work tomorrow and I still need to pack.'

He paid the bill and we left the restaurant. He walked me to my car and kissed my cheek.

'Thanks for a lovely evening,' he smiled.

'I enjoyed it,' I said truthfully.

'Let's keep in touch,' he looked slightly unsure of himself. 'I mean, as friends - of course.'

'Sure,' I nodded. 'Well… see you soon, then.'

'Yeah,' he watched me climb into my car. 'Have a nice holiday, Frankie.'

He shut my door and I watched him walk towards his dark blue Audi.

I felt strangely cheerful as I drove home, maybe because we had briefly discussed what had happened between us - I wasn't so sure about us being friends, but I felt less of a bitch.

I was running very late the following morning. After answering a million questions from Maggie when I had returned home the night before, it had gotten rather late, then I remembered I hadn't washed a couple of Gracie's things I wanted to take on holiday and put them on a quick cycle, not wanting to go to bed until they had finished. I slept through my alarm, and by the time I had dragged a sleepy and grumpy Gracie out of bed and showered and dressed in record time, then hung out my washing so it was ready to pack after work, we had barely two minutes before school started. Then I realised I had left my laptop at home - it had been playing up and Paul said he had a mate who could look at it for me - so I drove home as fast as I dared and arrived at work nearly twenty minutes late.

'It's OK,' Bea looked up as I slipped into the office, feeling overly warm and flustered. 'Mr Windsor isn't in yet.'

Jamie put a hand up in greeting to me from across the office, I smiled, then noticed Louise staring at me and I dropped my smile and disappeared behind my monitor, surreptitiously powdering my shiny nose and trying to tame my still damp curls.

Mid-morning, Paul wandered over and I handed over my laptop.

'Thanks, Paul,' I said gratefully. 'Let me know how much it's going to cost before he does anything though.'

'Sure,' he lowered his voice, 'Listen, Chel wants to invite you and Jamie over for dinner when you're back off your holiday - I said I'd check with you first, seems a bit like a double-date type of thing, I didn't think you'd be too happy.'

'Oh,' I said in surprise. 'Well... it's OK, I guess. I think Jamie knows how the land lies,' I looked over at him, he was talking to Joe and being gazed at by Sophie. 'Yeah... why not?'

'Great,' Paul straightened up and went back to his desk, my laptop case under his arm.

As soon as five o'clock arrived I clapped my hands gleefully.

'That's me done for a whole week,' I said to Bea as I shut my computer down.

'Lucky you,' Bea rummaged in her bag then handed me a bag of wrapped sweets. 'For the journey, for my little Gracie.'

'Thanks Bea,' I shoved them into my bag.

'Hey,' I looked up, Jamie was standing there. 'Walk you to your car?' he said.

'Bye, Bea,' I called as I left.

'Jess keeps on about Gracie,' Jamie told me as we headed towards the reception area. 'Do you want to do something soon?'

'Sure, Gracie would like that,' I nodded. 'I'm not sure when my ex has got her, he's being an awkward sod at the moment, but yes, that'd be good.'

'And dinner at Paul's next Saturday?' he gave me a sideways glance. 'You OK with that?'

'Yeah,' I said lightly. 'I'm home in the morning and won't have time to shop, I will need feeding.'

'Very funny,' we stopped as we reached my car. 'I know it's the fantastic company you're looking forward to.'

'Of course,' I patted his arm. 'Paul's great company.'

'Oh, you are a horrid woman Frankie Quinn,' he grinned. 'Go home.'

'Sorry,' I giggled. 'Well, see you in a week then.'

'Have a great time,' he started walking backwards. 'Bring me back a stick of rock.'

'Sure.'

CHAPTER TEN

Mine and Gracie's little holiday was just what I needed - the only thing that spoiled it was the mysterious withheld number ringing every now and then. On our third day I answered it, grumpily asking who it was, but whoever it was ended the call - it was becoming such an annoyance I was considering changing my number. But, at least I didn't feel as uneasy and vulnerable, as I was away from home. I kept thinking about it though and wondering if it was somebody I knew, playing silly buggers. For some reason my thoughts kept taking me to Robert, but it really wasn't his style. I knew it couldn't be David, he hadn't had my number when the calls had started and there seemed no good reason why he would be doing that to me. Could it be Louise and Sophie in their childish spite? I had no idea, but I was hoping that whoever it was, would get bored and very soon.

We got home around lunchtime, and I made Gracie have a bath and a little nap as Robert was picking her up at six o'clock. Jamie was picking me up at seven-thirty. I wasn't feeling much enthusiasm about the upcoming evening, I was tired and couldn't be bothered to get myself looking decent.

Gracie curled up on the sofa with Yellow Bunny and I started unpacking, wishing I could join her. I decided to do one load of our washing and hang it out before I went out; it could stay out all night if I was home too late. I went and had a quick shower and threw on some old shorts and a T-shirt, put away all our toiletries and opened our bedroom windows to air them, then went back down to hang out my washing. I was half-way across the lawn with my plastic basket when I noticed the side gate was open very slightly. Suddenly I felt sick - I knew one hundred percent I had bolted it at the top and bottom before I left home. Dropping my basket, I went over to the gate and pulled it open and looked around the drive-way. My bin still had a dent on the lid, I couldn't tell if it had been stood on again. I slammed the gate shut and bolted it then walked around to the back looking for anything that might have been disturbed, but nothing looked out of the ordinary.

'You back then?'

I nearly yelled in fright - Clarissa, my next-door-neighbour had put her head over the fence.

'Yes, hi,' I went over. 'You haven't seen or heard anything whilst we've been away, have you?'

'No,' she frowned. 'You OK, Frankie?'

'Yeah,' I looked up at my house. 'My gate was open, that's all... I'm certain I locked it.'

'Maybe you were in a rush when you were leaving?' she shrugged. 'Kids are distracting little turds, aren't they?' She had two young sons and a baby daughter.

'Yeah... maybe,' I murmured. 'I'm sure I did though. Never mind... you OK then?'

She started chatting - she was very hard to get away from. I starting to peg my washing on the line, only half listening to her, thinking about the gate and the calls... I felt foolish, but I couldn't help thinking they were connected.

I was nearly done when I heard her husband calling her, she excused herself and went indoors, I shot back in and locked my backdoor. I couldn't shake off my bad feeling. I poured myself a gin and sat down for a bit, telling myself I was being paranoid and ludicrous.

I woke Gracie up an hour before Robert was due to pick her up, she seemed refreshed and happy to be going to his. We went and packed her weekend bag, making sure she had the tin of fudge she had brought him and the photo I had taken of her sitting next to her sandcastle on the beach.

He arrived promptly at five.

'Hello, darling,' he hugged Gracie. 'I've missed you - did you have a nice time with Mummy?'

'Yes!' she yelled. 'I got you a present... can we watch Frozen tonight? What are we having for tea?'

'So demanding,' he chuckled, then looked at me. 'Was she good? You've got a nice tan there.'

'Yes, she was fine,' I nodded, smiling at her, then stuck out an arm. 'More freckles, you mean.'

He glanced down at my bare legs then smiled lazily, 'You look well.'

'Thanks,' I handed him Gracie's bag. 'Well, see you tomorrow then.'

'Yep,' he took Gracie's hand. 'Give Mummy a kiss.'

I waved them off, then fetching my drink, I went upstairs to get changed, tiredness and worry washing over me - maybe a night out was just what I needed.

Jamie was five minutes early, I invited him in while I finished brushing my hair and double-checked the doors were locked.

'You look nice,' he strolled in, nosily looking around. 'Lovely house.'

I'd put on a pale green summer dress; I was wondering if it was too short, I didn't want him getting any ideas.

'Thank you,' I waved vaguely at the sofa. 'I'll be two minutes.'

I ran upstairs to find some sandals and spray on some perfume, and returned to find him wandering around looking at my various framed photographs of Gracie. There was a new addition - us with Will and Lennie at their wedding.

'Who's that?' he asked.

'My stepson and his wife,' I jangled my house keys. 'I'm ready.'

He turned back to me and followed me to the hall.

'Oh, I nearly forgot,' I said as we reached the door - I pulled a stick of rock out of my bag. 'For you... or Jess.'

'Ha, you remembered,' he took it and grinned in delight.

Chelsea, Paul's wife, greeted us at the door, hugging me and kissing Jamie. I had met her on a few occasions, but I'd only been to their home twice. I had often thought they were a mismatched couple - no offence to Paul, but he was *average* looking I suppose you'd say, and she was simply gorgeous. She was very petite; I felt like a giant next to her, with long shiny chestnut hair and long-lashed aqua-green eyes, and despite having four young children - the youngest only a few months old - she always looked fresh and glamorous. Tonight, she was wearing an ankle length maxi dress, showing off her very tanned shoulders, her hair in two plaits. I wondered briefly whether Jamie fancied her, I imagined it must be very hard not to.

'Hello, you two,' she beamed. 'I hope you're starving, Paul cooked up a feast. I've shipped the boys off to my mum's for the night so I can drink a lot,' she giggled. 'I think I might pass out before washing-up time... ooo lovely, you've brought more wine.'

We followed her through to their spacious living room, the patio doors were wide open showing an extremely tidy back garden.

Paul appeared in the doorway, wearing an apron and a glass of whisky in his hand, looking tired as usual.

'Hello,' he greeted us. 'What do you want to drink? By the way, your laptop's all fixed, Frankie.'

'Oh, what was it?' I asked. 'What do I owe him?'

'Nothing,' he said. 'My mate said it just needed a clean-up and a new charger, loose wires or something.'

'Really? Well tell him thanks,' I said gratefully.

Chelsea disappeared into the kitchen with Paul after sitting us down and returned with two glasses of wine.

Her and Jamie were soon chattering away, they obviously knew each other well. I settled back on one the sofas, only half listening. My mind had started to wander again and I felt tense and worried about my possible intruder and the phone calls.

'You OK?' Jamie asked as Chelsea disappeared to fetch more wine. 'You're very quiet.'

'Yes,' I smiled weakly. 'I'm fine, sorry, tired after my holiday.'

'You sure?' he frowned. 'Gracie get off with Robert OK?'

'Yeah,' I shrugged, then stared at him. 'Robert? I've never told you his name,' I suddenly felt sick again.

'Oh shit,' he sat up straighter. 'Paul's mentioned him a couple of times... actually I was being nosy, because... well, you know -'

'Right,' I studied his face, my stomach knotting up.

'Sorry,' Jamie dropped his eyes. 'It was ages ago, before we were friends... I mean, me and you... Frankie?'

'Sorry,' I shook my head. 'It's just... I think someone is messing with me and I'm just a bit edgy... don't worry.'

'Well, now I am,' he got up and came and sat next to me. 'What do you mean?'

'It's probably nothing,' I tried to sound off-hand. 'Just a prowler in my garden. Probably kids... but I've had all these phone calls too -'

I broke off as Chelsea came back.

'Oops, sorry to interrupt,' she eyed us sitting close together.

'Well, that's it,' Jamie threw his hands up. 'Moment ruined!'

I giggled as Chelsea frowned, then realised he was joking.

Paul must have been cooking all day, he'd made a feast, enough food for triple the amount of people: Mexican chicken with rice that was so spicy it took the roof of your mouth off, nachos, stuffed peppers and salad and homemade strawberry ice-cream. We ate outside on their large patio, enjoying the last rays of sunshine. Chelsea was drinking a lot and kept topping up our glasses, Jamie reluctantly declined after a couple of glasses as he was driving.

Paul disappeared out the front for a cigarette, and Jamie started taking plates indoors. Chelsea, looking full of curiosity, leant over the table and grinned at me.

'So,' she said, 'what's with you two?'

'Nothing,' I smiled at her eager face. 'We are just friends.'

'Shame,' she looked disappointed. 'He is *so* cute… and he really likes you.'

'I like him,' I shrugged. 'As a friend. He's way too young for me.'

'Just a number,' she said impatiently. 'Do you know what he said the other day?'

'What?' I felt curious despite myself.

'He said that he knows you are out of his league,' she whispered, 'but, he can dream… how sweet is that?'

'Hmm, I suppose,' I hedged.

At that moment Jamie trotted back outside and Paul reappeared from having his cigarette - Chelsea put a finger to her lips and sat back.

They both sat down, Jamie groaning and rubbing his stomach.

'I'm so full,' he stretched contentedly and smiled at me - I smiled back and ignored Chelsea, who was avidly watching us both.

We sat outside until it began to grow cold, then went and sat in the living room. Chelsea was beginning to slur a little. We discussed our kids - I had to smile a little as Jamie joined in about Jessie as if she were his - and predictably work. I couldn't help noticing that Chelsea seemed a bit distant towards Paul and I wondered if everything was OK. She also seemed slightly flirtatious with Jamie too, the amount she had drank was probably fuelling it.

'Where did you get your shirt from, Jamie?' she asked.

'Oh,' Jamie looked down at himself. 'River Island, I think,' he shrugged.

'Better than TK Maxx,' she looked at Paul. 'I do like a nicely dressed man, don't you Frankie?'

'Clothes are clothes,' I glanced at Paul. 'It's what underneath that counts,' Jamie started sniggering. 'No, I didn't mean *that*… shut up… I meant, personality and all that.'

'Coffee, anyone?' Paul stood up abruptly.

'I'll help,' I got up and followed him to the kitchen, leaving Chelsea and Jamie chatting. 'Is everything OK, Paul?' I watched him fill the coffee percolator.

'Yes and no,' his shoulders went up a fraction. 'Nothing major.'

'Hmm, OK,' I started to load their dishwasher. 'Well, you know where I am if you need an ear.'

'Don't tempt me,' he muttered.

'Is it serious then?' I said, feeling alarmed.

'No… no,' he turned and leant back against the worktop, frowning slightly. 'I don't know what's up with her.'

'Have you tried asking?'

'Yes, of course,' he smiled wryly. 'She says nothing, so I'm like OK then… but then she gets huffy. God, you women confuse me.'

'It's what we're best at,' I said lightly, then noticing how miserable he looked, I went and gave him a hug. 'She's probably tired with the boys and things,' I stood back and smiled at him. 'You'll be alright, you two. Marriage is tricky… I *know* that much.'

'Yeah, well, Robert is a fool,' he shook his head.

'Talking of him,' I eyed him cautiously, 'no biggie but - please don't say I asked - did you tell Jamie much about him?'

'Not really,' he looked apprehensive. 'Not the ins and outs, that's your business. Just that he's a bit of a tosser and you're better off without him… sorry, is that not OK?'

'No, it's fine,' I assured him. 'It's just… oh please don't mention it, but he mentioned his name earlier and I'm sure I didn't tell him his name and there's been a couple of weird incidents lately… you know what?' I sighed. 'I don't even know what I'm thinking. Forget it.'

'Now *I'm* worried about *you,*' he crossed his arms and stared at me. 'What's up?'

'Nothing,' I lied. 'Really… come on, get those coffees done before Chel passes out.'

Jamie and I left a little before eleven o'clock, Chelsea seemed ready to pass out soon and Paul looked exhausted.

'Wow, was it me or are things a little strained?' Jamie said as he pulled away, putting his hand up to Paul in the doorway, Chelsea swaying behind him.

'I gather there's a few problems,' I said sadly. 'I hope they're OK, such a nice couple.'

'Nice, yeah,' Jamie paused. 'So… you going to tell me what's up with you?'

'I'm being daft,' I knew he was talking about our interrupted conversation earlier. 'It's just I had someone in my garden one night a few weeks ago, I've had security lights fitted… but I still feel uneasy, I think someone was in there again while I was away… and then there's these calls… it's probably nothing.'

'Nothing?' he glanced at me. 'Enough to worry you.'

'I'm fine,' I said automatically.

'No, no you're not,' he said quietly. 'Listen, I have a mate who does security alarms, I can have a word, if you want.'

'Oh, no,' I said. 'Honestly, who would want to break into my poxy little house?'

'Frankie,' he genuinely sounded concerned, 'you live in a nice area, you have an expensive car on your drive… and you're vulnerable on your own with a child.'

'I'm not vulnerable,' I bristled slightly.

'Don't get all offended,' he chuckled. 'I'm just worried about you, that's all.'

'Sorry,' I murmured - unexpectedly I felt my eyes fill with tears and I looked out of the passenger window, blinking rapidly.

'Just don't feel like you can't ask for help,' he said.

'Thank you.'

We drove the rest of the way in silence and I tried to compose myself, telling myself it was the wine making me feel emotional.

As we pulled up outside my house, I felt the unspoken fear rising again.

'Did I switch the hall light on before we left?' I asked, my mouth feeling dry. I stared at my front door, there was a dim light shining through the patterned glass at the top - I was certain that I hadn't switched the light on.

'I don't know,' Jamie looked past me at my house, then unbuckled his seatbelt. 'I'll see you in.'

I didn't argue, although I wanted to. I climbed out and marched to my front door, my legs shaking and my heart hammering in my chest. Jamie watched me unlock it, then squeezed past me. I followed him, trying to look unconcerned. He stepped into the living room and walked through to the kitchen, switching the light on.

'Want me to look upstairs?'

I shrugged, and he disappeared. Leaving my laptop on the table, I checked that both the kitchen and utility room doors were locked and went back into the living room, starting to feel embarrassed. Jamie came jogging down the stairs again.

'No bogie man up there,' he smiled. 'You must have switched it on.'

'Yeah,' I couldn't look him in the eyes. 'Sorry, you must think I'm stupid.'

'No,' he frowned and walked over to me. 'I'm not trying it on,' he held out his arms, 'but come here.'

I walked over, and he put his arms around me and I felt close to tears again. Wrong or right, it felt so good to have a proper cuddle and I buried my face into his shoulder, revelling in the feel of his warm breath on the side of my face and the musky smell of his aftershave.

After a few minutes, he gently pushed me away and held me at arm's length, his eyes solemn and watchful.

'Look, don't read anything into this… please… do you want me to stay?' he asked softly. 'Kip on the sofa?'

I gazed at him for a moment, fighting down my stubborn streak - I looked down and nodded.

'I promise I don't have an ulterior motive,' he said. 'I just hate seeing you like this, Frankie.'

'Thank you,' I looked up at his face, he did look concerned.

'I'll go and get you a duvet,' I went upstairs and pulled a spare duvet out from the top of my wardrobe and fetched a clean cover from the airing cupboard - as all the single covers were Gracie's, it had Moshi Monsters printed on it.

'Thanks,' he had taken off his trainers and socks and was sitting on the coffee table. 'Is it OK if I have the television on low? Else I can't sleep.'

'Of course,' I handed him the remote control. 'Do you want a drink or anything?'

'No, I'm good,' he grinned.

'OK… night, then.'

'Night, Frankie.'

I woke up at six, groggily aware that something was out of kilter - it took me a while to remember why. I had fallen asleep surprisingly quickly, I wasn't totally comfortable with Jamie staying overnight but I had obviously felt safer with him there.

After deciding I wasn't going to fall back to sleep, I had a shower and pulled on some jeans and a vest top and ventured downstairs, feeling awkward. Jamie was still fast asleep, I noticed his clothes discarded on one of my chairs, he was curled up on his side, one arm over his head.

I went into the kitchen and filled the kettle, unsure whether I should wake him up or not. Instead, spotting my laptop on the table, I went and switched it on, then made a mug of tea before settling myself on a chair, thinking I would do a little Amazon shopping to lift my mood. As my laptop came to life, I almost screamed with laughter, my previous screen picture of a view of a lake with a sunset, had been replaced with an extreme close-up of Jamie's face, cross-eyed and his mouth wide open - he'd clearly been at Paul's house when my laptop had been returned.

I soon got engrossed, perusing autumn clothes, when I heard noises from the living room. I leant back a fraction in my chair and looked to my right - Jamie was stretching and yawning from under the duvet - I tucked my chair in a bit, feeling I would be embarrassed if he got up and saw me, particularly if he was in his boxer shorts or worse, naked. His mobile started to ring.

'Hi Mum,' I heard him say. 'Did you get my text?... Yeah, I crashed at a mate's... yeah... no, I haven't... OK... is she OK?... Good, see you later.'

I smiled to myself.

'I'm in the kitchen,' I called, not wanting him to wander in undressed. 'Do you want a cuppa?'

'Please,' he answered.

I went and switched the kettle back on, keeping my back to the archway between the kitchen and the living room. Eventually I heard him plodding in and I turned around, he had put his jeans on, but his shirt was undone showing a tanned chest. I averted my eyes quickly.

'Morning,' he sat down and yawned.

'You sleep OK?' I asked as I made his tea.

'Not bad,' he said. 'Your sofa is comfy... you alright then?'

'Yeah,' I set his tea down and sat down, feeling ridiculous again about my wobble the night before. 'Actually, I have a bone to pick with you,' I tried to keep a straight face.

'I didn't sleep-walk into your bed, did I?' he grinned cheekily.

'No,' I tutted. 'Has someone been messing with my laptop?' I drummed my fingers on the table. 'I had a bit of a surprise this morning.'

He burst out laughing, 'Ah, yeah, couldn't resist, sorry.'

'Hmm,' I smiled. 'Well, my password is back on.'

'Blame Paul,' he said. 'He should have stopped me, I have no self-control.'

'Uh huh.'

'So,' he looked serious suddenly. '*Are* you OK? You didn't seem it last night.'

'Yes,' I tried to sound off-hand. 'I was being daft, I'm fine.'

He drank some tea and continued to look at me.

'I know you said no,' he said, 'but I'm going to call my mate about an alarm, see what he says,' he put his hand up as I started to protest. 'No, I am. Stop being stubborn.'

'But, it seems a bit extreme,' I argued. 'I probably left my gate open before I went away and I must have switched on the hall light last night… and the calls are probably nothing to do with anything.'

'And I hope you're right,' he said slowly. 'But, in this day and age it wouldn't hurt, and surely you'd rather not be worrying all the time, eh?'

I half nodded, half shrugged.

'And as for those calls,' he continued, 'even if they're withheld, if they become sinister, the police can trace them … I know because my ex had the same problem - turned out to be her ex being a dick.'

'Really?' I said. 'Because it has crossed my mind it's my ex… well my friend reckons it's him anyway. I even wondered if it's Louise and Sophie.'

'Why would you think it's them?' he looked puzzled.

I hesitated. I didn't want to tell him about their over-heard conversation, not just because it had been the reason behind me agreeing to a date with Jamie, but also because I was mortified about what they had said about me.

'Oh, I don't know,' I hedged. 'I've been over-thinking it. I even wondered if it was my ex before Robert, we've bumped into each other a couple of times… it's probably not even anybody I know.'

'Probably not,' he drank some tea and continued to stare thoughtfully at me.

'So, what are your plans today?' I changed the subject.

'Not much,' he said. 'Just chilling. And you?'

'I need to go shopping before Gracie's home,' I got up to rinse my mug. 'And it's my stepson's birthday next week, I need to get him a present.'

'I was wondering,' he said hesitantly, 'on Wednesday evening at the leisure centre, there's an autism-friendly session at the swimming pool... do you fancy it?'

'Um,' I sat back down. 'I'm not sure if my daughter is very "autism-friendly", would she be allowed?'

'Yeah, there's always siblings there,' he suddenly grinned wickedly. 'And I would *love* to see you in a bikini.'

'And then he goes and spoils it,' I shook my head in despair.

'Oh, come on,' he continued to grin. 'I'm allowed to slip up every now and then.'

'I suppose,' I giggled. 'OK, yeah, Gracie would like that.'

'Great,' he looked really pleased. 'Make sure it's super skimpy, please.'

'Jamie,' I said warningly.

'Sorry.'

CHAPTER ELEVEN

On Tuesday after work, I picked Gracie up from Rachel's and drove over to Will's house to give him his birthday card and gift. He'd told me that him and Lennie were having some people over later in the evening - Lennie didn't feel like going out, as apparently she was feeling "shit and tired".

Will answered the door, wiping his eyes and chuckling at something.

'Hello, you OK?' I asked, bemused. Gracie threw herself at him.

'Yes,' he stood back. 'We've, um,' he glanced at the top of Gracie's head, 'broke the news to Adam, and he's... well, come in. You'll see.'

I cautiously put my head around the doorway to the living room and nearly burst out laughing - Adam was sat on the sofa next to Lennie, his arms around her and noisily sobbing his heart out. She was gingerly patting him on the back, looking torn between laughter and despair.

As usual, when Lennie saw me, she looked cautious and her big, dark green eyes became guarded. I wished she wouldn't react that way, it always felt like she was dragging Robert into the room with us - but I supposed she couldn't help it.

'Adam!' Gracie exclaimed running over to him, her face a picture of concern. 'Why are you sad? Did you hurt yourself? Mummy... why is Adam sad?'

I looked at Lennie and she shrugged, 'He's not sad, he's happy,' I tugged Will's arm. 'We're going to have to tell her,' I added in a whisper, he glanced at Lennie, then nodded.

'Hello, little G,' Adam unwrapped himself from Lennie, wiped his eyes on her shoulder, was reprimanded with an 'Ew, Adam, you dick,' from her, then gave Gracie a little stroke on her cheek.

'Will?' I nodded in their direction, looking far from happy, he went and sat on the other side of Lennie.

'Come here,' he pulled her over and onto his knee. 'We have something very exciting to tell you.'

'What?' Gracie looked avidly at him.

'Lennie is going to have a baby,' he said, smiling at her.

'Really?! Is it a boy baby or a girl baby?!' she clapped her hands together, looking beside herself with delight. 'Mummy, Lennie's having a baby,' she told me importantly - Lennie giggled and Adam started sobbing again.

'Well, isn't that lovely?' I said, sitting down on the other sofa, trying not to laugh at Adam.

'When is it coming out?' Gracie looked at Lennie's stomach. 'Can I help you look after it?'

'Not until after Christmas,' Lennie told her, 'and of course you can.'

'Gracie,' I said, watching Will's face. 'Can you take Adam to the kitchen, so he can blow his nose, and maybe Adam can get you some juice.'

Gracie jumped off Will's knee and took Adam's hand.

'So, you're telling everyone, I take it?' I looked from Lennie to Will.

'Rosie kind of guessed,' Will said, putting his hand on Lennie's leg.

'She noticed I haven't been drinking,' Lennie shrugged. 'And, well... it's me. Adam would have clocked it sooner or later - also,' she glanced at Will, 'I'm beginning to show a little,' she smoothed her T-shirt over her tummy and sure enough, there was a hint of a bump.

'OK, I know you don't want to hear this,' I paused, then plowed on. 'Gracie will tell her dad and I can't really stop her.'

Lennie's hands went, instinctively it seemed, to her stomach and Will's face clouded over for a second.

'Well, if she does, she does,' he said shortly. 'It doesn't matter.'

'No, it doesn't,' I agreed lightly. 'Don't make it your problem - right, enough of that... happy birthday, Will.'

I got up and handed him his card and his gift-wrapped present, a bottle of his favourite aftershave.

'Thanks, Frankie,' he looked delighted and got up to hug me.

Adam came back with Gracie and he sat next to me, his face rather blotchy. Gracie wriggled her way in between Lennie and Will and started playing with Lennie's bracelet.

'So, who you got coming over later?' I asked.

'Dan and maybe Carla,' I noticed Lennie wrinkled her nose a little, I knew that she didn't always get on with her sister-in -law. 'Dom, when he's finished up at the Lizard,' Will continued, 'and my mum and stepdad. I've got to put my head in the restaurant for a bit, Adam's supposed to be helping Len make dinner.'

'And so I will,' Adam piped up. 'Lens shouldn't be cooking, she should be resting and practising her breathing.'

'You haven't met many pregnant women, have you?' Lennie shook her head in despair.

'I'm buying a book about it tomorrow,' Adam said happily. 'I wonder how hard it is to knit?'

'You can borrow Will's,' Lennie told him - I giggled, I don't know how she kept a straight face with Adam, but I supposed she was used to his peculiarities.

'I better go,' I said reluctantly.

'Aww, no, stay,' Adam turned to me.

'I want to stay,' Gracie implored.

'No, I really can't,' I patted Adam's arm and stood up, Gracie folded her arms and glared at me.

'I'll walk you out,' Will got up too. 'Be back soon,' he bent down and kissed Lennie.

'See you soon,' I said and pulled a reluctant Gracie to her feet.

'Lens,' I heard Adam say as we left. 'Do you think midwifery training takes long?'

'I love him,' I said, as we stepped outside.

'Got to really,' Will chuckled.

'Will,' I paused between our cars on the driveway. 'Sorry I brought up Robert, I shouldn't have.'

'No, it's fine,' he frowned then smiled sadly. 'As much as I'd rather forget he exists,' he watched Gracie, who was kicking gravel about, for a moment. 'I just don't want Lennie stressed out, she's gone from throwing up constantly to being exhausted - her midwife says it's normal, but I keep worrying.'

'It is completely normal,' I assured him. 'She'll be fine. She's tougher than you think, I reckon.'

'Yeah,' he nodded slowly. 'Yeah, course she is. I just want everything to be perfect.'

'It will be,' I touched his cheek. 'She's got you.'

I felt a little down and wistful that evening - a mixture of envy at Will and Lennie - so young and in love and starting a new adventure together - and my own sad regrets at how my life had turned out… and also the fact I didn't feel entirely comfortable accepting Adam's invitation to stay. I really would have loved to. I wasn't family though, not really.

Gracie played up at bedtime, still sulking because she had wanted to stay. Not feeling especially tired, I curled up in the living room with my laptop and started looking at clothes again. I was just dickering over a beautiful but expensive pair of leather boots, when Maggie rang.

'Have you got Gracie this weekend?' she asked without preamble. 'There's a singles night at The Engine.'

'Yes,' I said. 'And I wouldn't go anyway. Why don't you ask Sally?'

'You're joking, right?' Maggie said, sounding scathing. 'She's got a face like melted misery, she'd scare all the good blokes off.'

I laughed, 'She might scare them into your direction.'

'She's no fun,' she grumbled. 'I want *you* to come.'

'Well I can't,' I said. 'And singles nights are so tacky, seriously. If I'm going to meet a man, I want to do it the old-fashioned way... chance meeting, getting to know each other whilst being wined and dined... most the guys there are probably married anyway.'

'Still got dicks, haven't they?'

'Maggie!' I laughed. 'You're worse than my ex.'

'Don't compare me to that slimy bastard,' she hissed. 'Talking of that waste of air, you had any more calls?'

'Actually, no,' I said slowly, thinking about it. 'How weird... not since Saturday. They must have got bored, I guess.'

'*He* got bored, you mean,' she said.

I told her about my panic on Saturday and Jamie staying over.

'And you kept your hands to yourself?' she sounded disappointed.

'Yes, I'm not interested in him like that,' I sighed. 'Kind of wish I was, he is so sweet.'

'Go for it,' she laughed her dirty laugh. 'At least get your stabilisers off.'

'I wouldn't use him for sex,' I said laughingly. 'And he does genuinely like me, I'm not that mean. Plus, he's too young.'

'Robert was too old, it didn't stop you,' she pointed out.

'That's completely different,' I argued. 'I fell in love with Robert.'

'Love, lust - same thing.'

'No, it isn't,' I said. 'OK, I'll admit it, Jamie is fanciable - and fun. But not settling down material. I can't casual date with Gracie, she's screwed up enough as it is. I need a grown-up, who's fun and spontaneous too. And as that probably doesn't exist, single I will stay.'

'Woman, you depress me sometimes,' she grumbled.

'I depress myself,' I giggled. 'I'm going. I need to buy some stuff I don't need and cry in the bath thinking about my lonely existence.'

'Knock yourself out.'

I'd just started scrolling through Amazon again, when my phone rang. This time it was David.

'Hello,' I said in surprise. 'How are you?'

'Really good, thanks,' he sounded cheerful. 'Did you have a nice holiday?'

'Yes, lovely,' I said politely. 'Thank you for asking.'

'Good,' he hesitated. 'I was wondering if you're busy tomorrow night? Maybe we could meet up for a drink?'

'Ah, I actually am,' I said. 'I'm doing something with Gracie early evening, but I wouldn't be able to get a sitter for later anyway.'

'Never mind,' he said. 'What about the weekend?'

'I've got Gracie this weekend,' I bit my lip waiting for him to suggest the weekend after.

'OK,' he paused. 'I'm Harry-free. Would you believe, my mate's trying to rope me into a singles night on Friday.'

'Really?' I set my laptop aside, 'Maggie's just been on the phone asking me to go to one at The Engine.'

'Christ, that would have been funny, if we'd both turned up,' he chuckled.

'Yeah,' I agreed.

'Not really my thing,' he said. 'I prefer the traditional method.'

'Yeah, me too,' I said.

'OK, well, I won't keep you, Frankie,' he said. 'Give me a ring sometime, if you fancy doing something. I'd love to see you again.'

'Sure.'

'OK, see you soon.'

'Bye, David.'

I ended the call and stared at my screen for a second. It seemed strange that he'd called after the conversation I had with Maggie... was fate trying to tell me something? The truth was, David had hardly crossed my mind since we had gone out for dinner, and I was still undecided about how I felt for him. He would be an ideal dating candidate, safe and reliable. I stared into space trying to picture his face, and before I realised it, I was thinking about Jamie. Giving myself a little shake, I stood up and decided to get ready for bed. Out of recent habit, I checked I was locked in, even though I had checked the doors earlier, and headed upstairs, pushing any thoughts of men out of my head.

Jamie had arranged to meet Gracie and I outside the leisure centre entrance the following evening. I was a little early and managed to park nearby to the doors in the child-parking area, so I decided to stay in my car until they turned up.

After all the beautiful summer weather we had been lucky enough to have, it had turned cool and cloudy, almost autumnal. *Typical*, I thought, with weeks left of the school holidays. Pink blossom from the trees lining one side of the carpark drifted across the ground like confetti, some of it had settled on the windscreens of cars that must have been parked for a while.

Gracie, already dressed in her red and white polka dot swimming costume with her leggings and T-shirt over it, was very excited and talking ten to the dozen. I turned the radio down but only half-listened, I was thinking about Paul. We had had lunch together earlier and he was still very morose about things at home. Apparently, Chelsea was still being distant and cool, and he was now paranoid she had a thing for Jamie, which I quickly quashed, pointing out it had been her idea that we came around for dinner, and that she had been avidly asking me questions, and had looked disappointed when I told her nothing was going on between us. I liked Paul a lot, and I was worried about him. On a happier note, however, we had discussed Joe and Sarah; he had *at last* asked her out. The pair of them had been disappearing together at lunchtime and re-appearing looking pleased with themselves.

'Nice to know *someone's* getting some,' he had grumbled.

I spotted Jamie driving into the carpark and I got out to get our bags from the boot as Gracie unbuckled herself and scrambled out, looking around on her tiptoes trying to see them. I took her hand and walked over to the doors, I soon saw them making their way over. Jamie was dressed in jogging bottoms and a Nike T-shirt and holding Jessie's hand, who was clutching a pink swimming bag and had her head turned away, looking down.

'Hello pretty ladies,' he greeted us.

'Hi, hello Jessie,' I said - she stood a bit closer to Jamie and mumbled 'hello,' - Gracie looked at me with a puzzled expression.

'She's had a rough day,' Jamie said to me in a low voice.

'Hold my hand,' Gracie said bossily, and grabbed Jessie's hand. 'Can you swim? I'm a very good swimmer... can you swim Jamie?'

'Indeed, I can,' he chuckled. 'Come on then.'

Jamie disappeared to get changed, I offered to take Jessie into the changing rooms with us, but he declined. I slowly got ready, feeling slightly shy after Jamie's comment about seeing me in my bikini - even though he had been messing around. I had deliberately brought my less revealing tankini though.

As we left the changing rooms, I spied Jamie sitting on the edge of the shallow end, both him Jessie had their feet in the water, she was clutching his arm very tightly. As we approached he seemed to stare at me for a moment, then grinned broadly.

'Took your time,' he said. 'We just have to sit here for a bit, don't we Jess? We'll join you in a minute... Gracie sweetheart, come here a sec.'

Gracie knelt down next to him.

'It's a special night here tonight, for children that are a little shy,' he said. 'You can still have lots of fun, but try not to splash anyone too much - except Mummy,' he glanced at me, 'can you do that for me?'

'Yes,' she replied, unconcerned.

'Good girl.'

I led her away to where the pool was empty, and holding hands, we jumped in together. Gracie loved the water and had had swimming lessons from the age of two, swimming was one of the activities Robert and I had enjoyed as a family. I glanced around the pool, a little boy was doggy paddling around a middle-aged man nearby, and a man and woman were treading water watching an older boy holding his nose and going under water, then resurfacing and laughing and shouting. Most of the children were at the shallow end, and two women with their daughters were sitting in the baby pool.

'Mummy,' Gracie yelled. 'Watch me!' She began to swim away, doing a near-perfect breaststroke, then disappeared under the water, swimming back towards me. She grabbed me around the middle and I went under water and we both broke the surface, Gracie giggling.

I looked behind me to see where Jamie was, he was standing chest deep in the water, Jessie was floating on her back, smiling dreamily up at the domed ceiling. Jamie looked up at me and waved.

'Can we play with Jess now?' Gracie draped her arms around my neck, water clinging to her dark lashes in shiny droplets.

'We'll go and see,' I said.

We swam over and stopped a few feet away.

'Sorry, she doesn't like the deep end,' Jamie said apologetically, he gave me a small smile and looked back down at Jessie.

'That's OK,' Gracie said, I looked at her in surprise, I was expecting her to pout and complain. 'Can we throw a ball then?'

'Sure,' Jamie said.

I swam to the side to clamber out and went to fetch a blow-up ball from under the lifeguard's platform. When I returned, the three of them had moved further into the shallow end so the girls' feet could reach the bottom. I threw the ball to them and sat on the side to watch them for a bit - Jamie soon had them shrieking with laughter with his antics.

As I looked on, I couldn't help but notice that he had a surprisingly nice body. Not in a muscle-bound super-fit way, but his shoulders looked broader with nothing on, and his stomach was flat and slightly toned - not quite a six-pack but kind of *just right.*

Realising I was studying him a bit too much, I diverted my attention to the girls. Gracie was becoming a bit too boisterous, but Jessie didn't seem to mind - she was slowly becoming less reserved. I honestly didn't know that much about autism, but there was something about her that pulled at my heartstrings a little and I had vague tugs of affection towards Jamie at how sweet he was with her.

'Mummy,' Gracie yelled, 'come and play with us.'

I waded in and stood a little behind Jamie, suddenly noticing two small tattoos above his shorts.

'You've got a tattoo?' I tilted my head as he pulled his shorts up a fraction.

'No,' he turned to face me.

'Yes you have,' I tried to walk around him but he backed away.

'No, you're seeing things,' he splashed water at me and backed into the side of the pool.

'Come on,' I laughed, feeling perplexed. 'Why are you hiding it?'

'Hiding what?' he feigned a puzzled face.

I grabbed his hands and pulled him away from the side, he resisted, laughing along with me but also looking embarrassed, then came towards me, stopping just short of us touching - as I looked up into his bright blue eyes, the laughter died on my lips as he stared at me, almost looking pained.

'Pussy cat!' Jessie yelled from behind me.

With effort, I snapped out of my daze and turned around.

'Sorry, Jessie?'

She giggled and stuffed her fists under her chin.

'A drunken bet,' Jamie said. 'It's two cat paws, the girliest tattoo in the world.'

He turned around and yanked down his shorts an inch, there was indeed two cat paws right above his buttocks. He quickly pulled them back up and gave me a wry smile.

'I got off lightly, my other friend had a fairy on his arse.'

CHAPTER TWELVE

Over the next few days, I was very aware that my feelings towards Jamie were becoming muddled. Such was my strict determination to avoid anything that even hinted at romance... lust... whatever you want to call it, whenever my mind began to wander into unsafe territory, I brutally stamped on it.

The day after we went swimming, Jamie came shooting over to me at work, telling me his car had been "keyed", which he hadn't discovered until he got home.

'All the way from front to back on the driver's side,' he said, looking infuriated.

'Probably bloody kids,' I shook my head.

'Yeah,' he agreed. 'By the way - if it's OK, my mate, Baz, can come to yours Friday after work about the alarm.'

Baz, a tall bearded guy, turned out to be probably the most excruciatingly boring man I had ever met. He turned up with his catalogue under his arm, and even though I emphatically told him that I wanted the most basic and simplest alarm he had to offer, he insisted on going through every alarm he had ever fitted, explaining how I would benefit from each one in minute detail - only pausing for breath as he devoured half a packet of chocolate digestives, and slurped the two cups of tea I ended up making him.

While I was making the second cup, I texted Jamie, asking him where his off switch was, then worried after I sent it, thinking it sounded ungrateful. But within a minute he had replied with three laughing faces and about twelve x's.

In the end, I think he conceded defeat as I wouldn't budge from my decision to have his standard alarm, and with a slight air of that I didn't know what I was missing out on, he arranged to come and fit it on the second week I had off work.

I was just waiting for Robert to bring Gracie back, when Jamie rang, his voice full of laughter.

'Sorry, I should have warned you,' he said. 'He goes on a bit.'

'A bit?' I giggled. 'I feel qualified enough in the world of alarm systems to go into business myself.'

Jamie laughed.

'Look,' I said, 'thank you so much, Jamie. He told me I'm getting mates rates, as you're a friend. I really appreciate it.'

'No need to thank me.'

I hesitated - 'Would you let me cook you dinner tomorrow night, as a thank you?'

I wasn't sure what I wanted his response to be in all honesty, but I felt it was the least I could do. And I felt relatively safe as Gracie would be about - not that I didn't trust him, *or myself,* a little voice said.

'Oh,' he sounded surprised. 'I'd really like that. Yes, thank you very much.'

'Good,' I said, then as I heard a knock at the door, 'hold on a minute, Gracie's home.'

I answered the door, hoping Robert wouldn't hang about when he saw I was on the phone. Gracie barged in and hugged my legs.

'Look, I won't keep you,' Jamie said. 'Shall I come over about seven?'

'Perfect,' I told him, very aware that Robert was watching me.

'Who you talking to?' Gracie demanded.

'Jamie,' I murmured - I couldn't really lie as Jamie had probably heard her.

'OK, see you tomorrow.'

'OK, bye.'

'The famous Jamie, eh?' Robert raised his eyebrows as I ended the call.

'Yes,' I said defiantly - it hadn't occurred to me that Gracie would have talked about him, I wasn't terribly surprised though.

'So,' he gave me a twisted smile, 'Gracie tells me she's going to be an auntie.'

'Yes,' I watched his expression, he looked like he was going to say something else, then dropped his cold gaze.

'Give Daddy a kiss,' he squatted down.

'Bye Daddy,' Gracie wrapped her arms around his neck, then went to take up her position at the window to watch him drive away.

'I'll be picking her up on Thursday and having her through to Monday,' he informed me. 'I'm very busy so you can tell Rachel I won't be having her for a whole week.'

'Sure,' I shrugged.

'I will be taking her to the seaside Friday until Sunday, so pack her swimming things.'

'OK,' I had the impression he was waiting for me to argue - I just smiled blandly.

'Right,' he started towards the door. 'I'll get her from Rachel's and swing by here to pick up her bag on Thursday then.'

'Yep.'

'Bye, then.'

'Prat,' I mumbled, as I closed the door, surprising myself.

Jamie knocked promptly at seven o'clock the following evening, dressed casually in beige shorts and a blue polo shirt that matched his eyes, reeking of expensive aftershave and clutching a bottle each of red and white wine. I hadn't bothered to get tarted up, I'd just showered and changed into a pair of jeans and a loose top that made me look flat-chested.

'Jamie!' Gracie pulled him inside, talking her head off.

'Don't worry,' I laughed over her chatter. 'She'll be in bed before we eat, I've been wearing her out today.'

Gracie took him outside and I took him a glass of wine before disappearing to check on the food - I was making chicken in a white wine sauce, a recipe that I could make with my eyes closed, and warm bread rolls.

The weather was still a little cool, and it wasn't long before they came back indoors. Seeing that I had set the table, Jamie offered to read Gracie a story in the living room before I took her to bed.

'Oh, yes,' I said gratefully. 'Thank you.'

Gracie belted upstairs to fetch a book and was soon snuggled next to Jamie on the sofa, giggling as he read parts of the story in silly voices. I bustled about in the kitchen, taking repeated sips of wine, trying not to keep looking at the pair of them - also trying not to think how unbelievably adorable he was with her.

'Mummy,' Gracie bellowed a few minutes later, 'can Jamie take me to bed?'

I looked at him.

'I don't mind,' he shrugged. 'You get on with my food,' he added cheekily.

Gracie ran to me and kissed me and pulled Jamie up. 'Can I have another story in bed?' she asked as they disappeared into the hall.

Fifteen minutes later he came back down, chuckling to himself.

'She's great, isn't she?' he leant against the archway watching me.

'She's a madam,' I said, as I cut up the rolls.

'Do you need a hand?' he asked.

'No thanks,' I shook my head. 'Sit yourself down though, it won't be long.'

He both ate and talked a great deal, making me laugh like I hadn't for a long time. We got onto the subject of Louise and Sophie.

'I get them muddled up, to be honest,' he poured more wine. 'Looks like I'll be needing a taxi... I don't know where one ends and the other begins.'

'They're young and silly, that's all,' I didn't want to bitch about them.

'The other morning,' he said, 'I was getting out my car and saw Sophie sitting in hers, in the weirdest position, I thought she was having some sort of fit,' he started buttering his third roll, 'then I realised the silly cow was trying to take a selfie, making sure her Starbucks cup was casually just in the shot, I knocked on her window and shit the life out of her.'

I giggled, 'The pair of them are always taking selfies in the ladies,' I told him.

'Sarah can't stand them,' he confided. 'They're a bit bitchy to her.'

'Probably jealous,' I frowned, thinking about what they said about me. 'Sarah is so much prettier than them... don't you fancy them a *little* bit though?'

'God, no,' he looked affronted. 'They're so false. If you took away the make-up, the hair extensions, the fake tan, and whatever else it is they do to themselves, you probably wouldn't recognise them.'

'All girls tart up,' I said, not sure why I was defending them.

'You don't,' he took a mouthful of chicken.

'Well, I'm hardly a girl,' I pulled a face. 'And I tart up a bit.'

'You're naturally beautiful though,' he said bluntly, then dropped his eyes.

'Hmm,' I took a slug of wine. 'Well, it's just their generation.'

'Maybe,' he put his knife and fork down. 'God, that was bloody nice, I want to marry you,' he grinned. 'But... they're still awful. And I don't like what they say about Joe. He's a decent bloke.'

I knew he meant about Joe's weight - they had more than likely upped the spite since him and Sarah had got together.

'Yeah, he is,' I agreed. 'Actually, I remember you giving them a look when one of them said something when we went out for my birthday.'

'Did I?' Jamie frowned. 'I don't remember - but probably. It's not nice, I've been picked on and it feels shit.'

'Really?' I looked at him.

'Yeah, at school,' he nodded. 'I was a bit of a chubber until I hit sixteen or so.'

'You?' I felt taken back. 'I'd never have guessed.'

'Well,' he grinned, 'I *am* a bit of a fine specimen of a hunk now,' - I tutted - 'but yeah. I decided I wanted to lose my virginity at some point, so I sorted myself out.'

I found this information fascinating for some reason. I couldn't imagine Jamie being anything but, well, Jamie.

'What was you like at school?' he asked, looking curious.

'Well, it *was* a very long time ago,' I wrinkled my nose. 'Average, I suppose. Sporty... I was a bit shy.'

'I bet you was one of them pretty girls that I never had the guts to talk to,' he sighed.

'Well, you don't have trouble talking to girls now,' I said sardonically.

'Ah, I'm just all talk,' he laughed, then looked serious. 'I'm sorry if I used to annoy you,' he frowned for a moment. 'I don't blame you for thinking I was a complete knob.'

I laughed, 'I didn't think that, I just thought you were taking the piss.'

'Why?' he looked astonished. 'I fancied you... I still fancy you... I'm just a bit of an idiot.'

'Yeah,' I smiled serenely, and he threw his napkin at me.

'Come on,' he stretched his arms above his head. 'Make me a coffee and I'll wash-up.'

'Too right you're washing-up,' I stood up. 'I'll just check on Gracie.'

Gracie was fast asleep, curled up on her side cuddling Yellow Bunny. I gently moved her hair off of her face and went back downstairs to the kitchen where Jamie was busy scraping our plates into my recycling caddy.

'Do you want dessert?' I asked, switching on the kettle. 'I made apple crumble.'

'When we're married, can you make me that every day?' Jamie grinned.

'Pack it in. Ice-cream or whipped cream?'

'Both.'

'How on earth did you lose weight?' I asked in wonder, he definitely liked his food.

'I think my superb wit burns it all off,' he started rinsing the plates off.

'Uh huh,' I was just about to tell him he was full of himself, when the security light came on outside, making me jump. It was just growing dim outside, and feeling safe enough with Jamie there, I went outside to check.

'Peeping tom?' Jamie followed me, a tea towel still over his shoulder.

'Probably a cat,' I went to check my gate was bolted top and bottom; it was.

'Come on,' he put his hand around my upper arm. 'Don't get jumpy again, nothing's out here,' he pulled me back towards the door.

'I'm fine,' I said, letting him lead me back indoors.

'You had any more calls?' Jamie watched me as I made the coffees.

'Actually, no,' I said as off-handed as I could. 'Could you grab the ice-cream from the bottom of the freezer please?' I put our drinks on the table and went and pulled down my blind.

'Well, that's good then,' he put the tub of ice-cream on the side. 'Still, you'll feel better when your alarms installed.'

'Yeah,' I started dishing up two bowls of crumble, aware he was studying me. 'It's probably a waste of money though - I was being over-dramatic.'

'Of course it isn't,' he argued. 'Peace of mind and all that.'

'Yeah.'

'Frankie?'

'Mmm?'

'Can I have more ice-cream than that please?'

I giggled, putting in an extra scoop.

After coffee and dessert, I went to check on Gracie again, then pouring us a glass of brandy each, we went to sit in the living room. I had drunk way too much wine with dinner and was feeling a little light-headed - I decided this was definitely my last drink.

I curled my legs under me on one end of the sofa and Jamie sat at the other end, his feet up on my coffee table, looking relaxed and at home.

'So,' he said. 'Tell me more about your ex.'

'Oh, it's very boring,' I stared into my drink. 'I was actually supposed to marry someone else,' I looked over at his to see his reaction, but he just raised an eyebrow questioningly.

'I'm intrigued.'

Probably fuelled by drink, I ended up telling him briefly about David, then how my marriage went downhill after Gracie - then on a roll, I told him about Lennie. He listened intently, not interrupting once.

'So, that's her, in that photo?' he indicated to Will and Lennie's wedding photo on the sideboard. 'Not a patch on you.'

'She's OK,' I looked at my glass, surprised to see it was empty. 'She's young and naïve, right up Robert's street. She's actually a nice girl - a bit quirky, very shy. Will worships her,'

I felt tears fill my eyes unexpectedly and feeling embarrassed, I went to fetch the brandy as an excuse. I wiped my eyes hurriedly and took a deep breath, returning with the brandy.

'Let me,' Jamie said, taking the bottle from me.

I sat back down and he shifted over to re-fill my glass.

'Thank you,' I smiled at him and held out my glass. 'Not too much.'

He poured some in, and then settled back, not moving back over to the other end of the sofa.

'I've talked too much,' I muttered. 'You must be bored.'

'Nope.'

'Mmm,' I set my glass down. 'Go on, tell me about yourself.'

'Not much to tell,' he drank some brandy and set his glass down too.

'Oh, come on,' I glanced sideways at him. 'Any deep, dark secrets or drama? Where did you work before you come to ours? Any tragic love stories?'

'No,' he spread his hands. 'I had a very boring sales rep job, never had a serious girlfriend, the worst thing that happened to me was my dad dying and the love of my life is Jess. I am very basic.'

'I find that hard to believe,' I turned to look at him. 'Everyone has a story.'

'Not me,' he looked at me very solemnly. 'Frankie?'

'Yes?'

'I'm sorry.'

'What for?' I asked puzzled - then before I knew it, he bent his head and very gently kissed me - my brain started to tell me to push him away, but I suddenly felt a delirious rush of lust - something that had lain dormant for a very long time.

'For that,' he abruptly stopped and looked at me, almost with fear in his eyes.

'Oh,' I stared back, our faces inches apart. 'That's... fine,' I blinked stupidly.

'You smell nice,' he murmured, then putting his hands in my hair, he kissed me again, this time a little more urgently.

You're a little drunk, Frankie I thought, dimly aware that my hands had strayed to his chest, then around to his back, pulling him closer. *Probably best that you put the brakes on now, don't you think?* Instead, I kissed him back hard, thinking how soft his beard was when I thought it would have been scratchy - then I wanted to giggle.

'Oh, fuck,' he half-heartedly pulled away. 'Sorry, I couldn't help it... shall I go? I know you didn't want any of this.'

'No,' I shook my head slowly, and without letting myself think about anything but how good he was making me feel, I started kissing him again, my hands straying down his back and under his shirt. He was very cautiously - or so it seemed to me - edging his hands downwards to my waist, like a shy teenager and I fought the urge to giggle again.

'Come on,' I murmured. 'This is daft, let's go upstairs.'

'What?' he drew back, looking shocked. 'Are you sure?'

'I'm sure,' I nodded, deciding that putting the brakes on now was not really an option. I scrambled up and pulled him with me and kissed him again. I was very aware that he had an erection and felt a heady rush of irresponsibility. I led him upstairs, whispering that we had to be quiet because of Gracie.

'Frankie,' he said softly, pushing the door shut with his back, 'you've had a bit to drink, I don't want this to spoil anything - you know how much I like you... oh -' he stared mutely at me as I began to undress.

'It won't,' I assured him, starting to attempt to unbutton his shorts.

'You are so beautiful,' he gazed at me happily, then pulled off his shirt as I walked backwards to my bed.

I watched him wriggle out of his shorts, revealing black Batman boxer shorts - I suppressed a smile, trying to look wanton - or at least serious, and finally he came and lay on his side next to me, laying a warm hand on my stomach and gazing at me, his chest rising and falling.

'I'm really going to show you a good time,' he gave me a small smile and I felt butterflies taking flight and shivered.

It must have been nearly midnight.

'So… that just happened,' Jamie propped his head up on his hand.

'Yeah.'

I laid on my back, trying to catch my breath. I had more or less sobered up and was feeling slightly… *ashamed?* I wasn't sure how I felt, apart from a little shocked at myself. I'll give credit where credit is due, Jamie was very, *very* good in bed, and although I had never really thought about whether I was good, bad or average - after a very long dry spell, I had thrown myself into it like a wild animal. Maggie would be proud, I thought randomly, getting my stabilisers off in grand style.

'You OK?' Jamie stroked the side of my face.

'Yeah,' I looked at him, he suddenly seemed so young and vulnerable.

'You're regretting it, aren't you?'

'No,' I protested, not altogether truthfully. 'I'm just not sure it was the best idea in the world.'

'Maybe not,' he sighed, and his eyes wandered around the room for a moment. 'But it was really good,' he grinned. 'Can we do it again?'

'Oh, Jamie,' I found his hand and squeezed it. 'You're very sweet, but you do realise I'm just a crush, don't you?'

'No, you're not,' he looked solemnly at me. 'I like you so much, Frankie. I know you think I'm just young and daft, but I genuinely have feelings for you. And please don't say you don't have any feelings for me, because I know you do. You're just stubborn.'

'Of course I do,' I turned on my side, and he laid his head back down so he was facing me. 'I just think I'm too old for you and I'm not sure what I can offer you with Gracie and everything.'

'I'm not asking for anything,' he said. 'I know you wouldn't have slept with me if you hadn't have had a lot to drink, but I also think we would be really good together. And you aren't too old for me, I wouldn't care if you were twenty years older than me.'

'Now I feel bad,' I touched his face. 'It wasn't just the drink. I wouldn't have slept with you if I didn't like you, Jamie. I'm just not sure about a relationship.'

'OK,' he wrapped his arms around me and pulled me closer. 'We can be whatever you want, I'm not pushing it - just please tell me we can still be friends.'

'Yes! Bloody hell,' I buried my face into his neck. 'I'm not a complete bitch.'

'You are very sexy though,' he started to stroke my back. 'And very beautiful,' he tugged the back of my hair and began to kiss my neck. 'And I am definitely not finished with you yet.'

I half-heartedly thought I should resist, but as his kisses turned into gentle bites, and his hands began to wander lower, I began to feel that wonderful abandonment again, and succumbed to his love-making.

CHAPTER THIRTEEN

I woke up with a jump, Jamie was gently rubbing my upper arm.

'Frankie,' he whispered. 'It's nearly six, I better go before Gracie wakes up.'

'Oh Christ,' I sat up. 'You won't still be over the limit, will you?'

'No, I'm fine,' he threw off the duvet and sat on the edge of the bed, rubbing his face.

'I'll make you a quick cuppa,' I climbed out of bed, my legs feeling weak, like I had run miles.

Five minutes later he quietly crept downstairs, his trainers in one hand as I finished making his tea.

'Thank you,' he sat at the kitchen table, yawning - I leant against the work top looking at him, despite feeling half asleep, I had a strange sadness inside me.

'Jamie,' I began, not sure where I was going. 'Last night - I'm not sure if it should happen again… I don't want to mess you about.'

He stared at me, his expression unreadable.

'OK,' he said slowly. 'I get that. But - wow, don't pretend it wasn't good. It was very good.'

'Yes,' I said hastily. 'It was. Just please think about what you actually want… it might not be what you think it is.'

He stood up and put his hands either side of the work top trapping me. 'I meant what I said, we can be whatever you want us to be, just please, *please*, don't snub me. I told you last night, I more than like you.'

'I won't,' I frowned, I wasn't totally sure what he meant by *more than liking me,* but with my past experience with men… well, Robert… I was pretty sure he was just driven by lust - not saying he didn't genuinely like me, but I was certain that sex had a lot to do with it.

'Good,' he kissed me gently and smiled, his bright blue eyes looking soulful. 'Can I see you later?'

'Sure,' I nodded. 'Ring me later.'

'Cool,' he kissed me again and went and sat back down and started putting on his trainers.

We finished our teas, chatting about nothing in particular, I glanced at the time, it was nearly seven o'clock.

'I really have to go,' he said, looking reluctant.

'Sorry,' I murmured. 'It's just Gracie -'

'I know,' he leant over and stroked my cheek. 'I get it.'

'Have you got Jessie today?' I asked as he stood up.

'Nope, I'm a free man.'

I followed him to the door.

'I'll have a snooze and a shower,' he turned around at the front door and put his arms around me. 'I will call you later, OK?'

'OK,' I leant against him briefly.

Just as I was closing the door, he swore loudly, 'Frankie... for *fuck* sake... look -'

I opened the door again and looked at him confusedly.

'Look,' he said again, his face a picture of fury.

I gasped in shock - all of my potted plants that sat under my living room window had been knocked over and smashed, one of them was upside-down on Jamie's car bonnet, the mud spread out, fragments of the terracotta peppered it, the plant roots sticking up like tentacles.

'Oh,' I whispered, the feeling of dread that had been hovering over me vaguely in the last few weeks flooding back in full force.

'OK, this isn't funny anymore,' Jamie walked over to me and put his hands on my shoulders. 'Look at me,' he commanded, my eyes moved slowly from his car to his face. 'We are calling the police.'

'No,' I protested. 'It was probably kids -'

'Frankie,' he implored, his eyes full of concern. 'Please... you've had someone in your back garden, you've had all those calls... no, someone's messing with you.'

'No,' I tried to look away, but he grabbed my chin. 'Why would anyone do all those things? It's just a coincidence.'

'I don't care,' he said gently. 'You're going to call the police, whether you like it or not.'

'I feel silly,' I argued feebly.

Ignoring me, he let go of me and took out his phone. Instead of making a call though, he took some photographs of the damage.

'OK,' he looked at me, his expression grim. 'Call the police, please.'

'I will,' I sighed. 'Just let me get dressed.'

He followed me back inside.

'I'm going to go home and get changed,' he said. 'I'll leave my phone here with the photos - I'll be back in twenty minutes or so... no don't argue,' he smiled, shaking his head. 'For once, do as you're told.'

'OK.'

I had a shower, as I started getting dressed, Gracie came wandering out of her bedroom rubbing her eyes.

'Mummy,' she jumped on my bed and laid down. 'I'm hungry.'

'OK sweetie,' I struggled into my jeans, my legs still damp. 'One minute... listen, go downstairs and put the television on, mummy will be down soon.'

I sat on the edge of my bed, and feeling like a fool, dialled the non-emergency police number. Expecting that I'd speak to some call centre, I was surprised to be put straight through to the local police station. I explained the best I could what had happened and the police woman on the other end told me that somebody would be over some time that morning.

Jamie returned not long after, looking and smelling fresh, his hair still damp from his shower.

'Hi,' I let him in and he briefly put his arms around me and kissed my forehead.

'Is Gracie up?' he asked and I nodded.

'Is there any damage to your car?' I asked - he'd picked off all the bits of broken terracotta pot off from his bonnet earlier and only given it a quick brush off before leaving.

'A tiny scratch,' he followed me into the living room. 'Nothing terrible. Christ, my poor car, I only had it patched up on Friday after it was keyed.'

I had totally forgotten about that - I stared at him, my mind racing.

'What?' he frowned.

'Nothing,' I said hastily - but wondering... *could* this really be Robert? Was this his way of getting his own back and punishing me?

'Jamie,' Gracie appeared from the kitchen, still in her pyjamas. 'Why are you here? Is Jessie with you?'

'Oh, no,' Jamie widened his eyes at me. 'I, um, forgot my phone,' he spotted it on the arm of the sofa and picked it up. 'Silly me. How are you sweetheart?'

'Look how wobbly my tooth is now,' she opened her mouth and pushed it with her tongue. 'Mummy, can I play Minecraft on your laptop and show Jamie?'

'Go and get dressed first, sweetie,' I said. 'I'm going to make Jamie a coffee.'

She ran off upstairs and Jamie and I went into the kitchen.

'So, you rang the police, then?' he asked in a low voice.

'Yep,' I filled the kettle and turned to look at him. 'Someone's coming this morning... I feel so idiotic though -'

'Stop it,' he interrupted, grabbing both of my hands in his and then pulling me towards him. 'If you hadn't of rang them, I would have,' he rested his cheek on the side of my head and I melted towards him a little, thinking how reassuring it felt and how nice it was that he didn't tower over me like Robert had.

'Sorry,' I mumbled, closing my eyes.

Gracie started thundering down the stairs and Jamie let me go, sitting himself at the table and smiling wistfully at me.

Gracie sat next to him, now dressed in khaki jeans and her Hello Kitty T-shirt.

'Mummy, can you put your password in?' she opened my laptop. 'Minecraft is my favourite game,' she told Jamie. 'Last week I built a big bridge, it took me ages.'

'Great,' Jamie shifted his chair closer to her, still smiling at me.

A little after eleven, there was a loud knock at the door - by that time, Jamie had got very engrossed in Minecraft and seemed to be having more fun than Gracie. I opened the door, my feeling of foolishness returning, a young uniformed guy introduced himself as PC Blunt and I showed him in, offering him a tea or coffee, which he declined politely.

'You reported some damage to your property?'

'Yes,' I said a little breathlessly, indicating for him to sit down.

Jamie hovered between the archway with Gracie, who looked rather intimidated.

'Sweetie,' I looked at her. 'Go and play your game for a minute,' she drifted back into the kitchen.

I explained what had happened that morning and Jamie showed him the photos on his phone.

'And this happened sometime between -?' PC Blunt looked enquiringly from me to Jamie.

'Well, we went to bed around ten-thirty,' I could feel myself blush, which was ridiculous - he didn't know that we weren't a couple. 'And we found the mess about seven this morning.'

'OK,' he nodded. 'I can ask your neighbours if they heard or saw anything. I'll give you a crime number, but in all honesty, love, pointless vandalism like this rarely results in the culprit being found.'

'Frankie?' Jamie came and sat next to me. 'Tell him the rest.'

'Oh?' PC Blunt paused half-way through returning his notebook and pen.

'It's nothing,' I glared at Jamie, who stared stubbornly back, I let out a shaky breath. 'I had a prowler a few nights a go… maybe more than once, I'm not sure.'

I briefly explained what had happened but didn't mention the calls - I didn't want to sound like an hysterical woman.

'Right,' he said eventually. 'Anymore disturbances, you ring straight away, keep your property secured as you have been. Anything else, love?'

'No,' I shook my head.

After I saw him out, Gracie crept back in.

'Why was that policeman here, Mummy?'

'Somebody was naughty and kicked over my plants on the drive, that's all,' I sat down and held out my arms and she came and sat on my lap, her large eyes concerned.

'Why?'

'I don't know, sweetie,' I looked at Jamie and he shrugged.

'OK ladies,' he suddenly said brightly. 'I think I'm going to take you out for dinner, what do you reckon?'

'Yes,' Gracie yelled, and went to sit on his lap instead. 'Can we go to Pizza Hut?'

Jamie laughed, 'I expect that will be OK… Frankie?'

'Sure,' I said. 'Gracie, go and wash your hands and brush your hair.'

'Why didn't you mention the calls?' Jamie asked as soon as she was out of earshot.

'Because they've got nothing to do with it,' I said firmly, getting up and going into the kitchen to rinse our mugs.

'Why are you so stubborn?' Jamie followed me, putting his arms around my middle from behind.

'I'm not,' I craned my neck to look at him. 'Seriously, I just didn't think it was worth mentioning.'

'Mm,' he let me go and leant against the worktop.

'Can we drop it?' I put the mugs on the draining board and turned around.

'OK,' he continued to look at me. 'God, you are beautiful.'

'Jamie -' I began.

'I'm allowed to say things like that now,' he smiled, then suddenly looked serious. 'Don't over-think this please.'

'I'm not,' I dropped my eyes and tried to gather my thoughts.

'Do you want us to talk later?'

I nodded, and when I looked back up he was still looking solemn.

'I'm not blowing you out,' I frowned, he looked a little sad and I didn't like it.

'Well… good,' he gave me half a smile and walked back into the living room. 'Gracie? Hurry up or all the pizza will be gone,' he yelled up the stairs.

I hesitated for a moment, full of confusion and doubts, then followed him out to the hall.

Dinner was fun. I decided that Jamie could probably make a funeral seem like fun, he just had that way about him. We sat opposite each other, Gracie sitting very close to him.

I felt strange, and I couldn't really make sense of what my head was doing - I felt happy, because Jamie was making me happy - he was funny, easy-going and extremely good company. I also felt a little sad and lost, which was confusing, mingled with my contented little spark of happiness he had ignited. I kept thinking about the night before and random thoughts kept creeping in, like, *I've seen you naked, and from a lot of different angles* and could feel myself growing hot and bothered… I really wanted a repeat performance but then I felt like I was hitting a wall… it couldn't go anywhere, and it was unfair to lead him on.

Could we go back to being just friends? *Yeah, as long as you remain sober and don't find yourself alone with him…* I suddenly appreciated how much easier it must be to be a man. I felt sure that a night of passion didn't evoke these stupid thoughts.

'Frankie?'

I realised I was staring at him.

'You OK?'

'Yes,' I forced a smile. 'Off with the fairies, sorry.'

Our food arrived, and I found I was hungrier than I thought - Jamie demolished his pizza and had two trips to the salad bar.

'I think last night gave me an appetite,' he grinned over at me.

'You're a human dustbin,' I said in amazement.

'My tooth!' Gracie suddenly cried. 'It's come out,' she held it in the palm of her hand, looking over-joyed.

'I don't think the tooth fairy works on a Sunday,' Jamie teased.

'I'll go and get a clean napkin,' I got up and went over to the counter.

'Frankie?'

David was sitting at the booth on the other side of the counter with Harry and another boy.

'Hello,' I said in surprise.

'We need to move to a bigger town,' he grinned. 'Or are you stalking me?'

I laughed uncomfortably.

'How are you?' he asked.

'Yeah, good,' I glanced at Harry, he was looking down at the table. 'I'm just here with a friend and my daughter -' I gestured behind me. 'How are you?'

'Great,' he nodded. 'Give me a ring soon, yeah?'

'Sure,' I nodded and grabbed a napkin. 'I better get back.'

'Of course,' he agreed. 'Catch you later.'

I went back to my table, looking back at David; he was chatting animatedly to the boys. I sat back down - Gracie was busy telling Jamie all about the tooth fairy.

'- but she's not like Santa, it doesn't matter if you're naughty. She still brings you money. Last time she brought me a pound.'

'Wow,' Jamie beamed at her. 'A whole pound?'

'Yes,' Gracie nodded happily

Jamie dropped us off home, saying he'd come back later to talk - I wasn't sure if I felt up to it. What I really wanted to do was have a nice long discussion with Maggie about the latest developments and try to sort out my confused brain.

I spent the afternoon catching up on chores and laundry, and after I had put Gracie to bed, I had a long hot bubble bath and tried to relax myself.

Jamie turned up at eight, looking pleased to see me, clutching a bottle of wine.

'I know it's a school night,' he followed me in, 'but one glass won't kill us.'

'No,' I agreed.

He sat down on the sofa while I went to fetch glasses.

'So,' he took a glass from me and patted the sofa. 'Break my heart then,' he smiled crookedly.

'Oh, for goodness sake,' I giggled and sat down, twisting to face him.

'Before you say anything,' he took my free hand and held it gently, 'I just want to say that I know what I feel for you isn't what you feel for me, and that's fine... well, maybe not fine, but I'm a big boy, I can accept that. And whatever you want to do, I just want to be friends... you know, either way. And last night was perfect, just perfect. *You're* perfect.'

'Jamie,' I murmured, slightly stunned. 'You are very sweet. I do like you - I like you a lot. I just don't know what I can give you. Gracie is my priority, and I can't get into anything that will muddle her... she's had such a hard time.'

'So have you,' he frowned. 'Just don't hold back because you think I will hurt you. I'm not *him*.'

'Oh God, I know,' I searched his face. 'I'm just not ready.'

'Right,' he paused. 'Do you still love him?'

'I'm not sure,' I looked at our hands, not wanting to see his reaction. 'I hate him sometimes... it's just really hard.'

'OK,' he said quietly. 'That sucks, but OK. But... can't we just, take it slowly, and see? No big announcements, no pressure, no labelling it... just see?'

'You mean friends with benefits?' I said, sharper than I intended to.

'What? No,' he looked angry. 'I can't believe you'd think that.'

'Sorry,' I bit my lip. 'No, I don't think that.'

'Christ, he really did a number on you,' he said sadly. 'Just trust me, OK?'

'OK,' I sat up straighter and looked at him squarely. 'I'm sorry, Jamie.'

'It's fine,' he smiled, looking more like his usual self. 'I get it.'

'Thank you,' I relaxed a little and put my glass down. 'Hug it out?'

He laughed and put his glass next to mine, then wrapped his arms around me.

CHAPTER FOURTEEN

During the following week at work, I really felt like all eyes were on us - of course, they weren't, but I almost felt a *guilt*, like I was in the throes of an illicit affair.

I was trying my hardest to go with the flow and not over-think or label what was between us, but my naturally logical mind *wanted* a name for it. I was also finding it near-impossible to concentrate on my work, knowing Jamie was a few feet away from me. We both seemed to find our gazes drawn to each other. My thoughts kept drifting towards sex, then I'd feel ashamed, like I was using him for that - I knew it went deeper than that, but as soon as I probed my feelings, I'd feel a shutter coming down.

At first, I thought it was my imagination that Paul was giving us thoughtful looks, by mid-week I was convinced that he knew something was going on. Feeling like a naughty school girl, on Wednesday morning I texted Jamie from under my desk, asking if we could go for lunch together, I suppressed a giggle as I peered around my monitor and he gave me a double thumbs-up with his usual mischievous grin.

We drove in my car to a very nondescript sandwich bar in town, and after getting our coffees and a roll each, we sat in a corner away from the window.

'Alone at last,' Jamie leant across the table and kissed me lightly, then sat back and stared at me happily.

'It's been weird at work, hasn't it?' I said.

'A little,' he agreed. 'I have a very nice view of your legs from where I am, under that desk of yours. It's cute when you kick your shoes off and wiggle your toes when you're concentrating.'

'Now that's made me self-conscious,' I took a bite of my roll and wiped my fingers on a napkin. 'Jamie… have you, er, said anything to Paul?'

'I may have done,' he said annoyingly.

'Jamie-'

'No, I haven't, as per your instructions,' he rolled his eyes.

'Don't make it sound bad,' I looked down at my roll, suddenly I didn't feel hungry.

'Sorry,' he grabbed my hand. 'I just want to shout it from the rooftops… Frankie look at me… we will play by your rules. *You want private?* We will be private. But please understand it's hard for me.'

I stared mutely at him.

'So,' he said in a more matter-of-fact voice, 'have you told anyone?'

'My friend, Maggie,' I confessed.

'Ah, OK,' he nodded. 'What did she say?'

'You don't want to know,' I chuckled.

Maggie, in fact, had wanted to know every single detail - from who said and did what, to length, girth and technique, all of which I deflected in between fits of laughter.

'Knowing what you women are like, I probably don't,' he agreed. 'You eating that?' he indicated at my roll, and I pushed the plate towards him.

As Robert was having Gracie from Thursday to Monday, we made plans to see each other. Jamie came over for dinner Thursday evening, and this time I made a bit more of an effort. I laid the table with candles and cooked a rather impressive roast dinner, and we ended up in bed before I had even begun to clear away the plates.

He had to look after Jessie on Friday night until around ten o'clock, I declined him coming over late, as I wanted an early night - he had decided to take me out Saturday night to 'wine and dine me' and 'treat me like a lady' and despite myself, I was curious to see this side of Jamie.

It was strange, arriving at work when he had only left my bed two hours earlier, to see him sitting there at his desk. I glanced up in his direction as I sat down, he was sitting with his chin propped in his palm, smiling dreamily at me. I smiled back and busied myself, aware of his every move and my thoughts still in the hours we had spent making love. I spent a lot of the day yawning and wistfully dreaming about my planned early night.

I followed him and Joe out of the office after work, watching him talking animatedly and laughing. As Joe went over to his car where Sarah was waiting, Jamie drifted over to me.

'I want to kiss you,' he murmured. 'I wish I was seeing you later.'

'Me too,' I confessed, 'but I need my beauty sleep, seriously.'

'Never,' his eyes raked my face. 'It's impossible for you to get any more beautiful.'

'Oh, Jamie,' I looked down, feeling stupidly embarrassed.

'Caught you!' Paul appeared on the other side of my car, grinning as we both started - even though we were standing two feet apart.

'What are you on about, you prat?' Jamie asked good-naturedly.

'Come off it,' Paul looked from Jamie to me, still grinning. 'As if it's not screamingly obvious, you pair of love-birds.'

'Shh,' I scanned the carpark, then realised I had just more or less admitted to it. I looked at Jamie and he shrugged, as if to say, 'oh well.'

'Paul, please don't gossip,' I implored.

'Of course not,' he was still looking pleased with himself. 'But it's pretty obvious to anyone with half a brain what's going on. Which means everyone except Louise and Sophie.'

'Right,' I muttered, and Jamie chuckled.

'About time too,' Paul smirked. 'Sarah owes myself, Joe and Bea a fiver each.'

'Oh, for goodness sake,' I said crossly.

'Well, that doesn't cheapen it at all, does it?' Jamie shook his head at me and frowned at Paul.

'Ah, sorry guys,' Paul spoilt the apology somewhat by still smirking.

'Well, you can piss off now,' Jamie said lightly. 'I want to say goodbye to Frankie.'

'Have a good weekend,' Paul put his hand up and walked off, looking like he was trying not to laugh.

'Don't look so worried,' Jamie took a step towards me and touched my arm briefly. 'Paul's not going to put an advert in the local paper, it's just them lot in the office.'

'Yeah, I know,' I agreed and tried to pull off a smile.

'Unless you're ashamed of me?' Jamie watched me closely.

'No!' I said in surprise. 'Don't be daft. They're probably saying I'm too old for you.'

'Rubbish,' he shook his head. 'It's only you that keeps thinking that. They're most likely wondering how an idiot like me managed it.'

'Now you're being daft,' I laughed softly. 'You're not a bad catch, I suppose,' I added playfully.

'Well… well caught, then.'

We stared at each other for a moment, Jamie was smiling but I thought he looked sad beneath it.

'I better go,' I open my door - I felt on the verge of asking him to come over later on, but stopped myself... *it's just casual, it's not a relationship, it's just a bit of fun,* I suddenly felt a knot in my stomach.

'OK,' Jamie watched me climb in. 'I need to pick Jessie up, I'm probably late. We're going to McDonald's then I promised her a match of Hungry Hippos.'

'No cheating,' I closed the door and opened the window. 'I'll ring you later, before I go to bed.'

'Good... talk later,' he blew me a kiss and walked away, looking back at me twice.

My kitchen was still in a mess after the night before, so after eating a quick cold chicken sandwich and pouring a glass of wine, I spent an hour cleaning and tidying, then another hour gossiping on the phone to Maggie before she went off onto her night-shift.

I found myself fighting sleep whilst watching EastEnders, so I decided to have a bath, do my nails, then ring Jamie before collapsing into bed. David rang while I was running my bath, with a slight guilty twinge, I ignored it.

While my nails were drying, I curled up on the sofa and rang Jamie.

'Hello, I was just thinking about you,' he said happily. 'Are you naked?'

'No,' I laughed. 'In my jammies.'

'I'm going to pretend you said, 'yes Jamie, I am naked' - you should *always* be naked,' he sighed.

'Behave,' I giggled. 'Did you beat Jessie at Hungry Hippos?'

'No,' he laughed, 'she's unbeatable... I'm bored, she's been asleep for an hour.'

'You should have an early night too,' I suggested. 'You must be knackered.'

'Nah, I don't need much sleep,' he said. 'I'm going to have a shower and then think about you naked.'

We chatted for another ten minutes before we said our goodnights, he reminded me to wear something dressy for our upcoming date, then refused to tell me where we were going.

Feeling slightly more wide-awake than I had earlier, I went to make a hot drink to take up. I checked my doors were locked and was just putting the chain on the front door, when car headlights lit up my hallway, I heard a scraping kind of *crunch* and then whoever it was, turned the engine off.

Cautiously, I pulled back my living room curtains a fraction, and was shocked and surprised to see Paul more or less falling out of his car. In bewilderment, I opened the front door - he had straightened up, but was swaying, clearly extremely drunk.

'Oh my God,' I exclaimed, I hurried over bare-foot, wincing as I stepped on a stone. 'Did you drive in that state? What the hell-'

'Alright, Frankie?' he seemed to be having trouble focusing his eyes. He looked very dishevelled, his shirt untucked and rumpled and he absolutely reeked of whisky.

'You idiot,' I hissed, taking him firmly by the arm and guided him indoors, not without difficulty, as he swayed and stumbled.

'Whassa time?' he pulled back his right sleeve. 'I've losht my watch,' he hiccupped.

'It's on your other wrist,' I steered him into the living room and pushed him on the sofa. 'What the hell are you playing at?'

'So it is,' he giggled as he held up his left arm. 'I don't think it'sh working,' he squinted intently at it for a second, then letting his arm drop, he looked up at me. 'She's kicked me out,' he stared at me, his eyes red and crossing slightly.

'Oh,' I moved my hands from my hips, and went and sat beside him, he tried to follow my progression but ended up throwing his head back on the sofa and staring at the ceiling. 'What happened?'

'I have absho... absholutely no idea,' he mumbled. 'One minute we were talking, then she starts shouting. She said I don't pay her any attention,' he brought his head back up and looked at me, his eyes suddenly filling with tears.

'Oh, no, come on,' I took his hand, trying not to breathe in whisky fumes. 'Things seem worse when you're drunk, you had a silly row, that's all.'

'Nah,' he blinked rapidly. 'She told me to go, she... she said she's sick and tired of me. I haven't got a bloody clue what I've done wrong.'

'Well, I don't know,' I squeezed his hand. 'But it sounds like she's been bottling it up. I told you before, it's hard with kids and when you're tired... it'll be OK.'

'I love her, Frankie,' he mumbled miserably.

'I know you do,' I said, consolingly. Privately I thought that it was most likely that this had been brewing for a while, and like most men, he hadn't been reading the signals. 'I'm going to make you a coffee, then I'm going to ring Chelsea... yes I am,' I added as he looked at me in horror, 'so she doesn't worry.'

As I stood up, he struggled up with me, saying he needed to pee. As I went to fill the kettle, I smiled to myself, listening to him trying to navigate the stairs. I made a very strong and sugary black coffee and left it on the kitchen table, deciding I didn't want most of it spilled on my pale cream sofa. Realising I didn't have Chelsea's number, I rang Jamie.

'Bloody fool, driving in that state,' Jamie sounded shocked. He gave me her number, and I said I would ring him later.

I heard Paul plodding heavily back down the stairs, and he reappeared, rebounding slightly off the kitchen archway.

'Drink that,' I ordered, pointing to his mug of coffee.

'Thanks,' he swayed. 'You're lovely, you are.'

Suddenly, he very clumsily grabbed me around the waist, pulling me towards him.

'Paul!' I gasped in shock. 'What are you playing at?'

'I've always liked you, Frankie,' he staggered and attempted to kiss me. Without thinking, I slapped him hard across the face, then put my hands to my cheeks in horror as he let go and stumbled backwards.

'Shit,' I gasped as he righted himself and looked comically surprised.

'Oh, I'm so sorry,' he said, almost politely, like he'd just accidently knocked into a stranger.

'Paul,' I admonished, wanting to laugh, 'we both know that you didn't want to do that.'

He sat down very suddenly on the nearest chair and looked up at me - I could see a red mark blooming where I had slapped him.

'No... but I do like you,' he frowned. 'Always fancied you a bit. Jamie's a lucky bugger.'

'It's just the drink talking,' I folded my arms and tried to look stern. 'What are we going to do with you, eh?'

'Please don't kick me out too,' he implored. 'I don't know where to go.'

'Hmm,' I giggled. 'You can kip on the sofa if you promise not to throw up.'

Leaving him to drink his coffee, I disappeared upstairs to ring, first, Chelsea, then Jamie. Chelsea sounded really angry.

'Well, you can keep him for all I care,' she said shortly, after I explained that Paul had turned up at mine.

'He's really upset,' I baulked slightly.

'Good,' she replied. 'I'm going to bed.'

Feeling like I had done something wrong, I meekly said goodbye.

'Hello,' Jamie answered straight away. 'Is he OK?'

'Not ever so,' I told him what had happened.

'He did what?' Jamie sounded furious.

'Oh, no, he's so drunk,' I started to feel sick. 'Please don't be mad at him. He won't even remember it in the morning. He's harmless, you know he is.'

'Well, I'm not happy,' he muttered. 'I'm coming over.'

'No, really, it's fine,' I said in alarm.

'See you in ten minutes.'

I ventured back downstairs to find Paul laying face down on the sofa, one shoe off. I took the other one off, threw a blanket over him and went to fetch a bucket, just in case.

Fifteen minutes later, Jamie was hammering at the door.

'There was really no need,' I walked backwards into the hall as he strode in unsmilingly.

'I want a word with him,' Jamie shut the door and frowned.

'Good luck,' I said. 'He's passed out.'

He went into the living room and surveyed Paul, 'Christ,' he muttered.

'See?' I mocked. 'I was in no danger.'

'It's not funny,' he looked at me. 'I can see straight through them pyjamas too. What the fuck did he think he was playing at?'

'Jamie,' I said slowly. 'Are you jealous?'

'Yes.'

'You're being silly,' I shook my head. 'Come on, forget about it. Honestly, he was so drunk, he didn't know what he was doing.'

'Hmm,' he narrowed his eyes at the sleeping Paul, then bent down and started taking his trainers off.

'I take it you're staying?' I eyed him in amusement.

'Yes,' he straightened up. 'I'm not leaving you alone with him.'

'How did I cope for forty-four years without you to protect me?'

'Stop taking the piss,' he came towards me and put his arms

around me. 'He was out of order.'

'I'm sorry,' I smiled into his chest.

'I'd feel better if you said that with a straight face,' he murmured into my hair.

After I had switched the lights off, leaving a side lamp on in case Paul woke up and needed to see where the bucket was, I followed Jamie upstairs. I left him in my bedroom while I went to shower my feet, they were filthy after walking around outside bare-footed. I returned to find him undressed and in my bed, propped up on my pillows, still looking grumpy.

'Are you going to stop acting like a teenager?' I laid on top of the duvet, propping my head up on one hand.

'I'm not,' he looked at me, his expression softening.

'I don't get why you're so mad,' I said.

'Because,' he began frowning again, 'Paul, out of *anyone*, knows how much I like you. And for how long. And I don't want him looking at you like that.'

'Uh huh,' I smiled a little. 'Well, for one, he didn't know what day it was, let alone what he was doing, seriously. And also... you can't stop anyone looking at me, in any way. Not that they are... but you can't get mad about it.'

'I suppose,' he stared above my head for a moment, then looked back at me. 'But I bet everyone fancies you. I've got my work cut out.'

I laughed, 'Everyone, eh? That's a lot of people. And why have you got your work cut out? Jamie, I've been celibate for a long time. I'm not going to start putting it about now. I'm not like that.'

'So,' he stared thoughtfully at me. 'Are we exclusive?'

'Jamie -' I begun, but he cut me off.

'OK, OK... don't say anything.'

'I just need some time -'

'Yeah,' he smiled grimly. 'I know.'

We were silent for a moment, then his natural humour re-surfaced, and he grinned at me.

'I should thank Paul really,' he reached down and stroked my shoulder.

'Why?'

'It got me in your bed tonight, didn't it?'

'You're an idiot,' I laughed.

'Yeah,' he agreed, then flung the duvet off himself. 'Get naked and come here.'

I woke up early - Jamie was still fast asleep, his arm under my pillow - I crept downstairs to find Paul had gone. He'd neatly folded up the blanket and I discovered the bucket, thankfully empty, in the kitchen. I also found a scribbled note with the word 'sorry' on the table.

I switched on the kettle and went back upstairs and climbed into bed and lay for a while watching Jamie sleep. As if he could sense my gaze, he suddenly opened his eyes and smiled at me sleepily.

'Hello, beautiful,' he murmured.

'Hello.'

'I have an erection,' he said happily.

'Well, it would be a shame to waste it,' I giggled, and wriggled down to face him.

'You are marvellous, aren't you?' he sighed.

'I try.'

CHAPTER FIFTEEN

I had all good intentions of going to the gym that afternoon, but after a morning in bed with Jamie, I decided that I really needed a nap - a nap that turned into three hours. I woke up just before five o'clock and panicked that I only had two hours to get ready.

Just as I was blow-drying my hair, Paul rang me.

'Hi,' he sounded sheepish.

'Hello,' I said. 'Are you OK?'

'Define OK,' he said, and I laughed.

'Well, you're alive, at least.'

'Listen, Frankie,' he plunged straight in, 'I remember very little of last night, but I'm pretty sure I tried it on with you.'

'Kind of.'

'Which means I did,' he groaned, 'and I'm sorry... more than sorry.'

'It's fine,' I said. 'You were drunk and upset... put it out of your head.'

'That's kind of you,' he coughed. 'I noticed that Jamie's car was there this morning... did you, er, mention anything?'

'Yes,' I decided not to beat around the bush. 'Sorry, I shouldn't have. He's a little hacked off... can you call him?'

'Yeah, I will,' he sounded upset. 'I'm such a prat.'

'Yes,' I laughed. 'No damage done though. How's Chelsea?'

'Frosty.'

'Oh dear,' I felt bad, but was aware of the time. 'Listen, I need to go, do you want to have lunch next week? I'm off work I but can meet you in town or something.'

'Sure,' he agreed.

I was full of anticipation and curiosity, wondering where Jamie was taking me and what his methods were of "treating me like a lady" - dressed in a simple knee-length dress, cranberry-coloured and low-cut, I waited in the living room with a gin and tonic and tried not to keep checking the time.

He knocked on the door a little after seven - he stood there with a bunch of yellow and white roses and a huge smile, looking handsome and clean-cut in a light blue shirt.

'Look at you,' he said in delight as I let him in. 'You look beautiful.'

'Thank you,' I stood back as he walked past me into the hall, not taking his eyes off of me.

'For you,' he said courteously, holding out the flowers, spoiling it slightly by staring at my breasts.

'They're lovely, thank you,' I walked through to the kitchen to put them in water.

'You smell sexy,' he stood very close behind me as I filled a vase and I experienced an unexpected swoop of lust as I felt his warm breath on my neck.

'So, where are we going?' I asked distractedly as I arranged the flowers.

'Well, I'd like to say bed,' he dropped a kiss on my shoulder and stepped back as I turned around, 'but first,' he smiled cheekily, 'I'm going to wine and dine you in style.'

Jamie drove us out of town and headed south down the country lanes - as we approached our destination, my heart sunk a little.

He had good taste, I had to admit, but The Peacock Barn, an expensive and extravagant restaurant set in the grounds of a seventeenth-century manor house surrounded by woods with a golf course beyond, was an old haunt of mine and Robert's.

'Very nice,' I murmured, not letting on I had been here on numerous occasions, and praying that he didn't ask me.

'I've played golf here before,' he indicated to the left of the restaurant. 'Always wanted to come here, hope you like it.'

'It looks wonderful,' I assured him, wondering if Robert still played golf here too.

We climbed out of his car and he shot round to take my hand, and gave me a happy little smile, clearly pleased that I was seemingly impressed.

We were seated in the Piano Bar to wait for our table, and Jamie ordered two champagne cocktails - I gazed around the familiar surroundings feeling unsettled, then realised he was studying me, and hoped my discomfort wasn't showing.

'You know what?' he said suddenly. 'I've decided to forgive Paul,' we had already discussed him on the journey, Paul had indeed rung Jamie, and Jamie had called him a "complete prick" for drunk-driving and informed him that it was only the fact that they were mates, and that Paul was drunk, that he didn't knock him out for trying it on.

'Oh?'

'Well, who can blame him for fancying you?'

'Stop it,' I shook my head. 'He doesn't, he was just very pissed.'

'Who says?' Jamie stared at me, a smile playing on his lips. 'How can he not? Look at you.'

'You don't half lay it on thick,' I laughed.

'I'm serious,' he insisted, 'why don't you take me seriously?'

'I do,' I said apologetically and put my hand on his. 'I'm just not used to the flattery. And I'm sure Paul *really* doesn't fancy me... look at Chelsea, she's gorgeous.'

'She's OK,' he said in an off-hand voice, and I giggled. 'Yes, she's a very pretty girl, but you have class as well as beauty.'

'Do I now?' I considered him for a moment, then crossed my eyes and stuck my tongue out.

'OK, I take that back,' he laughed, then leant over and kissed me, taking me by surprise. 'God, you make this hard for me.'

'What?' I frowned at his sudden serious expression.

Just then, a young waitress appeared, announcing our table was ready for us.

I ordered the mini lentil and spinach pancakes for my starter, which I already knew were delicious, Jamie wrinkled his nose in disgust and asked for the spicy beef skewers *sans* the salad.

'I hate mucked about food,' he admitted.

'You should live a little,' I admonished, dipping a pancake in the coconut sauce and pointing it at him.

'I'm a growing lad,' he buttered a roll. 'I need proper food.'

'Neanderthal,' I watched him stripping his beef with his very white and straight teeth at great speed.

'You love it,' he beamed.

'Hmm.'

As the starters were cleared away, Jamie ordered more champagne for me and orange juice for himself.

'Don't you mind not drinking?' I asked.

'I'm not a huge drinker anyway,' he shrugged.

'Good for you.'

'So...'

'Yes?'

'Well, this is a proper date,' he sat up a little straighter. 'Let's be proper.'

'As in -'

'Tell me more stuff about yourself,' he raised an eyebrow.

'Like what?'

'Something random,' he grinned.

'Umm... I'm scared of spiders,' I offered.

'Lame,' he tutted and continued to watch me.

'I can speak fluent Spanish, eso está major?'

'Very sexy... not a clue what you said, by the way... what else?'

'OK,' I thought hard. 'I won a trophy for gymnastics when I was fourteen.'

'Mmm, bendy,' he smirked. 'OK, let me ask you a question.'

'Go on,' I said warily.

'How many times have you been in love?'

'Oh,' I wasn't expecting that, 'twice... the man I was going to marry,' I paused. 'I *think*, and my ex-husband.'

'So,' he stared intently at me, 'if you loved *guy-you-was-gonna-marry*, why did you leave him for ex-husband?'

'It was complicated,' I said, not totally truthfully - it hadn't been complicated at all. 'Perhaps I didn't love David, the guy I was going to marry. Robert kind of swept me off my feet.'

'Uh huh,' he took a sip of his juice. 'Poor David. And poor choice, Robert sounds like an idiot.'

'Yeah,' I agreed, desperately wanting to get off the subject. 'Well, I won't ask you the same question, you've already told me that you've never had a serious relationship.'

'Doesn't mean I haven't been in love,' Jamie said.

'Right,' I frowned at him, he looked down for a second then grinned at me.

'Let's move onto safer ground,' he said.

'You have strange first date techniques,' I tried to smile back.

'Sorry,' he shrugged. 'It's hard to go back to basics when we've already... you know -'

'Yeah, I know.'

The rest of the evening was good fun. I wasn't sure if Jamie was sensitive to my uneasiness or not, but he kept the conversation on a more normal level - we talked about work, briefly, Gracie and Jessie e, and typical *small talk* - where we had been on holiday before, other jobs we had had, music and movies we liked. I was surprised to find we had more in common than I'd thought.

We left the restaurant just after eleven o'clock. The evening was cool and breezy, the skies a clear midnight blue and stars bright like sequins above us.

I wondered on the drive home if he was assuming he was staying at mine, and found that I wanted him to. I sat in silence, having an inner battle with myself - I didn't want to get attached... *you're already attached*, a little voice told me. *Come on, let's be honest about how you feel, eh Frankie? Drop the ice queen act...*

'You OK?' Jamie asked, startling me out of my thoughts.

'Yeah, I'm good,' I replied, pulling myself together. 'Thanks for a lovely evening,' I added.

'My pleasure,' he glanced over at me. 'I must have been the envy of every man in the room.'

'If you say so,' I studied his side-profile, wondering if he really did mean all the corny flattery.

'I do,' he said firmly, as he turned into my road.

He pulled up on the driveway and turned to look at me, 'Tonight was wonderful, thank you,' he said.

'Aren't you coming in for a coffee?' I asked puzzled.

'Of course,' he chuckled. 'We're on a date... I was waiting to be invited in.'

'You're such a gent,' I clambered out.

We didn't get as far as coffees, he started kissing me in earnest the moment I closed the front door, and within five minutes he had me upstairs and undressed. In his excitement, he didn't last long - I found that weirdly flattering.

'Sorry,' he lay on his side, gently stroking my thigh. 'We'll do it again in a minute.'

'Wally,' I giggled. 'It doesn't matter.'

'Yes, it does,' he didn't seem particularly fazed by, in his eyes, an unsatisfactory performance, and I thought it was rather endearing, his confidence that we could "do it again".

'Are you missing Gracie?' he asked, catching me off guard.

'Yes and no,' I said, then felt that sounded bad. 'Of course, I am, but it's nice to have a bit of freedom.'

'She's great though, isn't she?'

'She has her moments.'

'Is Quinn your married name?' he asked, looking curious.

'Yeah,' I pulled a face.

'How come you've kept it?' he propped his head up on his hand and started playing with my hair.

'Well,' I said hesitantly, 'two reasons, I suppose. I want to have the same surname as Gracie. Doesn't seem right to not-'

'Unless you re-marry,' he interrupted.

'Unless I re-marry,' I agreed.

'And?'

'I don't especially like my maiden name.'

'What is it?'

'I'd really rather not say.'

'Oh, no,' he tugged a lock of my hair. 'You have to tell me now.'

'OK, don't laugh,' I looked at him and he automatically started to grin.

'I won't,' he said eagerly.

'Abbeywell-Bacon,' I narrowed my eyes at him.

'Bacon!' he said gleefully. 'My favourite food.'

'Hmm.'

'Well, that's not so bad,' he raised his eyebrows. 'Frankie Abbeywell-Bacon... it spells FAB.'

'Good eh?' I grimaced. 'Unless it's my full name.'

'Which is?'

'If you laugh, I *will* kick you out of bed,' I warned. 'OK... Francine... Louisa Abbeywell- Bacon.'

'Ha,' he looked delighted, then seeing my expression, he wrapped his arms around me like he was hanging on for dear life.

'You're horrid,' I giggled and wriggled until he let go.

'Sorry,' he kissed my neck and settled back down on his side, his expression suddenly tender. 'I'm only teasing. I wouldn't care if your name was Nigel, I'd still have you proudly on my arm.'

'Nigel?' I shook my head. 'You're a strange, strange man.'

'You like me though, right?' he gave me a crooked smile.

'You're OK.'

'OK,' he repeated. 'Just OK, or -' he left it hanging, his eyes serious for once.

'You know I like you,' I frowned, pushing away the unformed words that rushed into my head - I felt a tiny *tug* in my stomach.

'Let me in,' he said quietly. 'Just a little bit,' he held up his thumb and forefinger, opening them a fraction, like it was a struggle.

'Jamie-'

'No,' he closed his eyes for a second. 'Don't say anything.'

We were silent for a minute or two - I was unhappy how the conversation had gone from playful and light-hearted to this, whatever *this* was. Jamie looked sad, and I didn't want him to feel sad... I didn't want to be causing him any sort of unhappiness.

'Jamie?' I said tentatively. 'Are you sure that this is what you want? I mean... wouldn't you rather be with someone who could give you more time or commitment?' I wanted to add 'or younger' but stopped myself.

'No,' he said at once. 'We're fine.'

'OK,' I said, not sure what else to say.

'Bet you wish you never seduced me now,' he said, sounding more like his usual self.

'What?' I exclaimed. 'I did not!'

'Who dragged whom upstairs?' he playfully poked my side making me squeal.

'You kissed me first,' I tried to look indignant.

'You got me drunk,' he countered, moving a little closer until our faces were an inch apart. I stared up at him, thinking what pretty eyes he had... wasted on a man... blue as an exotic ocean, bright and clear.

'Damn, you've worked out my evil plan,' I whispered, feeling relief that his playful mood was back.

As he began to kiss me, and his hands moved over my body, I felt the tension leave me as I embraced him and sunk into the bliss that was his love-making.

We woke up surprisingly early on Sunday morning. Jamie guiltily confessed to having clean clothes in his car - I guessed he didn't want to appear too presumptuous, even if we both had known deep down how the evening would end.

While he had a shower, I went downstairs and decided to surprise him with eggs and bacon.

As I was drinking my tea and cooking, he came downstairs with just a towel around his hips, still wet from his shower.

'I could smell it,' he padded over, leaving drops of water on the tiles, and kissed the back of my neck.

'And you couldn't wait until you were dressed?' I laughed as I slid two eggs onto his plate. 'How many rashers?' I asked.

'How many are there?' he peered over my shoulder. 'I'm not that hungry. Five or six will do.'

'Bloody hell,' I shook my head. 'Human dustbin.'

We sat and had breakfast together, I'd never seen anyone so happy about eggs and bacon. He demolished everything, then shooed me upstairs for my shower while he cleared up. I came back down to find him dressed in black jeans and a white T-shirt, and my kitchen spotless.

'Wow, thank you,' I said as he handed me a coffee and gave the hob a final wipe with the tea towel.

'So… what are you cooking me for lunch then?' he beamed, then stepped away as I went to swipe him with my hand.

'Actually,' I settled myself at the table, 'I really should go shopping before Gracie's home tomorrow, but let me buy us lunch.'

'Well, if you're offering.'

Jamie reluctantly went home mid-morning, I said I'd go shopping and we would meet up later. The house seemed empty after he'd gone - I pottered about tidying up, trying not to think about him. I was becoming more and more muddled, one minute feeling light-hearted and contented, the next, uptight and… *scared?*

As I absently made my bed and picked up my discarded clothes, I started to get angry with myself. Why was I ruining something that was so sweet? Why couldn't I just *relax* into it? I'd told Jamie before that I wanted to keep this away from Gracie because she was screwed up enough, but if I were truthful with myself, that wasn't why. *I'm screwed up,* I thought sadly. My mind turned to Robert, and I directed my anger at him. *He's still controlling me, he's set me on this path, not letting anyone through my barriers.*

I sat down suddenly on the bed, feeling tears on my face.

CHAPTER SIXTEEN

I decided that I needed to talk to somebody, and I automatically thought of my friend Debs. Maggie was, and always would be, my best and closest friend, and I loved her dearly - but I knew exactly what she'd say. That I was being stupid, that I needed to live a little and then she would have her usual rant about Robert and tell me to move on. All of it true, but I wanted a sympathetic ear and a gentler approach.

I had been trying to cram in a lot of activities with Gracie on my last week off. I felt slightly guilty leaving her with Rachel for an hour on the Tuesday to have lunch with Paul - things were delicate at home, he said, but it seemed Chelsea's outburst the week before had at least eased the pressure Chelsea had clearly been feeling. I took Gracie to the zoo on Wednesday, and then met up with Jamie and Jessie at the swimming pool for the autism-friendly evening.

I arranged to go over to Debs house on Thursday afternoon, she had said it was fine to bring Gracie, her daughter was eleven and would probably enjoy entertaining her.

Baz, the alarm guy, came early in the morning to fit my alarm - it would have taken him less time if he hadn't have talked so much, then spent forever explaining how to operate it... I perused the instruction leaflet and pointedly kept checking my watch as he waffled on. He eventually left just before midday, I made Gracie a quick sandwich, then we headed off to Debs.

Debs, her husband Felix, and their daughters, Harriet and Iris, lived on the other side of Fernberry in a neat and tidy cul-de-sac. Out of the four of us old school friends, myself, Maggie and Sally, Debs was the only one that had had a successful marriage. Somehow, their little family unit gave me a sense of comfort. She worked part-time at the infants' school nearby as a teaching assistant and volunteered at a local animal shelter; Felix was in finance in London. Both their daughters, Harriet, sixteen and Iris, eleven, were pretty and well-behaved - Harriet had just got her first boyfriend and Debs had confessed to having a sneaky look at her phone to read their text messages, and reported that there was no 'smut', as she put it, and he seemed like a nice young man.

They took two holidays a year, abroad at Easter and had a caravan holiday in Devon in the summer and would do family activities like bike-riding, rambling and fishing at the weekends. Maggie was always taking the piss a bit, calling them "twee" but I thought it was wonderful - no drama, no upsets outside of the usual family ups and downs, just a contented and simple life.

Debs answered the door beaming, her King Charles Spaniel, Sully, joyfully leaping about greeting us.

'Hello,' she ushered us in. 'How are you? Hello Gracie, oh my gosh you look so pretty, how are you? Oh, I love your hair, Frankie.'

'We're good, thank you,' we followed her into her kitchen, which was both very modern and very immaculate. 'How are you lot?'

'Same as usual,' she indicated to a chair as she filled the kettle, telling Gracie that Iris was in the back garden if she wanted to go and find her.

I watched her as she took two mugs out of an overhead cupboard - she looked pretty and fresh as she always did, her dark, very cropped hair framing her elf-like face, her slim figure clad in tight jeans and a flowered blouse. I'd always thought she'd had an underrated beauty, nothing glamorous about her, just a clean-cut and simple elegance.

'I spoke to Maggie the other day,' she started opening a packet of biscuits with her teeth, 'she said you'd had a bit of trouble?'

'She did?' I said confused, then, 'oh yeah, just kids causing trouble I reckon.'

'That's not what she thinks,' she emptied some biscuits on a plate and put them on the table. 'She thinks you've got a stalker,' she giggled - she knew only too well that Maggie liked to dramatize. 'Most likely in the shape of Robert... what happened?'

'Just some stupid calls, and someone lurking in my back garden,' I said lightly. 'I had an alarm fitted this morning, and Will put up some security lights. I'm like Fort Knox now.'

'Well... that's good then,' she finished making the tea and sat down opposite me. 'She said your friend had his car damaged too?'

'Yeah,' I nodded. 'Jamie. Nothing major.'

'So,' she leant forward. 'Jamie... what's the gossip?'

'Hmm,' I smiled at her eager little face. 'I'm kind of seeing him. Kind of.'

'Kind of?'

'It's complicated.'

'Please don't tell me he's married or anything,' Debs widened her eyes.

'No! No, nothing like that,' I said. 'He's single… a little younger than me… really lovely…' I trailed off.

'So?' she looked puzzled.

'It's me,' I looked down and shook my head. 'I'm trying not to fall for him. Except I am… I have. I don't really know what the hell I'm doing.'

'Ah,' Debs leant back in her chair and studied me thoughtfully. 'I see. You're afraid… I get that.'

'Yeah?' I grabbed a biscuit and bit into it angrily. 'I'm being idiotic, I know I am, but it's like… like I'm tied down by a bit of elastic, and I can get so far… then I just get yanked back.'

'Oh, Frankie,' she smiled sadly. 'You're in a muddle, aren't you? You can't think every man is like Robert.'

'It's been said before,' I said wryly.

'It's true though,' she shrugged. 'Let me just go and check on the girls.'

She came back a minute later, 'They're playing with Sully,' she informed me, and sat back down.

'I really need some advice,' I pleaded, and proceeded to tell her about the dinner I had cooked him and how we ended up in bed, and the rest of our story.

'Hmm,' she sipped some tea and her eyes wandered around the room before coming back to me. 'You need a plan.'

'A plan?'

'Yes, a plan,' she nodded slowly. 'OK, you can't help feeling the way you do, and you can't do nothing about the past, but you can re-train your brain.'

'I can?' I said in amusement.

'Sure, you can,' she lightly banged the table with her palm. 'Baby steps… little things, a bit at a time.'

'Right,' I said. 'But you're going to have to expand on that.'

'OK,' she stared into space for a moment with a delicate frown. 'OK,' she said a little louder. 'So, like, think about when you first meet someone, and when you're kind of established… what kind of things do you do, to progress the relationship? Not bedroom stuff, stuff outside of the two of you.'

'I'm confused.'

'I mean like… meeting the parents, that kind of thing.'

'Oh, no,' I looked at her in horror. 'We definitely haven't got that far. It's very casual.'

'If it was *that* casual, you wouldn't be in turmoil over it now, would you?' she raised her eyebrows.

'I suppose,' I narrowed my eyes at her and she giggled.

'OK, so maybe not meeting the parents. How about going out with another couple?'

'Well, we had dinner with another couple, but that was before we slept together,' I grabbed another biscuit. 'I'm sorry, but I don't really see how this is re-training my brain, or whatever.'

'To make it seem more normal… natural… not something to be scared of,' she reached over and squeezed my hand. 'I know it must be hard not to over-think it, and not to worry that he will do what Robert did, but please try. You like him a lot, don't you?'

'Yeah,' I sighed, then squared my shoulders. 'I really like him, and I think about him all the time and I know he's fallen for me. He's funny and he's so sweet… he makes me feel special and I would be stupid to push him away. There, that's more than I've admitted to myself.'

'Good girl,' she beamed.

'And I know if I keep him at arm's length, eventually he will get fed up,' I continued. 'He's been honest with me, I should be honest with him. And if it goes horribly wrong, I'm a big girl, I'll just have to deal with it.'

'Hurray,' she clapped her hands. 'Frankie Quinn, you're talking sense.'

'Still hard though -'

'No, no, no,' she interrupted, looking cross. 'No. None of that. Listen… it's either try or be single forever. I *hate* Robert for what he's done,' she suddenly looked furious. 'Don't let him ruin something that could be good.'

'You sound like Maggie,' I chuckled.

'Well, Maggie is right,' she sat back again and folded her arms.

'I know,' I agreed. 'She gets so mad with me.'

'Because she loves you,' she said gently. 'And I do too. Go for it girl.'

I giggled, 'I can't really argue with that.'

'Then don't.'

We went and sat outside. Gracie was happily throwing a ball around for Sully. Iris, a miniature version of Debs, except she had long dark hair scraped up in a ponytail, was sprawled out on the lawn, half watching Gracie and Sully's antics, half scrolling through her iPhone.

'Come and have a drink, girls,' Debs called, putting two bottles of flavoured water on her patio table.

Having left my sunglasses in my car, I took a seat facing away from the sun, Debbie moved her chair slightly to the right, so she was in the shade.

'Seen Sally lately?' she asked, as the girls ran over, followed by Sully.

'A few weeks ago,' I must have pulled a face because she chuckled then clamped her hand over her mouth. 'We went for a drink.'

'She OK?'

'Same as usual,' I shrugged. 'That reminds me actually, I saw David,' I told her about bumping into him, then again outside the bar, and at the park, our meal out before my holiday, then again at Pizza Hut.

'That's weird,' she looked fascinated.

'Why?' I asked, puzzled.

'Well, he said he'd moved back here last year,' she looked thoughtful. 'You bump into him and then suddenly he's all over the place.'

'Fernberry's a small place,' I said.

'True,' she nodded, still looking lost in thought. 'You sure he's not behind your calls?'

'No,' I frowned. 'He wouldn't. Anyway, he didn't have my number until after Gracie and his son has their little altercation.'

'Mmm,' Debs absently watched the girls, now both sat under her pear tree, Sully panting beside them.

'Seriously,' I said impatiently. 'It wasn't him. It was more likely Robert than him, and I'm almost sure it wasn't Robert.'

'I always thought that David seemed pretty obsessional.'

'Really?' I felt surprised.

'Sorry,' she seemed to snap out of her thoughts. 'Just seems like a bit of a coincidence… no, you're right, David wouldn't do that.'

'What did you mean "obsessional"?' I asked curiously - I'd never once in the entire time I had been with David, thought that. Slightly clingy, maybe… attentive, maybe annoyingly so…

'I don't know,' she fidgeted. 'You never seemed that keen to start with, but he seemed to push things along.'

'Really?' I said again, truly perplexed. 'Of course I was keen, I wouldn't have wanted to move in together or agreed to marry him else.'

'Oh, yeah,' she looked tense. 'I didn't mean you were *railroaded* or anything. Just, I think you would have waited.'

'Maybe, maybe not,' I stared past her head, thinking about it. 'Neither here nor there now, is it?'

'I suppose not,' she agreed. 'He was a nice bloke, but I'm not sure he was for you.'

'Obviously not,' I sighed. 'I was easily persuaded away from him, wasn't I?'

'Robert has a big personality,' she mused. 'And seriously good-looking.'

'Hides a multitude of faults,' I said sourly.

'Well, yes,' Debs nodded resolutely. 'He has to have something going for him.'

I laughed, 'I was but one of many victims. His looks will go one day, I hope. And then what's he got?'

'He'll pay for it, he's rich,' she giggled. 'Anyway, he's the sort of cocky bastard that'll always land on his feet.'

'Everyone's luck runs out eventually,' I said firmly - although I didn't particularly feel that would be the case for Robert.

CHAPTER SEVENTEEN

September soon came around, with the start of the new school year and also Gracie's birthday. I had been thinking a lot about what Debs said regarding normalising mine and Jamie's relationship, and I had been trying to approach him with how I was feeling, but I seemed to get stuck. However, I decided that Gracie's birthday presented a good opportunity: her birthday fell on a Sunday - she was with Robert on Friday and he was taking her and her friend from school, Trixie, out to her favourite burger bar in town and having a sleepover at his. On Saturday I had booked a bowling party for her and ten of her friends, which my parents were coming along to, and on Sunday, her actual birthday, she had asked to have a tea party at home, with Will, Lennie, Bea, Maggie and Jessie... which Jamie was delighted about. And, as anxious as I was, I thought that he would be meeting people, thus "normalising it".

Gracie had wanted Jessie to come to her bowling party, but Jamie kindly explained to her that Jessie was very shy and wouldn't know anyone, and that the venue, Stars and Stripes - an extremely popular place locally with amusement arcades, soft play areas and an American diner - would be too much for her.

The weekend before, after we had been out together to the boating lake, I asked Jamie if he and Jessie would be able to come over for her tea party.

'We'd love to,' he said, grinning. 'Thank you, are you sure nobody will mind?'

'Why would they?' I asked cautiously.

We were making sandwiches for the girls whilst they played outside on Gracie's trampoline. I could hear Jessie squealing joyfully.

'Well,' Jamie put down his knife that he'd been spreading peanut butter with, and put his arms around me, 'that's not really keeping things private, is it?'

'So?' I looked steadily at him. 'People have got to know sooner or later, haven't they?'

'Have they?' he raised an eyebrow.

'Yes,' I nodded slowly.

'Hmm, some of them bricks are coming down, eh?' he dropped a kiss on my nose.

'What?'

'That wall of yours,' he smiled a little and let me go. 'I'll go and fetch the girls in.'

'OK,' I watched him through the kitchen window, biting my lip, thinking that he must think I was terribly hard work.

I was soon giggling, as he climbed through the net on the trampoline and started bouncing about with the girls, then diving at their knees, making them lose balance. Soon, he was flat on his back as they bundled on top of him, he started yelling 'help' at the top of his voice.

I was just pouring two glasses of wine when the three of them burst into the kitchen.

'Go and wash your hands, you two,' I ushered the girls upstairs. 'You hungry?' I asked Jamie; he had started poking around in the fridge.

'Always,' he answered, then laughed. 'What's this?' he held up four packets of bacon.

'Stocked up,' I looked at him over my wine glass.

'Well,' he smirked. 'I almost feel like I've conquered Everest. Showing me off to people, buying me bacon... what's coming next?'

'Shut up,' I sat down and put my nose in the air.

'I'm teasing,' he threw a packet of bacon on the side and put the rest back. 'Bacon butties?'

'Only if you wash up.'

Jamie and Jessie left around eight o'clock; Jessie had been yawning like mad. Jamie said he'd be back when Gracie was asleep later on. I felt a pang - that still seemed like I was keeping him a secret, but I appreciated that he understood it wasn't altogether straight forward with her.

I ran Gracie a bath, and started folding laundry whilst she splashed about, singing to herself. She came into my room to dry herself.

'Mummy?'

'Yes, sweetie?'

'Is Jamie your boyfriend?'

'Oh,' I continued folding, my back to her. 'Why would you ask that?'

'Because you like each other,' she said simply. 'And you smile a lot at him.'

I turned around and tried to gauge her mood by her expression, she looked innocently happy enough, drying between her toes, her cheeks rosy from her bath.

'Well,' I thought hard. 'He's a boy and he's my friend, so yes, I suppose he is.'

'Oh Mummy,' she said impatiently. 'I mean a boyfriend you kiss.'

I burst out laughing, 'Well, aren't you so grown-up?'

'I think he should be your boyfriend,' she wriggled her toes then looked up at me. 'You're not sad anymore.'

That statement took me by surprise, 'I wasn't sad,' I perched on the bed next to her. 'Why do you think I was sad.'

'Because sometimes you looked sad,' she blinked up at me. 'And I heard you crying before.'

'Oh, sweetie,' I kissed the top of her damp head, feeling a strange shame. 'Everybody feels sad *sometimes,* I wasn't sad all the time. So... you like Jamie then?'

'Yes,' she nodded. 'He's funny.'

'Yeah,' I agreed. 'He's very funny, isn't he?'

'Yes,' she frowned for a moment, her eyes pensive. 'Mummy, if he was your boyfriend, would Daddy be sad?'

'No, I don't think so,' I said quickly, thinking, *sad... no... pissed off... very possibly.*

'Good,' she jumped up and started pulling on her pyjamas, 'I wouldn't want Daddy to be sad, he's *never* sad.'

'Well... that's good,' I said lightly. 'Right, young lady, go and brush your teeth and choose a book, I will come and tuck you in when I've finished up here.'

'You need a heart to be sad,' I muttered to myself as I finished putting my laundry away. I started to wonder how he would react... probably with icy indifference peppered with passive-aggressive comments. *Oh well,* I thought.

The following Sunday, Jamie came over before everyone else to help me make Gracie's tea party food. She had insisted on a pink theme - unknown to her, Bea had made a beautiful pink and silver unicorn cake - so whilst she was with Robert on Friday, Jamie and I had trailed around two different supermarkets on a quest to find pink paper plates, balloons, streamers, as well as an assortment of party snacks. I ended up spending a fortune, unwelcome after splashing out on her bowling party and her gift, her very own laptop, as she was constantly bugging me to use mine, which was showing every sign of dying on me again.

Whilst Gracie and Jessie were playing upstairs, we laid the kitchen table, covered in a pink and white striped cloth, scattered with fuchsia glittery stars - which no doubt I would regret buying after a few weeks of finding them all over the house - leaving a big gap in the middle for her cake.

'I will need to do some boys stuff after this,' Jamie proclaimed, staring around the kitchen at the all the pink.

'God, she's so spoilt,' I muttered, as I loaded up some plates with some sausage rolls.

'Well, you're only eight once,' he chuckled.

'Can you get the door, please?' I asked as I heard a loud knock. 'It'll be Maggie.'

Maggie hadn't met Jamie before, but she'd seen him one time when she had popped into the office... he said he couldn't really remember her. I was curious as to how they would get on.

'Hello,' I heard her say, then Gracie screamed her name and came thundering down the stairs.

'She brought wine,' Jamie came back into the kitchen, brandishing two bottles.

'I think we'll need it,' I put them in the fridge, and surveyed the table. 'Uh uh,' I slapped his hand as it inched towards some mini pizzas.

'Can I open Maggie's present?' Gracie was pulling Maggie by the hand, a gift-wrapped present under her arm.

'No, we are waiting, aren't we?' I laughed as she pouted. 'Hello, you,' I leant over and kissed Maggie. 'No introductions needed, but Maggie, this is Jamie, Jamie... Maggie.'

'Nice to meet you at last,' Maggie beamed up at him.

'You too,' Jamie said, perfectly at ease. 'Frankie, I'm just going to get Jessie to come down,' he rubbed the top of my arm and disappeared, Gracie not far behind.

'Oh, well done,' Maggie looked after him admiringly. 'Cute, cute, cute, *and* fit.'

'Shh,' I giggled.

'He reminds me of that guy I went out with from Canterbury, Patrick...'

'The dick like a Pringle tube guy?' I asked, and she let out a squawk of laughter.

'Yeah, him,' she sighed. 'Had to let him go, my liver was going to pack up, the amount of paracetamol I had to take before, after and sometimes during.'

'Oh my God,' I wiped my eyes - I was still giggling when Jamie returned with Jessie.

'What are you cackling at?' he looked at us in amusement.

'Get me drunk, and I'll tell ya,' Maggie winked. 'Hi there,' she said to Jessie, who was standing very close to Jamie, clutching his arm. 'Shall we go and sit in the living room?'

Amazingly, Jessie nodded and trotted off with Maggie. Jamie's mouth fell open.

'She's got a way with kids,' I looked fondly after her. 'She's a nurse in the children's ward.'

'Wow,' he shook his head. 'She seems nice.'

'She is,' I said as I lined up some wine glasses. 'Don't get on the wrong side of her though, or she'll turn savage,' I nudged him.

'Noted,' he said, looking slightly alarmed.

Bea was the next to arrive, carefully carrying Gracie's cake aloft on a covered board.

'Happy birthday, sweet girl,' she trilled. 'Hello Maggie, hello Jamie dear,' she handed me the cake. 'I'll just get her pressie from the car.'

Gracie trotted after me, wanting to see her cake, Jessie in tow.

'Unicorn,' Jessie cried, looking thrilled.

'Mummy, Mummy, can I eat the head?' Gracie asked.

'Do you want to eat head later?' Jamie whispered in my ear, making me burst into laughter.

Maggie leaned forward in her chair, looking at us, smirking as Jamie stroked the back of my neck.

'Are we having a sleep-over?' I murmured.

'Oh, I think we are,' he grinned down at me.

'Hem hem,' Bea appeared in the archway and I jumped. 'You have guests.'

Will and Lennie had arrived, with an extra guest.

'Adam!' Gracie yelled, belting over to him.

'How about a hello to your big bro,' Will tutted.

I introduced everyone to Jamie, he shook hands with Will and Adam and kissed Lennie's cheek.

'Gosh, your bump's got big,' I studied Lennie. She looked better than last time I had seen her, not so drawn and pale, dressed in leggings and a long grey and white striped top, her dark hair in two plaits. She had a rather neat, round bump.

'I feel like a whale,' she grimaced. 'I can't believe I have nearly four months to go.'

'It'll zoom by,' I assured her.

'I hope so,' she stroked her stomach.

'We've got the scan next week,' Will told me.

'You going to ask the sex?' I asked.

'Yes please,' yelled Adam from the living room - he was ensconced on the sofa next to Maggie.

'I keep changing my mind,' Lennie looked at Will. 'Will wants to know, I kind of do, then think it'd be nice to have a surprise. Daphne keeps dropping hints, says she's knitting a blanket in "the relevant colour",' she giggled.

Daphne was Adam's landlady, Lennie had flat-shared with him before she had moved in with Will - she was a self-proclaimed psychic. I had met her at their wedding, she was a colourful character, extremely eccentric and very sweet. Lennie seemed to regard her as a mother figure, her relationship with her own mother was not a particularly warm one.

'Angela is insisting it's a boy,' Will frowned - Angela was Lennie's mother, I knew that Will was polite as he always was to her, but disapproved of her distant attitude to Lennie. '*That* kind of makes me want a girl... but I don't care really. As long as it's healthy.'

'Picked any names?' Jamie asked interestedly - both Lennie and Will looked at him in surprise.

'I like Arthur for a boy, but Will had a dog called that, so that's a no,' Lennie said. 'I *did* at the beginning like Harper for a girl, but now every time I think about it, it reminds me of feeling sick,' she pulled a face. 'We keep reading name books, but end up making up daft ones.'

'Mummy,' Gracie marched in. 'Can I *please* open my presents now, you've made me wait ages.'

Everyone laughed, and we went back through to the living room. Bea had taken the liberty of arranging her gifts in a neat pile on the coffee table.

She did well. Apart from her laptop, which she screamed with joy at, she got a unicorn onesie from Maggie with a matching blanket, a beautiful wooden jewellery box with a silver heart pendant necklace - and some bangles inside from Will and Lennie, Adam, probably not knowing what to buy and possibly inviting himself at the last minute, had very generously put forty pounds in a card and signed it, *lots of fabulous love from your best friend, Adam.* Bea had, under my instruction, brought her a board game she had wanted and a rainbow-coloured unicorn, ("my spirit-animal", Adam had said) and Jamie and Jessie had got, chosen by Jessie, a pink backpack filled with gel pens, stickers, pads of paper and the such.

Gracie politely thanked everyone, and hugged Jessie, who giggled and hugged her back. I ushered everyone into the kitchen, Jamie predictably started piling his plate up straight away.

'Hey, Lens,' Adam waved a sausage roll under her nose, she stepped back, looking revolted.

'I've gone right off pastry,' she complained. 'Adam, sod off,' she glared at him as he pursued her.

'I went off tea,' I said. 'Really hacked me off. You got any cravings?'

'Jam,' Will chipped in. 'She's started eating it out of the jar. I went and brought some cranberry sauce for dinners, we were entering the realms of downright disgusting.'

'Ain't me,' Lennie shrugged. 'It's your baby making me,' she leant her head on his shoulder and he kissed the top of it, looking affectionately at her.

I noticed that Maggie was throwing stony little looks in Lennie's direction, and catching her eye, I frowned and shook my head at her.

Jamie and Bea went back into the living room, both chatting away - Bea kept smiling at me, I wondered what they were saying.

'So,' Will said in a low voice, following me as I went to pour some wine. 'What's this then?' he nodded towards the living room.

'What?' I said innocently, and he nudged me.

'Your "friend",' he smirked a little. 'He seems nice.'

'Hmm, well,' I gave him a sideways glance. 'Early days, taking it slow and all that.'

'Yeah?' he smiled broadly. 'You look happy.'

'I *am* happy,' I looked up at him, realising I was. 'Can't sit on the shelf forever, can I?'

'Nope,' Will agreed.

After everyone had eaten and we'd sang happy birthday to Gracie and cut her cake, her and Jessie had got restless and disappeared upstairs to play.

Bea seemed rather taken with Adam, and settled herself next to him.

'You're a lovely young man, aren't you?' she patted his leg. 'Have you got a girlfriend, dear?'

Lennie nearly choked on a mouthful of her lemonade - everyone looked expectantly at Adam.

'You offering?' Adam beamed at her.

'Oh, you tease,' she tittered. 'If I were twenty years younger,' she sighed.

'Stop flirting,' Maggie directed at Adam. 'I'm first in the queue.'

'Actually, I'm taken,' Adam put his arm around Bea. 'But never say never.'

'What's the lucky girls name?'

'Dominic,' Adam said and both Lennie and Will burst into laughter.

'Oh, Bea,' Jamie shook his head.

It took a while for Bea to cotton on.

'Oh,' she said after a moment. 'You're the other way,' - Maggie actually screamed with laughter at that - 'well, I would never have guessed. I knew a gay once, we used to dog walk together. He always dressed nice.'

'Yeah, we do that,' Adam said seriously.

'I've always liked that Chinese fellow on TV,' Bea continued. 'What's his name... Gok,' she smiled. 'Always so lovely and dressed so well.'

Lennie excused herself to go to the toilet, her eyes watering from laughter - I got up too to pour more wine.

'You OK?' Jamie appeared behind me.

'Yeah,' I chuckled softly. 'Bea makes me die.'

'Funny old thing, isn't she?' he grinned.

'What time have you got to have Jessie home?' I asked.

'Around seven,' he snaked an arm around my waist. 'I'll be back before nine. Will everyone have buggered off?'

'You bored?' I glanced up at him.

'No,' he shook his head. 'They're a good laugh - I just want you to myself... I'm feeling very rampant.'

'Are you ever not?'

'Not really,' he squeezed my waist. 'And it's entirely your fault.'

CHAPTER EIGHTEEN

I was finding that I cared less and less about what people thought at work. Not that Jamie and I showed any public affection in the office, or openly discussed our relationship, but I resigned myself to the fact that over half of our work colleagues knew, and as long as they left us alone, I decided that it didn't matter.

Gracie hadn't brought up her question again, but I was carefully planning a little chat to have with her - I was confident that she would be OK about it, as she clearly adored Jamie.

My one blot on the horizon was that David had attempted to call me, on average once a week by the end of October, and I felt terrible. Maggie told me to just tell him: I have a boyfriend, and dinner or whatever wasn't appropriate. I felt decidedly uncomfortable with that - it seemed awfully arrogant to assume that David wanted to see me out of anything but old acquaintances; I supposed that the guilt from the past played a part in that.

On a whim one Sunday afternoon, while I was waiting for Jamie to come over after he had been to the cemetery to put flowers on his dad's grave, I decided to call David. I felt that it was just plain rude to ignore the missed calls that I had obviously seen. I asked how he was, and apologised for not getting back to him sooner, and that I had been *horrendously* busy - he was totally understanding and said he'd been busy himself, and hoped I was OK, and maybe we could catch up soon. I felt much better when I got off the phone.

I finally felt like my life was taking a path that looked promising. Jamie and I saw each other as and when we could - the weekends that Gracie was with Robert we would spend together, unless he was looking after Jessie, but he always would come over late in the evening and spend the night. On the weekends that I had Gracie, we would sometimes do something together - usually with Jessie, which Gracie loved.

What Robert knew or guessed, I didn't care. As long as his relationship with Gracie was consistent, and she was happy. In fact, I found that I was totally unconcerned - something that was foreign to me; I realised, as I never had before, how much Robert's influence… hold… *whatever* you want to call it, had directed my actions.

I began to stop analysing what Jamie and I had between us. It really didn't seem to matter anymore. He made me feel *young,* sometimes reckless… he made me feel desirable and important, and I liked it. The sex was incredible. Don't get me wrong, Robert had been good in bed, I would never deny that. But with Jamie, it was like he couldn't get enough of me. Where Robert had been so in control all of the time, and self-assured with his performance, Jamie was as enthusiastic as a puppy… always delighted at the sight of my naked body, his love-making was happy and joyful.

Despite this, I tried not to think about where we were heading. *Was the age gap still an issue?* Truthfully, yes.

At his age, he should have been thinking about marriage and having children in the near future - things that I felt unable to offer him. I didn't want to deny him those things, but it wasn't a discussion I felt like I wanted to get into. In the back of my mind, I feared that I was just a bit of temporary fun, but he didn't treat me as if that was the case. We hadn't said the 'L' word… any thoughts of mine that strayed in that direction, I pushed away. Falling in love meant being vulnerable. I had been there, done that, suffered the fallout. And did it really matter? In the great scheme of things? We were happy, we laughed together *a lot*, we had fun. Life didn't have to be about commitment and plans and seriousness… that was just a preconceived idea of what the natural progression of a relationship should be. And I had tried that - and look where it got me.

In the first week of November, Gracie was ill and off school with a nasty cold and cough. We were busy at work, so rather than use some of my holiday, I decided to work from home.

On her third day off from school, the Wednesday, she was feeling a little better and wanted to sit in the kitchen with me on her laptop too, which I said was OK - as long as she was a good girl and quiet as I was very busy - if she was, I promised I would order her a pizza later for tea, and we would watch a movie together with popcorn.

She sat in her onesie, engrossed in whatever game she was playing, while I worked away, trying not get distracted by her. At half-past ten, I heard the post landing on the hall mat, and asked her to go and fetch it for me. She returned a moment later, dropping the post on the table between us, I noticed a large white envelope amongst the smaller white and brown envelopes. Not wanting to stop in the middle of what I was doing, I carried on working, then sent an email to Scott, and stood up to stretch and switch on the kettle. I took my post over to the worktop with me, glancing at the time. It was eleven twenty-six and that exact time was imprinted on my mind for weeks to come.

There was a letter from Specsavers, junk mail from Capital One and some Christmas catalogue company, and the large white envelope, addressed to Mrs. F. Quinn, in untidy capital letters. I poured water into my mug, and carefully tore the envelope open. What I first thought were sheets of paper held together with a large silver paper clip, were large black and white photographs - three in total. It took me a confused moment to register what I was seeing.

The first photograph showed Jamie and a blond woman, her face in side profile, in his car. It was a little blurred as if it had been blown up in size. The view was front on, through the car windscreen, Jamie was leaning forward slightly, looking down. My legs started to tremble as I looked at the next photograph. In this one, they were walking with their backs to the camera, their arms around each other's waists and the woman's head resting on Jamie's shoulder. She was dressed in tight dark-coloured jeans or trousers, and high-heeled boots, her long blonde hair trailing down her back. Again, it was blurry, but they appeared to be walking in some sort of park and the path was covered in autumn leaves, so I knew it was taken recently.

My heart felt somewhere in the region of my throat. My mouth was dry and my whole body started to shake horribly. In the third and final photograph, they both stood facing one another, their arms wrapped around each other. She was leaning her forehead on his chest and appeared to be smiling widely. Jamie's face was buried on the top of her head.

'- Mummy, answer me!' Gracie's voice seemed to come from far away. I looked up feeling dazed.

'Sorry sweetie?' I turned the photographs upside down and tried to smile.

'I said, can I have lunch soon, please?' Gracie implored, her face puzzled. 'I asked you three times.'

'Yes,' I turned away, feeling nauseous. 'Sorry, in a minute, sweetie.'

I tried to breathe normally, tried to hold in a sob that was fighting to escape. I took a plate from the cupboard above and promptly dropped it; it shattered on the tiled floor, making Gracie jump.

'Sweetie, go and sit in the living room while I clear this up,' I was aware tears were forming, hot and insistent, I swallowed hard.

I began to blindly pick up the larger pieces, promptly cutting the side of my forefinger. Wrapping a tea towel around it, I fetched my dustpan and brush, the same word reverberating in my brain: *no no no... not this again... no no no...*

It was Robert all over again... how could that be? It felt worse, it felt more shocking... *I always knew deep down what Robert was, it hurt, it was awful, but I was expecting it. But... not Jamie... please, dear God, not Jamie...*

I clumsily made Gracie a sandwich, opened her favourite crisps, poured some orange juice and called her. I belted upstairs and shut myself in the bathroom, and with an awful relief, released the aching sob that I had been fighting down. I sat on the edge of the bath, my hands clamped over my mouth, feeling like my heart had been ripped into a thousand pieces. And how long I sat like that, I don't know.

I slowly began to calm down, a resigned numbness filling me. *How stupid was I?* I believed that Jamie, a man who was ten years younger than me, was interested in anything but getting his leg-over? *I bet he's laughed at me. I bet he's been so smug that a stupid, over-the-hill divorcee swallowed all of his bullshit.*

I washed my face in cold water, and stared into the mirror - stupid, stupid, *old* woman. I took a few deep breaths and went back downstairs.

Gracie had only eaten half of her sandwiches and a few crisps.

'Mummy, can I lay down with my blanket?' she asked.

I automatically felt her forehead, she didn't feel like her temperature had gone up again, but she looked pale and tired. I fetched her blanket and Yellow Bunny, and she snuggled up on the sofa with her Frozen DVD on.

I went back into the kitchen and sat looking at the photographs again. The temptation was huge to just rip them into pieces and throw them away - but I felt like I needed to come to terms with what I was seeing.

I stared at the woman's side profile in the first one. She looked vaguely familiar for some reason... I stared and stared, thinking hard. She looked maybe a little older than Jamie, but it was hard to tell as the picture was slightly out of focus. Her mouth was slightly open, like she was saying something, I couldn't tell what expression was on Jamie's face, as he was looking down. One arm was visible resting on the top of his steering wheel. I then looked at the second photograph, briefly wondering where they were... maybe the boating lake? It probably wasn't local though, I decided.

I glanced into the living room - Gracie looked as though she was dozing off. Impatiently brushing the fresh tears from my cheeks, I laid the final photograph on top of the others and let out a trembling sigh. It hit me that the image of Jamie resting his face on the top of her head was so familiar - how many times had he done that to me? I wondered why she was smiling. I gazed and gazed at her face until my eyes went out of focus, and stood up suddenly, my chair almost falling over backwards.

My mobile started to ring, making me start. It was Jamie. I rejected the call, knowing that in a moment the alert would sound that I had a voicemail. With fingers that were trembling worse than ever, I rang Maggie, not knowing what else to do.

'Hiya,' she answered straight away. 'You alright? How's the princess?'

'Maggie,' I tried to keep my voice steady. 'Can you come over?'

'What's up?' she immediately sounded concerned.

'Just come, please,' I started to cry.

'Give me ten minutes.'

Fifteen minutes later, Maggie was sat in the kitchen, looking at the photographs, her face pale.

'You have to confront him,' she frowned down at them.

'No,' I whispered sadly. 'I've already made a fool of myself. I'm just going to end it.'

'And not give him a chance to explain?' she looked up at me, her dark, usually merry eyes solemn.

'And listen to excuses?' I rubbed my temples. 'No. I want to retain some dignity. I don't want him to see I'm hurting... no, I want to control this one, I'm sick of being dumped on.'

'Frankie,' she grabbed my arm. 'Don't get me wrong, I know what men are capable of, but it might not be what it seems -'

'Yeah, right,' I laughed without mirth. 'Look at them! No... no, I'm not putting myself through it again.'

'Who the hell has sent these?' she murmured, more to herself than me.

It took me by surprise that I hadn't even wondered that. I supposed the shock had wiped everything else from my mind.

'It's got to be Robert,' Maggie picked up the envelope and examined the writing. 'Recognise the writing?'

'No,' I shook my head.

'It was posted locally,' she put it down again and turned her attention back to me. 'I'm so sorry, I really thought he was a good 'un.'

'Well, there you go,' I said, anger rising bitterly. 'I must have "push over" stamped on my forehead.'

'Hey, it's not you,' Maggie said forcefully. 'He's an idiot, look at you... his loss.'

'Yeah,' I tried to smile, then the tears started up again. 'But I really thought we were good together. He seemed so sincere.'

'Don't they all?' Maggie wiped my face with her sleeve, then stood up and come and put her arms around me.

'It's not fair,' I closed my eyes as she hugged me. 'I really liked him... so much. And Gracie... what will she think? She's got used to him being around -'

'Shh, now,' Maggie let me go and knelt down next to my chair, taking both my hands. 'Gracie will be fine, don't worry about that now, think about what you're going to do.'

'I can't face him yet,' I looked down into her worried face. 'I'll sleep on it... I can't even think straight right now.'

'No, of course,' she squeezed my hands and stood up again. 'Come on, go and clean your face, you don't want Gracie to see you like this.'

I obediently went upstairs and splashed my face with cold water - I looked terrible. I did a quick repair job, dabbing on some concealer under my eyes and powdered my face. I couldn't do anything about my bloodshot eyes, I just hoped Gracie wouldn't notice.

She was stirring under her blanket as I went back through the living room to the kitchen. Maggie had made two cups of tea and had tidied away Gracie's lunch things.

'Thank you,' I picked up my mug and wandered over to the window - it was a bleak and grey November afternoon, totally cheerless. I felt a wave of depression wash over me and shuddered.

'I need to go to work soon,' Maggie said, sounding guilty.

'Sure,' I said, trying to sound OK about it - I really didn't want her to go. 'I'll be OK.'

'Well, no you won't,' she came and stood next to me, looking outside too. 'I'll ring on my break.'

'Thanks, Maggie,' I glanced at her and she gave me a sad smile. 'Always here,' she assured me.

Feeling sick to my stomach, I texted Jamie saying I was feeling ill, I must have a touch of Gracie's cold, and I would speak to him the next day as I wanted to just crash out early. I read his reply with a pang; he said he would like to come and kiss me all better, and he hoped he could see me the following evening.

My evening was miserable. I ordered pizza, as promised to Gracie, but couldn't eat. I hoped I was imagining the quizzical looks she was giving me every now and then. I made popcorn and sat cuddled up with her, watching Despicable Me, not taking any of it in. All I really wanted to do was crawl into bed and stay there. Possibly for the rest of my life. But, because she had napped earlier, Gracie wasn't tired at her normal bedtime and wanted endless stories and kept chatting - I had to assert a lot of self-control not to bite her head off. When she finally fell asleep just before ten o'clock, I had a shower, and without drying myself properly, I laid on my bed, staring unseeingly at the ceiling, numb and dry-eyed, tired but knowing sleep wouldn't be coming anytime soon. I think it was around two in the morning when I finally climbed under my duvet and went to sleep, not even bothering to check I had locked the doors.

CHAPTER NINETEEN

I managed to put Jamie off seeing me until Friday, when Gracie was with Robert. I told him to come over in the evening in a brief conversation on Thursday while he was on his lunch break. If he thought I sounded off, he didn't say anything, and he was his usual jokey, cheerful self.

As Gracie was off from school, Robert had to pick her up from my house. I had a lot of time to think about whether he was behind sending me the photographs, and I had to resign myself to the fact, it seemed likely. I forced myself to be cheerful and chatty when he turned up - I would sooner slit my own throat than admit he had caused me more pain.

I had an hour to kill before Jamie was due, so I had a bath and made myself look presentable, drank two large gins which went straight to my head as I'd hardly eaten for two days, and then forced myself to sit and logically go through how I was going to play it.

When Jamie knocked, I counted to ten before letting him in.

'Hello, beautiful,' he came in, smiling and looking carefree and happy.

'Hi,' I said breathlessly, my heart pounding in my ears.

As I stepped back, he seemed to falter a little, frowning. I went into the living room, trying to clear my head, aware that I was shaking.

'You don't look good,' he said as I turned to face him.

'Jamie, can you sit down,' I said, my voice sounding higher than normal.

He sat on the sofa, his eyes not leaving my face. I perched on the chair opposite him, my mind struggling to stay focussed, trying to ignore the pain twisting in my chest. He looked so handsome, in his black jeans and an olive-green T-shirt that made his eyes look aquamarine.

'What's wrong?' he sat forward a little. 'Are you still poorly? You look really pale, Frankie.'

'I'm fine,' I cleared my throat, forcing myself to look him in the eyes. 'We need to talk. Actually... no, I need to tell you something.'

'Right,' he looked almost scared.

'Jamie, I'm sorry, but I want to end things,' I said, aware my voice was quavering with emotion. 'I don't think we should see each other anymore.'

'What?' he said after a stunned pause, he looked hurt and bewildered and I had to look away briefly.

'I don't want to see you anymore,' I said tonelessly, looking somewhere above his head.

'You're joking, right?' he said slowly, his eyes widening.

'No,' I shook my head. 'No... I just think it's for the best.'

'Why?' he burst out. 'Have I done something wrong? Have I upset you... I don't understand -'

I swallowed and thought about the photographs. Forcing the image into my mind... that last one. Jamie with his arms around *her*, his face buried in her hair, her smiling face...

'No,' I said, my voice clearer and harder. 'It's me. I don't want to be tied down... I just don't think it's working.'

'Not working?' he whispered hoarsely, and to my dismay, his eyes filled with tears.

'No.'

'Frankie,' he implored, 'I don't get it, we are working fine... please think about this.'

'I've made up my mind,' I stood up. 'Sorry, Jamie, but you need to go.'

He gazed up at me, his face a picture of confusion.

As I felt my resolve weaken, looking at his face, with his beautiful, *yes they are so beautiful,* eyes and his young unlined face, that I had taken, uncounted times, in my hands as we had made love, *oh, I shall miss that so much,* I began to feel a pulse of anger - and I honed in on that. He had played me, made me lower my guard... the walls that I had, oh so carefully, put up around myself to protect myself from pain and vulnerability... he had broken through that barrier... and then, what had he done? He had done what men do. Cheat, lie, cause heartache...

He stood up too and took a step towards me.

'Frankie,' he said in a low voice. 'I don't know what the fuck has happened here, but please, *please...* think about this.'

I stared mutely at him.

'Frankie,' he continued. 'I think we are good together... we are good for each other... please, don't do this.'

'Sorry,' I said firmly, my voice sounding like it was coming from far away.

'But... but, I love you,' he said, almost pleadingly.

'No, you don't,' I shook my head.

'What the fuck,' he burst out angrily. 'You can't even admit how *you* feel, don't tell me the fuck how I feel,' he suddenly looked furious and I tried not to flinch. 'You... you think it's all about you... you don't think anyone else is afraid of getting hurt? Nah... nah, because, oh, poor Frankie and her big bad ex... let's fucking tiptoe around you... you know what?'

I blinked at him, shocked into silence.

'Fuck you,' he snarled. 'I thought you were worth the hard work, but you ain't. You just used me, and now you're bored... yeah? Is that right? You enjoy your lonely little life, yeah? You've just done me a favour.'

He turned around abruptly and strode out of the room, knocking over a table lamp as he went. I stood, frozen to the spot, realising that he hadn't even slammed the door behind him... I heard his tyres squeal as he pulled away.

It's funny how the mind can blot out certain things, because the next day, all I remembered was crawling into bed and sobbing like my heart was breaking. It wasn't until later that I remembered slowly closing the front door, and sitting on the bottom of my stairs, too shocked and hurt to process what he had yelled at me, and sitting there for a long time. Then I had made a cup of tea, and sat in my dark kitchen, shivering and staring at my mobile phone, waiting... waiting for what? For Jamie to call? I don't know. Then, pouring my undrunk tea down the sink, I had gone upstairs, stripped off and climbed into bed. Then I had allowed myself the luxury of crying. Because, I then knew, I had fallen in love with him. And I was back to square one.

I spent the weekend with Maggie, thankfully she wasn't working. And bless her soul, she was a saint, doing everything to distract me. We went shopping in Cambridge, I spent an absolute fortune - spending away my woes. I must have spent at least £150 on baby clothes alone, along with a beautiful cream-coloured teddy bear, with "My First Bear" on its tummy.

Maggie brought us lunch in a small wine bar, not that I could eat much, or drink, as I was driving.

'Shall we go out tonight?' Maggie asked over her lasagne.

'If you want to,' I shrugged and picked listlessly at my food, then tried to smile, 'I have an entire new wardrobe to show off, eh?'

'Well, eat then,' she admonished, 'or they'll be falling off you next week.'

'I keep feeling sick about facing him at work,' I put my fork down.

'Oh,' she swallowed and put her fork down too. 'I didn't even think of that.'

'I don't want to see him,' I admitted - my throat started to ache. 'It's going to be so awkward. Worse if he just ignores me.'

'Can't you work from home again?'

'No,' I shook my head. 'I was at home all last week, I need to go in. Scott's understanding, but not *that* understanding.'

'Shit,' Maggie looked sympathetic. 'It'll get easier.'

'Yeah,' I sighed and picked up my fork and started pushing my food around my plate again.

Not wanting to spoil Maggie's evening, I decided to get rip-roaring drunk. I knew that I would feel much worse the next day, but I didn't much care.

We met up with some of Maggie's nurse friends, and they turned out to be even wilder than her. The youngest of the bunch, Ellie, cajoled us into going to Coco's Bar - the music bar in town that I normally avoided. It was loud and tacky, the bar staff wore bubble-gum-pink shirts and there were fake palm trees dotted around - in other circumstances I would have felt self-conscious, over-the-hill and way, way out of my comfort zone. However, my level of drunkenness was at a point where I was the first to agree.

Maggie, the man-magnet that she was, was soon talking to a group of guys that turned out to be on a stag-night, and before I knew it, we were sat with them, drinking cocktails and screaming with laughter. As one of them... I believe his name was Ethan, I could be wrong, started chatting me up, I felt a numbness spreading through me. As I tried to focus on his face and hold up my end of the conversation - I started to feel a little nauseous.

'I need some fresh air,' I announced suddenly, and stood up unsteadily. 'Back in a mo,' I called to Maggie, and made my way through the crowds.

The fresh air hit me, as it always does when you've had too much to drink, and I leant against the window, taking deep breaths, my head spinning.

'You alright?' the guy I'd been talking to appeared in front of me.

'Yep,' I wrapped my arms around myself, it was freezing. 'I just wanted some fresh air.'

'Come here,' he put his arms around me. 'You're shivering.'

I stiffened, as drunk as I was, I felt uneasy.

'You want to go somewhere quieter?' he pulled me away from the window slightly and placed a hand on my bum.

'Can you not do that?' I mumbled and moved my head back a fraction to glare at him. As I did that, he suddenly lunged and tried to kiss me.

'Piss off,' I tried to push at his chest, but my co-ordination didn't seem to be working. 'Let go of me,' I said a little louder.

'Oi, mate,' I heard an angry male voice somewhere in front of me; I tried to look over the guy's shoulder.

The next thing I knew, someone had roughly pulled him backwards away from me. I stumbled forward as he let go of me and then I hastily stepped back, as a dark-haired man punched him neatly on his nose, then shoved him heavily to the ground.

'David!' I gasped in shock as I realised who my saviour was.

'What the fuck?' the guy stood up and squared up to David - David aggressively pushed him, his face a picture of fury... even in my inebriated state I was flabbergasted, I had never seen him lose his temper before, let alone punch someone.

'Are you OK, Frankie?' he side-stepped the guy and walked quickly over to me.

'I'm fine,' I said breathlessly.

The guy, possibly deciding it wasn't worth the trouble, stormed back inside, muttering curses, throwing me a look of disgust as he went past.

'Thank you,' I said gratefully, David took off his jacket and handed it to me. 'Oh, crap... David, there's at least ten of his mates in there,' I pulled his jacket on clumsily, by now shivering worse than ever.

'Ah, crap indeed,' he agreed, grinning crookedly. 'Come on, let's go in there,' he gestured to the pub across the road.

He gently took my arm and led me across the road - I had to concentrate hard to walk straight. I glanced up at him, there was something very reassuring about his gentle pressure on my arm and the warmth from his body still lingering in his jacket.

'Oh, no,' I stopped abruptly in the entrance of the pub. 'My bag and jacket's still in there,' I fumbled under his jacket and pulled my phone out from my bra - he looked surprised, then chuckled at me.

Just as I was trying to focus on my screen, my phone started to ring; it was Maggie, sounding a little angry.

'Where the hell are you woman?'

'Oh, I'm in The Rose,' I hiccupped.

'That guy you were talking to said you were chatting outside and some man punched him,' she said, then shushed someone in the background.

'We were *not* chatting,' I said crossly, 'he was groping me, and David punched him. Oh yeah, I'm with David.'

'What?' she said loudly. 'Oh, come outside.'

I pushed my way out the door, David following me, and spotted Maggie stood outside across the road, one hand on her hip. I giggled and waved at her. She hurried over, shaking her head and laughing.

'Hello David,' she grinned at him and then tried to give me a stern look. 'I can't leave you alone for one minute, can I?'

'Sorry,' I swayed a little. 'Maggie, I don't want to go back in there, can you get my bag and jacket for me?'

'Yeah, yeah,' she frowned. 'So, what did that guy do?'

'Tried to kiss me and wouldn't get off,' I looked at David, 'luckily he came along and lumped him one.'

'Right,' she surveyed me for a moment. 'I'll grab your stuff and get the others,' she turned and went back across the road and disappeared into Coco's.

'Come on,' David held open the door. 'Let's get you a drink... a soft drink.'

Five minutes later, Maggie bustled in with the others, my jacket and bag under her arm.

'Well, I sorted him out,' she announced, looking pleased with herself.

'She emptied a jug of margarita over his head,' one of her friends gasped, in between laughter.

'A bit of a waste,' Maggie said. 'But they had paid for it.'

CHAPTER TWENTY

On Monday morning, I walked into the office looking neither left nor right, and sat behind my monitor, finding that my legs felt weak and my heart was beating out of rhythm. As I shrugged myself out of my coat, I dared to glance up - Jamie was on the phone, his left hand tapping a pen on his desk, his expression stony.

Bea wasn't at her desk. I quickly scanned the office for her, before hiding behind my monitor again.

'Morning, Frankie,' Sophie walked past, towards the door. 'Bea rang in sick, she has a chest infection.'

'Oh dear,' I murmured.

I started my work, trying to concentrate, aware of Jamie's presence and his every little movement. As the morning wore on, I started to feel like a Billy-No-Mates, over my side of the office, with no Bea to chat to. I didn't bother to have my tea-break, and continued working, although I sent a text to Bea, asking if she was OK, and if she needed anything.

I felt myself stiffen as Jamie walked past, deep in conversation with Joe, on their way to the coffee machine. I let out a shuddering breath and was irritated to find that my eyes were stinging with tears.

'Hey,' Paul appeared, and he crouched down, his face concerned.

'Hello,' I whispered, trying to get a hold on my emotions.

'I'm taking you out for lunch,' he said firmly. 'I want to talk to you.'

I nodded mutely.

Paul and I sat in the pub around the corner from work, the same one that we had gone to on my birthday. It felt like a century ago.

'Well?'

'Well, what?' I stared into my coffee. 'You've spoken to him, obviously.'

'He came around Saturday afternoon,' Paul sat back and folded his arms, I glanced up at him and he looked slightly annoyed.

'It's like I told him. It was never going to go anywhere. Better to end it now.'

'Nah,' Paul said. 'I'm not buying that. Frankie... look at me... he is *crushed*. The poor bloke is devastated.'

'He'll get over it,' I said in a forced hard voice.

'Yeah, sooner or later,' Paul said lightly, I tried not to wince. 'But right now, he's heartbroken. And so are you... I know you well enough to know *that* much. So, come on, what the hell happened?'

I looked into his tired, kind eyes and was on the verge of telling him - but then pushed that thought away. I didn't want to sound like a victim.

'Nothing,' I shrugged. 'I just decided it was for the best.'

'OK,' he looked exasperated. 'Have it your way, but Frankie, I'm telling you... You're a fool.'

'You've got that much right,' I muttered.

The afternoon dragged on. I kept thinking about what Paul had said - Jamie must have been upset, to pour his heart out, but why? He either had another woman on the go, or she was a one off... either way, he couldn't be *that* serious about me.

A headache started to nudge me above my left eye as I went around in circles in my head. I was so confused, torn between feeling heartbroken and sad, missing him already, and bubbling anger that he had betrayed me, fed me lies and acted so sincere about me. I kept picturing his face, bewildered and hurt, as he said, '*but, I love you.*'

As I stared unseeingly across the office, lost in thought, I came to slightly and realised that Jamie was watching me... maybe lost in his own thoughts... we gazed at each other for maybe three seconds and both looked away. I couldn't decide what his expression was, and I had no idea what my face was telling him. Feeling flustered, I forced myself to concentrate on my work.

At home time, I waited until everyone had left the office before getting ready to leave. As I went outside into the dark and windy carpark, I saw Jamie was still there, standing by his car, talking to Paul. They both glanced up as I walked to my car. I saw out of the corner of my eye Paul walking away, and on impulse, I called Jamie's name.

'What?' he said, somewhat aggressively, looking up as I walked towards him.

'I just wanted to say something,' I faltered as I reached him, his demeanour wasn't exactly friendly.

'Make it quick,' he said gruffly. 'I'm in a hurry.'

'Jamie,' I said as steadily as I could. 'I just wanted to see if you're OK... and I wanted to say sorry... you know... I would hate it if we never spoke again.'

'You're sorry,' he said, more to himself than me. 'Yeah, Frankie,' he said loudly. 'I'm great. I get dumped with no warning or proper reason, and then just left to get on with it. I am *fantastic*, couldn't be happier.'

'Please don't be like this,' I pleaded, close to tears again. 'It's not like we were serious... or exclusive,' I added.

'No,' he narrowed his eyes. 'We were whatever you said we were, wasn't we? So basically, I was your dirty little secret.'

'No,' I said defensively. 'It wasn't like that. It just wasn't realistic... come on, you know it wasn't.'

'Whatever you say,' he said coldly... his eyes were telling a different story though, even in the dim light. They were full of pain.

'Look,' I stood a little straighter. 'I just think we could be more adult and maybe be friends again at some point.'

He didn't say anything for a moment, and I continued to look at him. I wasn't even sure why I was asking him this - I was still unbelievably angry and disappointed. But, we had to work in the same office and it was in my nature not to hold grudges. As I waited for a response, I thought how thankful I was that I hadn't realised that I loved him and done something stupid, like telling him.

'Yeah,' he said eventually. 'Maybe.'

'Right,' I attempted a smile. 'OK, well... good.'

'Was that all?' he asked politely.

'Yeah.'

'OK. See you, then.'

And he climbed into his car.

I drove to pick Gracie up, feeling flat. *You're pathetic*, I told myself. *Worrying about how he feels... why can't you just toughen up?*

I turned my mind to David. Why couldn't I have just fallen for him again? It would have made everything so much easier.

On Saturday evening, he ended up staying in the pub with us, even though he had been on his way home when he had spotted me in trouble. All the girls had thought he was lovely, and after he had left, and Maggie had confided he was an old flame of mine, they all declared me mad.

At the time, I had thought this to be quite funny... but later on, back at Maggie's, I had mulled that over. He *was* lovely, in his own way. I wondered what I would think of him if I had just met him for the first time. On Sunday morning, I had rung him to thank him once again for rescuing me, and ended up agreeing to have dinner with him, the weekend after next, when Robert had Gracie again. I felt like I should be taking *him* out, we argued back and forth, until we settled on me going over to his flat for a meal… which still felt unfair on him. I was on the verge of saying I would cook him a meal at mine, but an image of Jamie swam in front of my eyes, and it just felt wrong having David in my home.

I couldn't wait until the weekend. Not that I had anything planned, but work was becoming slow torture. Jamie had defrosted a little, to the point of giving me a kind of nod in acknowledgement in the mornings, but he was yet to smile at me. It was all very depressing. The worse thing was just having to see him every day… how was I supposed to get over him? I idly thought about job-hunting, but then I felt a flutter of panic at the thought of *not* seeing him. I felt completely stuck.

I'd lay in bed at night, feeling sad, feeling furious… *why, why, why did you have to go and do that Jamie?* I had initially kept looking at the photographs, eventually I had forced myself to rip them up, into the tiniest pieces I could, and threw them away.

It was extremely difficult to not fall into the trap of self-loathing and self-pity, as I had with Robert, but every now and then, I'd hear that sly hateful voice. *It must be you, there must be something wrong with you.*

I hid this from Maggie, I didn't want lectures, or pity. Instead, I tried convincing myself that I didn't *really* love Jamie. He had just filled a gap in my life, and I had got used to the attention and sex. But I knew deep down that wasn't true.

Robert had dropped Gracie off at the usual time Friday evening, and I thought she seemed a little subdued for her.

As I was tucking her up in bed, she suddenly asked, 'Mummy, why hasn't Jamie been over?'

'He's just been busy,' I said casually, avoiding her gaze.

'Daddy was asking if I had seen him,' she said.

'Was he now?' I replied, my mind racing. 'What did you tell him?'

'I told him that I hadn't,' she said, twisting Yellow Bunny's ears around her fingers.

'Right,' I kissed her forehead and started to get up.

'Mummy,' Gracie frowned a little, like she was thinking, 'do you still like Jamie?'

'Of course I do,' I suddenly felt distinctly uneasy. 'Why? What else did Daddy say?'

'Nothing,' she said quietly, and pulled her duvet up to her chin.

'OK,' I said as cheerfully as I could. 'Goodnight sweetie.'

'Goodnight.'

As I made my way downstairs, I felt a surge of hatred towards Robert. I couldn't blame him for Jamie's actions, and maybe one could say he had done me a favour in the long-run, sending me the damning evidence… but to question Gracie to see what damage he had done? *Bastard*, I thought bitterly.

Maggie was working that weekend, and without her, I was determined as ever to fill every minute to avoid moping.

On Saturday morning, I took Gracie ice-skating, then to visit Will and Lennie - they proudly showed me the baby's scan image, they *hadn't* asked for the sex, then to lunch at Burger King, then we went to visit Bea.

She was feeling a lot better, she said, and Gracie had a wonderful afternoon playing with Prudence, Bea's Norwich Terrier. I told her a very edited version of the news that Jamie and I had broken up, she was very disappointed.

'Well,' she had said looking a little sad. 'If that is how you feel, it's probably the sensible thing to do.'

CHAPTER TWENTY-ONE

I did something very, very stupid...

I wasn't sure if I was looking forward to seeing David on Friday night or not, but it seemed better than staying home and feeling sorry for myself, and I had already been feeling sorry for myself *a lot.* I had got into the habit of having a couple of glasses of wine after Gracie had gone to bed; I found that it helped me go to sleep quicker - not an ideal method, but when you're in the midst of misery and heartbreak, *anything* is better than lying awake in the lonely and bleak early hours of the morning.

As I was leaving work on Friday afternoon, I was jolted to hear Jamie talking to Louise and Sophie as they walked out in front of me, arranging to meet up in town later. Louise had glanced behind at me and smiled - what I imagined to be a smug smile. I had kept my expression blank, as I had uncharacteristic thoughts of slapping her face. I watched Jamie as he amiably chatted away, wondering if it was for my benefit. As I decided it probably was, I felt a strange combination of anger and relief. *Two can play at that game,* I thought.

'What are you up to this weekend?' I asked Bea, as she caught up with me. I quickened my pace, so we were only a few steps behind Jamie.

'I'm going to Annabel's for the weekend,' she told me happily - Annabel being one of her daughters who lived a few miles away. 'It's her thirtieth birthday.'

'Lovely,' I said, still watching Jamie.

'What about you?' she asked.

'I've got a dinner date tonight,' I said lightly. 'And the rest of the weekend, who knows? I'm Gracie-free.'

'I see,' she glanced side-ways at me.

As we reached the carpark, and Jamie waved at Louise and Sophie before jogging over to his car, Bea put her hand on my arm.

'*Have* you got a date tonight?' she asked said in a low voice.

'Yes!' I exclaimed.

'Well, that's nice my dear,' she said. 'But if that was for young Jamie's benefit, don't play games.'

I felt a drop of shame but shook it off... she didn't know the facts. 'It wasn't,' I feigned a puzzled frown.

As I pulled up on my drive, 'Ho Hey' by The Lumineers came on the radio. It had been Will and Lennie's song for their first dance at their wedding. Initially, I had thought what a strange song choice; it's not your classic love song. But as I had listened to the words, watching them wrapped up in each other's arms, Will gazing down at her smiling face, like they were the only two people in the room, I had thought: how perfect.

As I smiled at the memory, and got as far as the line, 'I don't know where I went wrong,' I burst into noisy tears. I switched off the engine and sat, staring unseeingly in front of me, gut-wrenching sobs shaking my entire body. *It's not fair,* I thought in complete desolation. *Why can't I have my happy ending? Am I that unlovable? Why does everything have to hurt so much?*

I have no idea how long I sat there, but eventually, I pulled myself together with painful effort. Wiping my face and taking deep breaths, I got out of my car, trying to concentrate on my upcoming evening.

Before I had even taken my coat off, I poured myself a quadruple gin, and downed half of it. As it warmed my stomach and I felt the blessed first rush of alcohol, straight to my head but numbing my senses, I felt calmer.

I lay in the bath twenty minutes later, on my second drink, telling myself that I was going to have a lovely evening - a distraction that I needed - with a man that was good company.

One step at a time, I told myself. I was lucky *really*: I had friends that cared, a job that I loved, a beautiful daughter... I was going to be OK. I had survived worse.

As I sat in my towel, applying my make-up, I realised that I was getting drunk. *It doesn't matter... it's numbing that awful pain, isn't it?* I got dressed, having chosen a simple deep-purple dress that was neither too dressy or seductive, deciding that I could get away with another drink, as I was eating later.

Having originally planned on driving to David's, I ordered a taxi. At least I could drink as much as I wanted at his; I hated being a killjoy when I had to drive.

Just before eight o'clock, the taxi pulled up at David's, I gazed up at the building - it was on the outskirts of Fernberry, in an area I wasn't particularly familiar with. It was clearly a new-build, very modern without much personality. I paid and thanked the taxi driver, and climbed out, a little clumsily, pulling my jacket and scarf around me in the freezing wind. I tottered up to the double doors, and after locating the number nine, pressed the button and waited.

'Frankie? Hello, I'm on the second floor,' David's voice came through the intercom, a buzzing noise sounded, and I pushed the heavy door open. It was warm but not especially welcoming inside the entrance. A row of numbered mail lock-ups were along one wall, next to a large plastic plant in a black pot. There were some stairs to the left and lifts visible through a glass door straight ahead. I opted for the stairs, and clambered up, my high heels echoing eerily.

As I reached the grey-carpeted landing, I had to push my way through three fire doors until I reached the dark oak door with a brass number nine on it.

'Hi,' David answered almost straight away when I knocked.

'Hello,' I walked in as he stood back, and looked around.

'You look nice,' he led me in the living room, which was huge and minimalist.

'Thanks,' I brought my attention back to him, he looked happy to see me, casually dressed in dark jeans and a teal blue shirt with the sleeves rolled up. As he leaned forward and kissed my cheek, I realised that I had left the bottle of wine I was supposed to bring on the hall table.

'Oh, damn,' I said, 'I'm sorry, I left my wine at home.'

'Never mind,' he took my coat from me. 'I've got loads, come and choose one.'

I followed him into his kitchen, it was extremely clean and tidy and looked brand new. Something was simmering away on the hob.

'Here,' he indicated to a built-in wine rack next to his silver American fridge, complete with ice dispenser. He did indeed have an impressive selection of wines. 'Do you want a drink now? A gin?'

'Sure, yeah thank you,' I pulled out a bottle of red at random and squinted at the label, trying to read it without my glasses and feeling half-cut already wasn't easy.

'Good choice,' he looked over my shoulder. 'I'm cooking beef bourguignon, Bordeaux is excellent with that.'

'Great,' I suppressed a giggle, he was so endearingly pompous. 'Thanks,' I took my glass of gin and tonic from him and went over to the hob to have a look.

'How are you, then?' he took down some wine glasses and placed them next to the bottle.

'Yeah, I'm good,' I lied. 'How are you? How's Harry?'

'I'm pretty good, Harry is... Harry,' he chuckled. 'Me and Jen, his mum, are arguing about Christmas already,' he came over and stirred his beef and glanced over at me. 'Never easy is it?'

'We are yet to have that conversation,' I wrinkled my nose. 'It was a fiasco last year, I'm seriously considering just flying off somewhere last minute, and staying there until the New Year, but Gracie really loves all the traditional stuff. I seriously cannot be bothered with it,' as I said that, I felt a powerful aching sadness wash over me.

'Book us a couple of tickets,' he said jokingly.

I attempted a smile, then wandered away to look around, 'Nice place you've got,' I went back into the living room.

'Thanks,' he followed me, looking pleased. 'Still doesn't feel like home yet, got boxes I need to unpack. By the way, do you mind eating in the kitchen? I haven't got around to buying a dining table yet, although it seems pointless as it's usually just me and Harry.'

'No, not at all,' I said over my shoulder as I went over to the hall to peek in the bathroom. A door to the right was slightly ajar, a light was shining dimly in there.

'Harry's room, slash, office,' David said, as I poked my head in.

There was a bed in the far corner, covered with a navy and white striped duvet, with a large grey teddy perched on the pillows, and a white bedside table, with a desk lamp and books stacked neatly on top. Under the window there was a large desk, with a computer monitor, a few folders and three or four mobile phones - one of them in bits, and some small tools spread out next to it, all under a very bright lamp.

'My little side-line,' he explained as I looked at him. 'I've started repairing broken phone screens, quite a profitable business, as most places charge an arm and a leg.'

'I see,' I stepped in and looked down. 'I'll keep that in mind, I've cracked two screens so far.'

'Come on,' he tugged me away. 'Let's check on dinner,' he seemed a little uncomfortable... I supposed it was because it was the untidiest room in his flat, David had always been a complete neat-freak.

'Smells lovely,' I followed him out, he stood back so I could proceed him, then shut the door behind us.

Dinner was superb, but after another gin and tonic, and a few glasses of wine with our meal, I felt decidedly pissed. But at least I wasn't feeling as depressed.

'Gosh, I forgot how well you cooked,' I put my knife and fork together.

'Glad you enjoyed,' David refilled my glass, looking pleased at my compliment.

In my haze, I studied him, his intense dark eyes, rather boyish features and his dark hair - I wished that I felt something other than just friendship towards him.

'Shall I open another bottle, or do you fancy something else?' he asked as he started picking up our plates.

'Oh, you decide,' I started to help him, but he put his hands on my shoulders.

'Oh no, you don't,' he pushed me gently away. 'Go and make yourself comfortable, it'll take me two seconds to put this in the dishwasher.'

'OK,' I shrugged and went and collapsed on the nearest sofa, rubbing my stomach. 'I'm stuffed.'

'Then I did a good job,' he called back.

'I'll have to order my taxi pretty soon,' I glanced at the time, it was nearly eleven, I knew I'd probably have trouble getting one on a Friday night.

'Sure,' he appeared in the doorway holding two glasses. 'Cognac?'

'Thank you,' I took the glass, although thinking that the last thing I needed was another drink.

'Thank you for coming tonight,' he came and sat next to me and did his throat-clearing thing: one big one, two littles ones and another big one. I looked down at my glass, smiling. 'I'm so glad that we've become friends again.'

Have we? I thought. I didn't really know how to respond, so I looked back up and nodded at him.

'Robert's a fool,' he shook his head, his eyes wandering over my face. 'You haven't aged one bit. Still as beautiful as ever.'

'Oh, stop,' I giggled. 'And Robert's a bastard. Much better word.'

'Frankie,' he said in surprise, and laughed, 'you shock me. OK, yes, he's a bastard.'

'Life goes on, huh?' I sipped my drink, and sighed, snuggling back into the sofa. I felt terribly sleepy.

'Yes,' he sat back too and took my hand, squeezed it, then let go again. 'Don't you ever wonder-' he began hesitantly.

'Of course,' I turned my head to look at him. 'But you can't change the past.'

'No,' he smiled, his eyes thoughtful. '*I* would never have cheated on you, or hurt you,' he looked sad. 'You know that, right?'

'Yeah,' I patted his leg. 'I know. I was an idiot.'

'Perhaps it was me,' he shrugged. 'You weren't happy, else you wouldn't have... you know.'

'Oh, David,' I leant my head on his shoulder for a moment, then turned a little in my seat to face him. 'Let's not spoil a lovely evening by raking it all up... please?'

'No, sorry,' he frowned, then smiled at me. 'It's just sometimes, you think about things, when you're on your own.'

'Oh God, yes you do,' I agreed, and he laughed. 'You know,' I confided, 'quite recently I was kind of seeing someone, and he was just giving me the run-around. I've had some very dark thoughts about whether it's all worth it, relationships,' I wasn't sure why I told him that, but I suddenly felt like a little weight had been lifted. Not all of it, but drink-fuelled as I was, I felt a tiny bit better.

'Really?' he raised an eyebrow. 'Another fool. What happened?'

'He was just full of crap,' I considered spilling my guts, but reeled it in. 'You know what? It doesn't matter, it really doesn't.'

'Being single does have its advantages,' he said musingly.

'Like what?' I asked playfully.

'Bed space,' he chuckled. 'Exclusiveness to the duvet... you were always a terrible duvet hogger.'

'I was not,' I giggled.

'Bathroom time,' he continued. 'Now, you can't deny hogging the bathroom.'

'Well...'

'Pinching my razor?' he nudged me. 'Sneaking my favourite, special chocolate biscuits from my not very secret hiding place?'

'I didn't know you knew,' I burst out laughing.

'Well, I used to buy extra, so you didn't feel bad,' he confessed, then started to laugh too.

'I forgot about that,' I hiccupped and smiled in memory.

'Another drink?' he pushed himself up.

'Oh, go on, last one,' I sat back again, realising I was having fun. *Fuck you, Jamie,* I thought, *I hope you're enjoying what must be a very sophisticated evening with those two silly girls.*

'There you go,' David returned with our drinks and sat back down.

'So, what about you?' I asked. 'Any love interests?'

'No,' he put his hands behind his head and stretched his legs out. 'Last January I was very casually seeing a woman, someone from work. But, she left and moved a few miles away. I decided I didn't like her enough really to make the effort of travelling.'

'Fair enough,' I sipped my drink, deciding I was going to feel like death in the morning. I glanced at my watch, it was creeping up to midnight.

'So, what's new with Maggie?' he asked.

I filled him in with her latest love-life, he was soon roaring with laughter.

'I always loved that woman,' he said. 'She's one in a million.'

'Yeah, she is,' I agreed, looking at my watch again.

'Bloody hell,' David exclaimed. 'You're never going to get a cab, I'm a little over the limit to drive you.'

'A little?' I giggled, I got up to use the toilet, feeling very unsteady on my feet.

'Listen,' he said, on my return. 'Kip here, I don't mind sleeping in Harry's bed.'

'Oh, no,' I argued as I plopped myself back down. 'I couldn't kick you out of your bed.'

'You're saying that you wouldn't kick me out of bed?' he teased, then patted my leg as he stood up. 'I think we need coffee.'

'Yeah,' I agreed. I rubbed my eyes and sat up a little straighter.

'I've made it strong,' he came back, handing me a mug. I thanked him and put it on the floor.

'I've had such a nice time tonight,' I told him, linking my arm through his. 'We should have done this sooner.'

'Yeah,' he agreed, and kissed the top of my head.

We sat in silence for a moment, I felt extremely comfortable, I could have quite happily of fallen asleep.

'I'll go and find you a T-shirt or something to sleep in,' he said eventually.

'You sure you don't mind?' I asked sleepily. I sat up and reached for my coffee, I really wanted to sober up a bit before I went to sleep.

'Of course not,' he assured me.

I put my coffee back down and looked at him. He stared back. I could see such affection in his eyes. On impulse, I put my arms around him and kissed him. My mind was strangely blank, but it felt *nice.*

Without any hesitation, he began to kiss me back, and not really caring about what can of worms I was opening, I started to pull him down towards me. I felt a numbness, a bitter-sweet comfort… but not one drop of arousal.

'Oh, Frankie,' he murmured, his hands starting to wander everywhere, his breath quickening. He suddenly pushed himself up, and pulled me up by my hand, and then scooping me up in his arms, he carried me to bed.

CHAPTER TWENTY-TWO

'You can't avoid him forever.'

'I know, I know.'

I was sat cross-legged on Maggie's sofa the following afternoon, hugging a cushion, occasionally dipping my hand into the bowl of popcorn that sat in between us.

'Was it good?' she asked curiously.

'It wasn't good or bad,' I stared miserably into space. 'It wasn't *anything.*'

The worst part, after David and I had done the deed, was that he was so pleased with himself and happy. And the awful truth was, I had felt nothing at all. Apart from the fact I was drunk, I felt no pleasure, no emotion... nothing.

'I forgot how good you were,' he had murmured huskily afterwards, hugging me close.

I didn't reply, I wasn't sure how he could have deemed my performance as "good". My participation had been minimal. At one point I remembered admiring his lightshade and had wondered where he had got it from.

'Just ring the poor bloke,' Maggie's insistent voice brought me back to the present.

'I will,' I said grumpily. 'I've already texted him. Told him I would call him later,' I threw my head back and closed my eyes. 'Shit.'

'It *is* kind of funny though,' Maggie threw a bit of popcorn at my face, making me jump. I opened my eyes again and stared at her in disbelief. 'OK, maybe not,' she demurred.

'It's not funny, not one bit,' I covered my face with the cushion. 'Why? Why did I do it?' I mumbled.

Guilt was gnawing away at my stomach. Guilt at leading David on, and guilt towards Jamie - which was just plain idiotic.

I had fallen asleep... or passed out... fairly quickly, and had woken up with a jump, just as the early morning light was filtering through the curtains, to find David staring at me in joyful contentment. I sincerely hoped that my face didn't reflect the growing horror that I felt as my brain started to piece together the evenings events.

I had slid out of bed, trying to conceal as much of my nakedness as possible, and pinched his towelling robe, which thankfully was slung over a chair nearby, and escaped to the bathroom. When I had finally crept out, David was whistling cheerfully in the kitchen, making tea, like it was the most normal thing in the world.

As I perched on a kitchen stool, listening to him chatter away, my head had started to fill with panic, the only thing on my mind was escape. I had passed my quietness off as a hangover and after drinking my tea, and throwing on my clothes, I had somewhat sheepishly asked for a lift home. He had dropped me home, telling me how much he had enjoyed the night before, and asked if we could see each other later, to which I had replied we could. Coward.

'I'm going to suggest we meet for a drink, and tell him tonight,' I said as quickly as I decided it. 'Get it over and done with.'

'You really don't think it's worth giving it a go?' Maggie asked, looking thoughtful.

'No,' I said sadly. 'I just don't *feel it*... he's very lovely and all that, but no. I wish that I did like him that way. Oh God,' I groaned again. 'I'm such a slut.'

'You are not,' Maggie went into peals of laughter. 'Jesus, Frankie. What does that make me?'

'At least you fancy the guys you sleep with,' I countered. 'I did a terrible, terrible thing. It would never have got that far if I hadn't had drank so much.'

'Well, let's hope he's not too heartbroken.'

'Maggie,' I suddenly remembered Debs words. 'Would you have ever called David *obsessional*... when we were together?'

'Where did that come from?' Maggie gave me a surprised look. 'No... not really.'

'It's just something Debs said,' I muttered, and then shrugged it off. 'I better go and sort myself out,' I pushed myself up.

'Don't make yourself look too beautiful,' Maggie followed me to the kitchen as I fetched my coat. 'And do not, I repeat, do not drink too much.'

'I'm never drinking again,' I shuddered.

I rang David when I got home and arranged to meet him at the closest pub to his flat that I could think of. I decided that if I was going to come clean about how I really felt, and disappoint him, I didn't want to make him go far - but after I ended the call, I decided on reflection he might assume that I chose a pub nearby to him wanting a repeat performance of the night before.

I didn't even bother getting changed out of my jeans and jumper, and only minimally touched up my make-up and sprayed on some perfume out of habit. I dragged my heels, aware that I was going to be late; I really didn't want to go.

David was sat at the bar when I arrived, drinking a whisky and scrolling through his mobile phone.

'Hello,' he stood up as he saw me approaching, and leant forward to give me a kiss.

'Hi,' I tried to smile naturally and sound breezy.

'I hope you don't mind, I ordered us some food,' he snaked his arm around my waist. 'I know you love Mexican, they do a mean burrito here.'

'Oh,' I inwardly sighed, then remembered with a pang that the last time I ate Mexican was with Jamie at Paul's house. 'Sure, lovely, thanks.'

'I'll get you a drink,' he ploughed on. 'Gin?'

'Um, no,' I felt a wave of irrational irritation. 'Just a coke, please.'

'Still suffering?' he chuckled and squeezed my waist. 'Go and sit down, I'll bring it over.'

This wasn't going to plan.

'There we go,' he said a few minutes later, and sat down next to me, then grabbed my hand and kissed the back of it. 'I've been thinking about you all day,' he gazed soulfully into my eyes.

Not knowing how to respond, I smiled, probably somewhat wanly.

'Frankie,' he cleared his throat, one big one and two little ones, then a big one again, I cringed inwardly, then felt like the worse person in the world... last night I found his little ways endearing, one night of sex and he was bugging the life out of me. *I must be a man,* I thought, trying to find my humour, 'last night,' he continued, 'was wonderful. I never thought that I would be lucky enough to have you in my life again. Let alone, you know,' he smirked, 'have that beautiful body of yours again. Thank you for coming back into my life.'

Oh, fuck and shit, I thought.

'David,' I steeled myself, then as I tried to find the right words, a smiling barmaid appeared with two plates of food.

'Thank you,' he said to her, at least shifting over a few inches so I had some elbow room. 'Looks lovely.'

'Hmm,' I wasn't remotely hungry, but tucked in to delay conversation, and give myself time to think.

'What have you done with yourself today, then?' he asked, watching me.

'Went to see Maggie for a bit,' I swallowed too quickly and began to cough, he patted me on the back.

'Did you tell her our news?' he grinned.

'Well,' I hedged, not really sure what "our news" was, 'she knows I spent the night at yours.'

'Mmm,' he put his hand on my leg and started caressing. 'And what a night it was, eh?'

'Yeah,' I said weakly. *Is he stupid?* I thought, *can he not see I am not falling into his arms.*

'I've been smiling all day,' he started to dissect his burrito. 'I'm just so happy.'

I ate what I could, and apologised after putting my knife and fork together, 'I'm still feeling delicate,' I said.

'You always did get the worst hangovers,' he said affectionately. 'Remember that party in Hoxton we went to? You drank so much champagne you were in bed for two days.'

'Yeah,' I said, smiling briefly. 'Listen, David -'

My mobile started to ring, 'It's Robert,' I said, 'I'll have to get it, it might be Gracie -' I answered it, feeling both annoyed and relieved at the interruption.

'Frankie, listen, I need you to come here,' Robert said, sounding harried, 'my dad, he's been rushed into hospital… Gracie's fast asleep -'

'Yes, yes, of course,' I stood up. 'Is he OK? I'll be five minutes.'

'I don't know,' Robert said hoarsely. 'Thank you, Frankie, thank you.'

David was looking up at me.

'I'm really sorry,' I pulled on my jacket. 'Robert's dad's been taken into hospital, I have to go and look after Gracie,' I explained.

'Yes, yes of course you do,' he stood up too, his face quite expressionless.

As I drove down the dark country lanes towards Robert's house, I started to feel uneasy - I hadn't even been near the village since the day I had left him. As I pulled up on his driveway, he opened the front door, looking both pale and panicked.

'Hello, thank you,' he briefly squeezed my shoulder. 'She's fast asleep, I'll ring you, help yourself to anything you want,' he jogged over to his car and climbed in without a backward glance.

I watched him reverse out of the drive, his tyres crunching on the gravel, then slowly closed the front door. I don't know what I was expecting, but it looked exactly the same - the same black and white tiled floor in the large hallway, the plush cream carpet on the stairs, winding up with the glossy oak banister. I remembered how impressed I had been, the first time I had been here… well after we had made frantic love in the darkened living room, on his huge, soft leather sofa.

I pulled off my boots and left them next to the hall table and hung my jacket and bag on the newel post, before going upstairs to check on Gracie. Her room still looked the same too, apart from the addition of some new toys and a television on her white wooden bookcase. She was curled up on her side, looking lost under her big squashy duvet, Yellow Bunny under her arm. I went and turned her lamp off, before backing out of the room, leaving her door open a couple of inches.

I glanced over at our bedroom door, *no, not ours anymore, his,* and drifted over, not sure why my heart was beating so fast. I reached around the wall and switched on the light and stood hesitantly in the doorway. Nothing had changed, the king-size bed, the fluffy light blue carpet and the thick blue curtains, tied back to reveal a window seat. How often had I sat there, gazing out into the back garden, feeling sad, feeling lost? Feeling like an intruder, I switched the light off again and went downstairs. Not knowing what else to do, I went into the kitchen to make a drink.

One of the things I had missed the most about Robert's house was the kitchen. It had been *my* kitchen. When I first met him, I had playfully expressed my distaste of the out-dated light pine cupboards and beige-tiled surfaces, and when I had moved in, he had given me a free rein to do what I wanted to it. After endless searching and browsing I had chosen beautiful glossy, black marble work surfaces and white cupboards, filling it lovingly with potted herbs and all the little touches that made it mine.

I glanced at the stainless-steel range - it needed a proper clean, I thought absently. I went over to the window and pulled down the blind, noticing a framed photograph of Gracie and Robert on the sill, on what looked like a pier. Robert was crouching down, eyes narrowed against the sun and smiling his big smile, Gracie with her arms around his neck, wearing a yellow and white spotted sundress.

How can a man so handsome be such a bastard? I thought to myself. Turning away, I switched on the kettle and automatically reached to the cupboard above to get a mug. With my tea made, I went to fetch my mobile phone from my bag and wandered into the living room. The television was on; Robert had been watching some action film. A glass of whisky was on the side table, next to his reading glasses and a James Herbert book.

Restless and twitchy, I went over to the sliding patio doors at the far end of the room and gazed out. The patio was lit up by the lights that were sunken into the low wall that ran around it, I reached without looking to the switches to the left of the doors to turn them out, thinking what a waste of electricity.

It was so *strange,* being back in the house that had been my home for such a long time, everything so familiar, yet different somehow. I walked over to the marble fireplace to look at the framed photographs. There was the one of Gracie as a baby that had always been there, and Robert's parents, taken at our wedding. I was surprised to see one of Will - that hadn't been there before. I picked it up to examine it. Will must have been around sixteen, I guessed, standing on a log in some woods by the look of it, smiling at the camera with a baseball cap on backwards. I wondered how Robert felt when he looked at it. The photo next to it was of Robert's brother, Phillip, with his wife and two sons, now living in New Zealand.

I checked the time; it was gone ten o'clock. Deciding I might as well make myself comfortable, I curled up on the sofa and flicked through the television channels until I found some Julia Roberts film, and soon lost myself in that, trying not consult my watch every five minutes.

I was just starting to doze off, when I heard Robert letting himself in. I sat up and blearily looked at my watch - it was nearly midnight.

'Frankie?' he called and appeared in the doorway, looking shattered.

'Is your dad OK?' I stood up as he wandered over, then sat down again as he wearily sat on the other side of the sofa.

'Mini heart attack,' he said, rubbing his eyes with the heel of his hands.

'Oh no,' I was surprised that I felt sorry for him. He wasn't the kind to show emotion, but he looked upset and exhausted. 'What happened? Will he be OK?'

I won't pretend that I liked his father. Benjamin Quinn was an impatient, sour-natured and cold man, highly successful and seemingly driven by the desire to bully anyone in his way into submission.

'Yeah, he just needs to be kept in for a day or two,' Robert seemed to give himself a mental shake, and his voice changed to matter-of-fact. 'He's been short of breath, my mum said. Then earlier, he just couldn't get up, so she called an ambulance. He was mad as hell,' he smiled a little.

'I can imagine,' I said. 'Are *you* OK?' I hated asking, but it seemed the polite thing to do. He turned his head and looked at me, frowning, 'I'm fine,' he closed his eyes briefly. 'Just a bit of a shock, you know, seeing him in a hospital bed.'

'Yeah,' I said softly - then to my surprise and discomfort, his eyes filled with tears. 'Oh,' I reached over and touched his arm. 'He'll be OK, he's a tough old git.'

'He looked so frail, Frankie,' Robert looked down, shaking his head, as if in disbelief. 'I forget how old he is; he's such a cantankerous bastard, always on top of things.'

'Yeah,' I didn't know what to say. Reluctantly, I shifted over and put my arms around him and rubbed his back, very much in the way I did to Gracie when she was upset.

'Is Gracie alright?' he mumbled. 'Did she wake up?'

'No, and she's fine,' I said.

We sat like that for a minute or two in silence, then I withdrew my arms, 'I better go, it's late.'

'Don't go yet,' he blinked rapidly, then looked up at me. 'Just stay and chat for a while.' I looked into his dark blue eyes that used to melt my heart so much, feeling out of sorts. I could handle Robert when he was his usual tricky self, not this vulnerable version.

'OK,' I agreed quietly, and went to move away, but he stopped me, gently tugging my arm.

'Please, just hold me again,' he murmured, and drew me towards him.

Sighing, I closed my eyes, resting my cheek against his head, breathing in his familiar aftershave. Randomly, Jamie's face swam before my eyes, and I began to feel an awful lonely ache.

'I do miss you sometimes,' Robert said in a low voice.

'You don't mean that,' I said in a deliberately brisk voice. 'Come on, you're just upset about your dad.'

'I do though,' he insisted. 'There will never be another you.'

'Uh huh,' I smiled grimly. 'Well, we are in the past now, no point in thinking that.'

'I know,' he gave a little shrug and I was suddenly aware of his thumb tracing small circles on my back.

'Right,' I pulled away. 'Shall I make a cup of tea?'

Without any warning, he put his hands either side of my face, and kissed me.

'Robert,' I whispered in shock. 'No -' but he started to kiss me again, and I, with no idea what was going through my head, started to kiss him back. He was such a good kisser, I'd forgotten how good... he started to gently push me back, until he was on top of me, and I felt myself beginning to respond in earnest, arching towards him... I was full of sadness, and yearning and then... *no, no, no... this doesn't feel right...*

'Robert, no, stop,' I said angrily. 'Please, stop,' I pushed him away and tried to sit up. He looked down at me, he looked almost bewildered, then he pushed himself up. I quickly scrambled up onto my feet and stared at him, feeling shocked.

'I need to go,' I said numbly.

'Sorry, Frankie,' he ran his hands through his hair. 'I don't know what... I'm sorry. It's just you being here, in our house -'

So used to his clever little games, I wasn't entirely convinced by his seemingly sincere apology, and underneath my shock I was unbelievably angry with myself.

'It's not *ours* though, not any more,' I said, and sat down again. 'I *am* really sorry about your dad. I hope he's OK soon.'

'Thank you,' he nodded at the floor. 'Before you go, can I ask you something?'

'What?' I asked warily.

'Do you ever miss me?'

'I did,' I said shortly. 'But you did terrible things, Robert. That's why I left.'

'It wasn't what you thought it was,' he said quietly. '*She* spun herself a bit of a story. But of course, everyone would believe her.'

'What do you mean?' I said, my heart starting to pound.

'It doesn't matter now, does it?' he said in a harder voice, sounding more like his usual self again.

I stared at him, deciding he was just trying to draw me into something, and I was too tired and emotionally drained to play games.

'I'm going to go,' I got up and he followed me out to the hall, watching me as I pulled my boots on and shrugged on my jacket.

'Well, thanks for coming to the rescue,' he smiled sardonically. 'I will see you when I bring Gracie back.'

'Yep,' I opened the door. 'See you, then.'

As I backed out of his drive, Robert watching me from the doorway, the bright hall light spilling around him, I finally felt like I could breathe properly again.

You stupid, stupid, weak woman, I berated myself furiously.

CHAPTER TWENTY-THREE

I woke up with a start early the following morning, having had disturbing dreams about dark-haired men - whether they were Jamie or Robert, or both, or neither, I don't know, and the memory started to fade in the annoying way dreams usually do.

Maggie was coming over at lunchtime for news about my evening with David and I baulked at the thought of telling her what had actually happened. I considered heavily editing my story, but I felt so sick and full of shame, I had to get it off my chest.

I tried to busy myself all morning with some work, but my laptop was lagging again - I made a mental note to phone around the next day, as Paul's friend clearly hadn't done a good job - but I couldn't shake off the memory of Robert and I, and kept going cold.

I reluctantly rang David, apologising again and vaguely said I would see him in the week, if I could, which started me thinking about how I was going to tell him that me and him wasn't going to happen. Then, as I gave up trying to work, my mind turned to Jamie, and I felt a horrible weight of hopelessness engulf me. *You're just one big hot mess, ain't you Frankie?* I told myself bitterly.

Maggie turned up just after twelve, predictably armed with wine, and looking expectant.

'So?' she asked, before she'd even got as far as the living room.

'Let me pour a drink first,' I sighed, as she followed me to the kitchen and settled herself at the table.

I sat down and shoved my laptop out of the way, took one look at her face and promptly burst into tears.

'Oh, no,' she said, her face falling. 'Was it that bad? Whatever is wrong?'

'Oh, it's worse than that, but not because of David. I had to leave, Robert's dad was taken to hospital, so I had to watch Gracie,' I felt my cheeks colouring.

'Why? Is he OK?' she frowned.

'Yeah, he's fine. A mini heart attack.'

'Right. Good,' she gave me a worried look. 'So, why the tears?'

'OK, OK,' I muttered more to myself than to her, then squared my shoulders. 'When Robert came back, he was really upset. And, then he kissed me… and I think I nearly slept with him.'

There was a ringing silence as Maggie's expression changed from growing concern to mounting horror. In a different situation it would have been comical.

'If you're joking, Frankie,' she said, 'it's not funny.'

'I'm not joking.'

'Are you crazy?' she stared at me, almost in fright.

'Oh God,' I whispered. 'I don't know what I'm doing anymore. What the hell am I doing? What's wrong with me? What am I going to do?'

Maggie's appalled expression didn't change, but she at least took both of my hands in hers and squeezed them gently.

'Frankie,' she said slowly. 'I love you very dearly, and I mean this in the *nicest* possible way - but my advice is, keep your knees together. That's *one* thing you can do.'

'Oh God,' I repeated, not sure whether to laugh or cry. 'I just shouldn't leave the house.'

'But Robert,' she shook her head. 'David, I understand. And you were pissed. But *Robert?* He's the devil... after everything he's done and put you through! What the hell was you thinking?'

'Nothing happened,' I said pleadingly - Maggie seemed really angry. 'He just, kind of... ended up on top of me... but I stopped it!'

'Ended up on top of you?' she repeated. 'He just *ended up on top of you?* People don't just end up on top of people, Frankie.'

'You weren't there,' I snapped, starting to feel angry myself.

'I wish I had of been,' she retorted. 'I would have punched him in the back of his head, and told him to get off.'

'I don't know why it happened,' I rubbed my eyes. 'I'm so screwed up,' I started to cry again, and her expression softened.

'No, you're not,' she pushed my wine glass towards me. 'You've just had a hard time.'

'I'm missing Jamie,' I confessed miserably. 'I can't help it. I'm so... I'm just so sad.'

'Oh, Frankie,' she looked genuinely upset for me. 'Come on, you'll get there.'

'What if I don't?' I said, hearing and hating the drop of self-pity in my voice.

'You will,' she insisted. 'You're strong and beautiful and clever and worth a million more than those dicks.'

'It's too hard,' I picked up my wine glass and drained most of it. 'The one man that is the most decent of the bunch, I don't want. I just can't stop thinking about Jamie.'

'Frankie, listen,' Maggie topped up my glass, 'I know what you're going to say, but don't you think it's worth just confronting Jamie? It might not be what you think it is, it might have been completely innocent.'

'No,' I shook my head violently. 'And just get fobbed off? Again? No, if he knows I'm hurting, I'm just opening myself up. I'm done with that.'

'OK,' she said simply, looking like she wanted to argue.

Robert brought Gracie back at the usual time, and it was as awkward as I had been expecting it to be.

'How's your dad?' I asked, not looking at him as I unzipped Gracie's coat.

'He's OK,' Robert replied stiffly. 'I'm going up there now.'

'Right,' I crossed my arms and glanced at him. 'Send my best wishes.'

'Will do.'

'OK.'

Gracie went and held her arms up to him, and he picked her up, kissing her neck and making her giggle.

'See you on Friday, Daddy loves you.'

'I love you too,' she ran off to the living room to take up position at the window.

'Listen,' Robert said quietly, and I immediately went on guard. 'I'm away the weekend I'm next supposed to have her, can I have her this weekend?'

'Oh,' I relaxed slightly. 'Sure.'

'Thank you,' he nodded and left.

Just as I was running my bath later that evening, it occurred to me that I should ring Will to tell him about his grandad. Not that they were close, I think he occasionally rang his nan, but all the same.

'Hello, you alright?' he sounded in high spirits.

'Yes, I'm… OK… listen, I thought I should tell you that your grandad Quinn was taken ill at the weekend, he had a mini heart attack. He's OK though.'

'Oh shit,' he said. 'Thanks, I'll ring Nan. Frankie… I've been meaning to ring you, I bumped into Maggie the other day, she said you've been a bit down?'

'Uh, a little,' I hedged. 'I'm fine though.'

'Really? Because she seemed worried.'

'Mmm, well, I've been better, I suppose.'

'Right, I'm taking you out for dinner,' he said insistently. 'We haven't had a proper catch up for ages. Let me know what night you can get a sitter and I'm all yours.'

'Thanks, Will.'

I'm glad I had dinner with Will to look forward to, as my week was nothing short of horrible. Jamie barely glanced at me when he arrived at work Monday morning, nearly half an hour late and looking like crap - I was already sorely regretting mentioning my dinner date for his benefit, although I wasn't one hundred percent sure he had heard me.

David was texting me constantly, sending little kissy faces and trying to pin me down to arrange seeing each other. In the end I rang him on Tuesday lunchtime and said I would see him at the weekend as Robert was having Gracie, and I told myself no matter what, I would tell him that we weren't going to get back together. Such was my irritation, I wasn't even feeling that bad about it anymore.

On Tuesday, when I picked Gracie up from Rachel's she had been playing up again and had pushed another child over. As I drove her home, her sulking in the back with a pout on her face, I started to wonder if Jamie not being about was the issue. She hadn't mentioned him or Jessie, which seemed strange, but she had been rather subdued at home... and my guilt at disrupting her life even more intensified.

To top it all, as I was leaving work on Thursday, the guy from the PC repair shop where I had taken my laptop a couple of days before, had rung me and said I could pick it up the following day, and said there was 'a worrying problem', but refused to explain, saying it would be easier when I came in.

I drove to meet Will that evening at The Windmill, a restaurant in the neighbouring town of Chembury. The pair of us had dined there countless times before, when I had still been with Robert, and Will and I used to meet up.

It held bittersweet memories, it was there that I had poured my heart out to Will about the state of my marriage and where I had first heard Lennie's name, as Will, love-struck and under her spell, had talked endlessly about this beautiful girl, that he thought he would never have as his own.

I spotted his car as I parked and found him at the bar, reading a newspaper, his hair as untidy as always.

'Hey, my favourite stepson,' I tapped him on the shoulder. 'I need an enormous drink.'

'Hello,' he jumped up and kissed my cheek. 'Our table's ready.'

As we sat down, he studied me, looking troubled, 'You've lost weight again.'

'Have I?' I shrugged. 'How are you? How's Lennie?'

'I'm fine, Len's fine,' he picked up a menu but didn't open it. 'You're not.'

'What exactly did Maggie say?' I asked.

'Nothing really,' he continued to look at me. 'What's up?'

'Can we at least order first?' I patted his hand.

We both ordered the fish, mine with salad, his with chips, then after the waiter had brought us a glass of wine each, Will leant over the table, and put his head on one side.

'Where shall I start?' I grimaced. 'I'm not seeing Jamie anymore, I got drunk and slept with my ex and now he won't leave me alone, your dad tried it on with me and Gracie is being a nightmare.'

'Ah,' he sat back in his chair, looking alarmed. 'I'm not sure where to start... what happened with you and Jamie? I thought it was going well.'

'Me too,' I looked down, scared I was going to cry. 'I'm not sure I want to drag it all up.'

'Frankie,' Will said softly. 'I'm sorry. OK, you don't have to talk about it, but I hate seeing you sad.'

'I'm alright,' I tried to smile. 'I think Gracie is missing him though, and that's why she's playing up. He'd spent a lot of time with us and she idolised him... I don't know what to tell her. I'm missing him too... oh it's hard.'

'Yeah,' he agreed solemnly. 'OK... so... your ex?'

'David,' I sighed. 'We were engaged before I met your dad. He moved away but now he's back. I was upset over Jamie and got plastered... and there you go.'

'He bugging you?' Will asked shortly.

'No, no, not in any sort of way that's scaring me,' I smiled genuinely this time, Will sounded both angry and protective. 'He just seems to assume we are an item now. He's kind of annoying. I'll sort it, don't worry.'

'Well, you know where I am,' Will's face relaxed a little.

'Thank you.'

'So. My dad -'

'Yes,' I felt the awful shame creeping its way back. 'I did something stupid.'

'You didn't... did you?' Will looked horrified and I quickly shook my head.

'No! no, of course not,' I fidgeted, wishing Will wasn't looking at me. 'But... I kissed him back, and then... well... nothing happened. That's all you have to know. I shouldn't have even told you.'

'I kind of wish you hadn't,' he smiled crookedly. 'Frankie, can I ask you something?'

'Sure.'

'Do you still love him? Robert?'

'I thought I did,' I idly fiddled with the table cloth. 'Then... then Jamie came along, and I stopped thinking about him,' I swallowed hard. 'Then I fell in love with Jamie, like an idiot.'

'Oh,' he considered it for a moment. 'Don't let him creep his way back, my dad I mean.'

'No,' I sat up straighter as our waiter approached with our food. 'I won't,' I smiled in thanks to the waiter and waited for him to leave. 'It was just weird, being in his house, and he was so upset about your grandad... we were married a long time, it's very hard not to feel *anything.*'

I wanted to tell him about my ill-feelings towards Robert for sending the photographs of Jamie, but it meant raking it up, and I didn't want to, not in the shattered mood I was in.

'I suppose,' Will started to eat, still looking thoughtful.

'He started playing games though,' I said. 'I think he was pissed off that I rejected him. He said Lennie had misled everyone, and it wasn't what it seemed. I didn't believe him,' I said hastily as Will looked furious. 'It just shows what a manipulative, narcissistic bastard he is.'

'He is that,' Will stabbed at his fish. 'What he did... to you *and* Len, was the lowest of the low, trust me.'

'I know,' I started eating too, despite my angry and miserable mood, I was hungry for once. 'You don't need to tell me, I'm sure you know more than me.'

'Maybe,' he said. 'We had to thrash it out, I had to know. I couldn't lay it to rest else, and I wanted her back, so badly.'

'Yeah, I know,' I smiled a little, thinking what a beautiful human being Will was. 'Maybe I need to know the gory details, to shake off that last bit of him.'

'Even if it hurts?' Will raised an eyebrow. 'I could make you hate him in thirty seconds.'

'Really?' I felt a morbid curiosity, but I was also suddenly afraid. 'I wouldn't ask you, it's too painful for you.'

'Not really,' he shrugged. 'He's her ex... kind of. So, you know, you have to get past that. The fact it was *him*, made it harder to get my head around because he's despicable and I hate him. It was more the fact that she didn't tell me as soon as she knew he was my dad. But I understood why. I spoke to Adam and he told me she was in *bits*, scared to death.'

'Yeah,' I was strangely fascinated by this, it was the most Will had ever spoken about it. 'So, what's the worst you can tell me?'

'You *really* want to know?' Will shook his head.

'Kind of,' I pinched one of his chips. 'My life is a mess - how much worse can it get?'

'OK,' Will lowered his fork. 'He groomed her... I don't mean what you think it means, like a *paedophile*... reading between the lines, he targeted her, led her on, made her feel special... then pounced.'

'Right,' I didn't feel as bothered by this as I should have. 'It's not like she's not a grown woman though, she must have known what she was getting into.'

'Len's shy and awkward,' Will frowned at me. '*You* know that. I'm not making excuses for her, she knew about you. Kind of.'

'Kind of?'

'Well, for one, he said that you weren't married, just living together and on the rocks.'

'He got "on the rocks" right,' I muttered. 'God, he's a shit.'

'Yep,' Will agreed. 'Also, she didn't even know your name, he said it was Francesca... no idea why.'

'What?' for some reason, that bothered me more than anything. Like... I didn't even exist. 'Christ, did I even ever know him?'

'OK, no more,' Will suddenly looked distraught. 'This isn't helping anyone.'

'Did she love him?' I asked curiously, ignoring his worried expression.

'She thought she did,' he suddenly looked pained. 'I asked her if she did. She said she was in love with what she thought he was.'

'That's him all over,' I pulled a face. 'Does anyone know the real him?'

'Isn't this hurting?' Will asked gently.

'You know what?' I stared into space. 'Not really.'

'He's still Gracie's dad, you still have to deal with him.'

'Yeah, but I'd rather deal with him feeling indifferent towards him than not knowing how I feel,' I suddenly smiled. 'I don't even hate him, not really.'

'Is that... good?'

'Yeah, I think so,' I said. 'He can't hurt me.'

'A wise old thing, aren't you?' he looked relieved.

'Less of the old,' I laughed. 'So, anything else?'

'I don't know *all* the gory details,' he said. 'Not, you know, their sex life. I didn't need to know that.'

'No,' I thought he looked upset, and felt guilty for getting into this conversation.

'Anyway,' he said in a brighter voice. 'Enough of this, I didn't invite you out to talk about him. Any more of it, and I'll make you pay for the meal. And I *do* intend on having pudding.'

I laughed, once again feeling so thankful he was in my life.

CHAPTER TWENTY-FOUR

I left work early the following afternoon to go and pick up my laptop, wondering what on earth the "worrying problem" was. In all honesty, I was glad to escape. Bea had been organising our works Christmas meal for the second week of December, which was just reminding me how close it was, and that was depressing me further. She also was organising the decorating of the office for the following week, and our usual "Secret Santa". Louise and Sophie had been twittering on about Christmas and their festive plans - the only person to look sourer than me had been Jamie.

I drove into town, bad-tempered and wishing the thought of Gracie's excitement at the approaching holidays would cheer me up. I had the following Wednesday afternoon off to go and watch her in her school Christmas play; she was narrator this year, as her teacher had apparently told her, she had a lovely loud voice.

I parked around the back of Will's restaurant, thinking maybe I would pop in and see if he was there and have a drink after I had picked my laptop up. I had zero plans for the evening and I definitely wasn't looking forward to returning home to an empty house - and probably brooding some more. To further dampen my mood, I was meeting David Saturday night; something else for me to dread.

I walked through town, wincing at the freezing wind, pulling my scarf up around my face. Some of the shops already had their Christmas decorations up, reminding me that I had to go and drag my Christmas tree out of my loft. Maybe that could be something to do the next day, anything to take my mind off my impending "date" with David.

I entered the brightly lit PC repair shop and noticed the young guy behind the counter was serving somebody, so I wandered around looking at displays of second-hand tablets to kill some time.

'Mrs Quinn?'

I turned around; he had finished with his customer.

'Hello,' I walked over. 'You said there's a problem?'

'Yeah,' he nodded, raising his eyebrows. 'Can you hold on for two seconds?'

'Sure,' puzzled, I watched him walk out to the back of the shop, returning a moment later with another young guy, who walked away to the other end of the counter.

'Can you pop in here with me?' he requested, indicating to the door behind him.

Utterly perplexed now, and slightly anxious, I went to the end of the counter and followed him. He stood politely by the door, allowing me to proceed him. I glance quickly around. It was small and untidy with a large work bench dominating the far wall and two shabby-looking leather office chairs tucked underneath it. I watched as he crossed in front of me and pulled out my laptop in its case, from a large drawer.

'Sorry,' he smiled at me. 'I won't keep you a second.'

I loosened my scarf as he pulled out a note book and leafed through it. He was kind of good-looking in a nerdy sort of way, with untidy fair hair that reminded me of Will's, and big, innocent looking, light-blue eyes.

'So, it's fixed then?' I said, trying not to sound impatient.

'Oh, yes,' he gave me a glance that I couldn't decipher. 'Sorry, sit down,' he waved at one of the chairs.

'But there was a problem,' I stated as I perched on one of the chairs.

'Indeed,' he sat down also. 'OK, so basically, there was something slowing down your laptop.'

'Right,' I nodded.

'At first, I couldn't for the life of me see what was wrong,' he scratched his neck absently. 'So, I started looking through your event log.'

'OK,' I'm not particularly technology-minded, but I nodded along like I was following.

'And I saw that a software was starting up, every time you logged on, and that was the problem.'

'Right,' I frowned. 'So, you've sorted it out, yes?'

'Well, I've removed it and your laptop's fine,' he fidgeted. 'But, it's the software that's cause for concern. It's called SpyJack; it's a spying software that someone had put on there, and I am presuming that you were unaware.'

'What?' I had a brief moment of not being sure if I heard him correctly, then as I processed his words, I started to tremble. 'Are you sure? How?'

'I can only take an educated guess,' he reached out a hand as if to reassure me. 'Has anyone had access to your laptop and password recently?'

'No,' I said numbly, then with a jolt I remembered that I removed the password when I gave it to Paul. 'Yes, a friend had it fixed for me back in the summer. I took the password off.'

'Right,' he frowned. 'Do you know who fixed it?'

'No,' I shook my head. 'Some random guy... nobody I know.'

'Is it possible that anyone else could have had access to it?'

'Well,' I thought hard. 'My friend obviously... his wife... that would be it... I think.'

'Right,' he said slowly, 'OK, well you need to have a think. This might be a matter for the police.'

'Really?' I said, mind racing. 'So... so, how would they have done this, I mean, surely it's not that easy?'

'It kind of would have been,' he shrugged. 'The hacker would just need what's called an executable file; the easiest way would be to copy it over from a memory stick. Easy and it wouldn't take long. The file would then "nest" itself, in somewhere like the PC's C Drive... any number of places. That's why it was so hard to find.'

'So, I've been watched?' I said, it was truly starting to sink in. 'Sorry, could I have a glass of water?' I felt nausea rising in my throat as I tried to make sense of it.

'Yes, of course,' he crossed the room and fetched a lukewarm bottle of water from a small worktop with a kettle and a few mugs on it. 'Sorry, Mrs Quinn, are you alright?'

'I'm fine,' I said in a thin voice, feeling anything but.

'OK, so in answer to your question,' he said gently. 'You've been watched and listened to - but only when your laptop has been switched on... sorry, I know that doesn't make it much better.'

'No,' I agreed. 'I don't understand... can it... they be traced?'

'That's the clever part,' he grimaced. 'No, it's almost certainly impossible... it works by being triggered when you log in, right? Then the software sends the images, voices, whatever, the data, in what's called packets. The packets are sent over by a VNP: a virtual private network, and it hides the address. Virtually impossible to locate.'

'Christ,' I muttered hollowly. 'I'm sorry... so how would the police help? Is there a way to find them, something they can do?'

'No,' he said, sounding apologetic. 'But if you have *any* idea who it was, I would inform them. This is highly illegal.'

'Of course,' I stared at him; his concerned expression was

somehow making it much worse. 'Thank you.'

'I'm sorry Mrs Quinn,' he pushed my laptop case over to me on the desk, 'I wish I could be more helpful than that. I strongly suggest though, that you find out who originally repaired it - sounds like a good place to start.'

I drove straight home, my head spinning - I was so lost in thought that I almost didn't brake in time as I approached the round-a-bout to leave town, nearly driving into the taxi in front of me. I just couldn't make any sense of it. *Why? Why would someone do that?* I felt confused, unsettled and very, very frightened. I went straight to the kitchen when I got home, and poured myself a large gin, barely gracing it with tonic, and sat with my head in my hands, thinking hard.

The logical thing to do, I decided, was to ring Paul and ask him who his friend was... but as I thought that, something that had been in the back of my mind hit me. *What if it was Paul?* I suddenly took my hands away and sat up straight, my heart racing. He said he had always liked me, when he turned up at mine drunk... was he harbouring something more than that? *No, no, not Paul, he's too straight and steady...* as I tried to push that thought away, I thought of Jamie. He'd had access to it too... *that's ridiculous, Jamie never made any secret of his feelings...* but... I stared at my hands, still red from the cold, did I *really* know Jamie? He had had a secret woman on the go. I'd never thought he was capable of *that.*

I sat for a while, my mind going back and forth. I decided to ring Paul. I couldn't just do nothing.

'Hiya,' he answered straight away. 'You alright, Frankie?'

'Yes,' I lied, trying to sound normal. 'It's just a quick one... could I have the number of the guy that repaired my laptop? Your friend? It's playing up again.'

'Oh no,' he said. 'Do you want me to have a word and give it to him?'

'No, I don't want to put you out,' I heard my voice wobble, and took a deep breath. 'Send me his number; I'll have a chat with him.'

'You sure?' Paul coughed. 'Sorry, I'm having a fag outside... I'm meeting him for a drink in an hour or so... I could pick it up and take it with me if you want?'

'No,' I thought quickly. 'I'm popping out in a minute, could you just text over his number?'

'Sure,' he sounded puzzled. 'I'll tell him though, that you're going to ring him.'

'Thanks Paul.'

A couple of minutes later, a text arrived with the name 'Cal' and a mobile number.

I stared at it until my screen went blank. *Now what?*

CHAPTER TWENTY-FIVE

I spent a lot of time on Saturday picking up my phone to ring 'Cal', then stopping myself. I had absolutely no idea what to do. I had lain awake until the early hours, my thoughts running through it… *Paul, Jamie or the unknown 'Cal'?* I had no idea why somebody unknown to me would possibly do that, unless he was some sort of creepy pervert, and that thought made me want to contact the police. But what if it wasn't him? What if was Paul or Jamie?

In the afternoon, I decided to go to the gym - a sadly neglected activity. I ran for forty minutes on the treadmill and felt better afterwards, as if some of the tension had left my body. As I drove home, I decided to do this logically. First of all, get tonight and David out of the way. Then, tackle Cal. A thought had occurred to me as I had been pounding away on the treadmill: *if* the hacker was indeed him, then he would know the spy software had been discovered, as he would have seen and/or heard my laptop was being repaired. So naturally, he would avoid me at all costs. That decided, I turned my attention to the upcoming evening, and made the decision to play it as nice as possible. David was a decent and caring man, and didn't deserve to be messed about. *I* was in the wrong here, and I didn't want to hurt his feelings any more than I had to.

Just as I was getting ready to meet David, he rang full of apologies to cancel.

'I'm so sorry,' he sounded upset. 'I need to go and pick up Harry, Jen's been rushed into hospital and her mum's not well enough to have him.'

'Oh no,' I felt-light headed with relief, even though I knew it would be temporary - I had to face him sooner or later. 'What's wrong with her?'

'Apparently, she nearly knocked herself out after tripping over her cat,' he chuckled. 'Sorry, it's not funny really… she's been throwing up, so she needs checking out.'

'Oh gosh, yes,' I agreed. 'Well, let me know how she is, and I hope Harry's OK.'

'I was looking forward to tonight,' he sighed. 'I've been missing you.'

'Can't be helped,' I flinched a little. 'Well, I, um, better let you get on. Ring me when you can.'

'Sure thing.'

I'm ashamed to say, I punched the air after I had ended the call.

With an evening to kill and Maggie working nights, I decided to ring Debs, fully expecting her to decline an evening out at the last minute, but after a hurried discussion with her husband, she happily agreed to meet up for a bite to eat and a drink. I dickered with the idea of ringing Sally... then decided I *definitely* wasn't in the mood for her.

I went to pick her up, guaranteeing that I wouldn't drink, and we went to our favourite wine bar. It was the wine bar where I met Robert *and* first bumped into David in the Summer. I was hoping I wasn't jinxing myself, but I couldn't think of anyone else I didn't want to see.

She insisted on a soft drink, as I wasn't drinking, and we went and parked ourselves in a quiet corner to decide where to eat.

'So,' she eyed me shrewdly. 'What's been going on?'

I had already explained on the drive into town that I had been cancelled on, and no, it wasn't Jamie... and felt a twinge of guilt I hadn't rang her with updates. Then I had briefly told her about David and our fateful (for me, anyway) night at his, and how I needed to tell him that I wasn't interested in him.

I watched her as she unzipped her jacket and folded it neatly next to her. She looked very pretty, in a dark-red tunic dress and shiny boots, her boy-ish hair emphasising her high cheek bones.

'I'm not sure where to start,' I smiled weakly. 'The whole fiasco with David isn't even the worst of it.'

'I'm all ears.'

So, I told her about the photographs of Jamie, Robert nearly seducing me, and my mysterious hacker - then briefly about Paul's drunken pass and my suspicions that he *could* be responsible.

'That's a lot of things,' she looked rather astonished.

'I feel like I could lay down and sleep for a year,' I sipped my orange juice, wishing it had a healthy slug of vodka in it. 'I'm a mess.'

'Aw, Frankie,' she looked grave. 'Firstly, I'm so sorry about Jamie. And sorry I gave you bad advice.'

'You didn't,' I shook my head emphatically. 'It made no difference.'

'One thing that I don't get,' she frowned. 'Why didn't you ask him about the photos?'

'You and Maggie both,' I said. 'Because I didn't want to,' Debs raised her eyebrows. 'OK, because it... it felt like Robert all over again and I didn't want to listen to excuses.'

'Or a reasonable explanation?'

'You didn't see the photos,' I heaved a sigh. 'Really, there is no other explanation.'

'OK, fair enough,' she patted my hand. 'It must have been a shock.'

'It was horrible,' I blinked back tears. 'Sorry, I still keep thinking about it... and him. It's just been hard.'

'Yeah,' she nodded, looking sympathetic. 'I really wish you had rang me, Frankie. You've really been through it, haven't you?'

'Ah, I'm OK,' I shrugged. 'Tough as old boots.'

'If you say so,' she said kindly. 'Who on earth sent them though? Why would someone follow Jamie?'

'Follow him?' it occurred to me that I hadn't considered someone actually following him - but of course they must have... *Robert must have...* it was unlikely that he would just happen to bump into Jamie, while Jamie just happened to be with another woman.

'Frankie?' Debs waved her hand in front of my face. 'Are you OK?'

'Yeah,' I said slowly. 'I think it was Robert. Who else would do that?'

'I don't know,' she looked around, frowning like she was thinking hard. 'Where were the pictures taken?'

'I don't know,' I said. 'It looked like a park of some kind. But I don't think it was local.'

'Was Robert aware of Jamie, then?'

'Yeah, Gracie talked about him. He made some snarky comment.'

'So, he knows you work together?' she asked, still frowning.

'I really don't know,' I said. 'I don't know what Gracie told him or what he asked her.'

'Right,' she brought her attention back to me. 'I was just wondering if Robert knew who he was, I mean, what he looks like.'

'He could have watched my house, I suppose. Or my work.'

'Yeah,' she chewed her lip. 'Would he go to all that effort

though?'

'Who knows?' I laughed grimly. 'It's Robert.'

'True,' she said lightly. 'But… I don't know… it just doesn't *feel* like something he would do.'

'So… who else could it be?'

'Well,' Debs said cautiously, 'could it be Paul?'

'No,' I said straight away. 'He was trying to get to the bottom of why we had split up.'

'So?' Debs leant towards me. 'What if that was a cover-up? You already have your suspicions that he's your hacker.'

'Oh,' I considered that for a moment. 'Yeah, but he seemed a little annoyed with me that Jamie was so upset… surely he can't be *that* two-faced?'

'Why not?' she raised an eyebrow. 'He might be fixated on you… it happens.'

'OK, you're scaring me.'

'Sorry,' she immediately looked contrite. 'Me and my imagination, ignore me, I'm just blabbering like an idiot.'

'But… it makes sense,' my brain started to race. 'The weird phone-calls, my prowler-'

'No, no, no,' she looked distraught now. 'He's your friend, he wouldn't do that.'

'And he was really fed up, worrying that Chelsea fancied Jamie,' I continued. 'What if he's on a mission to get at him?'

'Oh, come on now,' she shook my arm. 'No. No, it's not him.'

'It could be,' I countered.

'It could be, but more likely Robert,' she said firmly.

'Yeah,' I agreed, but my mind was turning it over.

'OK,' she shook my arm again. 'So, what are you going to do about this hacker business?'

'I'm going to ring that guy tomorrow,' I said. 'And see what he says. If he's genuine, he will agree to look at my laptop. If he's the hacker, he's either going to ignore my calls or be weird about it.'

'Will he know that you know, though?'

'Yes,' I drained my juice. 'If he's been watching me and listening to me, he will know that my laptop was being repaired the moment the repair chap switched it on. And *if* it is him, I hope he's crapping himself.'

'Too right,' Debs agreed fervently.

'Right,' I gave myself a mental shake. 'Are we eating, or what?'

We ended up at the Indian restaurant across from the wine bar, and had a more light-hearted and rather giggly evening, talking about our school-days and some of our younger-selves' antics. I made a pact with myself not to bring up any of my woes, no discussions about Jamie, Robert, David, Paul, or computer hackers. Debs, taking my lead, kept things normal, and for that, I was grateful - although I thought I caught her looking at me in an anxious way a few times.

As I dropped her off home though, she leant over and kissed my cheek, 'You listen to me,' she said sternly. 'Stop worrying, and make sure you ring me… things will sort themselves out.'

'Yes, Debs,' I said in mock obedience.

'I mean it,' she opened the door and looked at me. 'You're not alone, Frankie. You need me? Then I'll be there, OK?'

'Thanks Debs,' I murmured, feeling touched. 'I know.'

'Goodnight, Frankie.'

'See you soon.'

The following morning, I felt a little more positive. I had slept surprisingly well, managing to push all of the disturbing thoughts out of my mind.

After I had showered and had a mug of tea, I attempted to ring Cal, with no joy. *OK,* I thought, *it's Sunday morning, maybe Cal likes a lie-in.* Also, I wasn't sure if I was ringing a personal number or a work number - if it was the latter, I might not get any joy until Monday.

David rang me in the afternoon to tell me Harry's mum was back home, and she was fine, but he was hanging onto Harry for another week, so we couldn't see each other until the following weekend.

'Oh no,' I feigned disappointment. 'I have Gracie, so unless I can get a sitter, I might not be able to.'

'Oh,' David said. 'Well, we will sort something out.'

After I got off the phone, unless it was my imagination, I thought that he didn't seem too concerned; maybe he was cooling off. It was hard to tell over the phone, but I clutched at that thought with hope in my heart.

With no plans for the day, I clambered into the loft to get the Christmas tree out and hid it in the utility room, so Gracie wouldn't spy it later and demand to decorate it that evening. Then I set about cleaning the house from top to bottom, did all of my ironing that had been approaching epic proportions and finally, I curled up with a glass of wine and a tube of Pringles and wrote out my Christmas cards.

I had just finished when Robert knocked.

'Mummy,' Gracie threw herself at my legs. 'Guess what? We went Christmas shopping and I got your present. Daddy says it's a secret though, so I mustn't tell you.'

'Well, aren't I lucky?' I kissed her head and she scampered off to the kitchen.

'You alright?' Robert asked, handing me her school bag. 'Her reading's done and there's a letter in there about her Christmas show.'

'OK,' I nodded. 'How's your dad?'

'At home and biting everyone's head off, so situation normal.'

'Good,' I said. 'I've got you a ticket for her show, if you can make it.'

'Of course,' he eyed me, half-smiling. 'I'll meet you there. Before I go, I wanted a word about Christmas.'

'Right,' I braced myself.

'I think my dad needs a quiet one this year,' he said. 'So, I'll have Gracie at mine until lunchtime, then drop her back… you at your parents?'

'Yes,' I said, trying to hide my amazement that he wasn't being his usual bullish and awkward self.

'Great.'

At work the following day, I attempted to get hold of Cal, ringing every hour or so with no joy. My suspicions began to grow as the day wore on, but I still kept looking at Paul and wondering.

Jamie was out of the office most of the day, which made working easier, but just being there was slowly grinding me down - I once again started thinking about job hunting.

At home time, I apprehensively approached Paul, hoping I seemed my normal self.

'You alright?' he looked up as I hovered near his desk.

'Yeah,' I thought he seemed edgy. 'I've been trying to get hold of your friend, he's not answering my calls.'

'Really?' he furrowed his brow. 'I told him you were calling him.'

'Are you sure you gave me the right number?'

'I sent it over from my contacts,' he stood up, and started pulling on his jacket. 'So, yeah. How odd… I'll call him later.'

'Right,' I watched him gather up his phone and keys. 'Is he a good friend of yours?'

'Yeah,' he gave me a perplexed look. 'He came to my wedding anyway… he's an old work colleague.'

'I see,' I couldn't really think of anything else to say without sounding weird.

'Must dash,' he said. 'We're starting marriage guidance counselling tonight,' he said in a lower voice. 'Can't say I'm looking forward to it, but it's what Chel wants.'

'Good luck,' I touched his forearm fleetingly and went to go and get myself ready to leave, feeling a bizarre mixture of suspicion towards Paul, along with guilt because he was my friend and I shouldn't even think he was my hacker, and a frustration that was like an itch I couldn't reach.

As I left, I glanced over at Jamie's empty desk, and noticed with a pang that his scarf was folded over the back of his chair - I had a random urge to go and steal it, then smiled dejectedly to myself. Bidding Bea a goodnight, I went out into the cold, wondering when my life would feel normal again.

CHAPTER TWENTY-SIX

Gracie's Christmas show was a welcomed break from work, even if it meant sitting next to Robert for two hours, with his arm casually laying along the back of my chair, which felt like a vaguely proprietorial gesture. It also meant that I could avoid decorating the office after work; Bea had bustled in that morning with a box of new decorations and some trays of snacks.

She had also written down everybody's names on pieces of paper and gone around the office for people to pick their secret Santa - I had thankfully pulled out Sarah's name, and breathed a sigh of relief that it wasn't Jamie's. I had discreetly watched Jamie's face for his reaction as he pulled out his piece of paper, and saw that he smiled a little, so he definitely didn't have me to buy for.

Paul had caught me before I left to go to Gracie's school to tell me that he'd had no joy getting hold of Cal, which seemed highly fishy to me. I thought it was all pointing to the allusive Cal, but that wasn't making my decision of what to do any easier. I considered telling Paul that my laptop had been hacked, but something made me hold back, so I decided to leave it for the time being.

The rest of the week was uneventful. Jamie was out of the office again all of Thursday and Friday morning. As everyone was getting ready to leave, Bea clapped her hands for attention.

'I've provisionally booked our table at Nova Bistro for the weekend after next,' she trilled. 'I just need to know who's bringing a plus one,' she looked around.

'I'm bringing Chel,' Paul said, and Bea scribbled it down in her pink notebook with an elephant on the front. 'Anyone else?'

'I'll bring my new boyfriend, Sebastian,' Louise waved her hand - I noticed Sophie rolling her eyes.

'Is that it?' Bea asked, her pen poised. 'OK, jolly good.'

The weekend came along, and I managed to finish my Christmas shopping, guiltily leaving Gracie with my parents on Saturday afternoon. There seemed to be an upswing in David's texting and I wondered if he was bored now Harry had gone back to his exes. Out of guilt I rang him on Saturday evening - as he waffled on about his week with Harry, I briefly wondered if it was acceptable just to tell him over the phone that a relationship wasn't going to happen between us… which was tempting but not really fair.

He started questioning me about what I was doing over Christmas and New Year. I was as vague as I could be, which didn't really deflect him, but I made an excuse to get off the phone, then chucked it across the sofa in irritation.

Suddenly, I made a decision and rang him back before I changed my mind.

'Actually, David,' I said rather breathlessly. 'Could you come over to mine, now, for a quick drink?'

'Really?' he sounded happily surprised. 'I'd love to! Give me half an hour.'

'Great,' I ended the call and went to check on Gracie in bed, then opened a bottle of wine. I had to tell him, I had to get it over and done with.

He arrived twenty minutes later, with damp hair, smelling strongly of Paco Rabanne and with a huge smile on his face.

'Hello, come in,' I forced a smile, and led him into the living room. 'I'll get you a drink, white OK?'

'Sure,' he sat himself down.

'There we go,' I said briskly, returning with a glass of Semillon.

'Thank you,' he took it from me. 'You look beautiful, by the way,' he took a small sip of his drink. 'Lovely, you always had great taste in wine.'

'Thanks,' I was wearing my comfiest grey leggings that I wouldn't be seen dead in outside of my house, a very baggy hooded sweatshirt and didn't have a scrap of make-up on - I felt an unwelcome wave of annoyance with no logic behind it towards him.

'I'm so glad you asked me over,' he said eagerly, as I sat down next to him. 'Couldn't keep away, eh?' he patted my leg.

Couldn't keep away? I've been avoiding you for two weeks, you prat.

'The thing is, David,' I said as gently as I could. 'We need to talk. I think you might be getting ahead of yourself. About us.'

'I don't understand,' he said, looking confused.

'Well,' I said slowly. 'I like you *very* much, but I'm not really looking for a relationship.'

'I see,' he said quietly.

'I mean,' I continued, 'we had a great time at yours,' I looked seriously into his eyes. 'But, I don't think I'm in a place where I can offer you much more. I'm really sorry.'

'Well, I won't pretend I'm not disappointed,' he said. 'But, OK, I respect that.'

'Really?' I inwardly breathed a sigh of relief.

'Of course,' he smiled. 'As long as we can still be friends. And who knows? When you're ready, we can try again.'

Oh crap, I thought.

'I'm not sure about that,' my brain was racing. 'I mean, yes friends… but I'm not sure if anything will happen between us again.'

'Oh, Frankie,' he sighed. 'I know you've been hurt and messed around. But I also know, that *you* know, I would never do that to you. Ever. And I'm prepared to wait.'

Well, that's it, I'm going to have to kill him, I thought randomly, and then wanted to giggle.

'Right,' I searched for the right words, but they wouldn't come.

'It's fine,' he reached over and stroked my cheek tenderly. 'Don't look so worried. I'm a very patient man.'

'David -'

'No, it's OK,' he smiled. 'Really. Come on, let's finish our drinks… as friends,' he winked annoyingly. 'And we will part the evening as good friends.'

'Right,' I said again, torn between wanting to laugh hysterically and wanting to punch him.

Surprisingly, the following week, I heard very little from David. I had discussed him endlessly with Maggie, and she was convinced I had driven him into a breakdown of some sort. I also rang Debs, and after she had finished laughing, her take on it was at least he hadn't been upset or angry. I supposed that was true, but his reaction had been so *peculiar*, like a stubborn refusal to face facts. But at least it felt like one problem was ticked off my list.

However, another problem… maybe not so much a problem, maybe a worry, was Jamie. I had thought for a few weeks that he had seemed rather insular - not just towards me, that was expected, but in general. I had supposed that being his usual life and soul of the office was hard with me sitting a few feet away from him, but I overheard a conversation between Sarah and Joe that he had lost weight and that he was drinking a lot. My first bitter thought was that he should be in high spirits with the pretty blonde woman in the photographs to keep him amused, but then I really did take a good hard look at him. He looked pale and had dark rings under his eyes, and he had indeed lost considerable weight. I caught him staring at me often, and I couldn't read his expression at all. I tried not to feel guilty… it was all his own doing, but my stupid soft heart didn't want him to be miserable.

The week seemed to go on forever, and I was looking forward to the weekend. Gracie was with Robert, and I really felt like I needed some "me time", before the craziness of Christmas descended upon me. I had planned for some final Christmas shopping and crashing out with wine and take-aways and shutting the world out. However, that was not to be.

Saturday afternoon was cold, wet and miserable. I had trailed around Fernberry town centre, buying a few last-minute gifts to put in Gracie's stocking and Sarah's secret Santa gift, a box of glitter-covered shot glasses and a bottle of tequila, planning to put it in a gift bag with a lime and a sachet of salt.

As I climbed thankfully back into my car, I decided to drop into Will and Lennie's, as I hadn't seen them for a while.

Lennie answered the door, looking flushed and uncomfortable, and wearing - despite how cold it was - a black vest top and leggings.

'Hi,' she stood back to let me in. 'Will's not here, he's gone to pick up our cot from Chembury.'

'It's only a flying visit,' I followed her in. 'How are you feeling?'

'Like shit,' she smiled weakly. 'Can't sleep, I keep peeing and my ankles are like balloons… do you want a cup of tea?'

'Yes, but let me,' I offered. 'You look shattered.'

We went into the kitchen, and she lowered herself onto a chair.

'I actually can't wait until this is over,' she winced and put her hands to her belly.

'You OK?' I asked in concern. I took a proper look at her face - her dark hair was up in a bun; the loose strands were damp with sweat and her cheeks were pink with high colour.

'Braxton Hicks… I saw my midwife yesterday and she said it's nothing to worry about… they just seem worse today.'

'Yeah,' I said sympathetically. 'I had them, used to wake me up in the night.'

'Well, they're making me dread the real thing,' she winced again.

'They bloody well hurt today.'

'Sorry Len, do you have sugar?' I dried up two mugs from the draining board. 'You just need to take it easy, hot baths and paracetamol help.'

'Two please,' she wiped her forehead and fidgeted. 'I keep cleaning… Will says I need to be pregnant more often. I tidied the airing cupboard twice last week.'

'Ah, you're nesting,' I chuckled, then looked at her in concern as she winced yet again. 'Do you want to sit somewhere more comfortable?'

'I'm fine,' she leant forward a little and bit her lip.

'How long have you got to go… three weeks?' I poured water into the mugs.

'Just under four,' she sighed. 'I feel like I've been pregnant forever.'

'The last few weeks are the worst,' I said. 'I remember being so uncomfortable, and it was so hot when Gracie was born, I was constantly standing under a cold shower.'

'I am *definitely* not doing this again,' she grimaced. 'I've already told Will if he wants anymore, it's adoption or divorce.'

I laughed and finished making the tea.

'Excuse me,' Lennie struggled up. 'Pee time again.'

I watched her waddle in the endearing way pregnant women walk, out of the kitchen, then put our mugs on the table and sat down.

A few minutes later she returned, her face pale.

'I'm bleeding,' she said, looking petrified.

'Oh,' I stood up quickly and pulled out her chair. 'A lot, or -'

'It's kind of *gloopy,*' she remained standing, her face a picture of panic. 'It looks like a lot.'

'OK,' I tried to sound calm. 'Well, let's ring your midwife, and see what she says.'

She suddenly bent over and gasped, holding her lower stomach.

'Len,' I walked over and rubbed her shoulder. 'I'm going to ring Will, you ring your midwife… where's your phone?'

'In the living room,' she started to tremble, her face all eyes.

'Ok,' I went to fetch it, and returned to find her sitting down, looking anxious. 'Ring her, I'll tell Will to come home, OK? Don't worry.'

I went into the hall and rang Will; it went straight through to voice message, I cursed under my breath and waited a couple of minutes, then tried again with no luck.

'He must be on his phone,' I said, trying to sound unconcerned.

'I can't get hold of my midwife,' she bit her lip.

'Maybe you should call the maternity unit, to be on the safe side,' I suggested.

'Oh God,' she stared at me. 'I can't be in labour, it's too early.'

'No, you're probably not,' I said calmly. 'But you might need to be checked out.'

'Yeah,' she went and pulled a folder out from a drawer.

'I'll try Will again,' I went back into the hall, having vivid visions of delivering the baby by myself on the living room floor. With shaking hands I tried Will again with the same result. 'Len,' I called, 'what time did he go to Chembury?'

'Nearly an hour ago,' she said. 'Is he not answering?' she wandered into the hall, her phone to her ear.

'No,' I smiled reassuringly. 'It's OK, I'll try the Lizard.'

'Yes, hi,' she said into her phone and went back to the kitchen. I rang the restaurant,

'Good afternoon,' said a female voice, 'The Lounge Lizard Restaurant and Bar.'

'Hello,' I said quickly. 'Is Will about, please? It's his stepmum.'

'Sorry, no,' she said in a slightly less formal voice. 'Can I help?'

'Um,' I thought hard. 'Is Dom about? Or Adam?'

'Yeah, one sec.'

'Hello?' came Dom's deep rumbling voice.

'Dom, it's Frankie, listen,' I lowered my voice. 'I think Len *might* have gone into labour, and I can't get hold of Will, if he comes back tell him to ring me please.'

'Hasn't she got another few weeks?' he asked, sounding concerned.

'Yeah,' I paused, I could hear Lennie still talking.

'Is she OK? Where are you?'

'At their house,' Lennie appeared in the doorway. 'Hold on, Dom.'

'They want me to go in,' she said, her eyes filling with tears.

'OK sweetie,' I told her, 'I'm just talking to Dom.'

'Frankie,' Adam's voice came on the phone, Dom had obviously filled him in. 'What's happening? Is she in labour? Have her waters broke?'

'Possibly and no, and calm down,' I said. 'I'm going to take her in… just try and get hold of Will, please.'

'I don't want to go without Will,' Lennie said, then gasped again, her hands going to her stomach.

'I know,' I was glad that the panic I was actually feeling was not showing itself in my voice. 'We can meet him there, where's your bag? I'll take you, and Will will be there soon, OK?'

Twenty minutes later, we arrived at the Maternity Unit. Lennie's panic seemed to have turned into slight rage, and she had been calling Will a few choice names.

'How can he not be answering his phone?' she stormed as we walked across the carpark, her folder clutched against her chest and me carrying her hospital bag.

'He will, don't worry,' I was starting to feel angry myself.

We entered the building and she went over to the desk - I stayed by the entrance and attempted to call Will, 'Oh, for fuck sake,' I muttered. Then looking up, I spotted Adam running across the car park - I wasn't sure if this was a welcome sight or a problem I could do without.

'Frankie,' he grabbed the tops of my arms, his pretty face pink from the cold, then he spied Lennie. 'Lens,' he let me go and rushed over to her. 'I'm here,' he announced unnecessarily, 'what can I do?'

'Pipe down, for starters,' she said, but I could see some relief on her face.

I followed him over, wondering if I should stay or go now that he was there.

'What did she say?' I nodded at the desk.

'They're going to check me over and put a monitor on for the baby,' she said, looking on the verge of tears again.

'You'll be in safe hands,' I rubbed her back as she winced. 'I'll go back to yours and see if Will shows up.'

'No,' she burst out. 'Don't go, can you stay with me, please?'

'If you want me to,' I said soothingly. 'Don't you want your mum? Shall I call her for you?'

'No,' she looked horrified at the thought - and I suddenly felt very sorry for her, not to want her own mum there with her, that she'd rather have the woman whose husband she had had an affair with to stay with her.

We went and sat down. Lennie had barely lowered herself down, when a young woman called her.

'Can you come?' she implored me.

'Of course,' I turned and hissed at Adam as I stood up. 'Keep trying Will.'

CHAPTER TWENTY-SEVEN

My veiled panic was mounting. After having her blood pressure and temperature taken, and having had her stomach gently felt, Lennie had an internal examination and was told that she was five centimetres dilated - halfway there.

'Fuck,' were Lennie's first words and then she promptly burst into tears. 'What if he misses it?' she wriggled back up the bed. 'What if he's had an accident, Frankie?'

'He'll be here,' I said bracingly, surprising myself at how confident I sounded, when I had been thinking exactly the same thing.

'This can't be happening,' she wiped her face. 'It's too early, what if something is wrong with the baby? I want Will here.'

I truly felt so bad for her and felt myself on the border of tears too. *I'm going to kill him,* I thought darkly.

We were taken up to the delivery suite, Adam following, talking a mile a minute. Lennie was told to make herself comfortable and wait for the obstetrician. After reassuring her that we would be straight back, I pulled Adam out of the room and into a small waiting area, where a pregnant woman was pacing about in pyjamas, talking on her mobile phone and eating a chocolate bar, and a middle-aged couple were sat, the woman engrossed in a book and the man watching the progression of the pregnant woman's pacing.

'Where the hell is he?' I murmured to Adam.

'He will be here,' Adam said with conviction. 'Will would not miss this, I know he wouldn't.'

'Adam,' I said in exasperation, 'either his phone is switched off or it's died on him, and he's not really on baby red-alert as it's not bloody due yet.'

'I know, I know,' he said, raking his hands through his hair. 'I'm just trying to be a positive Polly. I can't think about what if he doesn't show up because I will cry. I think I'm going to cry anyway.'

'I'm going to ring Daniel.'

Suddenly, a woman's scream drifted up the corridor from one of the delivery rooms and Adam clutched my arm, looking alarmed.

'I don't like it here, Frankie,' he whispered. 'I'm scared.'

I nearly laughed, 'Be brave for Lennie,' I patted his cheek as I pulled out my phone to ring Daniel.

'Hello?'

'Daniel, listen,' I watched as Adam trotted over to a desk where two midwives were sat, one on the phone, the other absently eating a biscuit as she read something. 'Lennie is in labour and we can't find Will.'

'What?' he exclaimed. 'But the baby's not due -'

'I know,' I cut in. 'Look, I'm here with Adam… he went to pick up a cot from Chembury, at "Bumps and Babies", do you know it?'

'Not really, but I'll find it,' he made a shushing noise, I could hear Carla in the background. 'I'm going now.'

'Thank you.'

Back in the delivery room, Lennie had a monitor strapped around her bump and looked white and fearful. The obstetrician wasn't overly concerned that she was only 36 weeks pregnant, apparently it was what they called "late preterm", meaning the baby was preterm but it wasn't considered risky.

'How could I not have known I was in labour?' she stared miserably at her red-painted toenails. She'd got changed into an over-sized T-shirt that showed off her tattoo of a gothic fairy that covered most of one thigh and had tied a black bandana on her head to keep her hair off of her face. She still looked hot, red patches standing out on her pale cheeks.

'Well, even your midwife thought they were Braxton Hicks,' I shrugged. 'Early contractions are not always painful or regular.'

'How long ago did you ring Daniel?' she asked.

'Twenty minutes ago.'

Adam was stood with his forehead leaning on the window, staring out at the carpark.

'Hi, all,' a midwife came breezing in. She'd already been in and introduced herself as Donna - she was extremely young looking, with a pretty face and blonde hair tied in a high ponytail. She checked that all was well with the monitor. 'We'll have that off you soon, so you can move about to get things going.'

'I don't want things to get going until my husband is here,' Lennie frowned at her.

'Bless you,' she perched on the edge of the bed. 'Are you still hot? Shall I go and find you a fan?'

'Please,' Lennie fidgeted then tensed up. 'Oh, fuck, that hurts,' she tried to sit up more.

Donna smiled absently, looking like she'd seen and heard it all before, 'When was your last contraction?'

'Twelve minutes ago,' said Adam from the window.

'OK, my lovely,' Donna stood up. 'I'm just going through your birth-plan, then I'll find a fan, then we'll chat about pain relief,' she pushed her way back out the door.

'I want Will here,' Lennie said miserably.

'I'll go and ring Dan,' Adam finally came away from the window and went and kissed Lennie's forehead. 'Don't worry flower, Dan will find him.'

Lennie heaved a sigh and threw her head back on the pillows.

Adam returned five minutes later, looking wary, 'Well, Dan went in and Will has picked up the cot,' he said.

'And?' Lennie stared at him.

'And that's it, so Dan's having a drive around, he's going to Will's mums first to see if he popped in there.'

'Oh,' Lennie whispered, and closed her eyes. 'He's going to miss it, isn't he?'

'No,' I stood up and went and sat on the bed. 'Absolutely not.'

Adam and I looked at each other in despair, as a solitary tear ran down Lennie's cheek.

Half an hour later, things weren't looking good. Dan rang to say that Will had indeed been to see his mum and had a cup of tea but had left ages ago. He was literally driving around and ringing everyone he could think of.

The midwife had removed Lennie's monitor and had encouraged her to walk around, which Lennie had stubbornly refused to do. Instead she was sitting on the edge of the bed, head down and had gone very quiet.

'Ow,' she gasped, and stood up.

'That was ten minutes,' Adam consulted his watch.

'Will you stop doing that,' she said through gritted teeth. 'They are lasting longer,' she looked at me, as if she wanted some reassurance.

'First babies are notorious for taking their time,' I assured her. 'Do you want anything? Tea? A snack?'

'No,' she lowered herself back down.

When the next contraction came, Adam didn't say a word, but he automatically looked at his watch.

'They are really hurting,' Lennie moaned. 'Can you get Donna please?'

'Sure,' I stuck my head out in the corridor and spotted her coming back down. 'I think she needs some pain relief,' I said.

'Is she coming?' Lennie was standing up again.

'Yeah,' I went and rubbed her lower back.

'Hello,' Donna come in with a small cup and some water, she rattled the cup at Lennie. 'A couple of paracetamol.'

'Are you *shitting* me?' Lennie looked thunderstruck. 'I take them for headaches... what the hell are they going to do?'

'Lens,' Adam tutted.

'Take them anyway,' Donna said cheerfully, winking at me. 'We can try some gas and air, if you want?'

'Yes,' Lennie sat back down.

'OK,' Donna opened a panel in the wall to the left of the bed and fiddled about, humming to herself, then pulled out a light-blue hose and fitted a mouthpiece on it. 'Right then, when you have a contraction, just have a nice long suck on this. You'll feel a bit light-headed, but it helps loads.'

As soon as she left again, Lennie took a hesitant suck, then blinked rapidly, 'Woo,' she smiled a little.

'Good, eh?' I chuckled.

'Let me!' Adam demanded.

'Bugger off,' Lennie climbed back onto the bed, stretching her legs out. 'Right, if I don't move, the baby will stay put.'

'I don't think it works like that,' I discreetly checked the time, Adam gave me another worried look.

As it approached seven o'clock, Lennie was getting frantic. Her contractions were coming thick and fast - Donna was now staying in the room, scribbling notes in the corner and reassuring Lennie.

Adam was sitting next to her, rubbing her back and looking as scared as she was - I had more or less given up hope of Will being found. Daniel had been texting me every ten minutes or so, he was running out of places to look.

'Oh God,' Lennie clutched Adam's hand.

'Is it hurting a lot?' he unhelpfully asked, watching as she sucked on the gas and air.

'Let me pull your foreskin over your head, and we'll compare notes,' she muttered. 'Oh, shit, shit, shit,' she squeezed her eyes shut. 'Where is he?'

'OK, shall we check your cervix, my lovely?' Donna put her notes down and came over.

Adam looked horrified and slid off the bed.

'Don't leave me,' Lennie implored.

I went and took Adam's place and she sought my hand, 'You're doing so well,' I told her. 'You're being really brave.'

'I want Will,' she said again, her big eyes full of anguish. 'It wasn't supposed to be like this.'

'I know, sweetie,' I exchanged looks with Donna.

'OK,' Donna pulled on a glove. 'After your next contraction, I'm going to have a quick feel, OK? I'll be in and out.'

'I feel sick,' Adam pulled his T-shirt up over his eyes.

Lennie was breathing very rapidly, her hair damp with sweat. After a moment she groaned and squeezed my hand.

'Breath through it,' Donna watched her. 'OK, I'm going to have a quick check, try and relax, good girl…'

I winced along with Lennie, suddenly feeling glad I was never doing this again.

'Right,' Donna withdrew and deftly pulled off her glove. 'You're at nine centimetres, you might feel like you want to push soon.'

'No, no,' Lennie began to sob. 'I can't, not without Will… I can't… Frankie,' she implored, I felt horribly helpless.

'Lens,' Adam stroked her head, tears in his eyes. 'We're here, it's OK, we'll look after you.'

'I'm scared,' she closed her eyes. 'I want him here, I don't want him to miss it… oh,' suddenly she opened her eyes and looked down.

'Lens,' Adam looked panicked. 'There's something coming out of you.'

'There goes your waters,' Donna smiled brightly.

Despite the fraught situation, I couldn't help but laugh at Adam's face, a mixture of repulsion and surprise.

'If I liked fannies to begin with, I wouldn't now,' he said solemnly - Donna shook her head and Lennie almost smiled.

'Oh fuck,' Lennie brought her head forward and held her breath.

'Suck on this,' Adam thrust the mouthpiece at her.

'Nice and gently,' Donna rubbed her legs, watching her intently.

'No,' Lennie gasped. 'Frankie -'

'It's OK,' I held her hand, almost feeling her pain.

'Is the baby coming out?' Adam shot round and stood behind Donna, tilting his head sideways.

'Not just yet,' Donna said quietly in amusement.

'Adam,' Lennie snarled, 'stop looking, other end.'

'Sorry,' he walked quickly back towards her. 'I'm really out of my comfort zone here, you know,' he directed at me, wringing his hands.

Lennie started to push again, almost clawing my hand, 'Ow, ow, ow,' she groaned. 'I don't think I can do this.'

'You *are* doing it, my lovely,' Donna reassured her. 'Try and keep your bum down, bare down with each contraction.'

I watched her face, her eyes were glazed with pain and her hair was now soaking, 'You're doing great,' I told her. 'It won't be long.'

'I need Will,' she started to cry again, I stared helplessly at Adam.

Suddenly the door was pushed open, and another midwife stuck her head around, 'Yes, in here,' she said - and Will burst in, a picture of panic.

'Will,' Lennie almost screamed. 'Where the fuck have you been? I'm going to kill you... oh shit -' she gasped and started to push again, half sitting up.

'Oh my God,' Will looked mortified and deathly white, he rushed over and took her face in his hands. 'I am so, so sorry, my poor baby', he kissed her forehead and I saw tears glistening in his eyes.

'Where was you?' she looked furious. 'I've been so scared -'

'My phone died, then I had a shunt in the car, no, no I'm fine,' he said as she opened her mouth. 'I'll explain later. I'm so sorry... what's been happening? How long have you been here?' he looked from me, to Adam and then Donna.

'I take it you're Mr Thomas?' Donna smiled. 'She's doing great, everything's fine... alright my lovely,' she said as Lennie started to yell and strain. 'Don't fight it, nice and gently.'

'I'm going to leave you with Will,' I stroked her forehead. 'I'll be back later,' I looked at Adam. 'Come on.'

'Thank you, thank you,' she whispered.

Daniel was sitting in the waiting area, looking exhausted.

'Is she OK?' he stood up quickly.

Adam threw himself down on the nearest seat and put his hands over his face.

'Yes, she's fine,' I said. 'What on earth happened? She was going out of her mind, asking for Will,' I took a shuddering breath, suddenly aware how emotional I was.

'Come on, sit down,' Daniel put an arm around me. 'I'll get some coffees first.'

So, apparently Will had picked up the cot as planned and then had driven over to see his mum and stepdad for a quick hello and a drink. Assuming all was well at home as Lennie hadn't rung him or anything, and not realising how low his battery was on his phone, he had then decided to drive into Chembury town to buy some more baby things and do some Christmas shopping. Bumping into an old school friend - Will had grown up in Chembury - he had then gone for a quick pint and lost track of time. Then, seeing that his phone had died, he had started driving home, only to have a car pull out on him. He was fine, his car was fine, and the other driver was fine - although Will had lost his rag with him a little bit, Daniel said. By the time that had been sorted out and Will had continued on his way home, Daniel had spotted him driving in the opposite direction and thankfully Will had pulled over, seeing that Daniel had seen him.

'He drove like a bloody maniac here,' Daniel said. 'I had a hard time keeping up.'

'Jesus,' I muttered. 'Will she forgive him?'

'Eventually,' Daniel chuckled. 'Let her recover first, poor Will.'

And so, we waited. Daniel rang his parents, and said he'd let them know when the baby was here, managing to talk his mum out of coming over.

'It's the last thing Len needs,' he said grimly.

As the clock hands on the wall above the midwives' station crept around to nine o'clock, Adam went to find some sandwiches as none of us had eaten. As he returned and sat down, an almighty scream echoed down the corridor.

'That's not Lens,' he said.

'I hope she's alright,' Daniel was very pale, clutching his sandwiches but not opening the packet.

'She'll be OK,' I said firmly. 'It can't be long now.'

All three of us watched a pregnant woman, in visible pain, being led up the corridor by a plump midwife and her husband carrying a bag.

Adam put his head on my shoulder and sighed. We sat in silence, when an almost primitive yell rent the air.

'Oh, that's Lens,' Adam sat up quickly, and clutched my hand.

I held my breath, then there was an even louder, angrier yell.

'Oh my God,' Adam sounded close to tears. 'I can't stand this. Oh, poor Lens.'

Daniel had gone very still, his hands in fists on his legs.

Almost fifteen minutes has passed, when I spotted Donna backing out of the delivery room. I stood up, and Adam and Daniel, upon noticing what I was looking at, stood up too. We all converged on her, talking at once.

'Baby's here,' she beamed. 'Everything is perfect. The new daddy will come and get you in a minute.'

'What is it?' Adam and Daniel yelled at the same time.

'I've been told to make you wait,' she put her hands up, and sidestepped them.

'Hey, guys,' we all swung around - Will was leaning around the door, red-eyed and grinning.

I hung back a little, as Adam and Daniel hurried towards him. As I entered the room, Adam had already burst into tears, gazing at Lennie holding a small bundle in a yellow blanket, jet black tufts of hair just visible.

'She's here,' Lennie smiled weakly. I'd never seen anyone looking so exhausted in all my life. The high colour had gone down in her cheeks, leaving her pale with dark shadows under her eyes.

'A girl,' I went and hugged Will, then approached the bed to take a look. 'She's beautiful,' I breathed in awe. She was tiny and pink, with a fuzz of black hair, her little face perfect - like a doll. She sleepily opened her eyes, unfocused and bleary.

'Six pounds on the button,' Will said hoarsely, perching on the other side.

'Well done, sis,' Daniel said, leaning over.

'You clever, clever girl,' Adam wiped his face. 'Oh... and you Will. Why are you so wet?'

'Len threw her cup of water at me,' Will chuckled and kissed the top of her head. 'We've made up now, haven't we?'

'For the time being,' Lennie glanced sideways at him.

'Can I hold her?' Adam asked.

'Sure,' Will tenderly took her from Lennie, and handed her to Adam.

'Mind her head,' Lennie said.

'I'm minding it, I'm minding it,' Adam murmured, gazing down at her, sniffing. 'Hello you precious thing. I'm your auntie Adam,' he said, tears running down his face. 'You're going to be my new best friend, you are. I'm sure mummy won't mind -' he began to sob again, I covered a giggle as I caught Lennie's eye.

'Take her,' he said to me, his body shaking.

'Oh,' I looked at Will and he nodded. 'Come here... Adam you soppy thing... hello,' I held her tiny body, swallowing hard. She blinked and yawned. 'Aren't you beautiful?'

Daniel stood looking over my shoulder, seemingly fascinated.

'Do we have a name?' I asked.

'Violet Willow Thomas,' Will said, not taking his eyes off of her.

'Gorgeous,' I whispered. 'That's perfect.'

'I better ring people,' Will said, where's your phone Len? Mine's still dead.'

'I'll ring Mum and Dad,' Daniel went out to the corridor.

I handed baby Violet back to Lennie, and for a moment we just stared at each other.

'Thank you,' she murmured. 'Frankie -'

'Yeah, I know,' I said softly, touching her hand.

'No, I mean... I'm just...I -'

'Len, I know... it's OK,' I sighed and looked at Violet again.

'Thank you,' Lennie wiped a tear from her cheek, smiling at me gratefully.

CHAPTER TWENTY-EIGHT

It took me a long time to fall asleep that night, it had been such a strange and emotional day. I had driven home a little after eleven o'clock, shattered, and with only half of my mind on the road, headed straight for the shower, then lay awake thinking about it all.

I couldn't wait to tell Gracie, but then my mind turned to Robert. What would his reaction be? Would he even care?

I thought about little baby Violet, I was already in love with her. *How lucky they are,* I thought, with a drop of wistfulness and envy, *a brand-new baby, unaware how lucky she is, having so many people to love her.* I'd had a hard time conjuring up an image of Lennie with a baby, but looking at her, gazing down at her precious bundle, with Will looking beside himself with pride, it had looked like the most beautiful and natural thing in the world.

I texted Will in the morning, enquiring after everybody, and asked when it would be OK to bring Gracie over. He replied that Lennie and Violet were doing well, and they were coming home later that morning, and that if I wanted to avoid the avalanche of grandparents descending on them that afternoon, after school on Monday would be fine.

I didn't feel snubbed, and I knew that he would consider me a grandparent as much as Lennie's parents and his mum and stepdad, he was just aware that I would be uncomfortable visiting while they were there.

When Robert dropped Gracie home later that day, I waited until Gracie was out of earshot, and told him that Will had a daughter.

'Wasn't it due after Christmas?' he asked matter-of-factly.

'Yes,' I tried to read his expression. '*She* was early.'

'Right,' he said. 'Is, er, everyone OK?'

'Yep.'

'Good... that's good,' he nodded. 'Have you got a photo?'

'No,' I lied - I had several, but felt it would be disloyal to Will to show him.

'Right,' he stared fixedly at me, I had the feeling that he knew I was lying. 'Has she got a name yet?'

'Violet.'

'That's... different.'

'It's beautiful,' I said sharply.

'Sure,' he said flatly. 'Right, I better go. Gracie darling,' he called.

Bastard, I thought.

After he had left, I pulled Gracie onto my knee to tell her the news.

'Can we see her now?' she looked simply beside herself with excitement.

'No,' I laughed, hugging her tightly. 'After school tomorrow, sweetie. And you must be on your best behaviour, Lennie is very tired.'

'Yes, Mummy.'

I couldn't wait to tell Bea at work the following day, and she was thrilled as can be, demanding details and to see the photos on my phone.

Jamie overheard as he walked past and actually stopped to speak to me.

'Tell them congratulations from me,' he said with, what I thought, some effort. Close up, he looked terrible.

'Yes, of course,' I felt an overwhelming urge to touch him.

'Can I see a picture?'

'Yeah,' I held out my phone and he leaned a little closer to look.

'Cute,' he muttered after a few seconds, then raised his eyes to mine and we just stared at each other.

'She's gorgeous,' I agreed, dropping my eyes.

'How's Gracie?' he asked, gruffly.

'She's OK,' I fiddled with my phone. 'Is Jessie OK?'

'Yeah,' he shrugged. 'Anyway -'

'Yes, I need to get on,' I nodded.

'Stop looking at me,' I said grumpily to Bea as Jamie walked away.

'I wish you two would sort it out,' she grumbled.

When I picked Gracie up from Rachel's, she was full of beans, showing me a picture she had drawn at school of her holding Violet.

As I pulled up on Will's drive, I reminded her to be extra good and quiet, just in case Violet was asleep.

Will answered the door with a tea towel over his shoulder, looking tired but happy.

'Well, hello, Auntie Gracie,' he picked Gracie up and kissed her.

Violet was indeed fast asleep in her white Moses basket, Lennie was curled up on the sofa with a hot water bottle on her back, still looking shadowed under her eyes. Gracie approached the basket and gazed down for a minute, then promptly asked Will for a biscuit.

'Yes, of course princess,' he chuckled and took her to the kitchen.

'How are you feeling?' I asked Lennie, who had sat herself up, her legs curled under her.

'Yeah, good,' she said, almost sounding surprised. 'My back's killing me though.'

'It takes its toll, childbirth,' I went and sat next to her. 'Don't be cross, but I've got a few bits and pieces,' I held up two carrier bags.

'Bloody hell, Frankie,' she beamed, peeking in one of the bags. 'You shouldn't have but thank you.'

'My pleasure,' I got up to take a look at Violet, then sat back down. 'She's beautiful.'

'Yeah,' she smiled. 'And good as gold, feeds and sleeps… well, so far, anyway.'

'Make the most of it,' I said wisely. 'Have you had lots of visitors?'

'My parents and Will's mum and stepdad yesterday,' she shifted and winced. 'Rosie popped in this morning and Adam's been here most of the day. After quoting his bloody pregnancy book at me for months, he's now educating me with his baby book,' she giggled.

'Bless his heart,' I laughed. 'He's lovely.'

I got up and went to look at Violet again, 'Who do you think she looks like?'

'Will, I reckon,' Lennie said, watching me. 'According to my mum she's the spitting of Dan,' she rolled her eyes. 'Emma says she's got Will's grandad Thomas's nose,' she giggled again, 'Adam says she's got *his* eyes, the idiot - and she looks a bit grumpy, so she must look like me.'

'Well, whoever she looks like, she's perfect,' I sat down as Will returned with Gracie.

'You talking about my daughter?' Will sat down carefully next to Lennie, squeezing her foot. 'Beautiful like her mummy,' he said, looking like the proudest man on the planet.

'I need a pee,' Lennie eased herself up, as Will jumped to his feet to help her. He watched as she walked slowly out of the room.

'Frankie,' he looked at me. 'I never said thank you properly. Lennie told me everything, how you looked after her... I can't thank you enough, I really can't.'

'Don't be silly,' I shook my head. 'It was a pleasure... scared the life out of me,' I laughed, 'but a pleasure.'

'So,' he smiled. 'Important question... is to be Grandma Frankie or Grandma Quinn?'

I started to laugh, then stopped, feeling incredibly touched as I realised that he was serious, 'I think Grandma Frankie sounds just perfect,' I said.

Violet had shifted all my problems to the back of my mind: Jamie, although I was still hurting, my hacker and my suspicions, and David - who was still texting me on and off. Throughout the following week, I had been attempting to contact the mysterious Cal, and becoming increasingly frustrated and angry. I was still unsure what to do.

Lennie had asked me to babysit while her and Will went to register the birth, which I felt honoured to do - she confided that both her mum and Emma, Will's mum, were "getting on her tits", locked in a battle of the grandmas. I took Friday afternoon off work to go over to their house, perfectly happy to get away from the office, as everyone was going on about our Christmas meal on Saturday night, which I was dreading slightly.

Robert had said that he couldn't have Gracie, so I had hesitantly asked Lennie if Gracie could stay over as Maggie was working and my mum had the flu, and she said she was more than happy.

I had been feeling a strange sense of closure about Lennie and Robert... like I had at last made complete peace with her. I supposed that you couldn't really go through what we had together, without bonding. And she, in her turn, had stopped looking so wary and awkward around me, and had been ringing for advice with Violet and sending me pictures of her every day.

I dropped Gracie off at Will and Lennie's before I had started getting ready on Saturday, they were having takeaway pizza and Lennie had promised to do Gracie's nails, and let her have one of her bath bombs, while Will was on baby duty. Violet was wide awake and laying happily on her changing mat; I was reluctant to leave.

I took my time getting ready. I had already booked a taxi, so I could have a drink, and was halfway through a bottle of wine before I left, wearing a brand new, very festive red dress and full of nerves at the thought of having to spend an entire evening near Jamie.

I arrived at the restaurant to find that everyone was there, except Jamie, and I experienced a confusing blow of disappointment and relief... maybe he had decided he couldn't face it.

I found myself sitting opposite Paul and Chelsea, who looked simply beautiful, in a black and gold, daringly short dress, showing off her lovely slender legs.

As I greeted everyone, I noticed Louise sitting next to her new boyfriend, a very hunky-looking black guy, and Sophie on her other side looking slightly huffy. There was an empty chair between her and Joe, presumably for the absent Jamie.

'Hi, everyone,' I squeezed in next to Bea. 'Hello,' I smiled at Chelsea and Paul - I thought that she seemed a little off with me.

'We've just ordered some champagne,' Bea said cheerfully. 'You look very nice, Frankie.'

'Thank you,' I said, aware that Chelsea was watching me, a slightly sour expression on her face. 'You too, Bea. New dress?'

'Marks and Spencer's,' she said complacently, smoothing down the front. 'Are you OK?' she mouthed, and I nodded.

Two smiling waiters approached, laden down with half a dozen bottles of champagne and a tray of champagne flutes.

After a glass, I started to relax a little, deciding that Jamie wasn't coming, and I could probably cope with the evening. But as everybody started studying the menu, I spotted Jamie weaving his way over to our table, looking handsome and slightly dishevelled, plainly very, very drunk.

'Hey, everyone,' he said loudly and cheerfully, squeezing himself around our table. 'Sorry I'm late... hey Frankie,' he exclaimed. 'Look, it's Frankie... how're you doing?'

'Hello,' I said shortly, aware that all eyes had turned to me.

'What we having?' he squinted at the bottles on the tables as he sat down.

'Champagne,' Sophie giggled. 'Here, let me,' she poured him a glass.

'Cheers, Loulou,' Jamie flung an arm around her chair, nearly losing his balance.

'I'm Sophie,' she giggled again. Paul and I exchanged anxious looks, and Bea put her hand on mine and squeezed it.

'Bottoms up,' Jamie raised his glass and drained it.

'What do you fancy to eat?' Bea said louder than necessary, staring intently at her menu.

'The lamb looks nice,' Sarah said, looking nervously at me.

I stared unseeingly at my menu, full of apprehension, I glanced up at Jamie, he was whispering something in Sophie's ear, she smirked, catching my eye, then covered her mouth.

'Excuse me,' Chelsea stood up, and headed off to the ladies' - Jamie wolf-whistled after her and Paul looked at me again.

I refilled my glass with shaking hands.

'He's very drunk,' Paul leant over towards me slightly.

'You think?' I whispered back. 'I knew coming was a mistake,' I glanced around the table, Joe was talking to Louise's boyfriend, Sarah was watching Jamie and Sophie, a frown on her pretty face. Bea turned to her and started asking what her Christmas plans were.

'Alright?' Paul pulled out Chelsea's chair as she returned.

'I love your dress, Chel,' Louise called down the table.

'Thanks,' Chelsea said brightly. 'Early Christmas present from Paul,' she put her hand on his.

'It's lovely,' I agreed, Chelsea smiled at me blandly and continued talking to Louise.

'I want to go,' I muttered to Paul, he shook his head.

A waiter appeared and looked expectantly around the table, 'Are we ready to order?'

'Absolutely,' Jamie peered up at him. 'A triple whisky, my good man, and the biggest steak you've got, with everything.'

'No starter, sir?'

'The whisky,' Jamie roared with laughter.

'Christ,' I muttered.

'What was that, Frankie?' Jamie blinked at me. Ignoring him, I gave my order of asparagus for my starter and roast chicken.

'Yum, asparagus,' Jamie mimicked my voice. 'Sounds spiffing.'

'Pack it in, mate,' Joe mumbled, surprising everyone, including himself, by his expression.

'Joe, that's not very gin and tonic, is it now?' Jamie said in a fake posh voice.

'I'll have the soup and lamb chops,' Chelsea said loudly.

'Now, Frankie,' Jamie said. 'You sure you won't change your

mind?'

Sophie coughed to cover a giggle and I felt a hot pulse of anger. The waiter stared fixedly at his order pad, clearly sensing the uneasy atmosphere.

'Soup and fillet steak, mate,' Joe mumbled.

'So, Soph,' Jamie said loudly. 'What you cooking me for breakfast then?'

'Don't rise,' Bea whispered to me.

I nodded, staring down, frightened I was going to cry.

'Frankie,' Sarah said. 'How's the baby?'

'Yeah, she's lovely,' I forced a smile.

'What's it like being a grandma, eh, Frankie?' Jamie smirked.

Sophie leant over Jamie and whispered something to Louise, they both cackled with laughter - I drew in a deep breath and stared fixedly above Paul's head.

'Come on, Jamie,' Paul said mildly. 'Pack it in now, yeah?'

'Of course,' Jamie focussed his drunken gaze on Paul. 'We know what a *big* fan of Frankie's *you* are, eh?'

'Jamie,' Sarah murmured, looking at him. Chelsea bowed her head, her hands clenched on the table, and there was an awful ringing silence as all conversations ground to a halt.

'Toilet,' Jamie announced, struggling up, one hand on Sophie's shoulder.

Paul went to put his hand on Chelsea's, but she snatched it away quickly.

'Excuse me,' I said quietly, and followed Jamie to the toilets, waiting outside, blood ringing in my ears.

'Hey, look who it is,' he slurred as he came out.

'Outside,' I snarled. 'Now,' I grabbed his arm above the elbow and shoved him in front of me, not caring that our entire table was watching us.

'What the hell are you playing at?' I shouted as soon as we were outside.

'Oh, I'm sorry,' he said in mock apology, 'am I spoiling your evening? Are we feeling uncomfortable? Is this not acceptable in Frankie-land?'

'Stop it,' I said furiously. 'Just go home, you're drunk.'

'Ah... yes,' he surveyed me, his eyes slightly crossing. 'We must do what Frankie says. What Frankie decides is law... right?'

'You're behaving like a child,' I snapped. 'Which is telling me I made exactly the right decision.'

'Whatever,' he stumbled backwards slightly. 'You know what? You are actually just a heartless bitch, aren't you?' he glared at me, then to my horror, his eyes filled with tears. 'Why? Why Frankie? Why did you do that?'

As I felt my anger melt, I resolved myself... I wasn't listening to anymore guilt trips or excuses, not anymore.

'You,' I prodded him hard on his chest. 'How fucking dare you? I've got news for you... I *know* you were messing me around. I know you were cheating, so don't you *dare* come the injured party with me.'

'What?' he stared at me.

'Oh, you know exactly what,' I spat. 'I saw you... I *saw you...* with that woman... you hypocrite.'

'What woman?' he looked utterly perplexed, which only increased my anger.

'At... at the park,' I stormed.

'At the... what?'

'Stop it,' I hissed.

'I don't know what you are on about,' Jamie run his hands through his hair.

'OK,' I breathed, trying to calm down. 'OK... someone... I don't know who... sent me pictures. Of you and some blond *slapper,'* I took a deep breath. 'All over each other. In your car... at some park... hugging and laughing.'

'What?' he said, his expression startled.

'Don't lie,' I yelled, glowering at a couple walking past who turned to stare.

'But,' he shook his head, as if trying to clear it, 'I didn't... who sent you pictures? I haven't been with anyone... oh,' he suddenly seemed to snap out of his confused state, 'hold on,' he glared at me, pulling out his phone, nearly dropping it.

'What?' I said, agitatedly shifting from one foot to the other.

'Is this her?' he thrust his phone towards my face, I took a step back and stared at his screen. It showed an attractive blond woman sitting in what looked like a pub, with Jessie on her knee... unmistakably the woman from the photographs.

'Yes,' I said thinly.

'That's my mum,' he said in a strangled voice. '*My mum.'*

'What?' I felt the blood drain from my face as I stared at his phone.

'This park,' he lowered his phone, his face white with rage, 'could it have been... a cemetery?'

I gaped at him, 'Maybe,' I whispered.

'So,' he said, his voice rising angrily. 'Someone, *no prizes for guessing who,* sent you pictures, and *you,*' he glared at me, 'you, without bothering to ask me, without trusting me enough to ask me, assumes the worse, and dumps me, *ruins my fucking life,*' he waved his arms wildly, almost losing his balance, 'is that what you're telling me? Is that what happened, Frankie, is it?'

'Jamie -' I felt a rush of relief, *he hadn't cheated,* but I was filled with horror.

'Oh, my fucking God,' he covered his face with his hands, then slowly lowered them. 'You must have been relieved,' he said in a low voice. 'Your shameful little secret... not good enough for *Frankie...* you know what? Go fuck yourself,' he turned abruptly and strode unsteadily up the road.

Not knowing what else to do, I went back into the restaurant. As I walked numbly to our table, the waiter was bringing our meals over.

'You OK?' Paul asked, earning a look from Chelsea.

'Uh huh,' I nodded, not trusting myself to say anything, aware that everyone was looking at me curiously.

My head was spinning... *what the hell have you done, you stupid, stubborn woman? All of this, for nothing...*

I picked my way through my starter, drinking more champagne, then tensed up as Jamie returned as everyone's plates were being cleared away.

'Hey,' he plonked himself down, waving a bottle of whisky.

'Sorry sir,' the waiter said. 'You can't drink that here.'

'Eh?' Jamie looked up. 'Sure... right... merry Christmas Mr waiter man,' he stretched out his arm to hand him his bottle.

'Right,' the waiter took it from him, smiling a wry smile.

'What's going on?' Bea whispered.

I looked down, shaking my head on the brink of tears.

'Great, my starter,' Jamie drained his glass of whisky. 'Merry fucking Christmas, everyone.'

'Come on, Jamie,' Sarah implored. 'That's enough now.'

'I'm enjoying myself,' Jamie exclaimed. 'Why all the sad faces? You're not sad, are you Sophie?'

'No,' she snuggled up to him and I had a very vivid image of breaking my glass over her head.

'You can sober me up later,' he told her.

I noticed that even Louise was looking uncomfortable, and her boyfriend clearly didn't have a clue what was going on. I dared a glance at Chelsea, she caught my eye, looking sullen.

Bea cleared her throat, 'Chelsea, dear, how are those lovely boys of yours? Excited for Christmas?'

As they started to chat, normal conversation seemed to follow around the table. I sat silently, staring unseeingly at my glass, wishing I could just get up and go home.

Our main meals came out, and I found I could hardly eat anything; my throat felt constricted and sore. Jamie had gone quiet, seemingly giving all his attention to his steak, Sophie was watching him fondly, a small smile playing round her lips. Louise was chatting to Bea, and her boyfriend and Joe were discussing football. I could almost feel waves of cold air coming off Chelsea, who was stiffly talking to Paul - he seemed too nervous to even catch my eye.

I played with my food, trying to keep my mind a blank, terrified I was going to break down. After giving it up as a bad job, I went to the ladies' without even excusing myself. I stared in the mirror, my eyes were glittering and bloodshot and my cheeks pale.

As I came out of the cubicle to wash my hands, Bea came in.

'Alright?' I muttered.

'What on *earth* is going on?'

'Oh, you don't want to know,' I closed my eyes, battling to fight down a sob.

'Indeed, I do,' she came over to me, putting a motherly hand on my back.

'Oh, Bea,' I whispered. 'I've done something bad... something really, really stupid.'

'You?' she looked genuinely surprised at my statement. 'I'm sure it can't be that bad, dear.'

'Remember what I told you, about why I finished with Jamie?'

'Yeah,' she frowned at me.

'Well, I wasn't altogether truthful,' I looked at my hands. 'You see... someone sent me these photographs of Jamie with another woman -'

'The rogue!' she burst out angrily.

'No, no,' I swallowed. 'The thing is… I didn't confront him, because I felt stupid. You know… with the whole Robert thing in the back of my mind. But,' I sighed despairingly. 'I've just found out that the "other woman" was… his mum.'

'Oh,' she looked startled. 'So… what were the photos of, exactly?'

'Them hugging… at the cemetery. But I didn't know it was a cemetery. And in his car… and walking with their arms around each other… it just looked like they were, you know, *together*.'

'Who on earth sent them?'

'Probably Robert?' I shrugged. 'And the worst part is, he hates me. He told me he loved me, but now he must hate me,' I swallowed. 'And I love him. But I never told him.'

'Oh, Frankie,' she rubbed the tops of my arms. 'I'm sure it can be fixed. From his behaviour tonight, the silly boy, I'd say he still loves you. Talk to him when he's sober.'

'I don't think there's much point,' I said sadly. 'I should have asked him. I should have trusted him… instead of assuming he's just like Robert. He won't forgive me.'

'Yes, he will,' she said firmly. 'I saw the way he was looking at you on dear Gracie's birthday. Isn't it worth trying? If you love him?'

'I don't know,' I mumbled.

'Try,' she insisted. 'What have you got to lose?'

Nothing, I thought, feeling very sorry for myself.

CHAPTER TWENTY-NINE

I spent a good hour first thing Sunday morning talking to Maggie on the phone, before she went to bed after her night-shift. I appreciated that she didn't say "I told you so", but I can almost guarantee that she was thinking it. And I didn't blame her.

Before she went, she implored, "Please, Frankie, listen to Bea. At least try to talk to him."

I agreed listlessly and went to make more coffee and take some painkillers for my hangover.

Curled up on the sofa, I stared at the over-decorated Christmas tree that Gracie had spent an hour perfecting. According to Will when I called him earlier, she had been as good as gold, helping Lennie tidy up and had gone to bed when she was told to. They had decided to take her out for lunch as a treat and would bring her home later on.

I sat for a long time, messing around with my phone, half-planned conversations going through my head, trying to pluck up the courage to ring Jamie. Every time I thought about it, my stomach flipped over, and I felt sick.

The rest of the evening at the restaurant had been horrendous. I made it through the rest of the meal, after I returned from the ladies with Bea, unsuccessfully trying to block out Sophie's giggles and Jamie's drunken comments. As we had left, and I stood alone trying to get a taxi, I saw Jamie and Sophie climbing into a taxi together, presumably back to hers and my heart went cold. Not only because the thought of him and her together was sickening... or him and *anyone*, if I were truthful, but also because I knew that Jamie didn't even like the girl, and would regret it heavily in the morning once he had sobered up.

My phone began to ring, making me jump. It was Paul, to my surprise.

'Hi,' I got up and headed upstairs, thinking I'd have a nice long bath.

'Are you OK?' he said, I could hear he was driving.

'I won't lie,' I laughed humourlessly. 'No, I'm not. Is Chelsea OK?'

'Hmm,' he coughed. 'I think she's a little paranoid about you since I, um, crashed at yours. I didn't realise how much until last night.'

'You *think?*' I flopped on my bed. 'You mean you've had a row, and in matter of fact, she *is?*'

'Yep,' he coughed again. 'Listen, the reason I'm ringing is to tell you something about Jamie.'

'What?' I sat up, butterflies starting up in my tummy.

'Last night, the prat,' Paul said, 'he was only all over Sophie because he was drunk and he's hurting.'

'Well, yeah,' I slumped back again. 'I worked that much out. Hope they had fun at hers,' I added bitterly.

'That's where I'm headed now,' I could hear laughter in his voice now. 'He threw up all over her kitchen floor and passed out and she's not very happy… he rang me a little while ago to apologise and asked me to come and rescue him as he has no money on him and has no idea how far her flat is to his house. She made him clear it up this morning and stood shouting at him. Disappointment is a hard thing, eh?'

The feeling of relief that he hadn't slept with her was huge.

'Also, he asked me to apologise to you,' he continued. 'I told him to do it himself, but he says he can't talk to you right now.'

'Tell him… tell him it's OK. Listen, Paul,' I stood up. 'Take your time, I'm going to see Chelsea,' I said it quickly, before I changed my mind.

'Is that a good idea?' he sounded apprehensive.

'Probably not,' I said. 'But this is ridiculous. I want to clear the air.'

After throwing on some clothes and tidying my hair, I drove over to Paul and Chelsea's house, thinking that this was the worst idea ever, but I needed to talk to her. She answered the door - even dressed in faded jeans and a baggy sweatshirt without any make-up on, she looked beautiful, although her face tightened as she took me in.

'Can I come in? Please?' I said resolutely.

'Paul's not here,' she considered me for a second. 'But, OK,' she shrugged and walked back into the hall.

I followed her into the living room, she had been evidently looking at a photo album, on closer inspection, I saw it was her wedding album.

'No kids?' I asked, it was very quiet.

'Still at my mums,' she said shortly.

'I want to talk to you,' I sat on a chair facing the sofa where her album was. 'You OK?'

'Fine,' she sat down, curling her legs under her, looking both defensive and sulky. 'My wedding photos,' she nodded at them. 'Our counsellor told us to think about happy memories.'

'Listen,' I cleared my throat. 'Last night... Jamie was *very* drunk. He shouldn't have said that. Paul and I are just friends, that's all there is to it.'

'You know,' she spoke like I hadn't said anything. 'I always knew he liked you... Paul. Always saying how smart and pretty you are. It's not nice being compared to someone else. Especially when you can't compete.'

'What?' I said incredulously. 'He wouldn't compare you! He loves you, and trust me, you've got nothing to worry about.'

'Really?' she pulled a face. 'He thinks I'm just a bimbo compared to you. Just fit for having babies and cleaning his house.'

'That's rubbish,' I was shocked by how insecure she clearly was. 'He loves *you,* he wants *you,* please believe that. Listen,' I stared at her for a minute. 'I really like Paul, he's a good guy. But if being friends with him is doing this to you, then I will stop being friends. I don't want to be the cause of you being upset. I really don't.'

'You'd do that?' she frowned.

'Sure,' I nodded. 'As a recent recipient of having their heart broken, I would do that.'

'There's absolutely *nothing* going on?' she bit her lip.

'Nothing at all,' I said firmly.

'Shit,' she rubbed her eyes. 'You must think I'm crazy.'

'Love does that,' I smiled wistfully.

'So,' she fiddled with her sleeve. 'You and Jamie -'

'Me and Jamie,' I shook my head. 'I made a mistake and now I'm living with the consequences.'

'You seemed so well suited,' she smiled for the first time. 'I love Jamie, he's so funny and sweet.'

'Mmm,' I said. 'And I will let you in on something. That is Paul's little insecurity, and I shouldn't have told you that.'

'You're kidding?' she widened her eyes.

'Nope,' I sighed. 'See? You and Paul need your heads banging together.'

'But Paul *never* gets jealous. I thought he didn't care.'

'Everyone gets jealous,' I chuckled. 'You two will be fine.'

'God,' she suddenly giggled. 'Do you want a coffee?'

'Please,' I smiled. 'May I?' I indicated to her photo album.

'Sure,' she got up and went out to the kitchen.

I started leafing through it. Paul looked handsome and less tired in his suit; Chelsea looked simply stunning in her white dress with orange and white flowers in her hair. I smiled, feeling melancholy. They looked so happy, and the day looked like it had been perfect wedding weather, sunny and bright. I got to the end of the album just as Chelsea returned with two mugs of coffee, I noticed some photos in a wallet tucked up in the last page.

'They're some evening pictures that people gave us,' she said as I pulled them out.

I leafed through, there were several of them alone on the dance floor, clearly having their first dance, the rest of them were mainly of groups of people, clutching drinks or dancing. I had nearly got to the end, when a picture of Paul standing laughing with three or four other men caught my eye. I squinted at it, suddenly feeling a chill creeping over me.

'Chelsea,' I held the photo up. 'Who is this?'

She gave me a quizzical look, and leant forward to take it from me, 'Who?'

'This guy,' I pointed.

'Cal,' she said, frowning. 'Paul's friend from his old job... he's the guy that fixed your laptop.'

'Cal?' I whispered, my heart pounding. 'His name's David. He's my ex.'

'David?' she looked at me in concern. 'Are you sure?'

'Yes,' I started to shake, 'I nearly married him.'

'Are you OK?' she came and sat next to me. 'You've gone ever so white.'

'No,' I rubbed my hands together. 'I don't know... and it was definitely him that fixed my laptop?'

'Yes, why?'

'Oh my God,' I whispered, feeling sick.

'Frankie?' Chelsea looked frightened.

'Can I wait for Paul? I need to speak to Paul,' I stared and stared at the photograph, my mind starting to run through recent events. *He knew... he knew I knew Paul... was it him who was in my garden and was calling me? No... David's straight, he wouldn't... but... he just seemed to turn up everywhere, like he knew... of course he knew. He's been listening to me and watching me... revenge. He wanted revenge...*

'Frankie,' Chelsea shook my arm.

I stared blankly at her, 'Can you ring Paul? It's urgent.'

'Yeah,' she leapt up, throwing me a scared and puzzled look.

Just as she picked up her phone, Paul let himself in, a second later putting his head around the doorway cautiously.

'Paul,' I jumped up, waving the photograph at him. 'This guy,' I pointed shakily, he glanced at Chelsea and she shrugged in confusion.

'What ever is up?' he took the photograph from me. 'Ah our wedding reception... that's Cal as a matter of fact, you know, the bloke who -'

'Mended my laptop,' I finished for him, aware my voice was unnaturally high. 'But his name is David, isn't it? David Callahan... oh my God,' I smacked my forehead. 'Callahan.'

'Oh yeah,' Paul looked at me in alarm. 'It is, everyone calls him Cal though, or Cally... sorry Frankie, do you know him?'

'Know him?' I laughed hollowly. 'I was engaged to him.'

'Small world,' Paul said. 'But, why are you freaking out?'

'I need to tell you something,' I turned away and sat down, mindlessly picking up my coffee.

Fifteen minutes later, both Paul and Chelsea were staring at me with a mixture of shock and disbelief.

'This can't be right,' Chelsea was sitting with her hands clasped between her legs. 'He's so nice... and normal.'

'Yep,' I was starting to calm down and anger was replacing my shock.

'It makes sense,' Paul stared into space. 'You need to contact the police, Frankie.'

'Yeah,' I agreed. 'But I'm not going to. I'm going to confront him.'

'Is that a good idea?' Paul looked at me.

'I'll know by his reaction.'

'So,' Chelsea said, 'do you think he was behind the photographs of Jamie?'

'I reckon so,' I said grimly. Then a thought struck me. 'Paul, remember the night you lost your phone? Back in the summer?'

'Yeah,' he nodded slowly, then comprehension dawned on his face. 'I was with Cal... sorry, David... the fucker,' he muttered. 'It was him, wasn't it?'

'That's how he had my number,' I said. 'My friend, you know, Maggie, said it might be him that was in my garden, but when the calls started up, I thought the two were connected, but he didn't have my number until I saw him at the park when Gracie and his son had a fight,' I sighed.

'When are you going to confront him?' Paul asked.

'No time like the present,' I replied, pulling out my phone.

Paul and Chelsea had looked at me in awe as I had calmly rung David, breezily asking him if he wanted to meet up for a quick drink at The Lounge Lizard at lunchtime. He had agreed, sounding delighted. I had then driven home to shower and change, with Paul's voice ringing in my ears, telling me to be careful.

I wasn't afraid, I was *livid*. I had chosen The Lounge Lizard because I knew I would feel relatively safe there, especially if Dom was behind the bar.

I arrived there just after eleven-thirty and was pleased to see both Dom and Adam behind the bar and a woman with short pink hair who I knew was friendly with Will and Lennie.

'Hello Frankie,' Adam said in surprise as I approached the bar. It was fairly empty in there, still too early for the lunchtime crowd.

'Hi, you,' I beamed. 'Can I have an espresso please?'

'What are you doing here, all alone?'

'I have a meeting... of sorts,' I settled myself on a stool, checking the time.

'Hmm, mysterious,' he trotted off to make my coffee.

I nodded and smiled at Dom and he wandered over, 'Hello,' he said gruffly. 'Will's been singing your praises, nice thing you did there.'

'Anyone would do the same,' I said demurely, 'poor Len was scared half to death.'

'Well,' he said, 'they are lucky to have you... went to see the little lady the other day, she's a little cracker.'

'About the size of your beard, eh?' Adam plonked my coffee down. 'Is this your meeting?' he looked over my head towards the door and I swung round.

'David,' I called, and spotting me, he broke into a grin. 'I'll get you a coffee,' I said cheerfully.

'Thank you,' he gave me a strange look, I guessed he was sensing something wasn't quite right. 'Shall we?' he waved a hand at a nearby table.

'Sure,' I carried our drinks over and sat opposite him.

'How are you?' he asked. 'You look lovely, by the way.'

'Yeah, I'm good,' I said impatiently. 'I haven't got long, so I'll get to the point.'

'Huh?' his smile faltered a little.

'Right, *Cal,*' I said softly, 'I need you to listen and listen good, because I haven't contacted the police, *yet*, and what you say in the next few minutes will help me decide whether I'm going to.'

'Cal?' he gave a puzzled laugh, but I noticed a small tic going in his left eye. 'The police? I don't understand -'

'Yes, you do,' I said clearly. 'You know *exactly* what I'm on about, so don't waste my time,' I watched his face closely, his eyes darted around briefly. 'I saw you in Paul's wedding photos.'

'Who?' he pulled a baffled face.

'Oh, stop it,' I said loudly, and Dom glanced over.

'You alright there, Frankie?' he called over.

'Yes, I'm fine,' I nodded, watching David take in Dom's height and girth.

'Frankie,' David said hoarsely. 'I think… that whatever you're thinking… I think you've got hold of the wrong end of the stick,' he sighed. 'Yes, yes, OK, I know Paul… but please listen,' he had started to sweat a little, 'he's an old friend of mine, and when I realised you work together, I kept it quiet… I was worried you'd think I had deliberately bumped into you.'

'I see,' I nodded, and he visibly relaxed. 'What a load of shit. You stole his phone, you broke into my garden, you hacked my laptop… *you* sent me those photos of Jamie… do you want me to go on?'

'No,' he gasped, his tic going worse than ever. 'I really don't know what you're on about,'

'David,' I interrupted, anger was filling every part of my body. 'Just stop. You got your revenge, well done… now just grow a pair and admit it.'

'Revenge?' he suddenly seemed to deflate. 'I wouldn't do that… I love you.'

'Love me?' I laughed derisively. 'So, let me see... you realised I worked with Paul, yes? He mentioned me, yes? But instead of doing what a *normal* person would do... like, hey Paul, I know her, say hi, ask if she wants my number and we can catch up... you, you... do *this?*' I was aware my voice was rising, and both Dom and Adam were watching us. 'Who the hell does that? You need help.'

'Frankie -'

'No,' I stormed. 'Either you admit it, swear you will stay the hell away from me and anyone that knows me... or I *am* contacting the police.'

He stared at me, then lowered his eyes slowly and nodded, 'I'm sorry -'

'I don't want to hear it,' I snapped, feeling mad enough to stand up and punch him. 'Just go.'

He stood up, looking at me beseechingly, 'I really do love you, you know -'

'Go,' I snarled.

He hesitated for a second, then strode away. I took a few deep breaths, rubbing my temples.

'Frankie?' Adam cautiously approached the table. 'Are you OK? Who was that man?'

'Oh, Adam,' I looked up and the ceiling. 'If I told you, you wouldn't believe me... Jesus fucking Christ,' I muttered, and Adam gave me a startled look.

'I'm knocking off in a mo,' he sat down. 'Do you want to come back to mine for a cup of tea?'

It was such a quaint offer, coming from Adam, and I started to giggle, 'Yeah, why not?'

CHAPTER THIRTY

While I waited for Adam, I rang Will to make sure that Gracie was behaving and to tell him I would text him when I was home.

I followed Adam's blue Corsa out of town towards the boating lake, then along the side of the park, furthest away from the lake to his flat that he shared with Dom. His flat was contained in a converted house, with a leafy front garden, and a large carport to the side. I parked on the road and hurried over to where he was waiting for me at the front door. We went up a flight of wooden stairs to a big dusty landing with potted plants and two doors, the one on the right being his.

Adam put a finger to his lips as he unlocked the door. 'Daphne's,' he whispered, pointing to the other door. 'If she's not with a customer, she'll be over in a shot. Nosy mare. For a psychic she doesn't half ask a lot of questions.'

I went in after him and looked around. It was large and open-planned, with beech floors and a huge black sofa covered in multi-coloured cushions, with a polished wooden coffee table sitting on a black and white rug.

'Nice,' I said appreciatively.

'It's a lot tidier since Lens moved out,' he went and switched the kettle on and leaned over the counter separating the kitchen from the living area.

'Of course,' I said. 'I forgot she lived here.'

I wondered if Robert used to stay there, realising with satisfaction that the thought didn't bother me.

'So,' Adam brought our teas over, sat on one end of the sofa, and turned to face me. 'Who was the mystery man and why was you looking like you were about to kill him?'

'That, was my ex-fiancé and most recently my stalker.'

'Oh?' he raised an eyebrow. 'Tell me more.'

So, I did. I told him everything, from the phone calls and the damage to Jamie's car… suddenly remembering when his car was keyed at the leisure centre, and swearing loudly… to the photographs of Jamie and my laptop being hacked.

'Wow,' Adam said. 'Is he safe to roam the streets?'

'As long as he stays away from me, I don't care,' I shrugged. 'I pity him, in a way.'

'You're too nice,' Adam frowned at me. 'You should have him arrested.'

'I'm sick and tired of drama,' I put down my mug. 'I just want to slink away now and nurse my wounds.'

'Jamie?'

'Jamie.'

'You need to win him back,' Adam suddenly sat up straight. 'Oh, that'd be fabulous... so romantic.'

'Adam,' I laughed, 'he might not want to be won back. I treated him like dirt, I never took him seriously and I clearly didn't trust him,' I felt a wave of grief. 'He thinks I was ashamed of him... I wasn't. I was just scared.'

'Because of Robert,' it was a statement, not a question. 'Robert's a knob. He doesn't deserve that kind of power.'

'You sound like Maggie,' I said. 'But it's true.'

'Too right,' Adam wriggled over and put his arm around me. 'He's lost Will, he's lost you, one day he'll probably lose Gracie... he's a prat.'

'Yeah,' I agreed. 'Perhaps he and Will will make it up again... they did before, you know, before Will found out about him and Lennie.'

'And Will was a prat too, letting him worm his way back, I wouldn't have, not after what he did. Who would do that to his own son?'

'What?' I pulled my head back and stared at him and Adam suddenly looked horror-struck.

'Oh, fuck,' he pulled my head down on his shoulder. 'Don't look at me... oh I thought you knew... bugger... nothing, nothing at all.'

'What?' I laughed, struggling away from him.

'I can't,' Adam pressed his lips together and shook his head.

'Adam,' I nudged him. 'Come on, it doesn't matter, I don't care anymore.'

'Really?' he looked at me sceptically.

'Really.'

'OK,' he lowered his voice dramatically. 'You know Will's fiancée?'

'Daisy?' I said, feeling confused. 'Sure... oh my God,' I whispered as I began to think back - before Will had disappeared all those years ago. 'He didn't?'

'He caught them,' Adam bit his lip. 'Sorry.'

'Poor Will,' I sighed. 'Oh, what a *bastard.*'

'You don't care?' Adam twisted his fingers together, his pretty face a picture of concern.

'Not for me,' I assured him. 'For Will, bless his heart.'

'I'm such a blabbermouth,' Adam snuggled up to me. 'You're very lovely.'

'I am,' I giggled, although I felt a little sick at his revelation... no wonder Will hated him so much.

'Anyway,' Adam said in a brighter voice. 'Jamie... how are we going to win him back into your arms?'

'Oh, Adam,' I said. 'I don't think I can. I will try and talk to him, but I think I need to accept it and move on.'

'No, no, no,' Adam said insistently. 'You love him, right?'

'Yes,' I sighed miserably.

'Then you get him back, even if it means stalking him and hacking his computer.'

I laughed, shoving him away, 'Pack it in.'

'I'm serious,' he grabbed my hands. 'He thinks you're ashamed of him, right? That you were just mucking him about? Then prove to him that you weren't... I'm thinking big gesture,' he swept his arm in an arc above his head.

'Like what?' I asked dubiously.

'You know him better than me,' Adam said. 'What's his thing? What would win him over?'

'Food,' I said jokingly. 'He talked about bacon a *lot*,' I smiled wistfully, then felt stupidly on the brink of tears. 'God, I miss the silly bugger.'

'Really?' Adam stared into space, then suddenly beamed. 'Ooo, I've got an idea,' he hugged himself, looking excited.

'What?' I said warily.

Ten minutes later, I was gazing at Adam in complete amazement.

'Oh, it'll be so *romantic*,' he clutched himself.

'No,' I breathed. 'That is the most ridiculous thing I've ever heard... I'd look like a complete lunatic. And my boss will sack me on the grounds of insanity.'

'No,' Adam implored. 'Don't spoil it for me.'

'For you?' I raised my eyebrows.

'Sorry, I'm very excited,' Adam blinked at me. 'Come on,

Frankie... let's do it, please, please, please... if it doesn't work, I will... I will... give you a million pounds!'

'Do you *have* a million pounds, Adam?'

'Well, no... but that's how sure I am that it'll work.'

'Christ,' I watched his expectant face. 'I can't believe I'm going to say this...but, OK.'

'Oh my God,' he hugged me, then planted a huge kiss on my mouth. 'This is going to be the most splendid thing ever.'

'If you say so.'

The atmosphere in the office Monday morning wasn't great, but I had other things on my mind. As soon as I saw Scott going into his office, I went and knocked on his door, feeling like a mad woman.

He listened to me, his expression changing from mild interest, to amusement as I talked.

'So, just for an hour?' he drummed his fingers on his desk.

'Yes,' I nodded. 'And please, keep it quiet.'

'I'm sure I can cook something up,' he chuckled.

'Thank you,' I turned and left his office, as I closed the door he broke into loud guffaws.

I sat down and looked across at Jamie, he slowly looked up as if sensing my gaze and I smiled a little. His mouth kind of twitched before he dropped his eyes. I noticed Sophie throwing him cold looks and generally looking dour.

At lunchtime, I grabbed Paul, 'Can you have lunch with me, I need a word?'

We ended up sitting in his car sharing a sandwich - firstly I told him about David in more detail, I'd already had a hurried conversation with him first thing.

'I still can't get my head round it,' he looked troubled. 'You *are* OK though?'

'I'm fine,' I said. 'And you and Chel?'

'I think you talking to her helped,' he smiled. 'I really do. I think we'll be OK.'

'Good,' I felt genuinely happy for them.

'On a not so happy note,' he sighed heavily, 'Jamie plans on handing in his notice after Christmas.'

'Really?' I stared at my hands. 'He told you that?'

'Yeah. Says it's too hard.'

'Well, that kind of leads me to what I needed to talk to you about,' I took a deep breath and explained, trying to ignore the odd chuckle from him.

'I'm not really sure what to say,' he said in amused tones. 'But, of course... just give me the signal. Tell me something,' he patted my hand. 'Have you totally lost the plot?'

'I think I have,' I said solemnly.

I woke up on Friday morning, my stomach in knots.

'I can't believe he talked me into this,' I muttered to myself as I got dressed, laddering a pair of tights with my shaking hands.

Adam had been over the evening before to pick up my bank card, visibly brimming with glee.

'I'm having second thoughts,' I had told him.

'I didn't hear you,' he had kissed my cheek before jogging back to his car, waving cheerily.

After dropping Gracie off at school, excited for her class party before breaking up later that week, I drove to work slowly, worse-case scenarios going around and around my head.

After lunch, Scott strode into the office, giving me an imperceptible wink, 'Jamie, can you come to my office at two, please?' he called over.

Jamie looked up, 'Yes, of course.'

I kept checking my watch, hoping Adam wasn't going to be late... although a tiny part of me was hoping he wasn't going to turn up at all.

The atmosphere in the office was a little happier as we were breaking up at three-thirty and not back in until the second of January. Bea had her box of our wrapped secret Santa gifts by her desk and was passing out mince pies. Louise was sitting with gold tinsel wrapped around her bun, talking loudly about what her and Sebastian were doing over Christmas. Sarah had excitedly told me earlier that her and Joe were going to Scotland for Hogmanay, and that they had started talking about moving in together.

Proved you wrong, girls, I thought happily, remembering Louise and Sophie's derision at Joe and Sarah as a couple.

At two o'clock, Jamie wandered towards Scott's office and I texted Adam.

'I am here xxx' he sent back, and I truly started to feel a nudge of panic.

I looked over at Paul, he stood up and stretched, then pulled the vertical blinds behind him a little, giving me a swift grin as he sat back down.

This is absurd, this is madness, I closed my eyes, feeling sick.

As quarter to three approached, Adam texted, making me jump. I read it quickly, then sat trembling for ten minutes, before getting up as casually as possible and walking out of the office. Paul gave me a significant look as I went out.

I belted down the stairs, nearly losing my balance at the bottom, and went outside to find Adam sitting on the low wall, shivering slightly in the cold.

'Oh my,' I gazed across the carpark, then up at the office window.

'Where's your coat?' Adam tutted.

'I couldn't bring it,' I walked slowly into the carpark, my heart jumping about. 'It would have looked suspicious.'

'Here, have mine,' Adam unzipped his Calvin Klein jacket and handed it to me. 'I'll go and sit in my car.'

'Thanks,' I shrugged it on. 'Right, oh my God… just beep your horn in a couple of minutes.'

'I'm so excited,' he squealed, jogging off towards his car.

I walked into the middle of the carpark and stared around, turning on the spot. In two-foot-high letters, Adam had spelt out "FRANKIE", and below that a giant love heart with an "s" beside it and then, "JAMIE"… with packets and packets of bacon. The insanity of the whole thing suddenly over-whelmed me. I had never felt so utterly ludicrous in my entire life. I turned towards Adam's car and he gave me a thumbs up, grinning from ear to ear.

I stood facing the building, shaking wildly, my arms wrapped around my body. Adam started sounding his horn, making me jump.

I waited, staring up at the window. I saw the blinds move, and somebody's outline, then saw it was Paul as he flung the window open, yelling Jamie's name. I waited, my face starting to feel hot as I saw outlines of more people appearing.

Adam stopped beeping his horn, and in the ringing silence, I heard female laughter from above.

'Oh, fuck,' I felt tears of mortification welling up.

Suddenly Jamie appeared at the open window. Without my glasses I couldn't tell what expression was on his face. He withdrew his head and disappeared again, leaving me so light-headed with panic, I felt like I was going to pass out.

Just as I was having vague thoughts about dragging Adam out of his car and beating him to a pulp, Jamie burst out of the door, stopped dead and stared at me, his face completely deadpan.

It seemed like eternity had passed, before he slowly walked towards me, his eyes on my face.

'You know,' he said, 'that's an awful waste of bacon.'

'If this doesn't work as intended,' I said in an unsteady voice, 'you are welcome to keep the bacon.'

He stopped in front of me and looked around at the huge letters.

'Do you mean it?' he asked huskily.

'Yes,' I took a deep breath. 'I love you, and I'm sorry… I am so, so sorry Jamie. I do love you, so much.'

'No, I meant about keeping the bacon?' his face was serious for a second, then he broke into his beautiful huge smile, a smile that I felt like I hadn't seen for a very long time.

'Oh… you -' I started to giggle, as he wrapped his arms around me, burying his face in my hair, then he grabbed my face and kissed me until my legs were weak.

I could hear wolf-whistling and cheering from above, and Adam had jumped out of his car to clap, yelling, 'I told you it would work!'

'I love you too,' he finally stopped kissing me. 'I really do… I love you more than… than bacon,' he pulled me against him, his heart was beating as fast as mine.

'Wow,' I murmured. 'That's a whole lot of love.'

THE END

ACKNOWLEDGEMENTS

So – I am at the end of my second adventure, and as before, this would have not been possible without the help of some wonderful people.

Once again, I would like to thank my editor, Ash Watson. I simply cannot express enough gratitude and admiration for her hard work and advice. It's been a pleasure working with her again.

Huge love and thanks to Natasha and Mark Woolcott for letting me invade their home (again) and for Mark's brilliant photography.

More love and thanks to Sam and Barry Haggerty for their own brand of support, and for the beautiful Sam for being the most fidgety and naughty cover model in the world, (sorry for kicking your leg a few times, Sam).

I had to pick the brains of a few clever chaps, and would like to thank the following: David Bressington, Dirk Schroeder, Nate Orrow, and in particular, the very thorough Jonathan Shields.

Thank you to my family and friends for their support and faith in me, and a few of you for being my brainstormers and encouraging my daftness.

And finally, last but never least, love and thanks to my poor long-suffering husband, Paul, the grown-up half of me that has pulled this madness that is writing a book together when I have been banging my head on my laptop. I love you with all my heart.

Printed in Great Britain
by Amazon